I0822749

The Seven Planes of Kalamar – Battle for The Third Plane

And Darkness Comes

A special thank you to Derek Gruen, mydeliumdesignllc@gmail.com and Erin Miller, erin.wordsmith@gmail.com. A wonderful and captivating redesign of the covers welcoming readers to **The Seven Planes of Kalamar – Battle for The Third Plane**.

In loving memory of my wife, Marsha Ann, 05.03.1951 — 01.02.2021,
and to all of those who've lost a loved one to Alzheimer's.

Thank you!

To family and friends for your support while writing this book.
To my editor, Meg Trast, at Overhaul My Novel.

Other books by Hansford Robert Hull

The Seven Planes of Kalamar – Battle for The Third Plane

Book 1 – And Darkness Comes
Book 2 – Rescue Times Three
Book 3 – Break The Darkness

The Seven Planes of Kalamar - Battle for the Third Plane

by Hansford Robert Hull

Book I:

And Darkness Comes

Table of Contents

Part 1

Prologue

Zorleg sat motionless, alone in his chambers, lost deep in thought. His long black robe disappeared into matching shadows on the floor. *How many years have I waited for this day?* he wondered silently. He rose slowly from his throne before he moved across the cold, damp cobblestone floor to one of the many windows and peered out. His deep black eyes stared into the unfathomable blackness he had created.

Mentally, he replayed how he had laid out his master plan of destruction. Out of the Seven Planes, by his choice, he had laid waste and conquered the Third Plane of Kalamar. This was where his teachings started long ago. He snickered at the memory of exactly what he was supposed to have been taught. He was so rebellious in his teen years, defying everything he was meant to know. Those thoughts had long since been replaced by his own evil thoughts, fueling his ego. Oh, how powerful and destructive he had become!

Zorleg no longer found any reason to remember exactly where he was when he placed his pieces of the destruction together. The Great City of Kalamar would lay in ruins. Even the mention of the city's name still caused his blood to instantly reach its boiling point. The thought of this great place having the same name as all the other planes provided additional fuel for its complete obliteration. Zorleg released a blood-curdling scream from the depths of his lungs, shattering the silence, when he remembered it. His scream transformed into a hideous laughter, his thoughts returning to the plan he had conjured up in the deepest recesses of his mind. His maniacal laughter reverberated off the cold stone walls of his chambers.

His vast army was positioned exactly where it needed to be when he ordered the assault to begin. Left behind was total devastation, cities, and villages alike. He had placed as the highest priority on his list the physical destruction of the Great City of Kalamar. His mind flashed back to the visions of the giant jasper walls as they turned into giant heaps of rubble. The joy of destruction continued to fill his soul. To see the city in such a state!

He, and he emphasized the *He*, created a combination of smoke, clouds, mist, and fog…a shroud, his shroud, that would hide the Three Suns and Moons of Kalamar. A simple edict…serve me or suffer, to those who survived. He felt the need for something more. Then it came to him to set the skies a-rumbling. Throughout the day and night, the skies rumbled to antagonize those who remained.

Without warning, Zorleg again broke the silence in the room. His laughter rose and fell, before it stopped as abruptly as it had started. He paused to cherish another memory.

Shaking his head, he slowly settled back into his throne. Many thoughts rapidly exploded in his mind. As great as his power had become, there was still much he did not understand. Who are those who are called *the Chosen*? Zorleg closed his eyes, slipping into deep thought. His bony fingers reached up to lightly stroke his temple. Uttering barely above a whisper, the words escaped his lips, "Who are they?" This was a great unknown that grated and angered him. So many questions passed through his mind. Silently he pondered, while his anger rapidly intensified. His nostrils flared as the passion of rage increased with each breath. From so long ago, one of the few things he remembered when he created his power of darkness was the story of the Chosen. Countless were the number of times the story was told at the Great Meeting Place.

Lord Zorleg rose from his throne, slowly standing, pacing around the room. He mumbled softly asking, “Where are their roots?” Wandering about, he spat out another question. “Who are these who have been called *The Chosen?* They are deeply entrenched, but deeply entrenched in what? Who would dare go against me and all my power?” Zorleg paused to ponder. “Whoever, wherever they are, I shall stop them. No one,” he paused briefly then defiantly shouted, “I shall remove them from existence! The Third Plane shall be mine! MINE!”

The First Attempt

The Guardian remained motionless after his unannounced and instant arrival. The long locks of his grey hair and beard held their pristine look. His purple robe reflected the bright rays of the sun on the bright day. Traveling as only he could, the only thing he could do at that particular moment was shake his head from side to side in disgust while he peered down intently at Benny. The look of grave concern and worry covered his face. He found the sight of Benny's body covered in so much blood acutely upsetting. While he looked down at Benny's lifeless appearance, he took a moment and thought things through rationally before he took any actions. *I should have arrived earlier! Had I gone with my gut instincts and done what I felt I should do, this would have been avoided. However, had I taken those actions, I would have created much greater problems for now and Benjamin's future. The temptation for me to interfere was so great. Why, out of all the things that were given, why did He create His rule of noninterference? I'm certain the minions of the Dark Lord had absolutely no idea who the three-year-old child was. The Dark Lord, however, knew exactly, even at his young age, who the child was. It is that knowledge and reasoning why he ordered his assassination. That is precisely why the Dark Lord sent two of his minions to carry out his bidding against the young child.* The Guardian pushed all his thoughts aside, paused for a moment and began to thoroughly survey the room and Benny's condition. He needed to formulate his plan before he moved, regardless of how much the sight of Benny's nearly lifeless body pained him.

First, The Guardian turned his attention to Benny and his condition. He immediately noticed how his shorts and t-shirt were soaked in a bright crimson. He also noticed how the pools of blood had formed around his left arm. Next, he looked at the wound itself and observed how the blood flowing from Benny's arm was nothing more than a minute trickle. The Guardian listened carefully, barely able to hear Benny's short and shallow breathing, his body remaining motionless. While it may have been faint, The Guardian confirmed Benny was still breathing He took the time and shook his head again, acknowledging this would be but the first of many dark days that awaited Benny as he grew and matured. The one thing The Guardian assured Benny in that moment of silence was that he was not alone now, nor would he ever be alone in the future.

The Guardian methodically crossed his arms and exhaled slowly through his nose. *Yes*, he thought, *the minions of darkness had left Benjamin for dead.* However, he felt the slight glimmer of hope that still burned deep within him. No, young Benjamin was not dead yet. The Guardian nodded his head. It was obvious that the young lad had been gravely wounded and was very near death. He emphasized, again, his vow that young Benjamin would never be alone again. The Guardian reached out his large hands and gently lifted Benny's bloody left arm. He held Benny securely in his left arm while he carefully extended the index finger of his right hand. Very methodically, The Guardian ran his finger lightly over the wound. He started with his finger in the meat of Benny's small hand, then followed the open gash down his forearm before stopping just above Benny's elbow. As The Guardian's finger delicately traced the open wound, the wound gradually closed before it suddenly started to glow a bright silver. It didn't take The Guardian long to trace the entire wound on Benny's arm. While his finger traced the open wound, The Guardian whispered words from the Ancient Language. When he had finished tracing the wound and his incantation, a brilliant flash filled the room. When the flash subsided, The Guardian smiled as he looked at the healed wound on Benny's left arm. The open wound was now closed and had been replaced with a distinctive brilliant silver glow. The Guardian's use of the Ancient Language had caused the bleeding to stop and left behind an unmistakable scar, exactly as he had intended. Effortlessly, The Guardian lifted Benny out of the pool of blood and off the kitchen floor, carried him in silence up the stairs, and placed him carefully in his bed.

It only took The Guardian a brief moment to secure Benny in his bed and cover him with blankets. After he had placed him in his bed, The Guardian knelt on one knee and spoke directly to him barely above a whisper. "This was but the first of many attempts on your life, an assignation attempt if you will, young Benjamin. While you sleep, I leave you with the memory that you will never be alone again." The Guardian slowly stood, now towering over Benny as he lay resting comfortably in his bed. As difficult as it had been, he took a great amount of pride in not violating the rule of noninterference. The Guardian needed to leave Benny alone for now and return to the kitchen to painstakingly observe the major havoc that had been left behind. He descended the steps in silence, breathing steadily through his nose, rotating his head slowly with every step, allowing his gaze to pierce every corner of the room. What he noticed was the multitude of glass shards and cookies scattered across the floor, a single chair on its back that had been tipped over, and the large pool of blood. He shook his head briefly, immediately lifted both of his hands slightly and temporarily closed his eyes. Once again, he spoke a few words from the Ancient Language softly. After the few words of magic left his lips, he gave a quick wave of his right hand, and it was finished. In that instant, everything in the kitchen had been returned to its rightful place. As he gazed around the room, there was nothing that remained of what had transpired only moments before. The Guardian's eyes scanned the room again to ensure he had missed nothing, and everything had been returned to how it was before he was attacked and left for dead. The chair Benny used to climb on for the cookies now rested under the kitchen table, exactly where it belonged. The cookie jar sat securely on the counter and remained just out of Benny's reach, fully intact. The pool of blood on the floor...gone. To the unknowing, nothing had happened in this room. The Guardian's long purple robe moved silently over the kitchen floor before he ascended the stairs and returned to Benny's bedside. It was comforting to see Benny sleeping soundly after his ordeal. The Guardian took great pride that the scar on his forearm continued to glow and pulse its bright silver. A smile crossed The Guardian's lips as he thought. *Sleep well, my child. You shall never be alone again.*

He watched Benny sleeping restfully for several moments. Almost unnoticeable, The Guardian moved his fingers slightly once more and whispered another enchantment in the Ancient Language. Silently he thought, no, commanded, *let me look into times past and see what happened before my arrival.* Directly in front of where he stood, a display instantaneously appeared, providing The Guardian with the means to see what was while he observed in silence. He remained deep in thought and motionless while he watched exactly how the events unfolded that preceded his arrival. Now he simply watched every moment, heard every word, of all the events that led up to Benny's injury and near-death experience.

Grink and Pounce arrived in what appeared to them as somewhat of a familiar place. It was like where they were before, yet it was different. Grink looked at Pounce and spoke with a cockney accent in a hushed tone just above a whisper, "I know we be where he sent us, but we where we 'posed to be? What tells us do that and where to do it?"

Pounce, without speaking, began to move to his right, cutting a path through the tall grass. Grink quickly fell in behind and followed Pounce's tracks. After running a short distance, they stopped and observed a small house in the distance. From what they could see, there was nothing that appeared to be significant about this small house. It was a plain white two-story house, with covered porches on the front and back. They instinctively knew, however, this was the home of the male child, one of those referred to as *the Chosen*. The two moved quickly and covered the distance from where they had stopped to hide behind a group of tall bushes located not far from the front entrance to the small house. It really was simple. From what they could see, it was a modestly furnished home with the needed bare essentials for comfort. They watched in silence, looking for the slightest movement from around the house. Grink felt an elbow dig into his side and looked at the outstretched arm and pointed finger of Pounce. In the distance, he saw Benny. "Humph, we found him. He looks younger than when we saw him before. How that be, Pounce?"

"Perhaps that makin' it easier 'n' better for us. Come, we need be closer." Pounce began to move as he spoke. His long legs made Grink move much faster than Pounce, who had short, stubby legs. Together, they reached the side of the house and peered inside through an open window. Benny appeared to be wandering aimlessly from one room to another. Grink felt another elbow in the side as he heard Pounce begin to speak softly, also in a cockney accent. "There! It appears he be looking for something, don't ya think? Oh, oh, oh...me has an idea." Pointing into the room, he continued, "See, there, be large jar, barely be out of his reach? If I be thinking correctly, he be tryin' to get to that jar and help himself. We, you, and me, we be his helpers for him, not only to be gettin' that jar but makin' sure the jar be fallin' from where it be. When it falls…BOOM! It be shattered into lots and lots of large sharp shards of glass scattered all 'cross the floor. Then, we be helpin' with a slight push. We be givin' a bit of guidance, and we be makin' certain he be fallin' on one of those pretty, pointed sharp shards." Both giggled with joy and wickedness over the plan they had concocted. "When others be returnin' to this dismal abode, there they be findin' him, awash in a pool of his own blood, all the life be drained out of him. He be dead, dead I tell ya! All the result of a simple accident we, you and me, orchestrated. He be tryin' to extract a morsel to enjoy from the jar. The jar falls and go boom, be brokin' on the floor, he be fallin' and go *splat*! He be landin' on one of those sharp, jagged shards of the jar. Be makin' me want to laugh and cry. Whatta 'bout you?" Pounce began to chuckle again as Grink joined in, so proud, the both of them.

Grink smiled. "So, you need be tellin' me, Pounce. Do I be the jar pusher, or I be doin' the cause of the boy's fall while you be guidin' his left arm to slice the wrist from finger to elbow?" Grink rubbed his hands together in anticipation, not caring which but overjoyed he was a vital part of this plan.

Benny, a small, young boy of three, was playing in his own world of make believe. A soft, gentle breeze pushed his blonde hair from side to side effortlessly. Dressed in a pair of cut off jean shorts, a t-shirt, and barefoot, Benny enjoyed feeling the cool grass between his toes as he ran around the yard. He wasn't running anywhere in particular, only running to enjoy himself and the dewy morning. Within his fenced-in yard, he had identified many special places he liked to spend a lot of time playing. One place, perhaps his favorite, was the old lilac bushes that had developed a growth pattern all their own in a corner of the yard. He enjoyed the multitude of fragrant blossoms covering the lilac bushes. In the spring, they filled his entire yard.

Within the yard were a few trees scattered about…trees that always seemed to beckon Benny to nothing but trouble. An apple tree here, a walnut tree there provided ample shade within the fenced yard, each provided a break from the sun and a place for Benny to rest. The trees also held a great temptation; Benny always heard them calling his name to climb. He had been warned on more than one occasion not to climb in the trees, but he couldn't help himself. Because he was told not to, he knew he must. He didn't try to climb too high but could never resist grabbing and swinging on the low-hanging apple tree limbs. He knew if anyone spotted him, a warning of concern about falling and breaking an arm would soon follow. Even though he was only three, he would always laugh at those who doubted him, but he wasn't sure why.

There were times, like today, when Benny would sit still and bask in the warmth of the sun. He loved mornings like this when he sat, watched, and observed everything around him. He could lean down and watch a worm as it worked its way out of the soil. Or maybe it was a butterfly that landed close by. There was always something begging for his attention. He heard and listened to the birds singing and dogs barking during his quiet moments. He really enjoyed the peace and tranquility it provided. He felt like he knew and understood exactly what each bird's song and dog bark was saying. He didn't understand why, but he knew he was right.

Should Benny happen to get thirsty while he played, and he often did, it was only a short walk from anywhere in his backyard to the old well. Old, yes, but it still worked. Benny knew the simple procedure of cranking the old iron pump to pull fresh, cool water from the well.

Regardless of how many times in the past he had done it, he still giggled when the water flowed out of the head and splashed onto the ground. Almost every time, he had forgotten to pick up the tin cup hanging alongside the pump to catch the water before it splashed everywhere.

It was easy for Benny to lose track of time when he played in the yard. He could run in the grass, jump over sticks, pick up rocks, or do whatever he felt like doing. He never questioned why he was left alone while others were out in the fields or in the barn. The morning had been full of hard playing, a lot of jumping and running about. Well, it was a lot for a three-year-old. Benny spent a lot of his energy and found himself getting hungry. Not really hungry, but hungry, nonetheless. He skipped over to the front porch, bounced up the steps, and entered his house. Benny's bedroom was on the second floor and overlooked the back porch. He always made it a game to run up and down the stairs, but he didn't need to go up the stairs to his bedroom now. He thought it a bit odd when he entered that no one was around, but he felt they were nearby, just not close enough to see or hear. *Maybe upstairs or visiting with neighbors*, he thought. Benny walked through the living room, past the sofa, and stepped into the kitchen. His brilliant blue eyes scanned the room and then suddenly stopped. There, on the counter, just out of his reach, he spotted the jar full of cookies. He thought for a moment, then sniffed the air. *Those are fresh chocolate chip cookies, too!* Even if he stood on his tip toes, he knew his small fingers would be unable to reach or move the cookie jar. Close, so very close, but the small distance might as well have been a huge canyon. The cookies and the cookie jar remained just out of the reach of his young hands and fingers. Benny looked around the room before his eyes stopped at the kitchen table. The perfect plan popped into his head. He walked over to the kitchen table and grabbed the closest chair. Slowly, using all his strength, he scooted the chair from the kitchen table over to the counter. This, Benny believed, would help shorten the distance from the floor to the kitchen counter. With great anticipation, he knew the cookies were now his for the taking. Benny crawled onto the chair and, just as he had expected, found the jar was now easily within his reach. He was so proud of himself and his accomplishment: his three-year-old arms now were able to reach the cookie jar!

Benny was completely unaware that he was not alone in the kitchen. He didn't notice the two shadowy figures while he devoted his full concentration on getting to the cookie jar and treating himself to a cookie or two. There were others hidden from his view, watching his every move. As they watched, they had plotted a very devious plan to inflict great pain and suffering, hopefully death, on young Benny. This was the moment they had been waiting for.

Grink and Pounce looked at each other and asked the unspoken question by the looks on their faces. *Now?* Silently they nodded their heads up and down in agreement when their eyes met. The meeting of the eyes, the shaking of their heads, gave the unspoken go-ahead for their plan. Grink grasped the legs of the chair and began to shake it violently. As the chair shook, Pounce pushed the cookie jar off the counter. Effortlessly, the cookie jar floated through the air until it landed on the hard kitchen floor. The sound of the cookie jar shattering filled the room. They looked at the remnants and smiled; the results were exactly as they had planned. From the shaking of the chair, completely unexpected by Benny, he lost his balance and tumbled to the floor. A second, maybe two, was all it took from start to finish. Everything passed through his eyes as if it were in slow motion. A broken jar and a floor littered with small and large jagged shards of glass formed the perfect recipe for disaster. As Benny fell, they guided his arm, so it landed firmly on one of the largest glass shards. Without a sound, the tip of the shard began to pierce the soft skin of Benny's left hand in the fleshy part of palm below his little finger, exactly as they had planned. The shard sliced deeper as it moved down his hand, traveling upward toward his elbow as he landed on the kitchen floor. Benny let out a blood-curdling scream from his tiny throat. Never had he experienced such excruciating pain. His little arm had been sliced open, blood flowing unabated out of the incision, rapidly creating a large pool on the floor. Young Benny continued to scream in agony from his wound. His young mind knew he was home alone, and all his screaming and crying were heard by no one. He continued to shriek and sob, sounds dwindling as he slowly began to fall unconscious from the bleeding. The pool on the floor grew larger with each beat of his heart.

The intruders, Grink and Pounce, moved off to the side, their view completely unobstructed as Benny lay sprawled on the floor. They watched with glee as the little boy bled. They were so proud of what they had accomplished. There was no one around to help, not a soul to hear his calls for help. Both watched with anticipation, clapping their hands together with great excitement. They watched and listened as his screams and cries became increasingly muffled, his life force slowly ebbing from his young body. With a nudge to get his attention, Pounce spoke to Grink. "Come now, we be leavin' him, leavin' him for dead. Not much good can come to him. He be dying soon." Letting out a joyful laugh, Grink and Pounce allowed big smiles to spread across their faces. "He be alone, no one be here to be helpin' him, not be anyone hearin' his screamin.' I be thinkin' His Lordship be pleased, very pleased, with us! We be doin' good, really good!" Pounce continued muttering.

"But what about her?" Grink asked.

"Oh, we be tellin' His Lordship that with how much we be doin' here there be no time lookin' for her…but we will."

"Yeah, we be so busy doin' so much that we be doin', but we did look, and we ne'er see her like we see him," Grink responded.

They both chanted, "Dead, dead, he be dead! One of the Chosen now be dead!"

As they had entered, so they returned, leaving the lifeless body of the small boy sprawled out on the kitchen floor in an ever-expanding, crimson pool. They gloated, smiled, and congratulated each other as they strolled casually back to the point of entry into his world. Both looked forward to the report they would give to Lord Zorleg. Neither bothered to stop and take a moment to look over their shoulders as they left the small dwelling. They knew he would shortly be dead. That's what they would tell Lord Zorleg, too. *He be dead but we not be havin' time to look for her. Time, we had no time, took long time, long time.* Now, they were more concerned about the trip back to the Lord of Darkness. It would have only taken a split second, the slight movement of the head to look over their shoulder to check. But no, they were too wrapped up in themselves and what they thought they had done.

The image The Guardian had been watching vanished. A smile covered his face while he spoke in a hushed tone to Benny. "Sleep well, young Benjamin. This was the first of many of your struggles and attempts on your life by the Dark Lord. While you sleep, remember, you will never be alone again. I was given the responsibility to teach and mentor the Chosen. It is a task that I shall not take lightly. Yes, the Dark Lord knows who you are, but he has no idea how great the power of the Chosen will become. I will be better prepared for the next attempt!" The Guardian left Benny soundly asleep but took great comfort that he had not left him alone. Whispering a few words in the Ancient Language, The Guardian magically returned to the Third Plane.

The First Warning

Slowly, Reevus stretched his arms and reached for the sky even before his eyes opened. Wriggling his fingers in and out, he listened to the birds, their joyful songs breaking the morning silence and filling the morning air. Slowly but surely, the same as every day before, Reevus lifted himself up from a restful night of slumber. First, he slipped one foot, then another, out of the comfort of his bed onto the cool floor. It was another peaceful morning after a very restful night of sleep. Reevus looked over his shoulder and chuckled as he stared down at Skippy. She was curled up in a ball on her pillow, sound asleep. Even with his movements, she never stirred. Letting out a short and quiet laugh, Reevus reached over and lightly stroked Skippy's back, making sure he did not disturb her slumber. When she was ready, and only then, would she rouse herself and get out of bed. Unless, of course, she was coaxed.

"Time to rise, my little friend. 'Tis another day." Skippy stretched out her puppy legs and rolled over on her back, ready to accept the loving touch of her master. Smiling, Reevus extended his hand and began to massage Skippy's stomach. "There you go, my girl. How does that feel? A good way to start our day, isn't it?"

After a few moments, Reevus rose from the bed and walked the few steps to his dresser. His sleeping room was very modest, with only his small bed tucked into one corner and a dresser up against another wall. A small table for two served as his breakfast table. On top of the dresser sat a glass pitcher and bowl. It was his nightly ritual making sure the pitcher was full of water, and positioned where it should be, before he turned in for the night. On the right side of the pitcher sat a large, empty bowl that he used to wash his face before he started his day. Silently, he lifted the pitcher in his left hand and filled the bowl two-thirds full before he placed the pitcher back in its place. He paused, looked out the window, then focused, allowing his eyes to drift to the design of both the pitcher and the bowl. Intriguing. He thought of the craftsmanship that laid out a pattern representing the great harvest. Reevus shook his head, leaned forward, and stopped to look at Skippy. "Time to get our day started, my friend?" Without waiting for a response, he dipped his hands into the freshly poured water and splashed it on his face repeatedly. The coolness was refreshing, and he continued the process for several moments before stopping. With his outstretched arm he reached for the towel that hung on the right side of the dresser. Vigorously, he rubbed the towel over his face. "Well, that should be enough to get me going!"

Located on the third wall of his small bedroom, Reevus had built his own wardrobe closet. Not that he was a carpenter, far from it, but he was proud of his work. It was a little something to give him a bit more space and help him organize his bedroom. He moved the few steps over to the wardrobe and pulled out one of his grey shirts with matching grey trousers. He always had a chuckle when he opened the wardrobe. It was filled with all grey except for one white shirt and a black pair of dress slacks. His daily attire for work was always the same and never wavered. Grey on grey. After dressing, he headed into his shop, picking up his apron as he walked out of the bedroom.

The rays of the morning sun filled his shop as Reevus paused to take a deep breath. "Ahhh, another beautiful day," he exclaimed. Without looking, he could hear the pitter-patter of little feet on the floor. Skippy was up and following his every step. Looking down, Reevus smiled as he greeted his four-legged friend. "Well, well, well, Skippy, it's gonna be another great day, isn't it? I'm sure you wouldn't mind a little something to start your day, would you?" Reevus bent down and patted Skippy on the head. "Yes, yes, I know…someone needs something to eat now, don't they? Go on now; it'll be in your bowl shortly." After Reevus had finished speaking, Skippy turned and took her spot in the corner of the shop on her day bed, as she awaited her morning feeding. Like clockwork, every day, the same routine for both. Reevus would be lost without her. They were perfect company for each other.

This day started like any other. Reevus turned slowly as he gazed around the room. There were many shoes to tend to and more canvases to mend for the farmers. This morning, however, something felt out of place. Exactly what it was, for now, Reevus couldn't put his finger on. He was certain the feeling would reveal itself before the day ended. It was not the first time he had this feeling, but like so many times before, he simply brushed it off. This time, however, the feeling had grown stronger, and he was unable to shake how uneasy it made him. He cleared his thoughts and began to bury himself in work. Even while he worked, the thoughts never drifted far from his mind and continued to linger through the day.

His foot moved methodically up and down, turning the wheels that caused the needle to rise and fall. The skill of the village cobbler was on display to anyone who walked by his shop. His body basked in the sun of a new day while he enjoyed its warming from the sun as it touched his skin. Merrily he went about his work as the day passed. He would always chuckle, sometimes only to himself, other times out loud, at something that struck him as funny. It was never too hot, never too cold, always the perfect temperature. Today time passed by quickly for Reevus as he tended to his daily routine. First one pair of shoes, then another, then another. Working with his skill and craftsmanship like no other, putting together again what was thought to be good for nothing. Not a new shoe, but a shoe as good as new, refurbished with either a new heel, a new sole, or both. Reevus smiled as he finished every piece of his work before moving on to the next.

Buried in his work, Reevus never heard the shop door open nor the footsteps of his guest when he entered. Skippy was never known to be a guard dog and continued to lie in her comfortable position, curled up in a tight warm ball, dreaming as only dogs dream. How long the visitor stood there, only he knew. Intently, he watched Reevus work as he placed a heel there, sewed a patch there. His mind on his work, Reevus hummed softly as he took one shoe after another to work on. Reevus looked carefully at each shoe to determine exactly what was needed and compared it to what the customer had asked for. Reevus quickly set about his work. Eventually, out of the corner of his eye, he finally noticed that he was no longer alone. Slowly Reevus turned, leaving a shoe secured in place in the sewing machine, and moved over to the counter.

"Reloc, why didn't you say something? It is always a pleasure to have you stop by! You do realize that your ability to remain so silent would startle someone, or worse yet, cause their heart to stop." After he finished his sentence, Reevus began to smirk, then he chuckled out loud.

Reloc, the youngest brother of Reevus, was dressed in his royal attire. He had served in the Royal Guard for the Emperor of Kalamar for many years. As a young man, he entered the service and slowly grew in knowledge, wisdom, and position. Now he not only was the leader of legions of men, but he was also in charge of the Great Fleet of Kalamar. Throughout the day one could see the Great Fleet loaded with the harvest from the fields sent to feed the other planes. Few knew the magical ability of the Great Fleet after they disappeared. Even when they watched the fleet, no one ever questioned why each ship was outfitted with cannons on both the port and starboard sides of the ship. To the untrained eye, the flaps concealing the cannons made each ship appear as if they were a loaded transport ship. The fully loaded great ships could only be seen leaving the harbor and heading out to the deep water of the Great Lake. What happened after they were out of sight was both a great mystery and a source of much local folklore. It was not uncommon for Reevus to mention them in his stories at the village inn about how they magically disappeared.

Reloc chuckled for a moment as he wondered how Reevus would morph today's meeting into another of those great stories. Reevus, known as a cobbler by day, was also the nightly entertainment to all who came to the inn to dine and listen to his stories. Reloc had always looked up to his older brother and admired his talents. He had his job and enjoyed serving but loved the moments when they could spend time together. Regardless of how busy Reevus may be, he always took time for the two of them to talk about things that were happening throughout the land.

Reaching out his hand, Reloc smiled, taking his brother's hand in his, greeting him warmly. "It is always amazing to watch you work. You are such a gifted craftsman. Methodical, tedious your work may be, but how gifted you are. Your expert craftsmanship is known wherever I travel." Reloc paused and slowly withdrew his hand. "Brother, do you mind if I might ask you a few questions?" Reloc's voice had changed to a hushed whisper, his eyes firmly locked his brother's.

"We have no secrets between us now, do we, brother?" Reevus replied softly. He could sense something different in the tone of Reloc's voice. Reevus kept his voice in a hushed tone. "Please, share with me what's on your mind."

Reloc leaned forward and placed his elbows on the counter. As if it were an unspoken signal, Reevus leaned forward so his ear was close to Reloc's mouth. Softly, Reloc asked, "Have you sensed anything different, anything off? While you are here daily seeing people come and go, my job takes me to other places." Reloc paused to take a breath before he continued. "Something just seems odd to me."

"Odd, what seems odd?" his older brother prodded.

Reloc continued, "Strangers. I've seen strangers buying up the harvest. First, it started with little, but they continued to buy more and more. A bit more concerning is the fact they are paying far beyond top price, sometimes five times more or greater. While the ships remain full, the amount of what is being gathered has changed. Secretly, I am trying to find out who is doing all the buying and why…it all seems so odd to me. Regardless of where we go, they have been there before us. My fear is soon we won't be able to load our ships full. My men have also noticed they have built great storehouses to hold the grain they are buying." Reloc drew another breath but remained quiet. His eyes met with Reevus's as they both silently stared at each other.

Reevus took his time to process what his brother told him. Finally, he leaned back, standing tall while he reached up with his right hand to stroke his cheek at the bone. "That does, indeed, seem very odd. Who would be interested in our harvest? And why? Odd, so very odd!" Like his brother, Reevus grew quiet as they continued to stare at each other. Neither spoke while they both processed the dark underlying meaning of their conversation.

Finally, Reevus broke the silence. "I do not understand the *why*, but I have had this feeling for some time now. What the feeling was, I knew not, but indeed it has been a very different feeling." Eyes firmly fixed on his brother's, his eyebrow moved upward as if casting a bit of doubt or seeking approval. "This morning, that feeling was even stronger." Without stopping, he continued and began to tell his brother, "When you return to bring in the harvest, give this message to the harvesters. Tell them to build storehouses of their own for their families. It is very important they are built out of sight, hidden, and concealed. We don't want whoever is doing the purchase to know they exist. Regardless of what else they do; it is extremely important. They must set aside 10% of every harvest and place it in the storehouse. No one, not even a neighbor, should know about the storehouse or where it is located. I have a feeling we will be facing very dark days ahead. Why, I don't know, but this feeling has grown stronger of late. The days of plenty from our harvest may soon come to an end. Answers will be given on another day." Again, Reevus paused. "I ask of you, brother, go and spread my words of wisdom to those who will listen. Is there anything else worthy of mentioning?"

"The buyers, regardless of where in the land they may be, were all wearing the same clothing. Each of them outfitted in black trousers with a gold stripe running down the leg, breaking at the knee to form a Z. I've seen it more than once myself. The first time I didn't give it much thought, but as I saw it more often, it began to pique my interest. No one knows the name of those who offer to buy, or who is doing the buying. Regardless of where they are encountered, it is always the same. The offer is too good to resist, and they are dressed the same…the black trousers and the bold, gold stripe and Z. Have you heard of any such thing?"

Reevus thought for a moment, then another, before he spoke in a voice no louder than a whisper, speaking to ensure that the words he spoke would be only for his brother's ears. "I have heard nothing, only the feeling. Something will be happening to what we know as Kalamar. My words may seem ominous, but the greater question will be…who will listen? With all the stories I have told, there is one that keeps coming to mind. Some will hear and scoff, others will hear and laugh, few will hear and take heed of the warning. They have laughed at my stories and were unable to separate fact from fiction. The one that seemed to have gotten the most raised eyebrows is when I told of The Chosen." Bewildered, Reevus slowly shook his head as he began to rub his left hand from his forehead over his scalp and then to his neck. "My brother, you need to be careful. I worry for you and about you." Silence again filled the room as Reevus stood motionless and quiet; his eyes fixed on his brother.

"I hear your warning, brother. But I, too, have a warning for you. In my travels, the same ones who do the buying have been asking questions. Strange questions, mind you. They ask who the greatest storyteller of them all is, the greatest in all the land. Resoundingly, it is your name they are given. For as you fear for me, I too, fear for you, brother."

"I shall heed your warning. From my time of telling stories, I will give a warning. Those who have ears will listen; others will ignore and go about their merry ways. We have only so much that we can do. But you, dear brother, I have this feeling that you will be taken care of. It's a feeling I can't explain or describe. When the happening comes, it will be swift and as sharp as a hot sword fresh from the furnace cutting through butter. By the time anyone remembers the stories and the warnings, they will realize something has happened, and by then it will be far too late."

Meeting The Guardian

Sitting on the west side of a small town was a simple, two-story, white house. You couldn't approach without noticing the multitude of flower beds surrounding the house. Spring flowers of all sorts were in different stages of bloom. Beyond the flower beds, at the edge of the property lay the freshly planted garden and more flowers. On the east side of the house, a wire fence separated the end of the driveway from this world of make believe. Between the fence and the back porch, right next to the lilac bushes, Benny, a young lad of five, was lost in a place and time of his own making. He was dressed comfortably in a pair of old jeans that he had cut off and made into jean shorts. He was mighty proud of himself, too; he cut them without any help. All Benny needed on this warm day was a T-shirt, leaving him barefooted. He couldn't get more comfortable than he was at that moment. He sat motionless, caught up in his own thoughts. He had surrounded himself with roadways made from rocks and sticks to form a maze of streets and city blocks in his imaginary town. With his small hands, he pushed discarded scraps of wood blocks he had turned into cars up and down his thoroughfares. Occasionally, Benny would stop and make the *vroom vroom* sound of a car engine as he drove about his town. To the side of his thoroughfare, he used some of the broken sticks to represent people or large brick houses. This was his world and his imagination for this moment in time.

Hovering above the treetops, The Guardian floated silently, transparent to the human eye. He looked down and smiled as he watched Benny playing in the stillness of the morning. He saw a small boy and remembered the first time the two met. It was not important to The Guardian that the Child didn't remember when or how they met. *In time, he will remember.* This was where The Guardian had hidden him, Benjamin, the Male Child of The Chosen, in time. He had returned to continue cultivating and bringing to life the hidden talents and traits Benjamin was given on his birth. One of two, he was given gifts that had not been heard of, let alone used, for over a millennium, if not longer. The gifts were only referenced in the magical ancient writings and the words of storytellers. The Guardian paused and took a moment to reflect, remembering how many times Zorleg had taken a messenger from him. It still pained The Guardian, but he continued to press on, remembering Zorleg could, and had, stopped a messenger, but he had never been able to stop the message. Now, looking down, The Guardian pushed those thoughts from his mind, as he felt quite confident Zorleg would not be able to stop Benjamin.

Through all time, on all planes of Kalamar, the message continued. With this thought fresh in his mind, The Guardian effortlessly descended and landed, silently, close to Benny. A few softly spoken words escaped his lips after he landed, allowing The Guardian to transition from translucence to a solid body which stood just out of Benny's view. The Guardian, firmly on solid ground, also noticed the two underlings of Zorleg, Grink and Pounce, hidden under the back porch. He knew exactly where they were, what they were doing, and why they were there. The Guardian could see them even now and noticed how they peeked from the abandoned and covered cistern under the porch. He wondered if the two would continue the charade they started at the farmhouse, having Zorleg believe Benny was dead. He paid no further attention to them and continued to watch Benny, undisturbed by it all, as he played.

Grink, the taller of the two, found his body cramped in the tight confines of the cistern. It was a struggle for him not to cry out in pain and agony, but he remained silent and endured. Pounce, on the other hand, being much smaller, had no difficulty with the space they found themselves in. Both pondered why Zorleg chose them, but they were extremely grateful for his recognition. Neither spoke, but they knew they could not report to Zorleg what they were doing, where they had been or what they witnessed. After all, they had told Zorleg years ago they killed Benny. They both saw how big of a lie they told, and they needed to correct things with Zorleg or face his wrath.

Neither Grink nor Pounce understood the significance of this young child, nor could they see how a young child could be a threat. They didn't understand it years ago, and they still didn't understand it now. They would not judge the *why*. Both hoped beyond hope they would be able to figure out some way to actually do what they told Zorleg was done. They were overjoyed with the gifts and rewards Zorleg had bestowed on them, but they also lived with a sour dose of reality. They knew exactly what would happen once Zorleg discovered the lie and deception. How thankful they were that he hadn't found out yet.

The Guardian took a few steps until he stood next to Benny. He spoke in a soft but encouraging voice. "You have created a very elaborate city, my child. Did you do that all by yourself?" As he spoke, the Guardian knelt in the dirt, placing his knee beside the young boy, not worrying about getting his robe dirty or whether the child would even notice the peculiar garb.

Without blinking an eye, Benny quickly responded in the innocent way that only a young child could. "Well, it's not real you know, and I can't drive. I'm not old enough yet. Here," Benny waved his hand over his city, "I have all that I need, and I can do whatever I want and be whatever I want to be." Benny smiled from ear to ear as he spoke rapidly; his face beamed with excitement while he talked, pushing one of his cars down the little street.

The Guardian kept his eyes on Benny while he slipped his right hand into his pocket and pulled out a stone. The stone was bright red jasper, smooth oblong, cool to the touch, and it was highly polished. The Guardian slowly reached out his hand to Benny. "Would you like a special stone, young man? Here, take this. You can use it as one of your cars, maybe a house, whatever you would like."

Benny's eyes grew wide and beamed with excitement. "Oh wow! Thank you, Mister! I've never seen a rock so perfect, so smooth, and it's so cold, too." It was hard for Benny to contain his excitement.

"And should you ever need a playmate, or perhaps someone to talk to, just rub your jasper stone in your hand, close your eyes and say to yourself, ***Dreams don't last forever, but dreams are not forgotten***. When you speak those very words and rub the stone, I will hear your voice and come. Then, at your calling, we will be able to talk again. There is something else I would like to share with you. If you place this stone up to your ear, if you listen closely, you may be able to hear it talk to you. Sometimes, though not always, you may hear it sing." The Guardian beamed with joy as he watched the excitement build in Benny.

Before Benny could speak, The Guardian's right hand reached into one of the many pockets of his robe and pulled out a small puppy. "Do you think you can watch my puppy for me? He'll make a very loving companion. I call him Cosmo, but you can change the name if you'd like. Perhaps the two of you would be good companions for each other?"

Benny turned and reached out to The Guardian and took the puppy in both hands. He sat down and placed the puppy in his lap and started to scratch the puppy's head with one hand and show him the stone with the other. He was overjoyed to have a puppy of his very own. Benny removed his hand from Cosmo's head and turned to say thank you again. Cosmo bolted to the back porch and began to bark loudly and nonstop. When Benny turned, there was no one there, and Cosmo wouldn't stop barking. The Guardian was gone and Benny, once again, was alone, except for his new puppy yipping at something under the porch.

Benny jumped up and ran around the corner of the back porch, through the back yard, to the gate, then out of the gate and to the front of the house. He looked everywhere, but the kind old man was nowhere to be found. Benny thought to himself that it was as if he had vanished into thin air.

The Guardian hovered above the treetops, once again transparent as he peered down at Benny. He couldn't stop smiling. *For this one it has now begun. Tonight, shall be his first night of dreams, beginning a long journey that will allow him to see what lies before him and the tasks that await him. While only a child, his mind had already grown well beyond the limitations of his youth, exactly as it was spoken on the day of his birth.* The Guardian calmly watched as Benny returned to his city of make-believe on the east side of the porch.

Under the porch, Zorleg's minions looked at each other and grinned. Their heads were barely visible in the shadows, shielded from the brightness of the day and the clutter under the porch. Cosmo's barking startled them both. How could that dog even know where they were? The Guardian, from his lofty perch, watched quietly as both spoke at the same time, "They know not that we be hiding here." Laughter escaped their lips as they patted each other on the back in the tight confines of the cistern. "They so dumb, they not suspect we even be here 'cept that stupid dog. What be with that dog? How he see us? How he knows we be hidin' here?" Quietly, they began to move. Not up, but down, deeper into the darkness of the cistern. Descending into the darkness, they began to plot how they would use this new knowledge to continue their great deception. The same magic that brought them returned them to where their secret journey had begun. It was their mission - and one that must be added to the things they intentionally kept from the lord of darkness.

Reevus - The First Story

Reevus walked through the inn's front door, turned to his left and took up his normal spot at one of the tables closest to a window. For the moment, he was lost in his own thoughts. What he would order for his evening meal could wait until he had taken a seat. Had anyone taken a moment and looked his way, all they would have seen was the village shoe cobbler settling in after a long day of work, getting ready to enjoy his evening meal. During his walk from his shoe shop to the village inn, he felt a calm and stillness wash over him. He immediately knew he was not alone. A calm and an assuredness would guide him as he told his story this evening, but only after he had finished his meal. This was not the first time he felt the presence and was thankful for its return.

Reevus was known for being a storyteller, though not any storyteller, but the greatest storyteller of them all. He was the greatest. He always had a new adventure to share at the inn, but tonight it would be a very special story for his audience. He knew, like other nights, every person huddled around him would be listening and watching intently. With every word he shared from his story of intrigue, magic, and enchantment, he captivated and drew all of them in. Unlike his stories before, his audience of young and old alike would grasp his tonal inflections. Unlike any of his prior stories, his voice would rise and fall when he emphasized his major points.

Reevus was fully aware on this night they would not be his words, even though he was the one speaking. They were words specifically crafted and prepared for him for this exact moment in time.

Reevus was thankful he was gifted with being able to tell stories. He was equally thankful for this unseen presence accompanying him, providing him with words like no other when he needed them the most.

When he began his story, Reevus would instinctively know what questions needed to be offered at the beginning to draw his audience of young and old alike into a web of fascination. Unlike what Reevus had said before, however, the ending of this story would be filled with warnings and unanswered questions sandwiched in between careful words. Provided to his listeners, between the beginning and the end, he would present another glimpse into *what was, what is, and what is yet to come*. What he offered on that night would be understood by many exactly as it was meant to be but scoffed at by others as only another story.

The barmaid, Miss Katie, quickly appeared on his right side, snapping him out of his trance. Reevus let out a soft chuckle, acknowledging her presence before she spoke, knowing exactly what Miss Katie was going to say before she even said it. Outwardly he appeared to be the same old jovial Reevus. Inwardly, he couldn't shake the feeling that pressed upon him with a great urgency, even with Miss Katie asking him the same questions she'd asked countless nights before. He pushed the thoughts out of his mind for the moment. He couldn't ignore what he felt, but for now it must wait as he turned his head and looked up at Miss Katie's gleaming smile.

"Well, top of the evening to you, Mr. Reevus. What will it be?" Miss Katie asked cheerfully.

Reevus couldn't help but let a smile spread across his entire face as he looked into Miss Katie's blue eyes. "Tell me now, what might you have back there that would fill a hardworkin' man's stomach and be savoring to my taste buds?" he asked. "You know, you're gonna be hard pressed to surpass that delicious chicken and noodles dish from last night." His voice trailed after a small chuckle while he awaited Katie's response to tonight's offerings.

She couldn't help but let out a small chuckle herself. "Not to be one to disappoint you Mr. Reevus, but we do have some delicious, mashed potatoes, peas, and a meatloaf that I am pretty sure will have you forgetting last night's meal in no time."

Reevus rubbed his hands together to show his appreciation for tonight's menu. "Say no more, say no more, that's what it will be. No, no, you won't have me trying to decide between such wonderful meals. My mind is made up…don't tempt me with anything else please." He held up his hands as if to stop her reply then put them back down on the table in good nature. Reevus leaned slowly forward and spoke in a voice no more than a whisper as he asked her softly, "Now my dear Miss Katie, you wouldn't happen to have some fresh apple pie hidden back in the kitchen, would you? Just in case I might need a little something sweet after such a delicious meal. You know, something I might need to clean my palate." Reevus was overly animated with his gestures as he teased Miss Katie.

Her blue eyes sparkled before Miss Katie leaned back, stood erect, and prepared to walk away. "Mr. Reevus, you know we always have fresh pies. I'm pretty sure the baker always, and I mean always, makes an extra one or two to be certain there is plenty for you." Before she moved away, Miss Katie leaned down close to his ear and whispered, "Truth be told, Mr. Reevus, I have heard there is a special pie made just for you. But no more from me. Not until you have finished tonight's meal will you know the surprise that awaits you."

"Well, that sure warms my heart, my dear Miss Katie, or would that be my tummy? I know it will hit the spot!" Reevus chuckled again as he reached down, picked up the napkin from the table, shook it, and tucked it into his collar, letting it flow down over his chest and stomach. He paused for a moment before he looked over at Katie again and asked, "was there something else, Miss Katie?"

Miss Katie's blue eyes beamed brightly at the question she was hoping he would ask. "Well yes, Mr. Reevus, actually there is." She raised her left hand just a bit, trying her best to be inconspicuous, and pointed to a corner of the room. "Do you see all the children gathered over there? I want you to know not one, but all of them, have been asking for quite some time if you planned to share one of your stories tonight." Miss Katie paused and smirked before she sheepishly asked, "If you would, that is, Mr. Reevus? Oh, but only after you have finished your piece of pie of course." Reevus noticed the twinkle in her eyes, the excitement in her voice, and the indiscreet wink when she asked her question. Yes, he knew she asked for the children, but she, too, enjoyed the stories he told. His stories put the entire room into a trance, every ear hanging on every word while he took them on a journey of make believe. He was a master at captivating the entire audience, drawing them deeper into his story.

Reevus, as he had always done in the past, mumbled humorously before he raised his head and looked into her eyes. "Well, Miss Katie, you march yourself right over to the young ones and let them know Mr. Reevus would be happy to share a story, a very special story, with them." He paused before he continued, "and yes, it will be for you, too, my dear friend. I know you enjoy them just as much as the children." Reevus winked at her when he finished telling her what he knew she wanted to hear.

Miss Katie excused herself, thanked Mr. Reevus for his order, and swiftly walked over to the children. Reevus watched as she leaned down and spoke to each child. "I want all of you to know Mr. Reevus will be happy to share one of his stories tonight with you after he finishes his dinner. He also wanted you to know this is going to be a very special story, too. Will each of you promise us, and all that has gathered tonight, that you will be quiet and still when he shares his story with us? Ok." Each child's head bobbed up and down as they nodded eagerly, showing they understood what was expected of them when Reevus began.

Now alone with his thoughts again, Reevus returned to planning how he would begin this evening's tale. Then it dawned on him: by simply asking a few questions. A simple first question, *"Who thought the stories I told were an embellishment of something that happened?"* He would wait to see how many hands were raised. He would follow the first question with his second. *"Or was it just an old storyteller making up a story to please you?"* Reevus would ask them to show, by raising their hands, if they believed his story had already happened, if the story is happening now, or was it something that had yet to happen in the future?" Now he had his plan in place.

Reevus knew the children were not the only ones filled with excitement. Before his meal arrived, Reevus discreetly glanced about the room and watched as the adults and older children alike covered their lips and motioned to every child to be silent in anticipation of tonight's story. Without a sound, Reevus picked up the glass and took a sip of cold water. He enjoyed feeling the water glide down his parched throat, refreshing him with its coolness. He watched as the children pointed in his direction, whispering to each other. He couldn't help but smile at the excitement slowly building around the room. For him, this was an unspoken acknowledgement that he was expected to take his normal spot shortly and begin his story of the night, to spin stories as only he could.

Reevus was cracking himself up as he thought. Regardless of what he would weave, they all waited anxiously for him to start.

Reevus chose to slowly savor each bite of his meatloaf while he gathered his thoughts. With each bite, he emitted a low grunt or humming, showing how much he enjoyed his meal. The right amount of seasoning, not too juicy and not too dry. Along with the mashed potatoes, it all dissolved in his mouth and left behind a very savory taste. After swallowing another bite, Reevus allowed his thoughts to return to his coming story. They spun in his mind as he considered ways to express his thoughts. Unlike stories before, he felt it very important to gauge what they thought and felt. Was he able to get his point across as he had intended?

The end of the story worried, puzzled, and intrigued Reevus most. He wasn't sure how telling a story that had a very different ending would be taken. Almost all his previous stories had an outcome that brought pleasure to those who heard them. Reevus wrestled with his thoughts and sought assurance everything would be as it should. He felt when they got up to leave at the end of the story they would be left with many thoughts as they tried to answer his questions. "*What if the story Reevus told was not a story at all? What if Reevus was telling us What Has Been, What Is, and What Is Yet To Come?*" Reevus liked how that sounded. If he had done his job correctly, he had painted a picture that would have left them all wondering. Carefully, very carefully would he speak the words that had been prepared. Dire warnings and the consequences of failure would be many of the words that Reevus used. Simply put, the Third Plane of Kalamar, as they knew it, would not exist. This was a story of a time long past but brought into the future. A story they all must hear and know.

Reevus' heart pounded. He reached for his glass, prepared to take another sip of the cooling water, but as quickly as he had started to lift the glass, he set it back down. His hands shook too much to even think about trying to lift the glass to his lips. His earlier merriment faded, for it was no laughing matter. The reality and the consequences of this story and its warnings weighed heavily on him, unlike ever before. Slowly, Reevus inhaled deeply before he softly exhaled to calm himself; his emotions must be controlled to effectively deliver this message in the form of one of his greatest stories.

The Great Deception

Grink and Pounce unceremoniously returned to The Third Plane Kalamar. Neither understood the *how,* but it didn't seem to bother either. They were sent by His Lordship to do his bidding, and now they had returned. Simple as that. What lay ahead of them, however, was a very sticky moment. Lord Zorleg had sent them to dispose of the male child called the Chosen.

During the brief time of travel for their return, Grink formulated and played out in his mind exactly how he would present the story in explicit detail of how they had left the male Chosen, recounting how they both had come up with the plan and the results.

Grink was full of confidence and excitement, unable to contain his emotions as they waited anxiously to be called before His Lordship. Pounce was exactly the opposite, quite a mess. Literally, he shook in his boots. He was so overcome by fear, he couldn't speak, only stutter. How thankful he was he had agreed to allow Grink to do all the talking to Lord Zorleg!

They were escorted into Lord Zorleg's chambers by one of his guards. Pounce couldn't speak, even if he had been asked to. Grink remained silent, awaiting Lord Zorleg's permission to speak. During the silence, Grink's eyes moved nervously around the room, glancing only briefly at the throne. He knew it was not his place to look at Lord Zorleg until spoken to. They both remained silent and waited for a moment that appeared to be frozen to both. Grink wondered if this was a ploy of intimidation by their master. He thought, *"I can wait as long as you want, but I shall not speak until spoken to.* Grink had heard stories of those who had displeased His Lordship, and he would do all he could so they would not suffer the same unpleasant fates as others before them.

Lord Zorleg placed both of his hands on the armrest of his throne and leaned forward. He spoke to neither, but both at the same time. "So, tell me, minions, what is your story? Lest you forget, should your words not be the words I expect to hear…" and then Zorleg's voice trailed off without finishing.

Pounce, again, was so thankful he did not have to speak. When Lord Zorleg had finished, he bowed before him, as did Grink. Grink stood, but Pounce remained with his knee on the floor and his head bowed. He felt as if he was going to throw up and fought with all his strength not to.

After he stood, Grink looked up and waited until he was prompted to speak. After a few moments, Zorleg raised his left hand and prompted Grink to speak.

Smiling, Grink looked up. "It be with great pleasure we returns to your presence, Great One. Such an adventure."

Lord Zorleg boomed from his throne, "Adventure? Is that what you thought this was…an adventure?"

Grink profusely apologized for his choice of words. "Begging Your Lordship's forgiveness for me poor choice of words. Let me starts over."

Zorleg motioned again with his left hand, and Grink continued.

"We found the young boy, 'bout in his third year, Your Lordship. Why, we know not, but when we found him, he be all alone. He be alone a long time, long long time. But we stayed hidden, watching. While we hidden, we, Pounce and me, Your Lordship, came up with a plan. We, the two of us, followed the young lad into his dwelling. Oh, Oh, Oh, we so proud of our idea. Poor boy he be hungry, but what he be wantin' be just out of his reach by this much." Grink held his hand up with his thumb and forefinger barely apart to emphasize how close the Chosen was to what he was after. "That be the beginning of our fantastic idea. Me, I be tellin' Pounce, *Now what if you and me give him a bit of help*. One of us shook his chair, it be causin' him to fall *Splat!* on the floor. While he be in the middle of fallin', we be pushing this big vessel onto the floor. Oh, how the noise fillin' the room as it shattered! Shards, big shards, be scattered all over the floor. We make sure he be falling right on one of those shards, Your Lordship."

Grink paused for a moment to catch his breath, wondering if he would be prompted to continue. Just as he was ready to begin telling more of the story, he heard Lord Zorleg's voice. "Hmmmmm, go on."

Taking a deep breath, Grink described how the Chosen had fallen and how they had directed his arm, so it landed on the largest shard. Grink held his hand up and pointed to a point just below his little finger. "Sire, be slit from here to here," he moved his finger down his arm, "and blood, oh, Sire, such a pool of blood coming from his wound covering all 'bouts him. Not one movement Sire, not one, I tell you. We, me and Pounce, we looked at him lyin' there, watchin' how the pool kept growing larger and larger." Grink now spoke with great excitement in his voice. "And, Sire, you be likin' this, he be home alone. No Sire, no one be even close. We checkin' on that when we arrived. He be alone, he be alone in his pool of blood, Sire. Big blood pool." Grink waved his hand far and wide to signify how large the pool was.

Pounce, head still bowed, had remained silent and motionless the entire time. Throughout Grink's retelling of events, not one word was incorrect. Now Pounce wondered if Zorleg would ask or if Grink would say, "He is dead." No sooner had the thought crossed his mind than he heard Lord Zorleg's booming voice.

"Then the male Chosen is now dead. Is that correct? And her, what about her?"

Grink smiled with glee as he lied the biggest lie of his entire life. "Yeppers, Your Lordship, he be dead, as dead as I be standing here right now. But beggin' the Lordship's pardon, it be takin' so long for us to do him in, we be left with no time to search for her, Your Majesty. If you be givin' us another chance, I'm sure we be findin' her and rid you of your worries of her too, Sire."

Silence filled the room after Grink had finished his great lies. Pounce trembled and wondered why they didn't pause, turn, and look to make sure they had actually killed the Child. Yes, yes, yes, he knew that anyone with those types of injuries should be dead…but he couldn't be sure. Oh lordy, he thought…her? They didn't devote one iota of time to searching for her. At least Grink was not lying on that aspect, just not really telling exactly how things were. Pounce trembled in fear, feeling his life ready to come to an end at any moment.

The silence continued until finally they heard Lord Zorleg speak. "Leave me now, I have much to ponder. When I am ready, I will send for you. Now, both of you, go."

Neither wasted a moment as they quickly left Lord Zorleg's chambers. Whether it was out of fear or common sense, they uttered not a peep as they scampered away. As far as Pounce was concerned, silence was necessary for now.

Now alone in his chambers, Lord Zorleg replayed the story over in his mind again and again. He concentrated on the male of the so-called Chosen lying in a pool of his own blood, his life slowly ebbing away. A smirk appeared across Lord Zorleg's lips. He was overjoyed but refused to allow any outward sign of emotion beyond the slight twisting of his thin lips. He stood and summoned his guards. Once they were in his chambers, he paused before he stood and slowly paced around the room.

"Word has come to me that the male child of the Chosen has met his demise. I do not find that it is an unfortunate happening but rather was exactly as I ordered." The smirk once again appeared on his lips, but still he contained his joy. "Your job is now to go out into the surrounding villages and hamlets and listen to the stories. Go, blend in with those who survived, and pump them for information. Then report back to me on what those few meager souls who remain have to say. Tell me how they react when they learn their so-called male Chosen is dead.

"First, the male child was found and disposed of at my orders, now to find the other. Female, hah, who would dare send a female to even try to come into my presence?" All the guards listened obediently to Lord Zorleg's orders. It was not their place to question or correct. Many, however, felt his scoffing of the power of the female Chosen was a huge mistake. They, too, had heard the stories, but they dared not interject, only to do as told.

Lord Zorleg dismissed them as quickly as they had been called. He milled around for a bit before settling back into his throne. As he did so, he lifted his left hand to his chin and stroked his beard. One of the Chosen was no more. While his desire was both of them, he excitedly accepted that one was dead. *And how hard can it be to find a girl?* he mused. Lord Zorleg was completely unaware that during this entire time he had been smashing his clenched fist into his open palm while he played the thoughts through his mind of the events that had taken place. Anxiously he would await the return of those he had sent to mill about in the crowds in the cities to see what the people of the barren world had to say. He could sense his power growing. With the Chosen eliminated, who could stand against him? Yes, another step closer to conquering all Kalamar. Lord Zorleg continued to pound his fist into his hand.

Part 2

His Beginning – Zorleg

Zorleg sat motionless, alone in his chambers, lost deep in thought. His long, black robe disappeared into the matching shadows on the floor. *"How many years have I waited for this day?"* he wondered silently. He rose slowly from his throne before moving across the cold, damp cobblestone to the window, and he peered at the darkness and destruction – the unfathomable blackness he had created.

He began to replay how he had laid out the plan of destruction. He had lain waste and conquered the Third of the Seven Planes, Kalamar, the same plane where his own teachings had begun long ago. He snickered, recalling that exactly what he was supposed to have been taught had long since passed from his thoughts. All formal teaching he'd replaced with his own ego, now fueled by how powerful and destructive he had become. "Children, please concentrate on the task at hand. We understand it seems mundane to you, but it is very important and part of your learning." How many times had Zorleg heard those words of instruction?

Bah, stupid! This is a complete waste of my time. Don't you realize how much more I can do? Zorleg thought as he grew impatient and angry with the repetitive teachings. It was monotonous and boring, the same mundane thing day after day. He knew he could do more, so much more. The rebellion and anger stewed within the inner recesses of Zorleg's mind.

Why can't they get it? It's so simple. Please can't we do something else? Zorleg remembered well his frustration with the teachings. He also wondered exactly what they were being taught and for what. Zorleg no longer found any reason to remember exactly where he was when he placed the pieces of his destructive plan together. His mind did not fail him for the plan itself, though. Methodically, step by step, he plotted and schemed. First, he would rid the air of the birds. He hated hearing their melodious songs. They seemed to bring great joy and happiness, so they needed to go. Next, he directed his attention to the water and removed a source of food. He laughed at the fishing fleets returning with empty holds, holds normally filled to the brim with the daily catch. He thoughtfully began to lay ruin to The Great City of Kalamar.

It felt like only yesterday, hearing the orders given and carried out.

"Trebuchet at the ready!" From one station to another, the same command was given.

When the last battalions report arrived, he smiled and waved his hand. His field commanders followed his instructions.

"Fire at will!" could be heard passing from one station to the next. Giant fireballs of burning oil bags and sulfur, or huge boulders, were launched nonstop. As rapidly as the trebuchet could be reloaded, it would fire again. From one, a boulder strikes the walls; from another, bags full of burning oil.

"Now we shall see how well the walls of jasper protect the city." Zorleg looked on in glee. He watched the wall slowly begin to break away.

"Move forward, move closer to the city. The walls are crumbling. Now for everything within the walls," he commanded.

He paused to wonder how fresh the air would be after he turned The Great City into ruins. He was quite certain the sweet fragrance of flowers that once filled the air would be no more, replaced by the foul stench of burnt sulfur. It would be another constant reminder of his great feat with every breath they took.

By his directions, all warmth from its three suns had been removed from the Third Plane. He replaced it with his creation of smoke, mist, and fog...*he did that.* His shroud would bring darkness to Kalamar for eternity. With their suns blocked, the people in this once-great city would be deprived of the warmth they had grown accustomed to.

"Welcome to your Lord Zorleg's world of Darkness," he could remember saying.

Even those deeds were not enough to satisfy his rage and anger; he needed something more.

"They see the darkness. Now let them hear my world of darkness!" Zorleg crowed. The skies would rumble both day and night.

"Listen to your new lives. Hear the sound as it moves across the sky, rumbling, never ceasing." The sound would move from east to west and then again from north to south to antagonize those who remained.

Zorleg enjoyed the view after his assault. Trees, bushes, grass, all burnt, charred, or dried and brittle. A dismal picture of the once-beautiful countryside, now nothing but a wasteland.

Those who dwelt on Kalamar had relished the warmth and light in the evening skies from the Three Moons since the beginning. Zorleg laughed, reveling in the knowledge that what blocked the suns would also block the moons.

He looked at his world of darkness. "First the suns, now the moons...all will be hidden from view. Me, I did this. Yes, I did it all."

Maybe it was part of him, maybe it was an afterthought, maybe it began during the mass destruction. He didn't know, nor did he care. This was his world of darkness, his creation. Zorleg slowly turned and walked away from the window. He paused every few steps to relive what he had planned.

He stopped in the middle of the room and began to rub his hands together.

"Where are they now?" Zorleg asked his question out loud. He rejoiced, for there were no more storytellers. "Where are their spun tales, casting out thoughts of magic and illusions, fairy tales, and myths when they told those stories?" A smile crept across Zorleg's face as he relished their extinction.

He felt – no, he knew – there was something more to the storytellers than just whimsy for children. Now that they were no more, how dismal were the meals at the inn for the wretched and meek who survived and came for a meal. Now they would eat what he decided they would eat, or they could starve. From his spies, he knew every inn had a storyteller to end the meal. Now that they were gone, Zorleg vowed whatever they kept, he would discover and add it to his growing power.

Zorleg was lost deep in thought. He didn't realize he had stopped, and his hand had moved to his chin, stroking the strands of his beard. As quickly as he had stopped, he began moving again. As he walked, he felt something gently pass over his ear. For whatever the reason, this had been a constant reminder that continued to infuriate him. *How could this be*, he wondered? Still, he could hear it as distinctly as if the words were spoken word at the very moment… The wind whispered his name!

"Zorleg."

When it first began, he thought it was his imagination playing tricks on him. It had gone on for too long for it to be something so simple. As time passed, this mysterious voice became both louder and more distinct. Zorleg was certain this did not come from his imagination, but from where it came, or whom, it puzzled him. For now, he allowed it to exist. *With the destruction, so too will be the removal of the breeze of Kalamar*. He detested its warm touch and wanted no part of it.

Without warning, Zorleg broke the silence in the room. From deep within, his laughter rose and fell, before it stopped as abruptly as it had started. He paused, and a snarl formed on his lips as he fought to recall the name they gave the wind on this plane. “Yes,” he murmured to himself, “the wind, too, will be gone.” How, he didn’t care, only that it, too, would follow the plan of destruction and be no more.

Zorleg moved to his throne and sat down. Shaking his head slowly side to side, he felt the many thoughts rapidly floating through his mind. As great as his power had become, there was much he still did not understand.

“The Chosen,” he whispered.

By his very essence, he knew there was something different about them. He didn’t know why, only that they were unique. Zorleg closed his eyes, mentally slipping into deep thought. He began to ask himself question after question but had no answers.

Uttering barely above a whisper, the words escaped his lips. “Who are they?”

The great unknown continually grated on and angered him.

“Where is the other?”

Silently he pondered while the intensity of his anger rapidly rose. His chest expanded and fell with each breath; his nostrils flared.

“How dare they even think of challenging me?”

From so long ago, one of the few things he remembered when he created his darkness was the story of The Chosen. Countless were the times it was taught at the Great Meeting Place.

Were they telling us a story? Zorleg wondered. *Or were they telling us what the future holds? If they could tell the story of The Chosen, did they not know it was me they would be facing?*

His nerves getting the better of him, Zorleg could sit no more. He stood up and frantically walked around the room, pacing from wall to wall. He began to mumble out loud.

"Where are their roots?" He spat another question as he moved about. "Deeply entrenched, but deeply entrenched in what?"

Perhaps even more perplexing, by whom? Who would dare go against all his power? Zorleg had never given a thought to anything other than his greatness and his power, but still the same questions returned repeatedly, causing him to take time to pause and reflect.

"Where are they?" Zorleg's other thoughts faded into deep contemplation.

Benny and the Darkness

Shortly after celebrating his seventh birthday, Benny stood motionless, trying to understand what was happening and where he was. His mind spun as he tried to comprehend his surroundings. His mind blurred. While he was only seven, he had the maturity of someone far greater in years than his young age. Benny found himself surrounded by total darkness and silence. He could hear and feel the beat of his own heart as his mind raced, searching for answers. It was important that he remained completely motionless.

"Where am I? What is this place?" Benny asked in no more than a whisper.

He had no sense of vision in this darkness. To test its totality, Benny put his finger on his nose, but he never saw his finger. He felt it but could see nothing. He blinked repeatedly hoping it would help, but that made no difference.

"Now you see me," Benny joked softly. There was nothing but darkness.

"Why am I here? Where is Cosmo? We are always together." No one answered.

While he wondered about where he was, he felt a calm cover him, providing an inner peace. He questioned why he felt an assurance, how he could even know where he was or why he was there. *What kind of dream is this?* Benny wondered. Instantly he knew he was not sitting on the old metal frame that he always slept in, nor did he feel the small piece of carpet he had grown accustomed to when he stepped out of bed. His small feet also did not feel the cool of the linoleum floor, but something entirely different.

Benny continued moving his head slowly side to side. At least, he thought he was moving his head. Without a point of reference, he wasn't sure if he had moved at all. Off in the distance, he noticed what appeared to be a very faint, small speck of light. He was positive it wasn't there a moment ago, but now, there it was. He closed his eyes and shook his head, unsure of what to do next. The curiosity and imagination of the young boy ran wild. In the silence, he could hear a name being called: "Benjamin."

His mind flashed back to another dream, another time when he was called Benjamin. It sounded so odd to him, so grown up, so different.

"Is this part of the same dream?" Benny questioned.

Finally, he decided he needed to move. Very deliberately and cautiously in the dimness, he began to slide each foot slowly, steadily, in the direction of the speck of light. With great apprehension, methodically feeling his way through the darkness, he moved forward.

His bare feet felt the cool moisture of the grass as it caressed his toes, yet his feet did not get wet. That seemed rather odd to him, but he allowed the thought to pass. He certainly was no longer in his bedroom, and he was certain he somehow continued from a dream he had before.

Benny took tentative, small steps, moving him nearer to the light. Like the dew on his feet, he could feel the crispness of the night, but he was not cold. Like his thought of the dew and the grass, he let this pass, too. To Benny, it felt like he had started to move faster, but he was still extremely cautious as he moved toward the light. He paused for a moment and lifted his head skyward; the heavens were filled with only a black darkness.

He felt the change and knew why there was only a deep darkness, apart from the single flame in the distance. He could feel the flame calling his name, drawing him to it.

He has heard the same calling before. "*Benjamin.*"

It was only a simple word that touched his ears, "Benjamin," nothing more, only his name. Benny felt the flame was the key to unlocking knowledge the closer he moved toward it. The faint speck continued to grow as he approached. His eyes adapted well to the darkness. What the flame revealed to him from afar was its blue brilliance, which danced to life from a pile of wooden logs that did not burn.

Cautiously, Benny continued to approach the fire. Now that he could see, he paused, turning his head from side to side to take in all of his surroundings. Now that he could see, calmly, he searched for something, anything, as his eyes gazed at everything around him.

Did I miss it before? He wondered.

Benny stopped moving his head, and his eyes fell upon him. There he sat, a single figure, The Guardian, next to the fire, as if he had been waiting. Confused, Benny thought of the many times he had looked at that very spot and hadn't noticed him. Was he always there, or had he just arrived?

Benjamin asked aloud question after question.

"Why am I here? Am I caught up in another dream? What is this place? How did I get here?"

Though only a child, in the deep recesses of his mind, he felt he knew the answers to his own questions – but now was not the time to ponder them.

The stillness was broken not in a word, but in sound that gently parted the golden locks of Benny's thin blonde hair.

I know I am Benjamin. The thought passed through his mind as he remained silent and listened.

Pure, rich, soft at first, notes of purity began to fill the void of darkness and silence. Benny found every note comforting, soothing, relaxing. The crescendo of notes appeared to open the heavens from a deep slumber. The silence and darkness were being pushed aside.

Benny sat still, holding his eyes tightly closed. "This is the awakening, this is my awakening, the awakening of The Chosen," he softly whispered. After speaking, he opened his eyes.

All around him, he could see bubbles of different shapes and sizes filling the air.

Benny stood motionless and watched them appear and then burst. When they broke, a distinct note pushed through the silence. Remaining motionless, Benny watched as more bubbles filled the air before bursting, filling the silence with different tones of purity. Listening to the notes, Benny started to run, cautiously at first, then faster, quickening his pace, running towards the flame and the Guardian. Approaching the fire, it was easier to make out shapes gathered nearby and standing close to the Guardian.

Arriving at the pile of burning logs, Benny paused and stood motionless. After he had absorbed all that was around him, he finally worked up enough courage to speak out loud. Softly, not wanting to disturb the one seated by the fire, confidently, knowing exactly who he was speaking to. But still, he questioned.

"Are you The Guardian?"

"Yes, Benjamin."

"You call me Benjamin? I didn't know that name, but I know that's me, and you have called me here. Just like Reevus called me before." He paused and bit at his lower lip before he continued. "Is it time?" He knew it was an important question.

The Guardian stood before he stepped up on a stump that rose a good two feet above the forest floor, with two smaller stumps on each side. His dark purple robe flowed over his shoulders, stopping at his ankles just above the ground. Strands of his grey hair flowed beyond his collar and reached a few inches below his neckline. Like his hair, his grey beard cascaded freely and rested on his chest. The only trace of movement Benjamin could detect was the slight movement of The Guardian's fingers, a raised eyebrow, or curled lips as a smile formed on his face. With each movement of his fingers, bubbles continued to magically appear, floating effortlessly upward as they moved toward the heavens.

The flame jumped, and then another bubble burst and released a note. As the flame grew in size and intensity, Benny found himself standing next to the fire on one of the other stumps. *Odd*, he thought. *I don't remember moving, but here I am.* He gazed in awe while he observed the light reflecting off the pure white coats of two horses that knelt in the grass behind them.

He remained motionless, mesmerized by the sight, as he watched and listened. Benny knew even before this moment that Benny and Benjamin were one and the same, exactly as Reevus had told him. Benny closed his eyes and processed all that was around him. When he opened them, he remembered the little spark in the distance. Now he stood next to a fire that burnt brightly while the darkness was being replaced by a shimmering white light. He noticed when each bubble burst, another part of the heavens glowed.

Benny saw that within each bubble, when it burst, a star was born and began to shine. As he watched, the stars danced in the night sky, joined by the moons as they rose high into the heavens. Moonbeams covered the countryside with a soft blue hue. Benny was able to look into the flame and feel it envelop him. He had never experienced this warmth before, but he sensed it touching the very essence of his heart and soul. His ears listened as the sounds, words, and magic filled the air. He now saw, heard, and felt what the Guardian had created.

Softly at first, words began to appear out of nowhere, and they joined the music filling the air. The words were clear and crisp, with a growing intensity, louder with each passing second. The Guardian continued to cast his magical spell and speak words that reverberated in Benny's ears.

Listening to them, Benny turned and broke the trance, asking humbly and softly, "Guardian, have they always been with you?"

Benny raised his left arm, pointing his finger at the figures that stood behind The Guardian. The scar on his wrist began to glow and pulse to match the chorus of The Guardian. To him, just out of sight, they seemed both so majestic and proud, standing quietly, bathed in the light from the fire and the blue moonbeams. Their coats glistened in the rich light cast from them both. Benny followed closely behind The Guardian, and he timidly caressed the horn of the unicorn. As he moved, he remembered the encounter with Reevus and Wren. He knew that he was Benjamin, not Benny. He felt the magic of its horn move up his arm when he touched the creature. There was a magic that was not meant to leave young Benjamin. Benny smiled as he welcomed a new gift.

The Guardian spoke softly as he looked on.

"Yes, Benjamin, for they are as much a part of me as I am of them. As you feel now that oneness has become part of you. I know you felt the warmth as it flowed up your arm when you touched the horn of the unicorn. Others will need to believe as you now believe. They are part of our being. Unfortunately, others will see and choose not to believe. But many will see and believe.

All have been given the freedom of choice, and the door is always open for them. For you and me, we shall touch hearts and souls throughout time, awakening their freedom. They will be given an inspiration for joy, allowing them to feel warmth. The warmth is given to replace the hurting, placing smiles on faces of the sad, or to dry tears from the cheeks of the crying. It shall provide comfort in a time of sorrow and create happiness in a moment of love." The Guardian paused for a moment. "But there is one who has removed it all from the Third Plane of Kalamar. This one has risen to be great in power, repressing the desire to create, dream, and imagine, snuffing the life out of the ability to enjoy what the Great Storytellers provide."

Was it Benny's imagination? It appeared to him The Guardian was having problems getting his words out. Was he crying? Benny did not speak but continued to listen and observe.

After a few more moments of silence, The Guardian continued.

"He has replaced the light and warmth of The Three Suns and Three Moons of Kalamar with his own darkness. He searches for what is not his, all to increase his wicked power. While it is his desire, he will learn there is no one who will be able to master the magic of the Great Storytellers of Kalamar. The Dark Lord has decided that which he cannot have, no one else shall either."

As The Guardian spoke to him, Benny knew this was a moment he had been prepared for. He knew his rightful name was Benjamin. It was from the calling of The Guardian, and those from Kalamar, that he, as Benjamin, came to life. "You, and Reevus have opened my eyes and mind," said Benny. "On Kalamar, I am Benjamin, but outside of there I am still Benny. I know it is who I am, and it has now begun. They said that night in the Great Forest, 'They shall be given what is needed when it is needed." Benny looked at The Guardian. "I remember those words, even as a newborn baby."

The Guardian listened intently as Benny talked. He waited until Benny finished before he stood and began to speak again.

"It is by our touch that we shall give it to others when it is needed. As you have heard, they, too, hear a tone, the music, and feel the inspiration. They will hear words and feel what came from deep within their own souls. Our purpose, yours and mine, is to leave them so moved they enjoy the moment and where they are. When they have those great swings of emotion, unknowingly tears shall also drench their cheeks. But there shall be a noticeable difference. These shall be different tears…tears not of sadness but of joy...for they are the tears of healing. In this time of rule by the Dark Lord, everyone will have been put through trials and tribulations. They will be overwhelmed with feelings of guilt, doubt, and hopelessness. When that time comes, you, Benjamin, as one of The Chosen, will fill their hearts with the truth, and they will understand the tears of healing. Unquestioning, they will know that they are loved, a feeling long removed since the Dark One rose to power. But beyond the knowledge of love, they will now know who loves them. For the One of Ones holds all the keys and shall give them His true love that started before time began and is never ending."

"Guardian, I know I am Benjamin. In the world you have hidden me, my name is Benny. When I am called from this world where you have placed me, will I always come as Benjamin?"

Benny settled in next to the fire and basked in its warmth. He closed his eyes and allowed his mind to drift and enjoy each note as he sat by the fire. *Do re me la so fa ti do*…repeatedly in different sequences as The Guardian orchestrated the notes and they filled the skies. While he listened, he felt coldness on his forearm, a nudging, and then a wet nose pressed his arm.

The Guardian spoke softly, "For as it was written, he has always been and shall forever be Benjamin of Kalamar." After he spoke, he listened contentedly to the excitement in young Benny's voice.

"Looks like I have company. How did Cosmo get here?"

The Guardian continued to fill the air with music and light. He turned his head to the left and a warm smile covered his face, and a slight chuckle joined the chorus. "It is my gift to you, Benjamin. Would it surprise you to know that there is another time, another place, where I gave him to you? He has a very special talent. Yes, that is the name you gave him when I presented him to you, too."

"Cosmo has been a very good name for him, don't you think?" continued The Guardian. "He shall be with you and give you comfort as you remain hidden in time. Even hidden in time you are still not safe. The Dark Lord will never stop searching for you. I'm certain you have already discovered Cosmo has a unique ability to warn you when he senses the presence of those sent by the Dark Lord. Listen to him, and you will come to know and understand his warnings. I have much to do for you to do, and we do have much to talk about before then, for I need to prepare for what is to come."

Petting Cosmo's back, Benjamin looked at The Guardian, puzzled. "What do you need to prepare me for? What do I need? Reevus mentioned the same type of thing."

The Guardian turned and looked deep into Benny's eyes. "Benjamin, you will have to deal with being rejected. The depression will attempt to overwhelm you. There are many other things that would take too long to describe. Your journey will not be easy, but it is meant to prepare you to make the right decisions at the right time. You are correct. When it is needed, gifts will be given to you. Gifts to help and guide you on your journey. I know you have many questions, and over time I shall do my best to answer them for you. For tonight it shall be but a dream, a dream you will remember, and with each dream you shall understand more of your calling. We shall reach out to you, calling you by your rightful name, Benjamin. I shall mentor you in the Ancient Ways, but not by myself. Many others will assist."

Silently, The Guardian reached out and placed Benny's hand in his. "The road you will travel will be filled with much strife, rejection, pain, agony, loneliness. Regardless of how bad things may seem, remember I am always with you, we are always with you. You shall never be alone. Even in the midst of your storms, you will not be alone. For within you, there will always be a part of me. Wherever you are, there I shall be also!"

Benny watched, dumbstruck and unable to move, as The Guardian dipped his hand into the fire. As he watched intently, the flame jumped from the fire, almost as if on command, into The Guardian's hand. Benny watched the flame dance and burn brightly in The Guardian's hand but not burn him or his robe. Benny sat mesmerized.

He looked briefly into The Guardian's eyes. During that one moment, the flame jumped from The Guardian's hand and into his own chest. It was like it happened in slow motion; the flame slowly rose up from The Guardian's hand and moved the short distance between them, before effortlessly entering his chest. There was no pain or discomfort. Benny's eyes had not moved from The Guardian as they began to recite:

> "*For as I have always been, for as I am, so you shall be. Many listen, but few can hear. The gift that was given to me in times past has now been given to you. Our flame is bright, our*

flame is light. For you have always been and you shall always be the One who is one of the Chosen."

Dazed, Benny looked down and saw, as well as felt, the eternal flame glowing within his own chest. He felt no pain, only the warm glow that now covered his entire body. Slowly, The Guardian lowered his arm, a smile etched upon his face. The flame remained alive within Benny's heart.

He now had a better understanding of who and where he was. He heard the calming voice of The Guardian touch his mind without moving his lips. *"Come, sit my child."* The two of them moved closer to the fire and took a seat on one of the large logs. As they sat, the deep purple of The Guardian's robe shimmered. Silently, Cna and Dorlie, their equine companions, moved and stood next to them, nuzzling against both as if they were asking to join, knowing they were always welcome without ever a word being spoken. The Guardian reached out and touched Benjamin's mind again. *Remember, your strength shall flourish in threes, for it was so deemed long ago and shall remain throughout all time.*

Benny opened his eyes and quickly pulled the covers back before he sat up in bed. He turned to his left and slipped out of bed. Once again, he felt the familiar coolness of the floor against the soles of his feet. His small hands began to rub his eyes as he stood, motionless. Looking out his bedroom window, he wondered about his dream and why it felt so vivid and real. There was so much he didn't understand about this dream and that night. He placed his hand over his heart and felt its warmth. Instantly, his mind returned to the burning fire and the scene, watching the flame jump. He now felt that same warmth glowing from within.

Talking silently to himself, he repeated, *Here I'm Benny, but there I'm Benjamin. They will guide, instruct, and prepare me, but who are they, and for what are they preparing me?* He slipped back under the covers and pulled his puppy close. It didn't take long before he quickly fell fast asleep. As he held Cosmo tight, he had a feeling this was not a dream.

While he slept, Cosmo kept a constant watch over him, alert to the movements around them, always searching for the presence of the Dark Lord's minions.

Nafari Fall From Grace and Beauty

Zorleg stood alone, hidden in his secret hiding place in the rocks. He marveled at his secret hiding spot. He needed anything to get away from the Great Meeting Place and the mundane teaching. How he hated the repetitiveness of the teachings.

Don't they realize how great my mind is? Don't they realize who I am? he thought.

Alone in his small fortress, he reveled at its appearance and how he had designed it perfectly for himself. His eyes had adjusted to the minimal light inside. He couldn't remember exactly when, or how, his power started, but he knew it was in there, growing, evolving. Maybe it was his anger, his wrath at the teaching.

Regardless of the how and why, he felt it must be related to the first time he entered his secret space located off the path to The Great Meeting Place. He enjoyed the coolness within the chamber and the smoothness of the rocks surrounding him. This was where he secretly slipped off to in his free time to develop his craft, his skills. He raised his arm before staring intently at his right hand. A chuckle escaped his lips. This was not the first time he had accomplished this feat, no, far from. With each succeeding attempt, he felt the power of darkness surge through his veins. His chuckling subsided for a moment while his mind zeroed in on how he had discovered dark matter. How many cursed flowers had he held in his hand and then turned into a powdery dust after his discovery? Flowers had become too easy. No one else could ever accomplish what he developed with a simple thought and an intense stare.

Zorleg broke his own silence as he shouted, his voice reverberating off the walls. “More, I need more!” he bellowed, letting his need consume him. Along with the intense burning for more power, he needed something other than a flower to wield it upon. Oh, but the power! How he loved what he had conjured up! His mind filled with thoughts of his revenge upon the teachers from The Great Meeting Place. They would regret the days they ignored him.

Zorleg concentrated and planned his next move. Deep in thought, he discovered that somehow, he had managed to freeze everything surrounding him. In their frozen state, he could freely walk around, pausing here and there to look at anything and everything. He enjoyed a great amount of pleasure as he moved about unnoticed. Time had stopped for them, but not for him. He never questioned the how, attributing it to his power alone. He found that he was no longer within the confines of his secret enclave but walking freely about the grounds of The Great Meeting Place. His presence, evil plans, and intentions were held within his mind.

You fools, he thought. They didn't realize he was among them.

He paused to observe every animal and person he came upon. By his power, through his own evaluation, he decided what and who would be the first. If they did not survive his test, it did not matter to him. Animals were not much of a challenge, but still a good beginning. No one would miss a squirrel or a rabbit. Oh, but a dog or a cat, someone’s pet. That was a different matter. They would be larger and more of a challenge for him, too. Regardless of what he chose, their death would only mean they were unworthy anyway and not fit for serving him.

Zorleg's eyes darted about, looking for something, or someone, whose being he could dramatically alter forever. He refused to allow failure to enter his thoughts. He paused and chuckled for a moment, so proud of what he had grown capable of doing all by himself. His mind raced and spun with excitement as he searched. He rejected one, then another, until finally he came across the perfect subject. She appeared to be perhaps a year or two younger than he was – if her age mattered at all. She caught his eye immediately. There she sat, youthful, with long locks of golden blonde hair that twinkled in the sunlight and flowed down to the middle of her back.

His gaze did not move from her as his mind whirled, passing through one name, then another until he finally whispered her name. "Nafari." He grunted in disgust. He was pleased with the name he had chosen for her, but how he loathed the brightness of day and sunlight.

Zorleg continued to move about undetected. He also noticed how things continued to move around him, but he remained unnoticed even with time resuming. He watched his newly named Nafari.

"Ah yes, so simple but so perfect. Nafari, my witch of darkness."

She sat with her friends and appeared to have been giggling about this, about that, talking in hushed tones amongst themselves. Unlike her friends, her eyes were an enchanting blue that sparkled in the sunlight. She and her friends ran their toes in the lush green grass, chuckling and giggling all the while.

None of them had a care in the world as they waited patiently for the day's studies to begin. She had no idea they were being watched. All of them were content, happy, energetic, and full of life, as they enjoyed what they had learned from the teachings of the elders. Their smiles beamed brightly with the dawning of a new day, showing glistening white teeth. Laughter filled the early morning air. None of them had an inkling of the evil darkness that lurked so close, so very close to each one of them. How could they? *Evil* was an unknown presence on the Third Plane of Kalamar.

Yes, Zorleg decided. She would be the perfect subject. He waited for a moment pondering whether his work should be a slow or rapid turn. He was certain the one he had named Nafari had no idea who he was, or that he even existed. That, however, would soon change.

Zorleg stood still to reflect on this special moment. He stretched out his arm and raised his hand to his mouth. A slow deep sucking sound pierced his stillness when he inhaled. He paused for a moment, and then exhaled, blowing outwardly across his hand. It was only a few seconds, a brief moment ago, that a live flower rested in the palm of his hand. Like he had accomplished many times before, the life of the rose had ended, turning it into a fine powdered dust.

This time, instead of scattering the dust to the wind, he had a very specific purpose for what he had now labeled as his dust of darkness. He had chosen the young girl now named Nafari because of her beauty. As the flower had turned into ashes, the ashes of his creation stole Nafari's beauty, and she would now fall under his power of darkness.

Zorleg took another deep breath before he exhaled across his hand. The dust, his dust of darkness, had been aimed precisely toward her. It followed his guidance, and when she inhaled, the dust embedded itself deep within her lungs.

It has begun.

Zorleg was so proud of himself. He would now begin to mold her, turning her into his witch of darkness. Together, both would grow great in power. With her as his servant, he would cultivate her powers to instill fear and horror in all who heard her name. *From fear will come obedience, both from her and from all that are converted to follow.*

Reevus – The Greatest Storyteller

It was another typical day for Benny. Enjoy the sunshine, play in the yard, drive in his make-believe city. He tried to remember if it was yesterday, the day before, or maybe even last week when the stranger visited and gave him a puppy. Actually, Benny didn't care how long ago it was that Cosmo came to be his puppy. He was ecstatic to have a puppy to call his very own. They were inseparable… If you saw one, you'd see the other. Cosmo, always full of energy, ran ahead, followed, or walked next to Benny wherever they'd go. His head was in constant motion, always on the lookout for Benny. Cosmo would bark at anything he did not like. Benny had grown accustomed to hearing Cosmo's alarm and knew if he barked, he barked for a reason, and Benny needed to pay attention.

The day was beautiful, and Benny couldn't wait to take Cosmo for a walk. There wasn't a plan of where he'd go, perhaps the park. Cosmo enjoyed getting splashed when the kids jumped in the water at the city pool. Benny knew not to be gone too long, though. He knew it was up to him to always be home on time. With Cosmo at his side, he left his bedroom and headed downstairs. Before continuing his thoughts about what he wanted, he needed to make sure he didn't have chores that needed to be done. Then, if allowed, he would take Cosmo to the park.

Cosmo scampered down the steps ahead of Benny, running over to his bowl for a bit of breakfast and a drink of water.

Stepping off the last step, Benny smiled. "Good morning, Grandma. Something sure smells good. Pancakes maybe, or waffles?"

The aroma coming from the kitchen made Benny's stomach growl. Grandma made the best waffles. They were so delicious.

"Well good morning, Benny. Nothing gets by your nose now, does it? We'll see how many pancakes we can get in that five-year-old stomach." Grandma smiled at Benny as she watched him slide up to the table. *He has sure been a blessing to have around the house*, she thought. She never asked why the county needed to find a home for him, but she was more than happy to open hers. She thought it was someone from the county who stopped by when she was at the store and left the puppy, but they assured her it wasn't them. Regardless of where Cosmo came from, the two of them made a great pair. Cosmo was the perfect companion for Benny.

"Anything you need me to help with around the house, Grandma? I can pick up the eggs after breakfast."

"Would you like a cold glass of milk to go with your waffle, Benny?" Grandma smiled, knowing the answer would be yes. "How many waffles do you think you'll eat this morning?"

Benny's eyes lit up. "Well, I think I can eat three, but if that's too much, two will be just fine."

Grandma looked down on Benny. "My goodness, boy, how can someone so young and small eat so much? But if you eat them, I'll make them. Don't let your eyes be bigger than your belly." Grandma headed into the kitchen, wiping her hands on her apron.

It warmed her heart to watch how Benny devoured anything she made. She often wondered if he came from a home where they didn't have much. Not that she had much compared to others, but she had all she needed. Mercy, what an appetite he had for a five-year-old!

Benny did exactly as he told Grandma he would do. He enjoyed two of her delicious waffles with butter and warm syrup but knew he could've eaten three. When his glass of milk was nearly empty, she filled it up. She was so thankful the county had called her to see if she would accept the boy. It brought so much happiness into her small house.

After Benny had finished his breakfast, he helped Grandma clear the table. "Was there anything you'd like me to do today? I thought this afternoon I'd take Cosmo to the park and watch the kid's swim."

Grandma thought for a moment, tilted her head, and looked down at him. "You know, it would be a big help to me if you'd pull the weeds from the small flower bed on the side of the house. The morning is still cool, and you'll be in the shade. Maybe that will help you work off that big breakfast." Grandma reached down and gave Benny a big hug. "I sure do enjoy watching you eat."

Benny, with Cosmo close behind, headed out the front door and to the flower garden, stopping to pick up a coal bucket to place the weeds in. There was no hurry, and Grandma was right; it was cool, he was in the shade, and Cosmo took a nap close by. Benny had completely lost track of time. It wasn't long before he heard Grandma calling him for lunch. He looked at the pile of weeds he had pulled.

"Cosmo, I think you've slept through the entire morning." Benny laughed as he picked up his pile of weeds, placed them in the coal bucket, and took them to the compost pile, dumping them on top, over everything else already there. Like Grandma had shown him, he sprinkled a bit of lime on top to help everything decay faster. "Ok, boy, you ready for lunch?" Together they ran into the house, Benny stopping in the bathroom to wash up before sitting down at the table.

It was a modest meal but one of Benny's favorites: bacon, lettuce, and tomato sandwiches. He had helped Grandma pick the tomatoes and lettuce from the garden last night. Not this time, but there were other times when Grandma made her own bread and cinnamon rolls, too.

"You know, Benny, you've worked awfully hard today. Why don't you and Cosmo take a nice nap after lunch before going to the pool?"

"Sure, Grandma. I put all the weeds in the compost pile, too. And sprinkled some lime on top, just like you taught me." With that, Benny and Cosmo headed upstairs.

Benny lifted Cosmo onto his bed, then slipped in beside him. With Benny's arms wrapped around Cosmo, it wasn't long before they were both sound asleep. The next thing Benny heard was Grandma calling up the stairs.

"Benny, are you still asleep?"

Benny rubbed his eyes while Cosmo got his big stretches in. "I'll be right down, Grandma! Guess we must have been tired from the weed pulling, huh, buddy?"

Cosmo enjoyed it when Benny lifted him and set him gently on the floor. Together, off they went, racing down the stairs.

"Hi, Grandma."

"Benny, I don't think it would be a good idea for you and Cosmo to go to the pool today." She took Benny's hand in hers and led him to the back porch. Off in the distance, even at five, Benny could see the storm clouds rising and turning a darker shade of grey.

"Hmmmm, yeah, I don't think that would be good. We'd probably just get there, and the storm would arrive. We'll just stay home. Cosmo and I will find something to do."

Benny kept himself occupied through the afternoon and evening. It didn't take long, even with his nap, before Benny was feeling tired after they had eaten dinner. He said his good nights and headed up to bed, Cosmo racing ahead of him. Benny didn't understand why he should be so tired after taking a long nap. He figured it was because he was a young, growing boy.

After Benny had lifted Cosmo onto the bed, Cosmo immediately rolled over on his back, the unwritten Cosmo notice of, "I want you to scratch my belly."

"What, you want your belly rubbed, Cosmo?"

Benny curled up in bed with Cosmo curled up next to him on his own pillow. It wasn't long before both Benny and Cosmo were in a sound sleep.

"*Benjamin.*"

Benny wondered if it was part of a dream. *Who is Benjamin*, he wondered? He ignored what he heard. He was almost asleep when he heard it again.

"*Benjamin.*"

This night was like many other nights before…moonbeams covered the countryside from the Three Moons of Kalamar, growing brighter as they ascended into the evening sky. They kissed the landscape, gently nudging it from its slumber. Tonight, the forest began to dance in anticipation. Each leaf shimmered, with the moons of Kalamar slowly ascending effortlessly higher into the dark heavens, illuminating everything they touched. At the edge of the forest sat the small and quaint village of Carillon, home to someone they had always considered very special with indescribable talents. After the evening meal, he could always be found sitting near the fireplace at the village inn. He was plump, balding on top, and always sat in his favorite chair from where he would share his stories. With short, grey hair, trimmed tightly above his ears, combed from right to left, he rested comfortably in the wooden chair reserved especially for him. His forearms were thick and exposed, the sleeves of his shirt rolled up just above the elbow. With every word, those closest were drawn into another of his tales. Those who sat too far away to hear his words moved quickly after the meal and worked to be within earshot, so they wouldn't miss a word. All listened intently as he spun his yarns. Running his hand over his balding head, crossing his arms over his pot belly, he would lean forward as he pulled each listener into one of his many sagas.

Benny sat in silence as he watched and listened. *"Am I in a dream? But it seems so real, so lifelike."* Benny remained motionless, taking in every word of the story that was being told.

"It was a night such as this, all three moons of Kalamar bright and full as they climbed into the sky. Those moonbeams cascaded down from the heavens and covered the countryside in their magical blue hue." Reevus moved his hands from above his head to his toes to emphasize the moonbeams flight before he waved his hands above his head. "Not a cloud in the sky." Reevus paused and took a deep breath. He turned his head slowly from left to right as he methodically looked around the room and to every eye. He smiled when he saw the intended look on his listeners' faces – exactly as he had planned. Reevus cleared his throat before he continued, "I was walking through the forest late, very late at night, mind you, when I noticed the leaves begin to move, just as though they were being blown by the wind. I tell you on this night, I found it odd, very odd, because on that night the air was as still as the calmest day. Not one bit of wind blowing from any direction, mind you. With each step I took, the only sound that broke the silence was my feet touching the ground as the grass crunched or a twig broke under my feet. There was nothing else moving in the stillness of the night. Having walked a fair piece, I figured it was time to pause for a bit to rest my weary feet." As he often did, Reevus began a conversation with himself about an event. "Now did I stop and sit on a log, or was it a rock? No, no, it was a log; yes, yes, a log it was that I sat on." Reevus paused for a moment to collect his thoughts and pull his audience deeper into his tale.

Looking around the room again, Reevus rubbed his face, smirking under his hand, before he continued. "Now I can tell you I am one of the finest cobblers in the land. No, no, no, I am the finest cobbler in the land, but that doesn't mean my feet won't get tired or hurt when I walk." Reevus began to chuckle at himself, hearing the laughter from the audience as it joined him. His thoughts were interrupted by a young blond-haired boy sitting at the front who wanted to ask a question. His hand was held in the air as high as possible, but he didn't say a word. Reevus smiled to acknowledge him, nodded, and allowed him to ask his question.

"So, tell us, Mr. Reevus, what happened next?" A young lad of five, Little Benny's blue eyes beamed brightly as Reevus reached out and patted him gently on the head before he began to answer his question while he kept the audience fascinated with his tale.

Benny wondered why he was brazen enough to ask such a question. He didn't remember putting his hand up in the air. No one else put their hand in the air. Surely this must be a dream. He had no idea where he was or who these people were. Why did he know the storyteller's name? Reevus? He knew no one named Reevus. Benny sat quietly, motionless, as he listened.

Reevus promptly returned to the story. "Well, there I was sitting on the log - no, it was a rock, a pretty big rock…yes, that was it. I was sitting on a big rock when I noticed how the leaves moved and the light shimmered, reflecting off every leaf. 'Twas absolutely breathtaking, and so beautiful, but something I had not noticed before. I put my hand up on my chin and began to think about what I was witnessing. How can leaves move like that without wind? Hmph! Why are the leaves shimmering so brightly under the moonlight? Questions I asked out loud, hearing my own question the same as you hear me now."

Reevus stopped, rubbed his chin, sighed, and mumbled again. "No, no, no, it was a log I was sitting on, a log, not a large rock. Why would a large rock be in the middle of a forest? Yes, yes, yes, that was it. I was sitting on a log." Laughter erupted in the inn. Everyone was very familiar with how Reevus jumped back and forth between what is, what was, or what may have been, never really settling on one or the other. It was a part of his storytelling that everyone loved.

Reevus looked again at Benny and continued. "Then I looked up at the trees, and that's when I first saw it."

Silence filled the room. Everyone now sat on the edge of their seats with anticipation, wondering what it was that he saw. Reevus worked his magic as only he could, each person drawn to the magical web of Reevus, the Storyteller, not the village cobbler, as he told his story. His antics didn't change; his hands moved through the air with grand gestures to go along with his story. His eyes never moved from Benny's for more than a moment after Benny had asked his question.

While everyone in the inn heard the story Reevus was telling, Benny was hearing and feeling something completely different. Reevus was telling a story about being in the forest, and while Benny heard his story, he also heard something else. Something more real, something that transported him out of the village pub and into the very forest Reevus spoke of. *What type of dream is this?* he wondered.

"Benjamin, the Guardian has sent me to bring you here. Others laugh and think they are stories from my imagination. But you see through the ramblings of an old shoe cobbler and decipher the real meaning of the story." Benny's eyes did not move from Reevus as he spoke. While others heard his story of intrigue and imagination, Benny heard about the journey Reevus and others have made through time specifically to guide him, and his mind filled with so many questions.

Reevus slipped out of his chair and moved closer to the fire, rubbing his hands together. Everyone always wondered why he would do this, since the fireplace was only for aesthetics. They all felt he did it for effect. "Aye, this I tell ya, I saw people walking in the forest, but not just normal people. While they may resemble us, they were ones with pointed ears, with hair as fine as silk, slender and not an ounce of fat on them. And, oh mercy, could they run! They ran as if they were carried by the wind. With my own eyes I watched many of them as they dashed across the meadow. I saw it all with my own eyes, yes, my own eyes; I could hardly believe what happened before me. Every one of them, all of them mind you, pulled out arrow after arrow…had to be a quiver magically secured on their backs. Magical, I tell ya. It seemed to me it had been given a special incantation by someone very powerful, you can trust me on that, too. They repeated the same motion as they shot arrow after arrow." Deliberately, Reevus turned back to those gathered at the inn and jumped into the air before he shouted and made large circles as he waved his hands. "Thousands of arrows, thousands of them! I saw not one miss its target over a quarter mile away. Bam! Dead center every single time!" His hands slapped together to emphasize the accuracy of the shots before he moved his hand towards his head, fingers pointed to his eyes. "These eyes witnessed this feat for what seemed like hours. Was it an hour, was it a minute?" Reevus paused, calmed down, and spoke almost in a whisper, "How long I sat on the log, to be honest, I don't know. But this I tell you…if an elf is on your side, no mortal can stand against you. They have been blessed by the Most High to protect the Chosen Ones. Fleet of foot, they can outrun even the fastest horses. There is some very special magic about them. The bows and arrows entrusted to them never miss their targets, and their quivers never empty." Reevus paused and shook his head again before he repeated, "They never miss and carry a quiver that never empties!"

Reevus hesitated and took a moment to whet his whistle with a cold, fresh glass of spring water. After he cleared his throat, he continued to weave his story. "The elves were only the beginning of my long night."

Benny blinked his eyes. Or at least, he thought he blinked his eyes. When he opened them, he was no longer in the inn; no longer did he sit in a chair with a room full of people at the pub. *Was this all a continuation of my dream?* he wondered. But now, there he sat on a log in the midst of a forest. *Is this the same log Reevus spoke of and sat upon?* he wondered. *Is this the same meadow and forest?*

Benny heard the voice ringing clearly in his ears. "Behold! Let your eyes see what only the Chosen are allowed to see! From the Seven of Sevens, we bid you welcome, Benjamin."

The voice startled Benny. At the same time, it triggered an awakening, Benjamin knowing who he was. His eyes searched the area around him as he sat on the log. Feeling a nudge of a cold wet nose on his left arm, Benny calmly turned to look and standing beside him were two beautiful white steeds. *Where did the fire come from?* Benny paused to question. He didn't remember seeing the fire a moment ago. His eyes looked at the horses standing by the fire. One, with wings unfurled, was known as Pegasus, the flying horse. The other, its magical horn rising proudly from its forehead, was the mythical Unicorn. Why did he know this? His memory bubbled forth with a knowledge that he knew exactly who they were and remembered. Benny sighed as a whisper escaped his lips. "Ahhhhh, such beautiful, majestic creatures!" Words could not describe this moment, the beauty he experienced as the magic of the forest Reevus spoke of started to come to life before his eyes.

Benny blinked his eyes again and found himself back in the inn as Reevus continued to tell his story.

"But" Reevus paused before continuing in his soft voice to draw the listeners in, "there is one more thing that the night held in her hand. Shadows, shimmering shadows, white, with a ghostly aura that surrounded them. They moved without a foot touching the ground. It was almost as if they wanted to be seen, but then not really. I'll tell ya what I believe…I believe they were all apparitions, ghosts. They were put there more to scare those who saw them so the story could be shared with others." Reevus looked around the room with a very serious look on his face then raised his voice to almost a shout as he continued, "Sounds like the forest was haunted now, don't it?" His voice returned to a whisper. "Leaves moved without the wind, something walking in and out of trees. There were ghosts or apparitions moving around that you could see through." His face was covered with a very serious look before he asked a question. "Hmmmmmm, now who among you are feeling a touch of fear right about now?"

He stopped briefly to milk the moment for effect, before he turned and asked, "How many of you would be brave enough to spend the night in the forest? Remember, 'twas a night such as this. 'Tis not only me telling this tale. I only tell it in this city. Other storytellers, far and wide, are telling stories just like what I told you. Some are old shoe cobblers like me, but some are not."

Picking up his glass of cold water, Reevus took another deep gulp, then set the glass down and exhaled loudly. Slowly he looked around the room. "So, tell me, which of you young ones want to spend the night in the forest?" Pausing for a moment, Reevus corrected himself,

"No, no, no, it wasn't a stone, it was a log. Yes, I remember perfectly now. A log. So, who's ready for the forest?"

Reevus moved his head as he looked at each person in the room. One thing he observed was how every child's hands were tightly secured under their legs, holding them down. His head moved around the room until his eyes fell upon Benny, whose hand was held high, waving to and fro. No one heard the chuckle of amusement, but Reevus walked and stood next to Benny.

"So, young Benjamin. Are you brave enough to spend the night in the forest? If you were the bravest of them all, I wonder if you would do such a brave deed. Then you could share your story with us, too…that is, if you make it through the night. Be mighty scary for a young lad your age, such a mature and brave lad of five, to stay in the forest."

What? How did that happen again? Benny wasn't aware he had even raised his hand. Immediately he hung his head in doubt. Shyly, he looked up and spoke, "Oh, I am so sorry, Mr. Reevus. I was so caught up in your story. I didn't realize my hand was in the air. I think it would be an adventure, Mr. Reevus, but I don't see how I could do that. I'm sorry. That would be way too scary, especially alone." Benny felt so ashamed and embarrassed his hand was in the air. No one else even thought about raising their hand. Confusion filled Benny's mind, broken only when he heard Reevus speak.

Reevus looked at Benny and assured him, "Do not worry. I understood but wanted to ask. Out of all that are here, you are the only one to speak up. Be brave, young Benjamin, be brave!"

What kind of a dream is this? Benny wondered silently. It would have been such an adventure to spend the night in the forest, but not alone at five. *This is all a dream anyway,* Benny thought. He had plenty to do at Grandma's house. He was thankful he had a roof over his head and a bed to sleep in. Being only five seemed a curse to him. He was small enough to slip under the branches of an apple tree without the worry of hitting his head on the branches.

The story of the night over, Reevus mingled with young and old alike. Benny left the inn silently and unnoticed and began the walk to his home. He enjoyed ambling down the lane to the small house, but it felt so odd.

How can a dream be so vivid? How do I even know where I'm going? Benny asked himself. With each step, his mind raced back to the forest. He wondered if it was some sort of vision, or did he get so wrapped up in the story Reevus was spinning that he was actually living it? He chuckled to himself, thinking that really wasn't possible: this is all just a dream.

After arriving home, he poured himself a glass of water as he described Reevus' story of the evening with Grandma. While he told his story, a strange feeling seemed to wash over him. Shaking his head, Benny experienced the same feeling he felt at the inn. That was really odd, since the feeling was new to him, and he had never experienced it before. Now, looking at Grandma, he heard a whisper that he knew was only for him. "Tonight, we shall meet again."

When he had finished telling, actually retelling, the story of the night, he said his good nights and headed off to bed, Cosmo running ahead of him. The excitement of the story, spending a night in the forest, and the images he had experienced at the inn whirled around in his mind and kept him wide awake after he lifted Cosmo onto the bed. Silently, he lay in bed and waited until he knew Grandma was sound asleep. He felt a slight nudge from Cosmo. *Guess I must have drifted off.* Now he hoped he would be able to sneak away silently and return home before anyone even knew he was gone. Cautiously, careful not to make a sound, he slipped out of bed. He thought it was odd Cosmo didn't even stir when he slipped out of bed. In the moonlight he quickly dressed and moved to the open bedroom window. First one foot, then the other, ensuring he was very quiet, he climbed through the window and dropped silently to the ground and into the night.

Benny found everything in this dream difficult to understand, but he soon found that he was once again in the forest. There was the log he had sat on before. He had no idea how he was able to get from his house in Carillon to the Great Forest so quickly, but he was glad to be in the forest. He remembered feeling both feet touching the ground, taking a step and, before he took his second step, there he was.

He paused and questioned himself. "Why do I know the name of Carillon and The Great Forest?"

Benny could see the large log sitting close to a fire, the two white horses standing on each side of the log, with Reevus in the middle. Staring in disbelief, Benny hurried ahead to the fire. As he ran, he wondered, *how many times have I asked what type of dream have I found myself in?* Benny reached out his hands and slid them up and down the glistening neck of each horse. As if on cue, each horse bent its front legs and bowed down to Benny.

Benny didn't know what to think. He turned to speak to Reevus and was surprised to see the portly middle-aged-man with the large belly was no longer alone. Benny wondered if this was actually Reevus. Next to Reevus, sitting on his left, was a petite young lady with short, dark brown hair and eyes. Like Reevus, she, too, was dressed in a dark green outfit. Benny rubbed his eyes and looked on in disbelief and asked timidly, "Reevus? I am so confused. There's so much I don't understand."

With the same familiar voice he heard at the inn, Benny heard his new friend's voice coming from Reevus. Benny continued to speak softly, barely above a whisper before he started to stammer. "How, who, what? And her. Who is she?" But then Reevus gently cut him off.

"Benjamin, this is a good example of what is meant by "things are not always as they appear." What I tell you now may not make sense, especially to such a young lad, but I ask you to listen carefully. The key to life isn't the mistakes we make; it's how we choose to handle them. Sometimes the mistakes we make prepare us to help others at another time. It could be someone who had the same issue or faced a similar problem. It allows us, or more precisely, you, to be able to comfort and feel empathy only they can understand. For you will have walked the walk they have walked and understand what they are facing." Reevus reached out and touched Benny's arm. "I know it is difficult to understand, but all of it will come to you in time. From a day that has not yet come, we will walk with you in the future. From days long since gone by, we have walked with you in the past. Today is the day many have been told about. For now, for you, it is another beginning."

Reevus turned and faced the lady next to him as they both stood. She turned to face Benny. "Allow me to introduce you to my good friend, Wren. Like me, she is here for you. Again, this is not the day, but there will be days ahead when you will have need of her special talents." Benny noticed a quiver full of arrows tightly secured on Wren's back, a bow secured over her shoulder. He wondered if this was the same magical quiver and arrows Reevus spoke of at the inn.

Puzzled, Benny sat down on the log, looked up, and asked Reevus, "prepared? What am I being prepared for?" Slowly he lowered his head, even more confused now than he was earlier. This was a lot for a small boy to take in. Benny felt his mind begin to open, and all he could do was wonder, *What kind of dream is this?*

After a moment or two, Benny raised his head and looked around. He looked deep into the forest, his blue eyes glowing. For some reason he couldn't explain, he no longer felt the hardness of the log he sat upon. He watched as the glow from the fire reflected off the two mighty horses. He stood, walked over, and began to stroke both gently. He turned back to look at Reevus and asked, "What is the purpose of all this?"

Reevus and Wren stood, walked over, and joined Benny. "These are things we have brought into the past for you to use in the future." Reevus paused to laugh before he continued. "The magic of our mythical horses, my appearance…all were put in place now for another time, another place."

Reevus motioned for Benny to take a seat on the log. "This is only the beginning, Benjamin. Tomorrow you will remember your visit to the forest, me, Wren, and that your name is Benjamin. When the time comes, you will understand what you believe is a dream from this night. There will be other times when we come to visit you or when you have need of us. When the time is right and when you need us, our talents and skills will be there for you. For now, understanding is not needed. Let us leave you with these words as I bury them in your mind: ***Dreams will not last forever, but dreams are not forgotten.***"

Reevus slipped his hand into his pocket and pulled out a small bag. Without a word, he stretched out his arm and handed the small cloth bag to Benny. "Put this in your pocket, Benjamin. You will know the day when you realize what is in the bag and what it means without even opening it. As time passes, there will be others that will make fun of you, laugh at you, criticize you, bully, and even ridicule you. During those times, retreat within, and there you will find us to provide you the comfort and confidence you need for that moment."

Reevus put his hand under Benny's chin and lifted his head up until their eyes met. Reevus smiled and whispered. As he whispered, a white mist escaped his lips and covered Benny from head to toe. His young body was completely surrounded by the mist. His eyes closed instantly as he drifted off into a deep sleep. He never felt the hands of the storyteller he knew as Reevus, and Wren, pick him up. Nor did he feel any jostling as they covered distance, however far it was, from The Great Forest back to his bedroom in the twinkling of an eye. To go so far, so fast, without breaking a sweat or breathing hard still confused Benny. No one saw or heard when they placed him back in his bed. How long had he been gone? Did he really go anywhere, or was this night truly only a dream?

The sun slowly climbed in the eastern sky, kissing Benny's cheeks, gently waking him from sleep. Rubbing his eyes, Benny sat up in bed. Cosmo lay motionless, sound asleep. Everything in the dream was so vivid. Benny was amazed at how he could remember things in such detail. As he slowly slipped his legs out of bed, something caught his eye. There, sitting on the top of the small chair next to the bed, was a cloth bag sticking out of the right pocket of his breeches, the exact same bag Reevus had given him the night before. Benny's heart skipped a bit in excitement. No, no, it wasn't a dream at all.

Floating high above the treetops, invisible to the naked eye, a smile crept across The Guardian's face. Now he could share what was foretold by The One of Ones, to The Three of Threes, and written in The Seven of Sevens. *Another task has been completed.* This jump in time had served him well, and he couldn't have asked for anything better. The seeds of imagination and fear had been planted in time to grow, with its fruit to be brought forth again in the future.

Benny – The Formative Years

The sun was high in the afternoon sky. A soft breeze blew in from the outfield. Benny sat at the end of the dugout, lost in his own thoughts. *Why do I even bother coming to the games?* They never let him play.

More than once, he'd overheard the head coach telling the other parents, "I may have to have him on our team, but nobody will tell me who to play or when."

He allowed those words to process in his mind, a lot of cruel words to an eight-year-old. He never missed a practice, tried his hardest, but nothing changed. Several of his teammates seemed to relish pushing him around and roughing him up. Benny continued to wonder what he had he done. What made him the object everyone wanted to pick on?

They made fun of his clothes, but Benny knew nothing different. He thought it was quite exciting for the yearly shopping spree to buy clothes for the school year. He didn't give it a second thought. Oh, but how they did! Making fun of his clothes, making fun of Benny being the only one to carry his lunch to school, the house he lived in…the list went on and on.

Benny felt he was a pretty good ball player. He agreed some were much better, but he felt if he would ever be given the chance, he could show them what he could do. He liked playing catcher, but rarely would the coach even allow him to practice in that position. Instead, he'd be relegated to playing right field. That seemed to be the curse of death. The worst player was always the right fielder. Maybe it was because there were few, if there were any, left-handed hitters. Any ball that was hit to right field was completely by accident.

Even though it was a beautiful sunny day, and the wind felt nice, Benny could sense something was different, but he couldn't figure out what it was. The coach grumbled, like always, to the parents before the game even started about not playing him. The words still rang in his ears, "No one is going to tell me who to play." Every chance they got, the players would make fun of him, knocking his ball cap off, kicking dirt on his tennis shoes. They'd pepper him with comments about why he wasn't wearing baseball cleats. "Only girls wear tennis shoes to play baseball!" Benny never said a word and sat silently, alone at the end of the bench, watching the game.

Today, nothing had changed from the previous games or practices. He heard the same hurtful words and endured the same cruel actions. Still, he sat alone and felt a calmness come over him. A silence filled the air about him. No longer did he hear the ridicule or the cruel and mean words. To Benny, it was like a light switch that had been flicked on. He remembered the words of the Guardian and Reevus. "There will be times when you are made fun of, laughed at, and ridiculed. It is then that you withdraw into yourself and find your inner peace." There was no one to stick up for him, no one to intervene. The words and comfort continued to fill his mind. "Everyone is different, Benny, but we are all still the same. People should never be judged by where they worship, what their heritage and background may be, whether they are male or female…the list of comparisons goes on and on. Remember, all were created equal and shall always be equal. There are some whose hearts have been hardened and will never change. They take great joy in lashing out at those who are different, just as you are different.

Remember to never let the mindset of a few influence you. All are equal and should be treated as equals."

It seemed rather odd to Benny that he could feel the presence and calm from the words of The Guardian and Reevus while he watched the ballgame, as he listened intently to every play, as he watched and interacted with everything that was going on around him. He didn't try to understand the how or why what was happening. The one action he took was burying the words in his heart, "All are created equal." He wasn't going to let the few dictate to him how he should be, act, or respond. The dirt washed off, and the cruel words didn't break any bones. He could not change who he was, but despite their actions, he vowed it would make him better.

Benny watched as the game progressed. It really was an exciting game, with first one team leading, then the other tying it up before pulling ahead. He wasn't kidding himself. While he would love to be in the game, he knew it wasn't going to happen. Still, he sat and watched as the score moved from favoring one team to the other, tied, someone ahead. As the innings passed one after the other, Benny remained at the end of the bench, watching. Then the unexpected happened. A player from the opposing team hit a line drive off the second baseman's glove that careened into his face. He instantly fell to the ground like a rag doll.

The shortstop fielded the ball, and Benny could hear the coach yelling, "Ump, time out, TIME OUT!"

Led by the coach, everyone in the dugout ran to see the second baseman. All except for Benny. He was told to never move from his spot on the bench. As he was told, he remained in the same spot watching and listening. Even from a distance, he could hear the coaches arguing.

"I don't care if he is the only player on the bench, I'm not putting him in!" came the fiery words of the manager.

Oddly, Benny then heard the umpire tell the coach, "You must take your player out of the game and put in a substitute, simple as that. It's in the rules. He's an injured player and can't continue. Now get all your extra players off the field and back in the dugout. Your choice, substitute or forfeit." The umpire pulled his scorecard from his pocket. "Ok, your second baseman is out, and you have only one player left that you haven't played. Tell me where he'll be in the order and his position, and I'll mark it on my card."

The coach paused and thought for a moment, then pulled his assistant coaches over to the side.

"Ok, Benny will go to right field. Surely, he can't do any damage out there, and we'll make sure he's the last to bat. Got it?"

The coach turned to the umpire, gave him the position Benny would go to and where he'd bat, and how he had moved his other players around in the lineup. The coach escorted the extra players off the field and walked down to Benny.

"You couldn't even come out to check on our injured player? Just so you know, if it was up to me, you still wouldn't be playing. Now get off your butt and into right field."

Benny got up off the bench and looked at the coach. "I was doing exactly as you told me, sir. You told me to go sit on the end of the bench and don't get up for anything."

The coach bit his tongue and yelled at Benny, "Get your mitt and get out to right field!"

Benny grabbed his glove and ran from the first base dugout to right field. He really wasn't expecting anything more than standing around waiting for everyone else to make the plays. No one, and he repeated to himself, *no one* ever wants to play right field.

Benny couldn't believe it. They actually put him in a game. Of all things, he was really playing in a real baseball game. His first ever! Benny looked around to see where the other outfielders had positioned themselves and attempted to mimic where they were playing. He also took notice of the runner still on first. Standing in right field, all alone, he remembered what his coaches told the outfielders in practice. "Always keep the ball in front of you. Make sure you hit the cutoff man. Don't let them hit the ball over your head." Benny wondered if any of that would really matter to him. After all, he was the lowly right fielder.

Bending over at the waist, Benny kept his eyes glued on the pitch and followed every throw. He made sure that he was ready for anything, even the unlikely event a ball may be hit his way. When the pitcher started his windup, Benny bent slightly at the waist, crouched just a bit, and got himself ready for what might be. Most of the time, it was for naught. *Who would hit the ball to right field*? he wondered.

The pitcher seemed to be struggling with more balls and fewer strikes. No one hit the ball, but he wasn't getting anyone out either. Benny turned to look at the scoreboard. The game was still very close, with his team ahead by one run. When Benny turned his head around to follow the pitcher and the ball, he heard the coach yelling at him.

"Keep your head in the game, kid! Look at the pitcher and quit gazing into the outfield!"

Benny felt so picked on. He wondered if he should even be breathing. Looking at the scoreboard was something everyone did. But because he looked, he was chastised for it. Perhaps that was reserved for the "real" players in his coach's eyes. Why did he have to call him "kid"? He never called anyone else "kid," always by their first name.

Benny shook his thoughts and concentrated on the game. The pitcher was not doing well, walking the next two batters. Now with the bases loaded and two outs, the coach made a pitching change. It was a do-or-die moment, as intense as it could get. Bases loaded, two outs, bottom of the ninth inning. Benny chuckled to himself.

Isn't this exactly how dreams were made? This was every child's dream, Benny thought silently.

He got himself ready again and watched the pitch. Without question, things were getting tense. The pitcher threw one pitch after another until the count was full…three balls and two strikes. All the people in the stands were on their feet, shouting, clapping their hands, stomping their feet. The pitcher got set, looked at the runners, and threw what he hoped was his best pitch. The batter's eyes followed the ball as soon as it was released from the pitcher's hand. His eyes watched the rotation, picking up the spin of the ball. He swung with all his might, but he was behind on his swing. Flying off the end of the bat, the ball soared high in the air…toward right field!

Benny could hear the insanity of the crowd but kept his eyes focused on the ball as soon as it left the pitcher's hand. He watched the ball jump off the bat and had already started moving backwards and to his left, before the sound, the crack off the bat, reached his ears. Benny turned, took off, and ran at full speed. The base runners were off and running as soon as they heard the ball hit the bat. The crowd wondered if the ball would fall in for a base hit. Benny felt the excitement and anticipation of the crowd. Regardless of what happened, some would be happy, some sad. Benny pushed the thoughts from his mind, his eye trained on the ball as it sailed through the air. One foot in front of the other, Benny ran as fast as he could, never taking his eye off the ball. From the dugout, Benny heard the discouraging comments of the coach, already giving up on the ball and the game. He heard the head coach telling the players in the dugout, "Come on, guys, let's pick up our gear, we'll get 'em next time.'

The assistant coach had enough. He forced the coach to turn and watch as the events played out before them as if they were in slow motion. There was Benny, running at full speed tracking the ball, then at the last moment diving, stretching out as far as his eight-year-old frame would let him. Benny fell to the ground, his glove tightly wrapped around the ball that had fallen dead center into it. Benny held his glove closed tightly, placing his other hand to secure the ball inside. When he had completed sliding across the grass, he jumped up, took the ball out of his glove, held it high above his head and showed it to the umpire. As soon as the umpire saw Benny lift the ball out of his glove, he raised his right hand to signify the last out of the game.

Benny had made a fantastic play; his outstanding play actually won the game. He slowly trotted back to the dugout. Not one person on his team came to congratulate him. Instead, he was met with, "Get out of the way, punk." There were more jeers and snide comments from his teammates, but Benny didn't say a word. Instead, he walked over to the coach, handed him the ball, and thanked him.

"Thank you, coach, for putting me in the game and letting me play today." He stuck out his hand to give the ball to the coach. As expected, the coach slapped the ball away.

"Yeah, right, kid. You were lucky today. Now get out of here!" the coach angrily shot back.

Benny walked over and picked up the ball. This time he handed it to the assistant coach.

"I'm sorry, sir," Benny said before he turned to start his walk home.

It wasn't a long walk to his house, but Benny was certain it wouldn't be an easy walk. He knew he would be harassed on the way home by the same boys who always bullied him. What would they do this time? He didn't have his lunch, so they couldn't make fun of that. He didn't have his milk money, so they couldn't steal it. Oh, that's right. They didn't call it stealing; they called it his "toll" to walk on their sidewalk. He wasn't really dreading his walk home. He simply was tired of being picked on. How close would he get to home before they appeared this time? He really hoped to avoid them, but he knew his chances were slim to none.

Benny was a little over a block from his house when they came wheeling around the corner on their bicycles. Softly, all he could say was, "Oh great, what this time?" The oldest one in the group pulled his bicycle to a stop directly in front of Benny.

"What are you doing walking on my sidewalk, punk?" He jumped off of his bike and walked up to Benny, pushing him. Following his lead, a couple of the other boys also got off their bikes and joined in pushing Benny, taking his hat and glove, throwing them.

"Come on, please, give them back," Benny pleaded to deaf ears. So far, they hadn't started hitting him again, content to push him around and rough him up. Benny wasn't sure how it happened, but when the oldest bully pushed him, he lost his balance and fell into one of older boy's friends, knocking him to the ground. The sound of the boy's head hitting the raised concrete made a loud crack. From his lips came a muffled sound as he fell to the ground. Everyone was stunned. They all looked at Benny.

"You! You did this! Now we're going to make you pay!"

They pushed Benny to the ground and started kicking him. With every kick, Benny gasped for air, crying out in pain. He didn't know who it was, but someone was yelling at them, telling them to leave him alone, yelling that they had called the police. Close to unconsciousness, Benny lay on the ground next to the downed bully. Even in his state, he could see the pool of blood that had formed on the ground next to the other boy. Benny's eyes watched as the blood formed into a giant puddle. Sirens blared in the distance as he slowly slipped into a black nothingness from the brutal kicking he had been subjected to. All because a few bullies felt he was on the sidewalk they claimed as their property. Now both Benny and one of their friends were injured. The extent of the injuries couldn't be determined until both were at the emergency room.

The stranger knelt first over the boy from the bike club, then over Benny. The Good Samaritan had a very worried look on her face. Would the ambulance arrive in time for either, or both, of them? For her, it was like watching a horror movie.

It was only moments before she had sat and sipped her tea, looking out her bay window. Try as she might, it was impossible for her to get her frail old body to move any faster. She wanted to shout from her front porch but knew she would be too late with her warning. It felt like a premonition, knowing that the poor young lad would be the victim of another assault by these bullies. Then it happened…an accidental push by the one she assumed was the leader of the group. What was meant for Benny ended up causing one of the groups to stumble and fall, striking his head on the raised concrete.

She didn't know Benny at all, but she had seen him walk by many times and always thought he seemed to be a nice young man. She doubted if he would even know who she was, other than an old lady with gray hair that he would wave to when he walked by. Oh, how she hoped they would both be ok!

Before she walked out her front door, she set her tea down and dialed the police to report the incident and to say that they would need an ambulance or two. After she had hung up, she walked out of her front door, across the porch and down the stairs. She fretted. *Was she too late?*

"Oh, so much blood." She looked down and repeated, "Oh so much blood!"

Had they broken any of Benny's ribs from all the kicking? Had one of the broken ribs punctured a lung, or one of his vital organs? She couldn't stop the stream of dreadful thoughts that consumed her mind.

In the distance she could hear the wail of a siren, or was it more than one? Seconds seemed like hours, minutes seemed like days, as she waited for help to arrive. Some of her neighbors were slowly coming out of their houses to see what all the fuss was about. No one did anything; no one offered to help or console the boys. Were they afraid to touch them? Most of them milled about, looking at both boys, shaking their heads from side to side.

First one conversation, then another was whispered softly. "Why can't people respect one another? This is just another example of kids doing what they want. They need to be respectful to others."

Another person chimed in, "Isn't that the boy from down the street? What could he have possibly done to deserve this? He's in his ball uniform, too. I bet they decided to pick on him again as he walked home from the ball game, minding his own business."

Benny was unaware, but very aware, of all that was going on around him. Everything was shrouded in darkness, but his mind remembered words from before.

You will be bullied, ridiculed...

Benny remembered those words and thought that was exactly what had happened to him. Bullied, ridiculed, set apart from all the others was exactly what Benny had experienced. In his gloomy state, he wondered how he was supposed to help anyone if he continued to get picked on, mocked, made fun of? *What kind of help am I supposed to provide?* he questioned.

It was difficult for Benny to understand. Why couldn't he see? Why did he hear the conversations of the people that had gathered around him, but at the same time he heard the voices of The Guardian and Reevus talking? Was this what they meant…to be able to listen and help someone because he, too, had gone through the exact same thing? He thought about how the bicycle gang always picked on him and bullied him. His baseball coach plainly didn't like him, and he had no idea why. No, he didn't live in the best part of town in a big fancy house. But he had all he needed. He tried to understand and to find the answers to the *why* questions but really couldn't. Was he being picked on because he had no parents and lived with an elderly woman who graciously opened her home to him?

Why could Benny see his body and that of his attacker from above? Looking out of his eyes, he could see nothing but darkness, but his mind looked down on the two of them. The pool of blood was massive and still growing. Seeing it triggered a memory in Benny's mind. The memory had long faded away, but now it was as clear as day. He remembered reaching for the cookie jar and falling, landing on a large shard of the glass jar. Like his attacker, he lay on the kitchen floor, bleeding profusely. The memory was being played back in his mind. Like the feeling he experienced now, he was floating about when he watched The Guardian appear in the room. He was astonished to watch as The Guardian touched his wound and sealed it with magic, then picked him up and carried him to his bedroom. What The Guardian did for him, he must do for his attacker.

Looking down from above, Benny slipped his left arm under the head of the boy, placed his hand on his wound, and commanded the blood to stop. The scar on his left arm pulsed brightly, briefly, sealing the wound and stopping the bleeding. Benny instantly knew the young boy would now be safe, although he would undoubtedly have a very sore head. He didn't know him, but he also knew that what happened to him was entirely an accident. Benny hoped he had learned from his mistake and would choose a different path.

It wasn't much, but the help Benny extended to the young boy tired him significantly. His breathing became shallow and labored as the ambulance and police car pulled up. The Good Samaritan explained what she watched unfold. While she recounted her story to the police, the medics looked at the boy with a head injury. They lifted him up and placed him on a gurney and began to clean his wound, washing the blood out of his hair. They pushed the hair back to find just a small little nick in his scalp. Both wondered how such a small wound could have bled so much. They loaded him into the ambulance and turned their attention to Benny. From what they overheard the lady saying, they were both very concerned about internal damage and broken ribs. Benny's breathing was still short and labored. They both looked at each other and simultaneously said, "We need to transport him and get him to the ER as quickly as possible. He has at least four broken ribs," said one, "maybe more, and until he's in the ER there is no way to say or determine how severe his injuries are. Right now, all we can do is treat his broken ribs to make his ride as comfortable as possible. It will be up to the medical staff at the hospital to determine how severe his other internal injuries are."

While the medical team prepared to transport the two young boys, the elderly lady continued her story to the police. No, it wasn't the first time she or many of the neighbors had watched this group of boys pick on Benny. She couldn't understand why they had to be such bullies. All the neighbors knew Benny wasn't the only one they picked on either. She tried as best she could to describe the boys, their bicycles, and their clothes to the police. Even though she didn't know either of the injured boys, she was worried for both. She thought it odd how the medics thought it was nothing more than a small scratch on the boy who hit his head but was very concerned about Benny and his internal injuries. She had a very grave feeling about how his trip to the hospital would turn out, and she didn't like the feeling one bit. The feeling of death hung heavy in the air.

Reevus - The Second Warning

Today, like every other day, was busy. Reevus moved about his workshop, sweat dripping off his forehead as he moved quickly about his work. From his skilled hands came the tap, tap, tap of his hammer driving in nails to hold on a new heel. If it wasn't the tapping, it was the whirring of his sewing machine as he moved from one pair of shoes to another, sewing on a new sole. Some shoes received both new soles and heels, making them as good as new. For the farmers, Reevus had another machine that sprung to life as he repaired torn canvases. It was all in a day's work…his shoe, her shoe, child, grownup, all repaired as good as new. Quietly, methodically, Reevus went about his business fixing whatever was brought into his shop.

Anyone passing his quaint shoe shop on that beautiful afternoon would have looked on in amazement at Reevus, busy at his trade as the town cobbler. Nothing would have looked out of the ordinary. Reevus was deeply involved in his daily routine, whistling, or humming occasionally while he worked. Appearances were not everything, though. Reevus could not stop playing over in his mind the strangers and strange events he had seen. How many months had passed, he wasn't quite certain, but he knew it had been quite some time since he had shared his fear with his brother, Relocmor. He couldn't quite put his finger on it, but while he worked, the hair on the back of his head would stand straight up when the thoughts crossed his mind. Ever since he had talked to Reloc, he, too, had begun noticing things were not the way they used to be before he had been given his warning.

Today, he had an overwhelming feeling that something was going to change and change soon. It wouldn't be a change for the good, either. Reevus attempted to bury himself in his work and force the feelings from his mind. Try as he might, it made no difference, and he couldn't push away the thoughts that invaded his mind.

Reevus wasn't aware the shop door had opened, or that he was no longer alone in his shop. It wasn't until he heard the unmistakable sound of someone clearing their throat that he returned to reality. Startled, he gasped and quickly turned around. He was blinded momentarily from the bright light illuminating his shop.

Reevus broke the silence after his eyes had adjusted and he could make out his brother, Relocmor, standing on the other side of the counter.

"Reloc, you look good. I didn't realize you were back in town. It is always great to see you. Come, let me fix you some tea. So good to see you. How long has it been?" he continued as they moved toward his living space in the back. A few steps from his bed sat his kitchen table. He motioned for Reloc to take a seat as he went about getting the water started for their tea.

Reloc smiled and gripped his brother's hand firmly. "It has been too long, my brother, but it is always good to see you, too. Since our last meeting, I have noticed the buying of grain has increased significantly." Reloc followed Reevus as they walked into his back room, pulling out a chair and taking a seat at his small table. Reevus picked up the tea pot, a few tea bags, a couple of cups and spoons, and the honey. With his hands full, he moved to the table, placing each item on the table.

"Well, there we be…a cup, two tea bags, a spoon, and the honey. Can't ask for better than that now, can you, brother? Easily within reach for both of us."

Reevus smiled as he set the tea pot next to the honey. With his hands now free, Reevus poured the hot water first in Reloc's cup and then his own before sitting.

"Tell me, my brother, what news do you bring? But before you answer, I must share…I feel something is wrong, something is terribly wrong. I have had this feeling that something is going to happen, but I don't know exactly what. Whatever it is, it makes the hair on the back of my neck stand up." Reevus reached out for the honey and poured some in both his cup and Reloc's. They allowed the tea too steep as they both sat in silence for a few moments.

Reevus spoke first. "Has anyone followed my advice since we met last? Have they built storehouses to store grain?"

Reloc sighed. "Ahhhhh, my brother, how I wish all would have heard and heeded. Unfortunately, very few understood or complied. They were more than happy to get two or three times the normal payment for the crops. I was greatly saddened that the majority ignored what I told and asked of them. Out of all that I have accomplished serving our emperor, this has been my greatest disappointment. I have felt completely helpless that there wasn't more I could do." Reloc held the cup to his lips and sipped the warm tea.

"Perhaps, dear brother, it may be best that you get back to the fleet. I can't seem to shake this feeling of dread. Why, I don't know, but I feel it is the time, for your own protection, for you to be on your ship and be ready to sail." Reevus shook his head as he began to rub the back of his neck. "You've continued to see these strangers, too."

"Yes. Worse, they seem to have grown in numbers. Everywhere I go, I see them. It is odd. They wear black pants with what looks like a Z at the knee, but a shirt like any other farmer would wear. Perhaps they believe they would blend in with a simple shirt and hat like everyone else. Granted, others may not have noticed, but I have at every place I've stopped. If we were there to load the ships, they were there as well, buying everything they could and paying far greater than the price we offered." When Reloc had finished, they both sat in an eerie silence while they allowed what he had said to soak in.

Reevus broke the silence. "You know, I have tried to spread the word at the inn during the telling of my stories. Not a one would have anything to do with what I told them. They would laugh, scoff, and call me an old fool. There they all sat, dumb, and happy without a care in the world. Why should they worry? They believed not a word of what I said, thinking it was only another of my stories for the children. The children, at least, were kind enough to ask what they should do. I felt so useless that I couldn't tell them more. But I won't stop trying, and I will keep telling my stories."

They finished their tea in silence. Reloc stood and grasped the hand of his brother firmly. "Thank you for your warning, brother. I won't let you down, and I'll return to my ship and tell the fleet to make ready. At least I will feel safer on my ship than walking on land."

Releasing their handshake, Reevus led his brother to the door. "Thank you, my brother. Stay safe. Until we meet again."

Once the door closed, Reevus returned to his work, wondering silently how to best continue his story and warnings.

Skippy, curled up in her bed, slept through the entire meeting.

"Well, well, well, Skippy, fine guard dog you are. What are you guarding against? Someone coming to steal your nap?"

Reevus reached down and patted Skippy on the head as he chuckled.

"Yes, my four-legged friend, we'll make it through. Exactly what we'll make through and how, I'm not certain. But we will make it through."

Part 3

Zorleg - "Molded into The Lord of Darkness"

Zorleg, a young teenager, was on his way to another day of instruction at The Great Meeting Place. A smile curled across his face as he thought back to the first time, he discovered his uniqueness and power. It was a day no different than any other as he walked toward The Great Meeting Place. It would be another day of what he considered boring instruction. Oh, how he loathed this! But on that particular day, as he followed his normal path, he felt the desire – no, the need – to slip away, to be rebellious.

I am tired of doing what they say. They have no idea how great I am and what I can become. The words filled Zorleg's mind while he felt his desire to be someone, something different.

He didn't really know why, but he had a feeling it was exactly what he was supposed to do and where he was supposed to go.

There is something different about me, about this day. I can feel it growing with each step I take. As he moved further from the normal path, Zorleg thought it was funny how he had walked past this very spot every day and noticed nothing unusual. But today, after he wandered, he noticed a small space, a niche located within the rocks.

Well, this is interesting, he thought. This small space had really piqued his interest. How long had it been there, and why hadn't he noticed it before? Zorleg thought the spot appeared to have been expertly carved out in the rocks for someone, so why not him? It wasn't much, but this was his beginning, where it all started. Within this small space, he found privacy and was obscured from view in all directions. He could watch and observe everything about him, but no one could see him.

He was so tired, so aggravated with the mundane teachings he endured day after day.

They have no idea what I am capable of, he thought again. *But here I can watch, observe, and plot my revenge.* He could feel his rage and anger growing as the dark thoughts festered in his mind.

From the small space, barely bigger than he was, he noticed how it provided a clear view of where the Sisters of the Mist stood on the grounds of The Great Meeting Place.

"I am completely hidden from view. No one can see me at all." Oh, how Zorleg basked in his great find! No one could see him, but he was able to see everything around him clearly. He laughed to himself while his mind whirled in anticipation. He remembered the story of the Guardians, told many times. He could recite it from memory. They stood erect, each looking out to a different point in the compass, standing well over seven feet tall. This was another moment of amusement for him as he observed each one of these so-called Guardians.

Why? Zorleg thought. *Why do they appear to be dressed and equipped as warriors for a world covered in such a peaceful bliss? Odd, so odd.*

Each appeared as if they were protecting the Great Meeting Place. They stood on the teaching grounds, each with a dual-edged sword that reached from the ground to their shoulders.

Who were they supposed to be protecting and from what? Zorleg wondered. He paused again, recalling the story told so many times on their arrival to The Great Meeting Place.

The story had been repeated time and time again. "With a wave of his hand, The One of Ones had flattened this land, turning it smooth and level."

All, that is, except for The Great Meeting Place. Each of the Sisters proudly projected their prominence around the clearing. They rose well above the land after the words were spoken. Zorleg wondered who had placed them there and why. *Had The One of Ones placed them where they now stood? And why? Yes*, he thought, *there was always the "why."* To the eye and touch, they appeared made of solid stone.

Another story greatly intrigued Zorleg. It had been passed down overtime that each had been covered by words of enchantment, spoken by the elven Queen of The Great Forest.

Who is this queen, and what power does she hold? Zorleg had always wondered. *I must find the queen and The Great Forest. All those powers shall be mine!* Zorleg laughed, and his hands tingled with the thought of more power.

Yes, power, all power shall be mine. A smile of wickedness crept across Zorleg's face. *I will find this alleged great queen and her forest. Her power, her knowledge, and the secrets of the Forest will be mine!*

The Great Forest would be plundered, left in ruins with its trees burnt and covered by blackened, charred wood. He had no use for the queen, or the forest. It was only her power and knowledge that he thirsted for. Should anything happen to survive his attack on the forest, it would be quickly annihilated.

No mercy at all! Death awaits all who dare oppose me! Zorleg thought. *Power, yes, her power, shall be mine!* Zorleg wasn't aware he had started wringing his hands together as he lusted after her power.

Zorleg's mind quickly shifted away from The Sisters of the Mist, The Great Forest, and this so-called queen. He allowed his thoughts to return to his secret hiding spot.

Maybe, he thought, *maybe it isn't the right time.* Zorleg surmised that now, his being so tired and full of anger at not being recognized allowed him to see what he could not before.

Ahhhh yes, the timing, Zorleg mused. *I have become so tired of the teachings, so disgusted with all the goodie-goodie sayings.* Zorleg shook his head from side to side.

Ignore me, will they? Doubt my ability? I doubt if they will even notice I'm gone. Zorleg turned his attention to his new fortress.

He knew exactly where each stone bench had been placed for the teachers and the students. From there they taught the students day after day. Zorleg's mind flashed then to the memory of the daily ritual, watching The Three Suns of Kalamar rising. There appeared to be a calming of the minds of the students with peace and tranquility, but he wasn't certain if it was caused by the sun or something else.

Zorleg found it so tedious doing the same thing every day, over and over again. See the seed, make it grow. What was the purpose of this?

Thinking to himself… *Who really cares what the seed produces? What does that really accomplish? Why am I doing this? I can do so much more. Don't they know? Such fools!*

The very first time it happened, he thought it was an accident. His anger rose from within before it burst forth. He never questioned why or where his anger came from, only that it was something he had never experienced before, and he liked it. He knew the anger came from his rebellion against his teachers and everything on The Third Plane. He wondered if anyone else noticed the change in him.

Now Zorleg was hidden in his small fortress. He felt the desire to do something, something he had never done before. Looking down, he noticed he held in his right hand a fresh budding rose.

I don't remember picking a rose before. Did I make it appear in my hand? His mind raced as he felt a new power surging in his body. The years of frustration, anger, and resentment from not being recognized in the manner he felt he should be all came together. As quickly as a snap of his fingers, he had turned the flower brittle, dead. When he closed his hand, he felt the rose crumbling, turning into a light powder. The dust from the rose drifted slowly to the ground. Zorleg enjoyed a new feeling that coursed through his veins. He had never known such power and anger before but now… He inhaled deeply, opened the palm of his hand, and exhaled. He blew the remainder of the dust from his hand, watching it drifts downward before it settled on the rocks.

Zorleg was so proud of what he had done, the beginning of his power. In days to come, he continued slipping into his new-found hiding place instead of going to the Great Meeting Place. He doubted if they even missed him. He was far too excited to worry about that. He vowed he would perform his feat again and again, increasing his power with each repetition. It was important for him to keep his mind focused on exactly what he was doing. Zorleg felt the power growing after he completed the same steps repeatedly. When he had finished, he always looked at his hand. Like before, he created a handful of dust, snuffed the life out of another flower. He gloated over his great accomplishment.

For now, it was only a flower, but Zorleg started planning on bigger and more difficult objects, some alive, some not. He had become very good at turning flowers into powder, but he wanted more. Zorleg plotted on using the same power to crumble and destroy the Sister of the

Mist in the same exact fashion as he had done with the flowers. First, though, he needed to perfect it. He needed to choose his subjects of destruction carefully. With each exhibition of his power, nothing was left but dust, exactly like the rose. Now he felt positive he could develop his power to turn the stone statues on The Great Meeting Place into piles of dust. During his time in secret hiding, Zorleg worked hard as he developed and honed his ability to hide his true feelings, pushing them deep within, concealed from everyone. He had also developed an ability to look a bit into the future and could see his power grow. One by one, he would begin converting others to serve him. By his command, he would mold them into what would become known as Zoreans. The power of dark matter that manifested itself in him would continue to grow and influence him while he built his black army.

I shall not allow them to forget who I was and who I have become. It is through my power, my power alone, that I shall get my revenge! Zorleg smiled as he looked forward to the challenge ahead of him.

The Guardian - A Moment to Learn

Cosmo was curled up in a small ball on his bed, sound asleep and snoring softly, awaiting Benny's return home from his baseball game. How many times had Benny returned home from practice or a game and shared his feelings about how he was treated?

"Cosmo, I don't understand why the coach doesn't like me. He's new in town, so it's not like he really knows anything about us. But his words are so mean and cruel. I do my best to keep my chin up and not let it bother me, but it does. It's not like I'm asking to be treated special. All I want is an opportunity to play like the other boys on the team." Benny would reach out and caress Cosmo's back while retelling the story of the day. Cosmo's response was always the same, licking Benny's hand and cuddling up close to him.

Cosmo was aware of the difficulties Benny encountered when he left the house. It made no difference whether it was walking to and from school or baseball practice. The same group of boys continually harassed and assaulted him. They would take his milk money, make fun of his clothes and his lunch, and push and shove him. Even Cosmo couldn't make sense of why they acted that way and what caused such behavior.

Today, Cosmo woke from his deep slumber agitated and excited. He may be a small puppy, but he felt something was different. He sensed a multitude of emotions in Benny's heart. They were the same aches and pains Benny had experienced before, but Cosmo also detected a joy that he had not sensed earlier. Cosmo knew something good happened for

Benny today. But then tragedy struck. Cosmo knew something had gone wrong, very wrong.

Cosmo leapt out of his bed and began to run around the house, barking, trying to sound a warning. He was in the house alone, so his barks went unheard. Rather, the barks weren't heard by anyone in the house, but they were heard. His barks traveled across time, falling upon the ears of The Guardian. He, too, sensed the urgency of Cosmo's warning. He grabbed the staff of Kalamar, whispered a few words, and traveled to find out what had caused Cosmo to sound such an urgent warning.

The Guardian had chosen to first stop to visit Cosmo and allow his four-legged friend to fill him in. He picked Cosmo up and listened intently to his story of how Benny had been picked on, bullied, and completely ignored repeatedly. The Guardian let out a soft sigh. He should have known this type of encounter would happen, and it pained him deeply. But it was also part of the process Benny needed to understand as he developed a compassion and empathy for others. He would now be able to help those who were bullied and made fun of just because they were different. The Guardian stroked Cosmo's back with strokes of love and reassurance.

"Thank you, my friend. Yes, it was not easy for any of us, but it was part of his learning process. Through it all, he will come out a much better person on the other side." The Guardian placed Cosmo back in his bed. "You'll be all right now, Cosmo. Thank you again for reaching out to me and making me aware of the peril Benny has found himself in. Rest and rest well. Now, if you'll excuse me, let me go and check on Benny." The Guardian gave Cosmo one last pet. Then, as quickly as he arrived, he was gone.

He assumed his translucent appearance and floated within the trees. His view of everything below was completely unobstructed. The Guardian moved time backward so he could watch and observe how things had unfolded. He watched Benny innocently walking home. He watched as a gang of boys riding their bikes rounded the corner, cutting Benny off from his route home, all pre-planned by the leader of the group. Disgusted, he watched the boys pick on Benny before they pushed him to the ground and began to savagely kick him repeatedly. The Guardian had taken in all he cared to. With the slight movement of his fingers, he intentionally made the leader of the group accidentally hit one of his own, causing him to fall and strike his head on the uneven concrete to a resounding *thud* and small whimper. Blood instantly began to form a pool around the fallen youth. They screamed at Benny, "Look, see what you did!" as they continued to kick him repeatedly and their anger raged.

The Guardian was surprised when an elderly lady walked out of her house, sternly warning the boys they had better leave. She'd told them in no uncertain terms she had already called the police and now looked on, helplessly at the two boys.

Things didn't look good for either Benny or his attacker. The Guardian reached out to Benny, softly whispering words that could only be heard by Benny's mind.

"Benny." He paused. "Benny. Do not be afraid; I am with you." The Guardian assured Benny he was not alone. "Tell me, from this travesty, what have you learned?"

Benny heard The Guardian's words and began to share his experiences with him. "All people are equal. We shouldn't judge or make fun of others because they are different than we are. Everyone should be given the same opportunity and chance to succeed. They will succeed or fail based upon their abilities, not how someone else perceives them.

Everyone is equal. But I have experienced hatred, bullying, and revulsion because some of those perceived me as being different. The coach on the baseball team refused to play me because the family I live with isn't wealthy. I'm made fun of because, unlike the others, my school clothes are only bought once a year. The bullies have taken my milk money, made fun of my clothes and now, today, they beat me up. All because they thought I was different."

The Guardian smiled as he talked to Benny. "Tell me how this has impacted you, and how you look at things differently now." The Guardian grew silent.

Benny pondered for a moment before he gave his answer. "It all comes to…we are all equal and all should be treated the same. Everyone was created equal. While I can't understand some of the hardships others have experienced, it doesn't mean I can't listen to them and acknowledge we have differences. Together, we can learn from our differences and make each other stronger. What we learn, we pass along to make others better so we can live in harmony."

The Guardian asked, "And what of him, one of your attackers. How do you deal with him?"

Benny looked over at the young boy and the pool of blood. "I remember when I was young…you found me like this and healed me." The scar on his wrist began to pulse and glow. Benny reached out with his left hand and touched the spot on the back of the boy's head, sealing the wound and stopping the bleeding.

The Guardian observed Benny's action. "Why would you heal one who attacked you so viciously?"

Benny thought for a moment. "Because he really isn't a bad person. He wanted to belong to something, and he chose to belong to this group. Right or wrong, he chose to be part of a group that enjoyed bullying those they found different. He did what they did so he could feel like he belonged. My gift to him, by healing his wound, is to leave him with the knowledge that everyone is different. Being different isn't a crime; it's a gift. What one can do may not be what another can do. Together, through the blending of their skills, they accomplish more than either of them could have done alone."

Benny allowed himself a moment to rest, to think about what he had said before he continued. "If they had closed their eyes and listened, they would have seen the words and heard the meaning. They would not have allowed their judgment to be impaired by what they perceived as a difference. They would have been able to concentrate on the conversation instead of the traits, or appearance, of the other. That would have been the true ability to communicate with one another, pushing aside preconceived prejudices against others. All, all, are equal. But I also know there are some whose opinions will never change, unfortunately."

The Guardian enjoyed the words that Benny spoke. The words spoken by young Benjamin proved again that his knowledge exceeded far beyond his years. "Remember this day, young Benjamin. Place your thoughts deep within the recesses of your mind. As you grow, you will face many encounters like this. Look back at this moment, like you looked back at our moment at the farmhouse kitchen and use it to help others. Through your help, a healing will come, a healing that shall spread over the Third Plane of Kalamar."

"Why do I know these things? None of those my age seems to have the same knowledge that I do. Why am I so different?" Young Benjamin's questions didn't catch The Guardian off-guard. They were questions that he knew someday would be asked.

"Ahhhhhh, my dear young Benjamin. You, yet again, continue to amaze me with how wise you are and the questions you ask. The simplest answer that I can give you is this: When you were born, you were given knowledge far beyond what anyone had been given before. When it is needed, it comes forth or will be given. Does that sound a bit familiar?" The Guardian grew silent to allow young Benny to process the answer.

"It is because of who I am, isn't it? We, both of us, were gifted. Gifts are provided when they are needed."

It was difficult for The Guardian to contain all the joy he felt from the wisdom of young Benjamin's answer. "You are correct, my child. But now, we need to turn to things at hand. While you have helped your assailant, I am forbidden to do the same for you. Now had it been Zorleg's minions again, then I could have and would have. But this was a natural occurrence of this world. What I will share with you is, your injuries are serious, very serious. We can talk, but neither you nor I can actually see the extent of your injuries. For now, all I can say is the injuries you have sustained have me very concerned."

During a moment of silence, the ambulance arrived, and the medics started examining both children. Just as The Guardian had surmised, Benny's injuries were bad. He also found joy in knowing how expertly Benny had healed the wound on his assailant. Benny left only a small scratch for the medics to discover when they examined the boy. The Guardian was proud of how young Benjamin was able to reach back in time, pull forth the memory of his healing, and use it to heal the boy. He also knew he was the only one who noticed the scar and its brief glow when young Benjamin healed him.

Now it was a time of waiting. It had turned into waiting for The Guardian and for all of those on Kalamar. With the male child of The Chosen severely injured, the temptation to interfere was great. It took all of his power to resist the temptation and not break the rules of interference. The Guardian took a deep breath, held it, before letting it out slowly. The healing must be left to those in this world where Benjamin has been hidden in time.

Madison

It was another moonlit night in the Great City of Kalamar. Moonbeams cascaded downward from the heavens and illuminated Madison's room with a soft blue. She slept soundly in her large brass bed. If one listened closely, they could have heard the deep and comfortable rhythm of her breathing. Her long golden locks rested undisturbed on one of her king-sized pillows. The soft moonbeams caused her hair to give off a distinct glow in the darkness. A very light breeze blew in effortlessly through the window and circled the room before passing over Madison's sleeping body. The warmth of the sunbaked stones still filled the room, creating a perfect and comfortable environment for sleeping.

Carried gently and caressed by the wind, a small leaf entered through one of the open windows before it landed silently on the floor at the end of Madison's bed. No sooner had the leaf settled on the floor than it took on a life of its own. It commenced to vibrate on the floor as it moved this way and that, twisting and turning. Without a sound, it began its transformation. The leaf changed its shape as it morphed into a very large figure. An elderly man with long flowing gray strands of hair now stood at the end of the bed where moments before the leaf had landed. The Guardian smiled as he looked down on the sleeping Madison.

The Guardian raised his right hand and gently blew across it. As his breath passed over his hands, he softly whispered, "***Brestee' un mea***" three times. After he had spoken the words, a light-yellow mist formed above the head of the soundly sleeping Madison.

At his direction, the mist slowly descended, engulfing both her and her entire bed. With each breath Madison took, the mist slowly entered her body. The Guardian moved from the end of the bed to stand on Madison's left side. He reached out with his right hand and took her left hand in his. Softly, he spoke to the slumbering young lady.

"For now, our journey begins. Selected by the One of Ones, born the second child of Queen Rhianne, you are now one of his Three of Threes. What has been given to you is knowledge far beyond your years…perhaps even far beyond mine.

"While many will look at me and see only a foolish old man, they will look at you and see a beautiful young lady that is full of life, energy and excitement."

The Guardian released Madison's left hand. He paused for a moment, then he raised his left hand above his head. Silently, the words he had whispered a few moments ago reached Madison's ears. He moved his right hand, holding his hand a foot above her chest. Slowly, his hand began to glow. First, it appeared as a dull orange. Then it began to slowly change colors, until it radiated a brilliant white. Time appeared to stand still as his hand continued its transformation until it burst into a pure white flame, a flame so bright and so intense that it illuminated the entire bedroom. The flame neither burned his hand nor his robe but danced vibrantly in the palm of his hand.

The Guardian closed his eyes as he continued to whisper soft words for only Madison to hear.

"I was young, but I am older now…freely given, by my breath of life, I now give to you the eternal flame. The torch is now passed. For you, Madison, a special gift has been given. The eternal flame within you is carried by only a few. In your travels, you will be faced with many things, some good, and others that are not. I implore you to always remember whatever is before you. Regardless of what it is, your heart will always know. It is during these times that you must retreat deep within yourself and calmly, quietly remember. Your heart shall always know. Go within and garner warmth and strength from the flame. Allow it to light your path, especially during the darkest of times."

The Guardian hesitated before the flame left his hand and passed effortlessly into Madison's heart. Slowly he closed his hand and allowed his arm to fall by his side, the eternal flame left behind. He watched, seeing what only a few could see, as the flame burned brightly within her. His hand now empty, the flame now gone, the room returned to illumination only provided by moonbeams.

Softly, he continued, "within your heart now lives the flame of flames, created by The One of Ones. For my travels have placed many miles behind me, with perhaps just as many trials and tribulations that have been part of my life. I have felt the need to shed a tear to help me remember. But for you, Madison, I leave you with this…always remember, you have so much more to gain than you do to lose. A special gift has been given to you for a day that is yet to come. When it is needed, then it will be given."

The Guardian returned to the foot of the bed. Again, he stood between the brass bedposts. He crossed his arms over his chest and slid his hands into the sleeves of his robe. His softly spoken and distinctly clear words crossed silently across the room to Madison's ears. "Listen, my child, for these words are for your ears only. For as you sleep, your mind has been totally awake, and your ears have heard my every word."

As he spoke, Madison sat up in bed. To anyone else, she would appear to be fully awake. The Guardian knew that she sensed his presence while she remained in her deep sleep. Madison's eyes were locked on his while she listened intently to every word.

"In your time, you will see tears of joy and happiness, sadness and despair. Tears, I believe, are a very good thing. I call them the kiss of emotion. You shall see people who are good, bad and those who need healing. Sometimes it may only be one, sometimes two or more. Follow your heart because your heart knows and can see the difference. Use your flame then, its warmth and love…allow it to guide you along your path and in your decisions. Remember, your heart knows."

The Guardian paused once again before he moved his head from side to side while he spoke. Madison, like a sponge, absorbed every word and the instructions from The Guardian. "The one tear you shall see that no other can, shall be your tear of healing. In the deepest darkest point of their life, this special tear shall heal the broken heart. It is the gift of the tear of healing that has been given to you, so you may touch others in the moment when it is needed most. My dear child, so many treasures are awaiting you on the other side of the mountain. When you feel you can no longer go on, remember to trust your heart, for it knows, and allow it to guide and lead you."

The Guardian stopped, paused, and took a deep breath before he continued. "One of the most important things you must always remember, we have so much to gain as well as so much to lose. Defeat, while a very small word, is one word you shall never know or use. For it is his word, Zorleg's word, and for his sole purpose…to defeat all of us. For as I have prepared to leave you on this night, I leave you with these thoughts to carry with you and to remember. When you feel the sun kiss your cheek and as its warmth spreads across your face...remember. When you walk and feel as though your feet are not touching the ground...others are lifting you up…remember. Wherever you are…remember. Feel my presence, and remember I am always with you. Last and most important…remember this night."

The Guardian lowered his arms to his sides and bowed his head. He stood motionless and in complete silence. Madison's body silently and effortlessly returned to the mattress to continue her restful sleep.

Through the open window, a new sound permeated the room. The Guardian's ears picked up the soft sweeping sound of wings. He listened as they moved back, fanning the night air. He walked over by the window, bowed reverently to Madison before stepping on the window's ledge. He took a giant step from the ledge into the warm night air. Drifting downward, the mighty white steed Cna effortlessly pushed her wings into the night air. Her majestic white coat shone brilliantly in the moonlit night, navigating to slip directly under the Guardian, catching him in midair. Settling in the saddle, the Guardian patted her on the neck and spoke.

"This has been a good evening, my trusted friend. The evening's work is now complete. Another torch has been placed into the heart of a third. Let us take our leave, before we meet with Emperor Daniel and Empress Katherine."

Queen Rhianne looked on from afar, pleased with how the ceremony for her second daughter, Madison, had gone. Such gifts and treasures had been given to her!

"Yes, sleep well, my child. We have far to travel and much to do to help The Chosen. Sleep well, my child."

Another Meeting with The Guardian

The remainder of Benny's day was uneventful. Nothing out of the ordinary happened from the dinner meal until it was bedtime. There was nothing to compare to what he experienced in his play city in the old driveway. He was grateful for the gift of the jasper stone too. He was amazed at how smooth and cool it felt when he held it in his hand. Tonight, he was going to hold his gift tightly in his right hand as he slept.

Normally it wouldn't take Benny long to fall asleep but tonight was different. His mind kept returning to his visitor, the old man, and the gifts he had been given. Peeking under the covers, he ensured the rock was still secure, held tightly in his right hand, before he finally started to drift off to sleep. How could he forget the puppy, too, now lying comfortably beside him sleeping soundly? Drifting off to sleep, Benny was certain he saw the old gentleman standing at the foot of his bed, coaxing him to come and sit. Was what he saw real, or had he fallen asleep, and was he part of a dream?

When Benny moved, he quickly noticed he was no longer in his bed, or even in his bedroom. He found himself standing in the middle of a lush meadow. Benny turned slowly before his eyes were drawn to the glowing fire in front of The Guardian. Without being asked, Benny walked over and took a seat. After getting settled, he heard The Guardian begin to speak. Benny listened intently as he told him of What Was, What Is, and What Is Yet To Come. Attentively, he absorbed every word, his puppy nestled in his lap. Funny, he didn't remember picking up

Cosmo, yet, there he was. How did that happen? Then he figured that, if it were a dream, anything was possible.

The Guardian spoke softly, but forcefully, to him. "Benjamin, as you grow, there will be many times where you will feel a lot of things: pain, sadness, rejection. Some of those feelings will be your own, others will not. As you grow and mature, you will experience the feelings of a multitude of others as if they were your own. Their emotions will be emotions that we, you and I alone, must deal with. It is part of what makes us who we are. You will be scorned, ridiculed, laughed at, and made fun of, but what you must not do is shed a tear because of the feelings of others. There will be a time, and you will know when the time and place is right, where you can shed all the tears you have held back for so long."

The Guardian paused for a moment to allow what he had told Benjamin to sink in before he continued. "Strength will be one of the keys to success. It will not be a physical strength, but strength of your mind. You must always be strong and look beyond the moment, hold it in your hand before you hide it away in your mind. Gather strength from those moments, Benjamin. Absorb what they offer, allow the feelings of others to come and dwell within you."

The Guardian had stopped speaking. He needed the moment of silence to allow Benny's mind to process all that he shared with him. He slowly turned his head to look at Benny. It appeared he was asking for permission to continue.

Benny saw the raised eyebrow on the Guardian and nodded his head.

"All I can do is prepare you and make you aware. There will be times when you will feel as if a mountain has been placed upon your chest, pressing, and squeezing the breath and life out of your soul." The

Guardian reached out and gently patted Benny on the chest. "Within you, at moments like those, you could shake the heavens, make oceans swell and dams break should you choose to unleash the feelings you have harnessed. These are the type of emotions you have been given and ones that you must feel. They will all help you to grow into who you are. Use your feelings to guide others, to give them hope in the darkness. Help them to remember love, the enjoyment of playing with a child, seeing a friend that has not been seen for a long time."

Again, silence filled the air. The Guardian encouraged Benny. "Think and be in the moment. Allow what you feel to pass through your veins to be used in guiding you in your work. Open your heart and share your heart with others. Allow them to see, through your actions and words, that you are the hope of the hopeless. It is you who will be the voice of the ones who cry out and hear no answer. There will be some who will know your name, some will know who you are, and others will only know of you and pass along the stories of you and your amazing feats."

The Guardian paused, almost as if to catch his breath, and then slowly, softly, proceeded with his instructions. "There will be times when you will be overwhelmed with emotions that will rock your very soul. It will cause you to stop, pause, and wonder if you can continue to press on. Other times it will feel like a knife slicing into you, ripping you apart from the inside out. When you find yourself overwhelmed with so many emotions from others, look for a place of solitude. Then, during your moments of solitude, then and only then, shed your tears, releasing the feeling of anguish, the feeling of being distraught; feeling lost…but contain your feelings within you. It has been written no one shall ever see a tear run down your cheek nor the pain that has welled up within you…for I give you a special strength, and from this strength, you shall grow and become stronger. You shall go on like no other has before you, because that is who you have been from birth. I shall light your path and lead you through the darkness. Some will see your actions as a withdrawal, a depression, but it is not, for it is your gift given to you by The Great Storytellers of Kalamar. It is from within that we do our greatest work, taking the feelings of others and turning them into an inspiration for all…anyone that needs to be inspired to do a great work...just as the storytellers inspired and painted pictures in the minds of others through their stories. It is the process of returning what was removed from Kalamar by the Dark One and planting the seeds in return."

The Guardian stopped again, taking a few deep breaths, and then calmly picked up where he left off. "Benjamin, our work is not about us. No, it has never been about us, nor will it ever be about us. It is about them and allowing them to achieve the greatness they were destined to achieve. History books will never print our names…for that was the intention from the beginning. Our greatness, your greatness, comes through not only your work, but the work of others. We shall sacrifice our very essence to breathe life into another, whisper into their ear, a whisper only they shall hear. A whisper stirring a great awakening. As you grow, we shall grow together and two shall become one."

Benny's eyes never left The Guardian as he spoke. He heard every word as clearly as if they were spoken aloud: "For as I am, yet you will be; for as you are, yet you shall become, and even more. As I give to you, there is yet another waiting, hidden in time from the Dark Lord. Now I prepare you, so you will be prepared for the moments that await you."

Watching, listening, Benny saw in his mind something that he had experienced before. Calmly he watched as the Guardian's hand dipped into the flame before he slowly brought it out of the fire. Like he had experienced before, without a word, The Guardian's flame jumped from his hand into Benjamin's chest. Again, there was no pain; there was no fire on his clothes as The Guardian spoke the same words he had spoken before. "You will remember the flame, my child, for it is my gift to you. As it burns within you, you shall always remember. As I am, as you shall be, and you shall give to another. As you are now, your eyes shall be opened to reveal exactly who you are. Now, however, is not the time to reveal all. You will hear at the proper time, and you will know."

Lying in bed, Benny opened his eyes and wondered if it all truly was a dream. *What does it mean, "reveal who I am"?* Benny lifted his head and looked around the room. He looked to his left. Both windows over the porch were open halfway as they were when he slipped into bed. The same was true of the windows on his right and straight ahead. Everything was the same as when he slipped into bed. Cosmo, his new friend, was still sound asleep beside him, undisturbed by the events in Benny's mind. Reaching out, Benny pulled Cosmo closer to him before he settled in comfortably and quickly fell back to sleep. Drifting off to sleep, he wondered if it was real or if it was, as it seemed, only a dream.

Kay-Lee

Zorleg rose from his chair, and his hands relaxed after he released his death grip on the arms of the chair. His head turned when the head of the elite guard walked into the room. "Summon them!" Zorleg barked in a deep rumbling voice. "I have thought out my plan, and now they need to do my bidding." Without saying a word, the head of the elite guard bowed respectfully, or out of fear, then quickly exited the room.

The flame from the torches flickered, casting an eerie shadow into every corner of his chamber. Zorleg sat at ease on his throne. His dark black eyes pierced through the dimness of his sanctuary, looking at nothing in particular yet at everything. Unconsciously, he moved his finger up and down his cheekbone. The news from his spies excited him immensely. His eyes pierced each cold, dark stone, causing him to smile inwardly. "I have done this; this is what I created!" His chuckle was hard to contain as he rewarded himself, even though the sound reached only his ears.

His finger moved over his lips, wiping the smirk from his face as he formulated his next move. His sole purpose had always been to find those who were called The Chosen. From his spies, he had learned, and had proof, the male child was still alive.

Zorleg began to muse about the female child of The Chosen. *How is it that she has been able to avoid detection? What magic has been placed around her that keeps her hidden?* Zorleg, overjoyed with finding the male child, still sought to find the other one of The Chosen.

It is no concern to me how they are terminated. I need - no, I demand it be done, finished, completed! Death is the only choice for either of them! No longer shall a breath escape their lips!

Zorleg was unaware his fists were clenched tightly closed. *I found him before and he was left for dead. I continue to curse those who helped him!*

The spies Zorleg had sent out into the villages had learned he was not dead, but only severely wounded. But from Benny's near-death experience, he was left with a scar on his left wrist. A scar that forever reminded him how close to death he was!

Zorleg's thoughts churned in his mind; involuntarily, his hands now tightly clenched the arm rest, turning his knuckles white. His grip was not out of anger, but out of anticipation of the next step in his plan for the destruction of The Third Plane.

How long have I built my army? From a few in the beginning, I have grown it day by day. Zorleg reveled in how he had amassed such a huge following, all obedient and faithful to him.

Many days Zorleg found himself sitting alone on his throne. He would cup his hand against his ear and listen. *Ahhhh, there it is, the sound of the movement of my army.* Zorleg smirked. *Not only can I hear my army marching, but I can feel it, too!* The marching army's steps reverberated across the land, leaving no doubt who or what it was.

Yes, it was me, all me. I coordinated and planned exactly where they needed to be and when. Zorleg was proud of his army, his plan, and how well it was executed.

Across the land, those who heard the sound had long since forgotten the attack. Like a well-thought-out cadence, each step was orchestrated by him and him alone: methodical, never-ceasing. What fools they were! He created a great cloak of gray before the attack began.

They thought it was nothing more than part of the storm. Never in all of time had they figured out what he had planned.

Grink and Pounce were admiring how exquisite they looked in the uniform of the elite guard. The uniforms were fitted to the physical attributes of each.

Pounce was the first to speak. "Zorleg, he be knowin' before we returned what we be going to say in our report. His foreknowledge is why our uniforms be here waiting for us."

Grink chimed in, "And our rooms, they be ready with our new uniforms when we gets here. Always be perfect timing, everything be perfect, just like he be."

Before Pounce could answer, the head of the elite guard walked into the room, snapped to attention, and bellowed wryly, "Both of you! You have been summoned!" As quickly as he appeared, the head of the elite guard was gone.

Neither hesitated as they moved quickly to the door then down the hall. The door to Zorleg's chamber was wide open in expectation of their arrival. Moving swiftly, they stumbled through the door, both trying to enter at the same time with neither getting in. Grink allowed Pounce to go first, then both stopped before Zorleg's throne and bowed reverently.

Zorleg was already standing when they arrived and observed how they cowered before him. He smiled and chuckled to himself, pleased with his newest recruits. "You have served me well; however, you have not been truthful," he began, his voice echoing off the walls. "Again, I shall send you to find the female child. This time, I expect nothing less than her total eradication, total. Nothing less is acceptable. How you do that is up to you. Keep in mind I want her gone, completely wiped from existence! Do not, I repeat, do not return with the same actions that were a total fabrication of your minds." Zorleg paused and then motioned with his hand, directing Grink and Pounce where they needed to stand. "As before, I shall send you. Before you go, allow me to remind you again, nothing less than death is acceptable. You failed with him and did not follow through. Completely inexcusable. Should you not produce the result I demand, your life means nothing to me." With another wave of his hand, they were off to begin another journey. In the darkness, they sensed they were moving but had no sense of how or where.

This trip had sent the two to arrive in a somewhat familiar place, like where they were before, but yet different. Grink looked at Pounce and spoke in a hushed tone. "I know we be where he sent us, but we where we are supposed to be? What tells us what to do and where to do?"

"Who we supposed to be findin'?" Pounce asked. "All looks so familiar but different. Kinda like we be lookin' for him, but nothing like things about him seem right. You think maybe we be findin' her this time? He be mad, real mad at us me thinks. Me thinks he know you not be tellin' him the truth about him, too."

Grink asked question after question. "What we know 'bout her? She be like his same age? You thinkin' maybe they look similar?"

"Yeah, this be lot different than where we be for him. This time he know he be sendin' us for her. He know, warn us, too." Pounce scratched his head.

"Well, here we be, so let's see what we can see. We, you and me, we just be walkin' around. Come on, maybe somethin' good come of this." Grink turned and started to walk in one direction, Pounce in the other. "Pounce…this way!" Grink yelled.

Sophie lay on the front porch as Kay-Lee sat next to her, playing with her dolls. It was a warm summer morning, but Kay-Lee enjoyed the bright sunlight and the nice breeze.

Kay-Lee lifted one of her dolls and said, "Should we go to the grocery store today?" It was a question Kay-Lee's mom had asked of her for many days.

Kay-Lee's hair was lifted gently by the morning breeze. Her eyes sparkled in the bright morning sun. She was dressed comfortably in matching t-shirt and shorts. She had thought about putting on her tennis shoes but decided to go barefoot. Kay-Lee looked over at Sophie, curled up in a ball on her red mat, soundly sleeping.

"Heh, sleepy head. Are you going to sleep the day away? You aren't much help playing with dolls if you are sleeping!" Kay-Lee laughed, trying to rouse Sophie from her sleep. All she received in return was the opening of Sophie's eyes and a big puppy stretch. Sophie was now staring at her with her big puppy eyes but still lying on her red mat.

Kay-Lee looked over at Sophie and asked, "Did I tell you about the walk Mom and I had at the lake last week? I know Mom was pretty upset. She didn't really send me to my room, but she did tell me to go to my room and play with you."

Sophie looked at Kay-Lee without blinking. She lifted her head and turned it side to side, as if she were listening to every word.

"Would you like me to tell you about how different the trip was to the lake on that day?" Kay-Lee asked. "It was way different from any day before. And when I say any day, I mean any day."

Kay-Lee reached over and picked Sophie up, clutching her in her arms, and moved over to the porch swing. With Sophie safely in her arms she stared off into the distance and started telling the story as if had happened to someone else, not herself.

Along the shoreline, Kay-Lee, a young lady of nine, had walked with her mother, Mori. Unlike other morning walks, this morning Kay-Lee could hear music filling the early morning air, something she had never heard before on their morning walk. She slowly turned and asked her mother in the innocent voice of a child, "Momma, why is there so much music in the air? Can you hear it? It is so beautiful."

Mori stopped and looked down at Kay-Lee. Smiling, she asked her daughter in a soft loving voice that only a mother has, "Kay-Lee, what are you talking about? I don't hear a thing. Quit talking such foolishness, Sweetie." As she spoke, her voice began to change from the soft loving voice, that of a mother to her child, to a harshness only the child could detect.

"Momma, you don't hear the music? It's so beautiful. Can't you hear it?" Kay-Lee stopped, turned, and pointed. "Can't you see the man on the rock? Can't you see his arms moving? It's like he's a conductor and I hear the music, but I don't see any musicians. Are you sure you can't hear it Momma?" Kay-Lee asked.

"Kay-Lee, I think your imagination has gone wild again! I don't hear a thing!" Mori tugged on her hand gently, then looked down at Kay-Lee sternly and said, "now be still and come along. We need to finish our morning walk."

From his perch atop the rocks, the Guardian turned and looked at the little girl without stopping the movement of his hands and arms. From the distance, his voice was as clear as if he were standing next to her. While Kay-Lee was being pulled along, she watched and listened as she heard his voice call out, "Kay-Lee."

Wondering, Kay-Lee looked up at her mom and asked, "Mom, don't you hear it? He's calling out for Kay-Lee. How does he know my name?"

Feeling the pressure of her mom leading her along, Kay-Lee attempted to turn and listen, even though it was only briefly. She heard whispers only meant for her. "Kay-Lee, you hear what others cannot. You are seeing what others cannot. On this day, I have for you a gift."

She continued to listen intently as he quietly said, "This I give to you now. What you see, what you feel…all of this is your beginning, your awakening. Remember this day, little one. Remember your walk by the lake…for there shall be another time, another place, and another great lake for us. Then we shall have this talk again. It shall be at that time, my child, that all I do, all that I am, will be revealed to you. Then you will know your purpose in life."

Kay-Lee looked up at her mom again, pondering what she had been told. Before she could say anything, more words touched her ears. "Kay-Lee, your mother knows. She does see as you see, but for now, she has chosen to ignore it for a different set of reasons. In time, it will be explained to you, and you will understand."

Feeling a hard tug on her arm, Kay-Lee heard The Guardian tell her, "Before you go, remember these words and bury them in your heart: "***Dreams don't last forever, but dreams are not forgotten.***"

Kay-Lee felt confused as she listened to the words before she felt another strong tug on her arm. Mori continued to walk at a fast pace, putting more distance between them, the rock, and the Guardian, clutching Kay-Lee's hand firmly in hers. As they hurried along, Kay-Lee turned one last time to look at the stone, only to find nothing was there. The large stone and the one who stood on it were gone. The sweet chorus of beautiful music had been replaced by the sounds of the waves splashing against the shoreline.

Mori moved faster, quickening her pace as she hurried along, keeping her firm grip on Kay-Lee's hand. It wasn't until they were closer to her car that she slowed their pace. Her mind shot back through time as she took a deep breath. Oh, how well she remembered the old man!

Muttering to herself, Mori thought it was funny how he always seemed to appear as an old man. Even now she wondered if this was the form he enjoyed taking to give an illusion to more flair and mystery. How many times has this ritual taken place since they first met? Her task had always been different. Like the Ancient Ones, she, too, had transcended the bounds of time for the same reason, hiding one of The Chosen. How she had hoped this day would never come. Hiding in time had helped protect the young female of the Chosen, but what does the appearance of the Guardian mean?

"So, what do you think Sophie? Was that not quite the story?" Kay-Lee continued to stroke Sophie's back, pushing the swing with her feet.

Grink and Pounce had somehow managed to stumble to the exact spot they needed to be. The how of their getting there evaded them, but it was what they did now that mattered. Their minds raced ahead, thinking how great of a reward they would receive from His Lordship when they told him what they had found.

Grink looked at Pounce. "I sure that be her. Look, just like him, a dog. We no like dogs like they haves. They seems to know we be here."

Pounce scratched his head. "It was easy with him. He be young and we help him with the cookie jar. But her? What we do 'bout her?"

"Maybe all we can do be tell him here she be. He be smart, real smart, he figure out things. What you think?" Grink asked.

"I be seein' something we could do. We cause porch swing to break and cause her to go *boom*." Pounce offered.

Grink rubbed his hand over his face. "I be thinkin' that not do much for killin' her now, would it? And how we get close enough since the dog be in her arms?"

Both shook their heads in agreement before saying, "Yeah dog be a problem, a big problem."

Kay-Lee continued to talk to Sophie when the dog raised her head and started barking. Sophie jumped out of Kay-Lee's arms and ran to the edge of the porch, stopping before the first step.

"Sophie, what are you barking at?" Kay-Lee asked.

When she finished asking her question, the screen door opened. Her mom walked out onto the front porch and stood next to Sophie.

"Good girl, Sophie. Yes, I sense them, too." Mori knelt and stroked Sophie's back, then looked over at Kay-Lee. "Pick up your dolls, Sweetie. I think it's best we go inside now."

Grink and Pounce both heard the alarm sounded by Sophie.

"Grink, how she know we here?" Pounce asked. "We be so far away."

"Hmmmm now look, she be back in the house. No, no be no way we do nothin' now. Best be for us to report back and tell him what we sees and found," Grink replied.

"Yeah, he be makin' plan for her just like he did for him. He be knowin' what to do."

Together, they returned to where they had entered. They never tried to figure out or understand how they traveled. They accepted that it was as it should be and took them from here to there and back.

Hurriedly, they returned to Zorleg's presence. As always, Grink was the one to speak. He provided their account of the trip and where they had found the girl.

"We try plannin' somethin' but her dog, it be barkin' loud, very loud. Really loud for a small dog, too. Then someone be comin' out of the house. Nothin' we be able to do. We thought it be best if we come tell you. Odd, Your Lordship, she be old, much older than he be when we find him, but we not know why. You know, you always know what be best." They both stood motionless before Zorleg after Grink gave his report.

Zorleg rubbed his hand over his face. "Hmmmm. So, you found her. Interesting, very interesting."

He glared down at Grink and Pounce. "You may leave my presence now. I need to think, think and plan what I need to do about them both now."

Zorleg lifted his hand, motioning for them to depart from his presence.

They no sooner heard his chamber door close as they walked to their room than Pounce boldly stated, "Well that be good, real good. He not mad, not shout at us. You did good, Grink, real good." The remainder of the walk was in silence, not a word spoken until they had closed their door.

"Maybe we just sit and relax, Grink. If he be needin' us, he be callin' when he be ready," Pounce stated emphatically.

"Ya, we needs be ready. He smart, real smart and be wanting us when he ready."

Zorleg sat on his throne and pondered, asking himself question after question. *How? How have I not found her before now? Why has her hiding place been so well-guarded? Why is she so much older than he was when I found him? Well, my little dearie, you can hide no more!*

Zorleg continued to sit in silence, relishing his new discovery.

Nafari's Power Grows

Nafari wasn't sure how or when it started. She, as well as others, had noticed how her beautiful golden locks started to turn a deep, dark black.

"What is happening to me? Where have my beautiful golden locks gone?" It was difficult for Nafari to look at her own reflection in the mirror, questioning herself aloud as she gasped in horror.

Every time she looked at her reflection, she kept hearing a voice in her ear.

"All that matters is you are beautiful to me. Who would ever accept you as you are now? No one can love you as deeply as I. Remember your appearance and the power that I have given to you. It is all about me and the power I have given you. Accept your darkness and my gift of power to you. You could not be more beautiful in my eyes."

Nafari couldn't remember ever seeing anything that had such a dark blackness. It wasn't long after she noticed her hair changing color that she noticed the change was happening in her sparkling blue eyes.

Has this mirror been possessed? Why is my hair so black? And my eyes, where are my sparkling blue eyes? What is happening to me? Nafari watched as her transformation continued.

"What is happening to me? How have my eyes and hair changed color?" Nafari's concern and fear grew with each passing day. Both her hair and eyes continued to grow darker. She also was aware her physical appearance had morphed into something hideous.

With every question she asked, Zorleg filled her mind with his devotion to her and her new beauty. "It is my power that has changed you and given you a beauty that only I can truly appreciate. Together, we shall be unstoppable. There will be no one, no one that will have your power. Don't think of your features and the change as bad. Think of it as your power, your power over life and death, deciding who you would allow to live or whose life you will take. If they mock you, they mock your beauty and your power. The power I have given you is your beauty. Walk proudly with elegance and grace. You are exactly as I envisioned. We are in the darkness, together. Do you need or care what others think? Others will simply become jealous because of your rise to greatness under my mentoring."

Zorleg guided her transformation daily, making sure it was visible to others at just the right time. Her family and her friends also noticed the change but remained silent. They hoped that, by not pointing out the change, she wouldn't become upset.

What has happened to me? At first, Nafari was horrified by the change that had overtaken her. All she could do was take shelter in her room, afraid to leave or even open her door.

"Yes, this is exactly where I want you, my child. Oh, how wonderful the change is. This is far greater than I ever expected. Wonderful, just wonderful!"

Zorleg watched and observed how Nafari's physical features slowly changed.

"I should have written down my steps. This must be one of my greatest creations," Zorleg boasted.

Exactly how he was able to create such a dramatic change in Nafari remained a mystery to him. Oh, but he was pleased, extremely pleased, at how he corrupted her mind and persuaded her to believe his thoughts of her beauty and power were all to serve him. He made sure she understood no one could, or would, accept her the way she had been transfigured and how hideous she had become. *Together, it will become our greatest feat. She will grow to understand my love for her beauty and her love for power.* All that Zorleg cared about was her accepting the fact that he would be the only one that could and would love her, just as he made her.

Hmmmm, would it be possible that this all has come about because I discovered and harnessed the power of dark matter? Oh, how Zorleg loved that thought! This was yet another moment he would embellish to explain how he continued to grow in power.

Nafari looked in her mirror and gasped at the horrific person that looked back at her.

"Who are you?" she asked her reflection repeatedly. She saw the reflection of coal black hair and eyes, the physical deformities on her face.

"Who did this to me? How? Why me?" Nafari's facial features had changed too; her skin was no longer smooth and blemish-free, her nose no longer straight but crooked. She gasped in horror as she looked at her reflection, her hand touching her face. She had gone from being a beautiful young lady to a disgusting-looking old hag. She fell on her bed, tears flowing from her eyes as she cried uncontrollably. Over and over again, she questioned what was happening to her and why as she continued to sob uncontrollably.

"Oh, my dear, you are looking exquisite. You have become exactly what I longed for."

Zorleg felt he had broken Nafari, and she was now ready to begin to do his bidding. He called out to her.

"Nafari, why is it that you cry? Are you ashamed of how you look? I am responsible for making the changes in you. You are as I need you. Come, follow me, to do my bidding. I, I alone, will give you great powers as my obedient servant. You have seen your reflection and what I can do. Think how powerful you will become every time you use the powers I give you. Do what I ask of you."

Nafari did not understand. Timidly, her lip quivering, Nafari asked, "what, what do you need me to do? What do I need to do? I can't let anyone see me like this. I'm so hideous." She buried her face in her pillow as she continued to sob.

"Come to me, Nafari. I will make you both strong and powerful. You will have powers that almost equal mine. I will teach you how to use your new abilities to do what I need you to do. You will evolve, and as you evolve, you and your powers will grow greater. Now get up and go look at yourself in the mirror, and ask yourself who would ever want to be seen with you or to even look at you now? How could you continue to be friends to those who would constantly make fun of you? Come to me now, Nafari, and grow with me." Zorleg waited for her response.

Confused, Nafari asked timidly, "Come? How am I supposed to come? I will be missed; my family will worry. I don't know who you are, let alone where you are, but you ask me to come."

Nafari considered what he had said. How could she go out in public looking like this? She felt the ridicule, saw the fingers pointed in her direction, heard others whispering about her when she walked by. How horrific it would be for her to go through life completely shunned by society.

Nafari took only a moment as she pondered and spoke out loud.

"If he said he would take care of me and teach me, surely he has planned out how to explain my disappearance to both my family and friends." She fell silent as she waited for an answer, any answer, to her questions.

Instead of getting answers, Nafari felt she was becoming more bewildered by what had happened to her. She couldn't live looking like this. She felt going with whomever this was her only option. Already her thoughts turned to how she would lash out at all of those who dared to mock and scorn her. *He said he cares for me, appreciates the way I look, and my features.* She knew she must go where she would not be judged, into the comfort of the one who told her to be proud of who she is, embellishing the darkness and the power.

At that very moment, Zorleg felt a surge in his power. He knew exactly what she was thinking and how he had molded her into what he would use to fulfill his desires. Better yet, she was looking forward to lashing out at those who would shame her, accepting her hideousness as part of her power.

Zorleg placed his hands together and started rubbing them in anticipation. He was overjoyed with his biggest accomplishment yet. This was far greater than turning a flower into dust. He felt it surpassed making his secret place in the rocks. Now he had much more to do. First, he must make a place far from here to teach her the power of his darkness. For those she leaves behind, he would place fabricated stories to convince everyone she was gone and of how she disappeared.

Zorleg was so impressed with the way he had been able to disfigure Nafari. Now it was time for him to continue honing his skills and craft. With Nafari as his student, he knew what he wanted.

From the dark recesses of his cave, a smirk covered Zorleg's face. In the silence, he began to chuckle to himself. He lifted his right hand and began to move his fingers. With each movement, a small dark cloud began to form. His laughter ended as he looked down at the dark matter bubble, holding it in his hand. His eyes were fixed on the bubble as he commanded, "go, bring Nafari to me. You know what needs to be done.

Go, make it so." With that, his dark matter left his presence and returned as quickly as it had left. Nafari now stood beside him as the dark matter dissipated and left them alone.

Zorleg was pleased, very pleased, with his work on this day. To say he was proud of his work would not come close to the joy he felt. His heartbeat increased as his body surged with the newfound energy from this dark power. He was so proud of himself for the way he had crafted the dark power and used its dark energy. Now he had someone to teach his dark ways and how to use dark matter to make both of them more powerful.

Part 4

Kalamar

The bright moons cast their beams upon the rooftops as a gentle breeze blew over the city. On this peaceful quiet night, should one happen to look up into the starry skies, they would have seen the white coat reflecting the blue moonlight as Cna silently returned to the stable from his nightly flight. They would have also noticed a lone rider sitting high on his back. How majestic he appeared, gliding effortlessly and silently to the ground!

The prized pet of Katherine, Royal Empress of Kalamar, slowly walked into the stable after his rider had dismounted. His hoofed feet broke the silence of the night with a methodic clop, clop, clop. In the stall next to the royal steed was Katherine's other prized possession, Dorlie. Like Cna, her coat was also a brilliant white. The Emperor and Empress were so proud to have been chosen to house the last unicorn, Dorlie, and the last flying horse, Cna. Alone in the stables, the two greeted each other silently. Several stories above, Emperor Daniel and Empress Katherine had finished the evening meal and awaited the arrival of a special guest.

While he sipped from a glass filled with orange nectar, Daniel turned thoughtfully, letting the glass slowly drop from his lips. Before he could say a word, a soft knock could be heard coming from their chamber door. Daniel rose from his chair and moved across the room to answer the door. With each step he took on the wooden floor, the sound from the hard heel on his black boots echoed off the stone walls as he moved across the room. With each step, the gentle thuds of his feet rang out in the vast room. His long flowing robe skated gracefully behind him while he covered the short distance between his chair and the door to their private chambers. The sound of the fireplace crackled in his ear when he paused, took a moment and smiled at Lady Katherine before he spoke. "I believe our guest has arrived," he said with his smile still etched across his face as he opened the door.

The hinges squeaked slightly when he pulled the door towards him and enthusiastically greeted his visitor. "Ah, my old friend! Welcome! It has been far too long! We were expecting you. Please, come in, come in." Daniel's excited voice filled the great hall with joy and laughter as the two greeted each other.

Daniel closed the door behind his guest and paused after he had secured the door. Jokingly he asked, "forgive me, your eminence, but this is such an awkward moment. Do we bow to you? While we are the rulers and are accustomed to others bowing to us, I never know what we should do when you visit. Granted, your visits are not often, but still…"

The Guardian lifted his hand. "Please, please, my dear friend. Let those things pass and let those that should do as they should. For us, such formality is not needed. Perhaps, and you may agree, not wanted as well." All three fell into a jovial fit of laughter.

Daniel accompanied The Guardian to the center of the room, and the two of them joined Katherine in the three large chairs in front of the fireplace. The fire was more for aesthetics than warmth. As they gathered around, its flames illuminated each of them. As Katherine looked up, the reflection of the fire twinkled in her deep blue eyes and bounced off her long shimmering locks of blonde hair. Daniel turned to The Guardian, his rich brown hair and brown eyes also reflecting the same dancing flames.

Slowly, Daniel began to speak. "On a moonlit night, we are but three, joined together but none can see." And then he paused.

Katherine had risen when Daniel and The Guardian joined her. She continued, "From days gone by, placed in time, watched by The Guardian, this child is mine," and then her voice also paused.

The Guardian stood between and held his arms outstretched as he continued the chant, "the child I take, to hide in time. Waiting for the moment that is his time."

When The Guardian finished his words, a soft warm wind began to stir and fill the room. As the wind blew, the three of them stood and joined hands, then continued in unison, "placed in time for us to see, placed in a time that yet shall be. Three stones, three coins, a bracelet be…sealed together from the magic of a tree."

At the end of the brief incantation, The Guardian released the hands of Daniel and Katherine, stretched out his arm and opened his hand. With his fingers outstretched, in the palm of his hand sat three small stones and three small coins. Looking upward and speaking into the air, The Guardian's voice filled the room, "for I call on my good friend Mariah, for she is the wind of Kalamar." After he spoke the name Mariah, the wind drew inward upon itself, swirling tighter until it had created a vortex in the middle of them. The Guardian lifted his hand in the same direction as the vortex and gently blew across the coins and the stones. Daniel and Katherine intertwined their arms until the bracelets, one on each arm, touched. The room filled with a red flame that grew brighter and brighter as it illuminated the coins, the stones, and the bracelets.

Together, they spoke as one. "***Dreams don't last forever, but dreams are not forgotten.***" After each spoken word, the words floated in the air and swirled over them in a clockwise motion. They hovered for only a moment before they slowly descended, encircling each coin and stone. A flame shot forth, striking the edge of each coin. Like a finger in the air, an inscription was burned as the words that hovered in the air slowly were etched into the coins. At the same instant, the words encircled the stones before the words were absorbed into each of the three stones. Each stone was transformed from a deep dark blue to a brilliant color of jasper.

The room momentarily filled with a brilliant flash of white before it returned to normal. Quietly, the three moved to their respective places. Daniel and Katherine gracefully returned and sat themselves in front of the fireplace. The Guardian stood alone in the middle of the room for a moment. He raised his head and spoke softly, "thank you, Mariah. Go now. Prepare the way, please." And then he joined the other two, seating himself in his chair.

Looking at Katherine, The Guardian asked, "The child is ready then?"

Smiling tenderly, the room filled with warmth that could only come from one who had been a mother. Katherine responded, "She is ready and is completely unaware. As you directed, Kay-Lee has been protected and shrouded in the sleep of sleeps. Mariah will go with her to watch over her as you watch over him." We have found another place, in another time, for her just as you have for him," Katherine looked at Daniel. "What was that name?"

Raising his head, Daniel replied, "it is located not far from here, but it is the perfect place for her to hide. As it is here, it is covered with golden lush fields of grain. Taking a bit of our home world with us, so to speak, so we will always be reminded of this place. I have chosen a small place named after the freshwater wells that feed it, just as our wells feed us our pure water."

Looking at The Guardian, Daniel continued. "She will be hidden well, and we will have the ability to watch over her from afar. What we have found as we studied this location is a fear of things they are unable to explain."

The Guardian smiled broadly, chuckling, as he chimed in, "Ah, perhaps. Hopefully, she will blend in and go unnoticed. However, we may still have a few tricks up our sleeves that we could use. I shall remind you both, Cna and Dorlie will be accompanying us on this trip but will be returned to you as quickly as we can accomplish that. Your research of this world has given me a point in time to plant both of them and allow them to roam free."

"See, I told you so! He thinks of everything!" Katherine chimed in. Laughter filled the great hall.

"We will need them both when we are ready. For the travel to begin, Cna will use his wings to fan the winds of time, and Dorlie will use the magic of her horn to open a portal in time to transport them to where they need to go." Rising out of his chair, The Guardian looked at both of them and asked, "you are sure they are both well rested?"

Katherine rose from her chair first and put her hand gently on The Guardian's forearm before asking softly, "how will she know when it's time? So much for her to take in…how will she ever understand it all?"

The Guardian took both in his large arms and pulled them close. "So many questions, my friends. I have already set in motion the hiding of The Chosen and placed them in different points in time. His journey has already begun, but he is also young. Remember, when they were born, they both were given very special gifts and powers which were never seen before or since."

Daniel smiled and chuckled softly. "No one can ever out-think you, can they, old friend? You know what one will say before the words even form in his mind. Our only hope is that both of these children can do what has been set before them."

The Guardian rose and hugged each of his hosts. “It is time now for me to be on my way. Please, be seated. I’ll let myself out. There is much for me to do as things continue to move forward.” Silently, The Guardian moved across the floor, opened the door and was gone. By the fireplace, Daniel and Katherine smiled. They had faith and trusted in their old friend. They knew things would turn out for the best as they pushed their fears aside.

Kay-Lee – The Awakening

Kay-Lee felt her mom's hand in the middle of her back, nudging her into the house.

"Mom, why do I have to come in? It's not even lunch time yet." Kay-Lee wondered what she had done wrong that caused her to be ushered so rapidly inside.

Once she had Kay-Lee in the house, Mori stepped back outside and closed the door behind her.

Kay-Lee wondered what was going on when she heard the door latch shut. "What did I do? Everything was fine until Sophie started barking." Kay-Lee turned and watched her mom on the front porch.

Mori knelt down close to Sophie and scratched her back.

"Yes, I sense it too, little one. They are out there, aren't they?" Mori continued to caress Sophie's back as she looked one way, then the other.

As quickly as Sophie had started barking, she stopped. Her tail wagged rapidly from side to side.

"Are you giving me the all-clear, Sweetie?" Mori picked up Sophie and took her inside. She lifted Sophie close to her face. "You know we are going to have to tell her now. There isn't a doubt in my mind she will understand, but there still may be a lot of confusion."

Mori pulled open the screen door, and then firmly turned the doorknob to open the front door. Once inside, she set Sophie on the floor.

"Well, it didn't take long for her to bolt, did it, Pumpkin?" Mori looked at Kay-Lee while Sophie trotted across the floor to check and see if there was something new in her bowl to eat.

Mori reached out and took Kay-Lee's hands in hers. "Come sit on the sofa with me, Sweetie. We need to talk."

Dread instantly filled Kay-Lee's mind. "Mom, I didn't do anything. Why am I being punished? Why am I in trouble?" Kay-Lee was close to tears.

"Sweetie, it is nothing you did, nothing you have done. Please come and sit with me. We need to talk." Mori sat down on the sofa and patted the seat next to her. "Please sit close to me."

Kay-Lee slipped onto the sofa next to her mother. As soon as she sat down, Mori turned sideways so she could look directly into her eyes. Silently, she reached down and picked up her hands. Kay-Lee could see the troubled expression on her face.

"Mom, what's wrong? I've never seen you so upset."

Mori took a couple of deep breaths. "Sweetheart, this is going to be as hard for you to understand as it is for me to explain." Mori took another deep breath and held it before slowly exhaling. She found it more difficult than she had ever imagined, but she knew this day would come, and now it had.

"Mom, what is it? What is so important?" Kay-Lee was now beginning to get worried that this was really something big but had no idea what.

Mori looked over at Sophie eating a piece of her dog food. "You know, this will be a lot easier for me if you would join us."

"Mom, who are you talking to? You're looking right at Sophie. Why does she need to join us? She's only my puppy, and I love her to death. Oh please, don't tell me you are going to get rid of her!" Kay-Lee knew she would be lost without Sophie.

Sophie finished eating her piece of dog food, walked over, and jumped onto the sofa, putting her head in Kay-Lee's lap.

"Mom, please, I'll do anything, but don't give Sophie away!"

"Oh no, Sweetheart, we could never give her away, ever. And I mean ever! She is a very special dog."

Kay-Lee looked at her mom confused. "What? What do you mean? There's really nothing special about her."

"Actually, that's not true Kay-Lee. She is here to warn you, protect you. That's why she was barking on the front porch this morning. She senses things we cannot." Mori squeezed Kay-Lee's hands to assure her it was nothing she had done.

"Protect me from whom, Mom? From what?" Kay-Lee moved her head from side to side, up and down, looking at her mom, Sophie, at the front door.

Mori took a moment to gather her thoughts. Again, she looked at Sophie. "Really, anytime you want, you can jump in here and help out."

Kay-Lee looked at her mom. "Mom, Sophie is a dog. It's not like she's going to talk, you know."

Mori gasped before she blurted out. "Why is this so hard?"

Kay-Lee looked at her mom questioningly, "Mom, are you ok? You aren't making a lot of sense."

Closing her eyes for a moment, Mori gathered her thoughts. When she opened them, she looked Kay-Lee in the eye. "Sweetheart, we aren't from here."

"Mom, really! Of course, we aren't from here. You told me many times we moved here when I was young, like before I can remember. So that isn't such a big thing, you know." Kay-Lee raised her eyebrows at her mom. "So?"

"This is difficult for me to say, more difficult for you to understand. All I ask is that you listen with an open mind. Fair enough?" Mori paused to allow Kay-Lee to digest what she had said before she continued. "Yes, I did tell you that we moved here when you were young. That part is true."

Kay-Lee started to interrupt, but Mori held up her hand and then continued.

"When I say we came from a long way away, I mean a really long way." Mori looked at Sophie again, almost as if she was pleading. "A little help here, please."

Mori felt a clarity and confidence fill her when she felt Sophie's head on her leg. "Thank you. That will make it much easier."

She looked at Kay-Lee before she boldly continued, "Kay-Lee, do you remember when we talked about your dad? How your dad was someone very special? Well, the same is true for your mom."

This time Kay-Lee didn't let her stop her. "What do you mean? You are my mom, aren't you?" The confusion showed on Kay-Lee's face.

"Oh dear. No, Kay-Lee, I'm not your mom. Please let me continue and listen, listen closely to every word I say." Mori cleared her throat. "When I say we aren't from here, I mean it, and that is true. I don't mean another town or state. This planet is not our own, and you were not born here. You and I were sent away after your birth, for your protection. Your birth, as well as that of a male child named Benjamin, was very special and very significant where we come from."

Kay-Lee rolled her eyes. "Mom, please. Another planet? Really?"

Mori continued, working as best she could to dodge the questions and doubts from Kay-Lee.

"Let me talk about your birth for a moment. Your parents, and Benjamin's, came from The Seventh Plane of Kalamar. From their existence, on their plane they were gifted with powers far beyond any of the other planes of Kalamar. Not only were the two of you gifted with powers from The Seventh Plane, but from each of the Seven Planes. You were given gifts that had never been given before. Because of whom the two of you are, you have been hidden here, for your protection. The search for both of you has never stopped. The self-proclaimed Dark Lord, Zorleg, wants both of you dead!"

Kay-Lee sat in shock as her mind tried to process what her mom was telling her. But wait, her mom wasn't her mom, and she wasn't born here, she was from what…outer space?

Mori excused herself, got off the sofa and went into the kitchen. She reached into one of the cabinets and grabbed a large pot. After filling it with water, she set it on the counter. "Kay-Lee, would you come in here, please?"

Kay-Lee joined her mom in the kitchen. She looked at the large pot full of water, then at her mom. "Are you going to douse me with water?"

Mori laughed. Well, laughed as best she could, considering the conversation they were having.

"What if I can prove you do have powers that you aren't aware existed? Will that help you believe?" Mori looked at Kay-Lee, waiting for her to answer.

"Ok, that seems simple enough. Only don't pour the water on me, ok?" They both took a moment to laugh.

"I want you to pick up the pot of water and place it anywhere you want to. Why, you ask? So, you know that wherever you place it, I had nothing to do with what will happen next." Mori watched as Kay-Lee lifted the pot and moved it over to the counter where they normally sat to eat breakfast.

"You good with where you've placed it, Sweetie?"

"Yeah, I guess so." Kay-Lee watched while Mori pulled several tea towels from the drawer and placed them on the counter directly below where Kay-Lee had placed the pot. As she spread them out, she asked Kay-Lee to sit on the barstool directly behind the pot.

Kay-Lee didn't question her mother and sat down on the barstool.

Mori looked at her. "Now place your hands in your lap. Blow across the pot full of water."

Kay-Lee thought this was about the dumbest thing she had ever done. In the back of her mind, she thought of all those stunts people pulled on one another to make them really look silly.

Kay-Lee leaned forward, closed her eyes, and gently blew her breath across the water. Nothing happened. "Mom, is this a joke? I feel so stupid right now."

Mori didn't look at Kay-Lee. Instead, she closed her eyes and whispered, "***A mhuscailt***" (her awakening). After she spoke the words, Mori looked at Kay-Lee.

"Again, please, same as before."

"Mom, I feel really dumb. Are you sure you aren't going to dump the water on me?"

Mori gestured at the pot. "Again, please."

Like before, Kay-Lee inhaled then began to exhale. It felt like a flash of lightning before her eyes. Something happened, something really big that she had never experienced before. Her breath passed over the pot and the calm water began to churn and bubble, moving this way, then that, splashing over the sides.

"Mom, Mom!" Kay-Lee cried out. "Make it stop, make it stop!"

Mori put her hand on Kay-Lee's shoulder. "Only you can do that. It is all under your control. When it is needed, then will it be given."

No sooner had the words left Mori's lips than Kay-Lee's mind was filled with visions. Visions not of where they lived, but of the Third Plane of Kalamar. Her mind had now been awakened. Her purpose, her reason for being, was revealed to her.

Kay-Lee looked at Mori. "You, you have always been my protector. And you," Kay-Lee reached out and stroked the back of Sophie, "you, too, to warn and protect me from the Dark Lord."

The three of them returned to the sofa. Not a word was spoken aloud. Kay-Lee's mind was now filled with the knowledge of her birth, her parents, and knowledge of The Chosen. She wasn't sure how long they sat. Was it a minute, hours? She couldn't tell. She knew when her awakening had ended.

"They came looking for me, didn't they? The minions of Zorleg."

"Yes, they did. That is why Sophie was barking. She sensed their presence and was sounding the alarm. I knew you didn't understand, thinking she was only barking at something. But I knew exactly what it meant and who she was barking at."

"What do we do now?" Kay-Lee asked.

"We need to be careful, very careful. We have been blessed that it has taken them so long to discover you. Now they know we are aware of their attempts. They also know Sophie is by your side and will always sound an alarm. All of us, you, I and Sophie must maintain a constant watch of everything and everyone around us." Mori paused to allow Kay-Lee to ask any questions.

Kay-Lee sat silently, reserved, her mind being filled with who she was, where and when she was born. All things that were unknown have now become known. The other member of the Chosen knows who she is and why she was born. Her awakening continues.

Zorleg's Decree

For all have heard the decree of Zorleg...***Neathe eine de Soula, De Soula ist Minnen*** (death to the soul, the soul is mine). The decree had been posted on trees along every roadside, bellowed from town squares, plastered on the walls of every business in every hamlet and village. No one had an excuse for not knowing this decree, his decree. Those who did not follow it were dealt with harshly – and in full view of the public! People lived in constant fear of their homes being burnt to the ground, barged into by Zorleg's troops, children or parents removed from the home because they didn't follow the decree to his letter. Zorleg's power started slowly, but now he had become so much stronger. The power of dark matter continued to draw him deeper into its darkness as he succumbed to its power. All the while his army continued to grow. First was his growth, then his theft of the souls of the unknowing as he stole the very essence of life from them to grow his army.

Near the forest of dreams was a small hamlet, off the beaten path but not too far. Everyone who resided here and called this place home had heard the decree of Zorleg. Not many, but the few travelers that didn't stay had mentioned Zorleg's decree as they passed though. Most of the travelers found the small hamlet so warm and hospitable they never left.

Sitting by the fireplace, the hamlet's cobbler finished his dinner. With his stomach full, he pushed back from the table and let out a big groan. Almost as if on cue, the barmaid, Miss Katie, walked over and picked up his plate. She cocked her head to the side, a smirk crossing her lips as she looked down at Reevus, still seated but pushed back from the table. She politely asked, "How about a nice hot piece of apple pie to end your meal, Mr. Reevus?"

"Pie? Ummmmm. Oh, how I love apple pie!" It was difficult for Reevus to contain his excitement. "Now you wouldn't happen to have pumpkin pie, too, would you? Yes, pumpkin pie would be so good on a night like this."

Miss Katie had become accustomed to this moment of indecision. Without moving, plate still in her hand, she waited as Reevus continued.

"No, no, apple. What did I have last time? Wasn't it apple? Yes, I'll have a piece of apple pie. Well, if I had apple last time, I'll tell you it was a good one. Best piece of pie I've ever eaten, too. Maybe this eve I should enjoy pumpkin?" Reevus continued to struggle with what type of pie he desired while Miss Katie patiently stood and waited for his final decision. She knew from too many prior experiences that Reevus would go through this exercise many times before he finally decided what pie he really wanted. A warm smile crossed her face as Reevus continued struggling. With his mind thrashing about as he worked on making his decision, he added bits and pieces of different stories. His mind went back and forth between the choices of what he desired, and all the while his storytelling never stopped. Finally, the battle of making a decision came to an end. Reevus looked up rather sheepishly as a smirk crossed his face and he began to chuckle. "You know me oh too well. Now off to the kitchen, Miss Katie, and bring me one of those slices of warm apple pie."

Miss Katie scampered off to the kitchen and quickly returned, placing the warm pie in front of Reevus. "There you be, Mr. Reevus, the best apple pie around for the greatest storyteller ever. Hmmmm, looks like you've already got a large crowd to listen to your tales tonight, too."

As quickly as she arrived, she was leaving Reevus to devour his warm apple pie.

Slowly savoring every bite, Reevus felt the crowd growing restless waiting for him to finish his last bite. Finally, he pushed his plate back and pulled his chair from the table to a spot near the fireplace. His movement was an unspoken signal for all those with ears who wanted to hear to move closer. There wasn't a seat remaining in place as they all scooted closer.

Before Reevus could start his story for the night, someone called out from the back of the room, a voice he had not heard before. "Mr. Reevus, is this going to be another one of your farfetched yarns, or can you explain what happened in the forest last night? Why was there such a great light shining upward? Many of us heard Zorleg's army was at this very inn last night and a fight ensued."

Before he started speaking, Reevus brushed his hand over his face with his handkerchief. Methodically, he started at his forehead and moved back over the top of his head, rubbing his balding head. Looking at the visitor he asked, "Tell me, friend, what are the stories you speak of?"

The visitor pointed to one of the tables as he continued talking. "The way it was told to me is two strangers stopped here last night for food and drink. Both were seated when two of Zorleg's army barged in. Look at that door. You can see where the hinges have been repaired." His voice quivering, it slowly trailed off, unable to continue. His accusations caused quite a stir as many got up and began to look over the door.

Reevus started with a soft-spoken voice of authority. No one had to lean forward, his voice loud enough so that it was heard in every corner of the room clearly. "This evening, I am going to retell a story you have heard many times before. For it is not a story meant to scare or frighten, but rather one to give hope. All know of the fear, death and destruction across the land caused by Lord Zorleg. Evidence of his work is visible throughout the land." Reevus paused for a moment before he continued. "As our new friend has pointed out, his presence is always around us and, as he said, they were in this very inn. Before I tell you the story of things to come, allow me to regress and answer his question of the very things that happened in the forest. It is true. Zorleg's minions were indeed in this very room." Gasps filled the room as Reevus raised his right arm and pointed. "That very table is where one who is mentioned in many tales and legends sat enjoying a dinner meal." Again, Reevus paused before he lifted his other hand and pointed to another table. "Over there was a traveler who had stopped by the inn for a meal. Both were minding their own business when suddenly the door was kicked in. Arrogant and boastful, acting the part of the town bully, two thugs of Zorleg barged uninvited into this very room and demanded food and drink immediately."

Reevus turned and looked at Miss Katie, who nodded her head up and down in agreement. His eyes panned the room to see many others nodding in agreement as well. "There is no need to rehash the small battle. All of you have heard the story, haven't you? What I will tell you is that it was not someone's imagination; it was true. For those of you with doubts, I ask you to look at the floor and see the pattern of the arrows. Draw a line and connect them. 'Twas a short fight, but it was a good one. Perhaps that is a story for another day." Reevus' eyes scanned around the room before they stopped and settled on the visitor who broached the question. "That, my friend, is how it all began."

A roar came from the crowd. Many asked the same question. "Who could take down two of Zorleg's minions? It would have to be a small army to do such a feat, and you want us to believe it was only two?"

Again, Reevus raised his hands to quiet the crowd. He turned and looked at Miss Katie. "I think now would be a good time for you to tell your story." As if on cue, Miss Katie followed Reevus' request and began to recant the events. Her words were crisp and clear. Reevus pulled a chair up next to his own and assisted Miss Katie as she stepped up onto the chair, allowing her to be above the crowd gathered at the inn.

Timidly at first, she began to tell of the two travelers who entered the inn. "The first one to enter was dressed in leather with a bow and a quiver full of arrows slung over her back. She sat alone and enjoyed a bowl of soup and bread with a cup of tea. The other, dressed rather strangely, seemed to be waiting for someone.

"What I tell you now is: the unwelcome guests kicked down the door and barged in. Immediately, they demanded to have the table of the young lady as she sipped her tea.

"Pretty she was, very petite, but I felt she not be a lady, but rather a seasoned warrior. Now I don't really know what or how it happened. But in the twinkling of an eye, all of them were flat on their backs, arrows outlining each of them without breaking the skin. They were pinned to this very floor. What I found more amazing than the Zorleans lying on the floor was the other stranger. He was now standing with his back firmly wedged against hers, a sword held tightly in his hand. It appeared to me they had fought together before. Not that I know what they should look like, but both seemed to me to be highly trained warriors. I'm no warrior, mind you, but it surely looked to me as if they knew each other's every move before either of them moved or spoke a word. It has taken me longer to tell the story than it did for her to send the flurry of arrows pinning Zorleg's soldiers to the floor and for her companion to join her."

Someone else yelled from the crowd, “Where were the travelers sitting?”

Miss Katie raised her arm and pointed to thc other wall, a good thirty feet away. She continued to tell of the events from the encounter, ignoring the question for now. “‘Something very profound happened here, and when it was over, the warrior leaned over and told them who they were looking for was not here. She allowed them to live, telling them the next time things wouldn’t go so well for them. I heard her say they needed to leave and let the tales be told. Then they left quickly and, by the time I reached the door, they had already passed out of town heading to the Great Forest. It was later the same night that the bright beacon appeared, reaching high into the heavens.”

Stopping, Miss Katie looked down at Reevus. He lifted his hand, taking hers, as he helped her step down from the chair. Reevus sat back down in his chair and looked around the room. “Many times, I have sat before you and told stories. Tonight is a night to tell a different, far greater story. This is the story of the battle that is yet to come, what shall be referred to forevermore as the Battle of Battles.”

Clearing his throat, Reevus looked across the room. His eyes paused as he touched every person’s eye in the room. Leaning back, he placed his arms together and folded his hands over his rotund stomach.

“At a time known only to the One of Ones will be the day when the Chosen One, the One known to speak with the voice of thunder, will stand at the Seven Stones of Kalamar on the Great Meeting Place, in front of a raging sea that used to be the Great Lake. Billowing, dark clouds will gather where he stands by the raging sea as he feels Zorleg’s mighty darkness begins to pull, as it tries to pull him into the chaos and darkness Zorleg created. All the temptations of the world from the beginning to the end of time will flash through his mind. Who could blame him, a young lad experiencing the feeling of his world caving in around him? All because he has refused to give in and follow like so many others have before him. He will look out upon the sea, feeling the waves of a never-ending fear wash over him. Then, when his fear is at its highest level and he is at his weakest, she will return and join him. For this battle, he, they, will not be alone."

Reevus paused, thanking Miss Katie for the fresh cold glass of water. From somewhere within the inn, first one, then another called out asking, "Who are these people? Are they children?"

"Where did he come from?" asked someone in one corner of the room.

"Where is he now?" came from another corner.

"How old is he?" shouts someone across the room.

"Who is she?" asked another.

"Is she the one at the inn?" was the last question asked before the room fell silent, every eye fixed on Reevus.

Taking a sip, he placed the glass back on the table, took a deep breath and exhaled slowly before he continued. Reevus panned the room before he started speaking again. "Let me try to answer some of your questions before I proceed. The child has a simple name and is known by Benjamin. Doesn't sound very magical, powerful, or king-like, now does it? You need not know more for now. From where he comes and where he goes, his age…all are not important. He is only a humble child of meager means, but he comes with a heart and a desire to serve. His parents were chosen by The One of Ones, and their birth was here in The Great Forest. Benjamin knows it is not what he can do, but what can be done through him. He comes with an open heart, willing to serve."

Off to his right, Reevus heard someone else yell a question, "One of The Chosen? How many of The Chosen exist? Is he the leader of the army to protect and defend us? Is he a king?"

Reevus lowered his head, shaking it from side to side, with his bewilderment beginning to show.

"No, no, no, there is no army, there is no king. There are only two children who have been in training, being taught and schooled in the Old Ways, given gifts especially prepared for them at their birth. Allow me to continue as I tell you about her."

Silence filled the room as Reevus began to tell of the second child, the second of The Chosen. He also alluded to an unknown, that they may not be the last of The Chosen.

"The other Chosen One, Kay-Lee, will sense his need and join him at the Seven Stones of Kalamar. She will know the time has arrived and her gift, the parting of the sea with her breath, will be shared with him. In his hour of need, then and only then, shall she join him. Far and wide throughout the great expanse of time, he searched for her, but his search always ended up fruitless and in vain. Now he will discover and experience her appearance by his side when he needs her most. He will understand then that it was nothing he accomplished, as his efforts ended in failure. Instead, when faced with the uncertainty of the raging sea, she will appear by his side. How she came to be there, or how she got there, cannot be answered by a mortal man. What is important to one and all is that she will join him, as was foretold by The Ancients in the Seven of Sevens."

Reevus paused again, taking another sip from his glass, the water coating his parched throat, refreshing him. Looking over the audience, he observed how intent every man, woman and child hung on his every word. He set the glass down on the table then picked up his story where he left off.

"Together, they shall gather strength from one another as they await the arrival of yet one more. They will stand hand in hand, and waves from the sea shall crash against the shore, covering them with spray and fine mist shooting high into the air. Wave after wave will crash around them while they hold tightly to one another. If you look closer, impossible as it may seem, they will be completely dry; not a drop will have touched them. How can it be, you ask? In the midst of the storm, with waves crashing about them, not one drop can touch them. Why, you ask? How is it possible? Is it because The One of Ones holds them in his hands, giving them shelter from the storm? Are the Sisters of the Mist providing them with protection? That, too, is a possibility that cannot be ruled out, or perhaps both answers are correct."

Reevus paused, wiped his forehead before continuing. "As it is written in The Seven of Sevens, both shall hear, at precisely the same instant, something starting faintly and touching their ears above the roar of the waves. They will look at each other without saying a word, confirming they are both hearing the same tone. No one will know from where the tone came from, knowing only that it grew louder as it approached. Together, they will look into the storm and notice a very dim light far in the distance. Cutting through the darkness and through the storm, the light's intensity will increase as it descends. The volume of the tone will amplify with each passing second. The descent will be slow. The brightness and volume will grow until they become one. No more will the storm rage around The Chosen. The sound of the waves and winds will be replaced by the note of pureness. Then Madison, daughter of Queen RhiAnne, queen of the elves, will reach out her hand

and grasp both Benjamin and Kay-Lee's hands in hers. Bowing her head, she will reverently ***whisper ta se in am*** (It is time)."

Reevus had to stop, desperately needing another sip of water to quench his thirst after repeating Madison's reverent words. He placed the now half-filled glass down, cleared his throat, and spoke again. "Who remembers not? If it be the case, let me help you remember…from the book of the Seven of Sevens," Reevus' words filled the room. "It was written; my work is always done in threes." Reevus spoke softly, weaving his story as only a storyteller can. "In the moment, a gathering of three has occurred. For each has been chosen and accepted by their free will." Reevus quacking interjected, "Remember, The One of Ones has given everyone the right of choice, their free will." He paused briefly, inhaled quickly, before he continued, "They looked at each other and grasped each other's hands, placing what they have yet to do into the hands of the One who has always been faithful. Madison reverently continued to shower them with the words of enchantment given to her by her mother, Queen RhiAnne, for this very moment. They, The Chosen, will stand in hand, surrounded by love. This was not just any love, but a love that is rich and pure, for it is His love, long since gone from Kalamar. Then they will pass through Zorleg's raging storm and into its very eye. Kay-Lee, the one gifted with the breath of breaths, will exhale and blow across the raging sea. Her magical breath will part the waves, allowing her and Benjamin to walk from the rock of The Great Meeting Place out over the exposed shore to a place that has been prepared for them. From within the eye of the storm, they will turn back to see how they had crossed the deep. They see a horizon that is filled with massive waves, waves they have been through at one time in life or another. It was during those times they were never alone, for His hands comforted them, sheltering them from all the storms. Not just this storm, but all the storms that have raged around them as they were taught the Old Ways. They will now spend time reflecting upon the journey that has brought them here.

"Do you not remember the time as a child?" Madison asked Benjamin. "How many nights did the Witch of Darkness invade your dreams? For it was only a touch, a gift from the Old Ways that was passed to you. Still don't remember? The day when Zorleg tried to create great chaos by disrupting the lives of so many when the runways were covered with a layer of frost. Again, a moment of the Old Ways passed from The Guardian, Queen RhiAnne, Wren, and I, given to you when it was needed. It, too, was another gift from the Old Ways." Madison grew silent. Sometimes His gifts are simply a message in words that stirs your heart, covering you from head to toe with an emotion so great you feel as though you are going to burst. Madison grew silent, allowing everything around her to continue as it was planned.

"Whatever the task, wherever it may be in time, your heart always knows the truth," Reevus said. "There has been, and will always be, a feeling of disorientation. The weight of waves pounding against you, allowing you to see the flashback of the trials you have faced. As you look back at each trial, 'your heart has always known.' Many years, even centuries, were spent teaching you, The Chosen, in the Old Ways. Now your teaching has come to an end. Your awareness of all that was, all that is and all that is yet to come is with both of you now. Stories of the teachings were only a ruse to confuse Zorleg. Zorleg always thought there was so much to teach, which there was, but he thought it would take longer than it had. By using different points in time, methods, and friends, you have been schooled in the Old Ways. Not in the proverbial sense of a classroom setting, but rather in the way deemed best for them. For as Benjamin was taught, so they have taught Kay-Lee. Benjamin will share with Kay-Lee what she is missing and what she needs, while Kay-Lee provides Benjamin with the same. But not from a spoken word or a thought, rather the simple touch of a finger upon her forehead. The power unleashed when Benjamin touched Zorleg's witch Nafari on the forehead completely transformed her. To the untrained eye, it is a simple touch that happens so quickly it is not even noticed. From the Old Ways, the touch resounds throughout time, for his touch is the touch of The One of Ones. It was His in the beginning and created specifically for the Chosen."

Kick the Can

Benny walked down the alley in a pair of cut off jean shorts and a white t-shirt, repeatedly kicking an old tin can. Cosmo was either walking beside him or running off, only to quickly return to his side. Methodically, Benny would take a few steps to where the can stopped and kick it again. He repeated the same process over and over again as he walked to wherever it landed. Every few steps, Cosmo would raise his head and look about, as if he were looking or listening for something. Benny slowly placed one bare foot in front of the other with no particular destination in mind. The wind blew his silky thin blonde hair as it swished from side to side. His bright blue eyes twinkled as he meandered down an alley following the path the can seemed to have chosen for him. All around him, flower beds were in full bloom, and trees were full of a new year's growth of leaves in different shades of green. For some, being the new kid in town and a stranger would be difficult. For Benny, it was always a new adventure and exciting. Today, he immersed himself in a quiet walk with his best friend, Cosmo, entertaining himself by kicking a can, following it, then kicking it again. Benny paid little attention to what was going on around him. Cosmo was very aware, barking, stopping, then barking again. He could sense the presence of the Dark Lord in the air. Try as he might, all he could do was bark, attempting to alert Benny of the danger he felt close by. Every now and then, Benny would reach down, scratch him behind the ears, and whisper words of comfort and encouragement to him. Still, Cosmo was trying to warn him of the impending danger.

Grink and Pounce were hidden out of Benny's sight watching, waiting, and planning what they could do next. They watched Benny walking slowly, kicking the can again as he moved down the alley. Whispering quietly to each other, they agreed he was once again completely unaware of their presence. Turning toward one another, they ignored Benny for a moment to admire and embellish how well they looked in the uniforms of the Elite Guard of Zorleg. A touch of vanity overcame both as they fussed over every thread and the shine given off by the highly polished dark black boots.

Neither had noticed Cosmo. Had they forgotten how he was able to detect their presence when they were hidden under the porch in the cistern? Not only had they forgotten, but they didn't let the thought of Cosmo, barking, and running over to near where they were hidden, trouble them. Cosmo barked at them then turned and ran back to Benny's side, trying to warn him of the impending danger.

Grink and Pounce stopped preening over their uniforms, looked over to their left, and observed a group of boys that appeared to be much older than Benny. A devious smile formed on both of their faces simultaneously. They reached down and gathered a pile of rocks as quickly as they could. Hidden by the tall grass, they stood briefly and peppered the group of boys with rocks. Their aim was spot on, hitting each boy multiple times. One after another, they hurled a flurry of stones through the air, stopping for a moment before they made another assault until they had thrown every rock they had gathered. Hunkering down in the tall grass, they remained hidden and out of sight. From within the tall grass, they were able to see the havoc they had caused and the anger they instilled in the group of boys.

Neither Grink nor Pounce noticed how Cosmo had found where they were hiding. Cosmo stood just outside of the tall prairie grass, tail straight up in the air, ears pointed, as he barked as ferociously as a small dog could bark. Cosmo turned and ran back to be at Benny's side. Neither Grink nor Pounce noticed his presence or when he had departed.

From the yelps and screams of pain and agony, it appeared they had a resounding success in the group of boys. The boys were filled with anger and rage. They turned and charged in the direction from where they thought the rocks came from, running right past Grink and Pounce's hiding place. Having accomplished what they were instructed to do, the two left as they had arrived. Only Benny and Cosmo remained in the alley. Benny was left to endure the anger and wrath of the angered older boys.

Benny kicked the can again but didn't really notice the group of boys running at him, yelling and cursing. Cosmo, close to Benny's side, was barking nonstop. Confused, Benny became motionless and watched them approach. He wondered why they were running toward him and why they were yelling. The largest one of them dove head-first into Benny, his head hitting him directly in the stomach, driving him to the ground in a textbook tackle. Tumbling backward to the ground, he heard the yelling and shouting but didn't understand why. Why were they yelling at him? Why had they attacked him? He didn't understand. Cosmo had taken off before Benny hit the ground, running around the building and out of sight.

"Okay, you little punk, what's the idea? Why did you throw all of those rocks at us? Thought you could run and hide, did you? We'll show you what pain is!" He rolled off Benny and stood up before he was quickly replaced by another boy who reached down and grabbed Benny by his t-shirt and lifted him off the ground, shaking him violently before hitting him repeatedly in the stomach.

Benny's head was tossed about as his body reacted uncontrollably to being shaken. He had no idea how long they shook him or how many times he had been hit in the stomach. He didn't remember getting to his feet when another boy walked behind Benny and started slugging him in the back. The force of the punch knocked Benny to the ground head-first. He lay motionless on the ground for several minutes before he rolled over and looked up. The pain from the blows had Benny gasping for breath.

Another boy snarled, "Heh, isn't this the new kid that moved into town? Maybe we should teach him that we don't like to be hit with rocks around here, especially by little punks!" He reached over, grabbed Benny's hair, and pulled his head back. Shaking Benny by his hair, he turned to the others. "Well, would you look at this, guys. He has little pointy ears. What are you, a freak? Huh? You some kinda circus act or something? How's come your ears are pointed?"

Benny remained still and quiet. He had never thought of his ears as anything abnormal. They didn't look pointed at him. Why were they calling him a freak? Out of the corner of his eye, he watched as one of the other boys grabbed his leg and pulled, causing Benny to fall flat on his back. The fall knocked the wind out of him again. All Benny could do was try to protect himself. He closed his eyes and curled up in a ball waiting to feel the pain of a kick to his exposed ribs that he knew were coming.

Cosmo had dashed around the corner of a building and down the street until he found Reevus. He barked repeatedly at Reevus to get his attention. Reevus leaned down on one knee and asked, "What's the matter, my little friend?" Cosmo darted off then quickly returned. "You want me to follow you, boy? Well, show me the way then." Cosmo ran as fast as his short legs would carry him, Reevus following behind. When he got to the end of the building, it was easy to see what Cosmo was so upset about. He saw Benny lying on the ground and all of the other boys attacking him.

The first kick was in Benny's ribs. Excruciating pain shot through his body before he felt another kick to his head. He wasn't sure whether he was dreaming or not. He lost count of how many times he had been kicked. He thought that, right before he started to pass out from the blows and pain, he heard loud shouts coming from someone around the corner of the building. All he could do was try to breathe. He kept his eyes closed and couldn't see what was happening, but he could hear Cosmo and someone else rapidly approaching. Benny wondered who it could be coming to his rescue, or at least he hoped it was someone coming to rescue him and not another thug to beat on him.

Reevus and Cosmo rounded the corner and stopped. "Hey, you boys! What in tarnation do you think you're doing? Well, I'll just bet my last dollar all of you must feel real good about yourselves, all of you picking on a small defenseless young lad!" Reevus looked over at Benny, nose bleeding, hair in a mess, shirt ripped, curled up in a ball. "Any of you smart alecks feel big enough to pick on an old man?" Reevus walked over, leaned down and placed his hand on Benny's back before he offered words of comfort and encouragement. "It's okay, son, no more harm will come to you now."

Reevus stood up and placed his hands on his hips as he stared at the group of bullies. One by one, he looked at each of the boys. One by one, his eyes looked at one, then he moved on to the next. "What I think is you are nothing but a bunch of thugs and bullies trying to pretend to be tough." Reevus walked over to the biggest one of the group and dropped to his knees in front of him then placed his hands behind his back. "Go ahead, Mr. Smarty Pants. Give me your best shot. I'm on my knees, hands behind my back. Let's see how big and tough you really are!" Cosmo stood by the side of Reevus barking the entire time, not knowing whether to stay with Reevus or go over and comfort Benny.

The leader of the group snickered and started walking circles around Reevus and Cosmo. "You make this so easy, you old fool," he said as he reached down and picked up a two-by-four lying on the ground, grasping it firmly in his hands. He looked at Cosmo and kicked at him. Cosmo jumped out of the way before any of his kicks struck him. "Yeah, I'll knock your block off and then take care of your mutt, too."

Reevus never blinked as he looked into the eyes of the leader of the group. As he looked up, a smile spread across his face. "How many of you are there? Seven, eight? All of you against an old man and a defenseless young boy. Must make you feel mighty proud of yourselves, I'm sure. And then you add in the two-by-four you have in your hands. Well yeah, you are really bad and tough, aren't you?" Reevus paused before he looked up at the two-by-four and then back to the leader of the group. "You know, sometimes things are not as they seem."

"Shut up, you old fool! I'm going to knock your head completely off your shoulders!" The boy pulled the two-by-four back as he looked down at Reevus and swung with all his might. As he was swinging the two-by-four towards Reevus' head, Cosmo barked several times, then stopped.

"What? Where did they go? They were right in front of me! That isn't possible. I couldn't have missed! He could not have moved that fast! They were right there until that stupid mutt barked." In a fit of rage, he threw the two-by-four to the ground. The group turned and started to walk away. However, as they turned, a young lady stood in front of them with Cosmo, Reevus, and Benny standing by her side.

Dressed in a long, light-yellow dress, she smiled and spoke softly. “Remember, Reevus told you things aren’t always as they seem.” She lifted her left arm, opened her hand, and blew softly across her empty palm. Warmed by her breath, a fine dust rose from her palm, lifted into the air before covering the troublesome group. Without a word, each fell silently to the ground and quickly slipped into a deep sleep. Cosmo ran over, sniffed each one, and then returned to Benny’s side, barking nonstop.

Benny stood motionless. He didn’t know what to say or do. Then he heard Reevus and the young lady speaking to each other. He couldn’t remember their names, but the voices…he knew he had heard those voices before, but where, when? Why are they speaking so differently? Why did he understand every word they were saying? Benny had so many questions and his young mind sought to find the answers, but for a moment the answers eluded him.

Benny looked up questioningly at Reevus, as Cosmo rubbed his head against his leg. Before he could ask him one of his questions, he heard others coming up from around the corner of the building. A few elderly men rounded the corner calling out.

“Reevus? Reevus? Is that you? We heard there was a commotion going on back here with a bunch of boys.” They looked and saw the group lying motionless on the ground. “Well, I’ll be, looks like you have things well in hand. They all seem to be sleeping like babies! No need to be calling the sheriff on this.” The gentleman and his friends laughed. “I believe the shoe man can take care of this problem himself, gents. Well, we’re off to enjoy a walk on a nice day anyway. Take care of yourself, shoe man.” The group of men laughed, turned, and walked away as they continued their afternoon walk.

Benny's mind wondered about what had just transpired as he thought silently to himself. *Shoe man? Why is that so familiar? I don't know a shoe man. Why should I even know a shoe man?* His thoughts were interrupted when Reevus spoke.

"Yes, I know, it is difficult for you to understand, Benny. We told you then that when you needed us, we would be here for you. You need to thank your little friend, Cosmo, too. After all, he was the one who came and brought me here. Please, accept our apologies that we have interceded on your behalf before we were asked, though. But I took Cosmo's invitation to heart. Otherwise, I'm not sure how much of you would have been left." Reevus paused. "I know you do have a lot of questions. Come, walk with us to my shop and we'll talk there. Out in the open would not be a good thing." Holding his hand out, he took Benny's hand, with the young lady taking his other one. The three made the short walk to the cobbler's shop, Cosmo running ahead or following behind.

When they reached his shop, Reevus removed his keys from his pocket and opened the door, ushering all of them in. He looked down at Cosmo. "Well, of course you can come in." Reevus locked the door behind them and led them past the huge sewing machines to his back room. He stopped and pulled up a couple of chairs. After all three had sat down, he asked Benny. "Where would you like to begin? A story? Something to drink?" Cosmo curled up at Benny's feet and listened before falling asleep.

Return to the Forest

It had been a very busy and long day for Ben. He was swamped with what seemed like a million things that needed to be done before the close of business. He was so thankful when he was finally able to leave work and head home. Before he left the office, he called Marcie, apologized for being so late, and offered to stop on the way home to pick up something for dinner.

"Hey, Sweetie. I am so sorry I'm so late. Time really got away from me. I'm leaving work now; how does sweet and sour chicken for two sound? Egg drop soup and wontons?" A smile crossed Ben's face, knowing Marcie never said no to one of her favorite meals.

"I kinda figured something had happened at work," Marcie said. "Really, what would they do without you? You know I do worry about how hard you work! That sounds perfect for dinner. What would you like to drink? Iced tea, lemonade?"

Ben chuckled a bit. "Let me guess. That is some of your delicious solar-sweetened sun tea, isn't it?"

"Oh Ben, you know me too well. Yes, just for you, too!" Marcie always enjoyed how they were able to read each other's minds.

"OK, Sweetie, be home in a bit with our dinner. And yes, tell Cosmo he'll get something. Exactly what, I'm not sure, but whatever we give him he'll devour it."

They both laughed as Ben ended his call and walked to his car. Better late than never for getting out of work. He called one of their favorite spots, China One, and placed his order. China One was only five minutes from the house, so the food would still be hot by the time he arrived home.

He was thankful that traffic was lighter than the normal rush hour. He arrived at the restaurant, walked in, and the owners immediately recognized him. After a few moments of idle chit chat, he paid for his order and was quickly on his way home.

He was enjoying the aroma of the sweet and sour pork when he heard his name whispered, *Benjamin.* He listened to the voice, trying to determine who it was that was calling him. By now he knew when he heard "Benjamin" his presence was needed in Kalamar. He pushed the thought from his mind. He knew there was nothing he could do about the calling, but he wanted to get home and enjoy dinner with Marcie.

Ben thought it was a bit odd, or maybe funny, that when he thought of dinner with Marcie, he never heard his name called. Parking the car in the garage, Ben grabbed the bag of hot food and walked inside the house. When he opened the door, there sat Cosmo, tail whipping back and forth as quickly as he could wag it. Ben gave Marcie a hug and a kiss on the cheek and handed her the bag containing dinner. Kneeling on one knee, Ben teased and played with Cosmo while Marcie placed the food on the plates and set them on the table.

"Tell me, Mr. Fourlegs, have you had a good day today?" Ben looked over at Cosmo's bowl, almost empty. "Oh, my goodness, someone is almost out of food and water. Let me fill your bowls up, and you can eat your doggie food while the missus and I enjoy our dinner." Ben patted Cosmo on the head, stood up and did exactly as he said. He filled up both of Cosmo's bowls with fresh water and more food.

Ben pulled out Marcie's chair, then his own. They exchanged idle chitchat while enjoying the evening meal together, each sharing what they did during the day. When they had finished, Marcie looked at Ben.

"Why don't you go take your shower and relax? Sounds like it has really been a busy day for you."

Ben slipped out of his chair, helped Marcie clear the table, then headed for the shower. When he returned, he found Marcie was sitting in her recliner in the family room. Walking over to the coffee table, Ben picked up the evening paper before he settled in his chair. Ben thought it was a bit odd, or maybe funny, that when he sat through dinner with Marcie, he never heard his name called once.

"I'm going to read for a bit, Hon, so feel free to put on whatever you want on the tv." Before Ben could sit, Cosmo beat him to the punch and rested on the right arm.

"Well, well, well, guess someone wants to read the paper with ne," Ben said as he slipped into his oversized recliner and tilted it back. Cosmo didn't waste a second; as soon as the chair had reclined, he slipped next to Ben's right leg, his normal spot. Marcie had already placed a glass of sweet tea next to his chair.

"Thank you, Sweetie. Both of you know how to spoil me." Ben picked up the paper and started reading. With the TV softly humming, Marcie settled, and Cosmo happily snoozing in the stillness of the room, he heard his name called again. *Benjamin.* There was no mistaking hearing this voice, either at the office or again at home. He returned to reading the paper, Cosmo rubbing his head against his leg.

Ben was in the middle of an article when he blinked his eyes. Again, he heard the call, *Benjamin.* He thought he looked around the room but wasn't sure. He looked over at Marcie. "You know, Sweetie, I think I'm going to go ahead and go to bed. I can't concentrate on what I'm reading, and each blink gets longer and longer."

Marcie looked at Ben as he stood. "I know, Sweetie, you had a hard day. I'll be along later."

Ben, followed by Cosmo, walked down the hall. After helping Cosmo up in bed, Ben slipped under the covers, Cosmo quickly curled up in a ball between Ben's and Marcie's pillows. The race for who fell asleep first had started. His eyelids were heavy, Ben closed them. How long they were closed, he wasn't sure before he heard his name called again. *Benjamin.*

Ben opened his eyes. His mind flashed back to a memory from just before his 13th birthday.

Stopping in the middle of the lane, Wren reached out her hand to Ben. "Take my hand and run with me." With the words barely out of her mouth, they were off and running. Ben couldn't believe the ease and speed with which they moved. His mind suddenly returned to his childhood as Benny, another time when he was uplifted and ran faster than he had ever run before when he was returned to his bed.

Benjamin paused to remember. "You will be with me again, when I'm in high school at the league track meet, won't you? You will help me again, won't you? Reevus will be there, too. He sent a little girl to tell me to 'be ready'."

As they ran, Benjamin noticed how rapidly they traveled and here he was Benjamin and not Ben. The countryside had become a stream of colors as they passed, yet neither breathed hard. Wren continued to fill Benjamin in. Her words touched his mind as if spoken aloud.

"When that day comes, like today, Zorleg sent some of his stooges to disrupt things. I will tell you no more of what is to come. What I will tell you is that The Guardian will be extremely pleased with you that day."

"Thank you for explaining why things feel so familiar to me, Wren. But still, I have so many questions."

"Yes, I know you do. We shall be with Queen RhiAnne shortly, and she can answer and explain many things that I cannot."

Benjamin remembered everything as if it had just happened. Two of Zorleg's stooges at the inn, running with Wren. He felt like he was picking up their conversation exactly where it had left off before.

No sooner had Wren completed her sentence than they arrived in the meadow deep within The Great Forest. Sitting on her throne in front of her Tree of Life, Queen RhiAnne rose, the long emerald green robe almost touching the ground. Chairs similar to hers sat to her right and left. Wren left Benjamin's side and joined Queen RhiAnne. The great tree had a tremendous trunk in the center and two smaller trunks off to the right and the left, the smaller ones spaced precisely the same distance from the main trunk.

The Queen of the Elves bowed to Benjamin, who instinctively bowed in return. "Your Majesty, was it your voice that called me from my sleep?"

Queen RhiAnne motioned for Benjamin to join them, and another throne appeared. Queen RhiAnne began to speak. "Benjamin, Princess Wren you know quite well. Allow me to officially introduce my other daughter. Benjamin, Princess Madison." Queen RhiAnne waved her hand, pointing to the right of the Tree of Life. Princess Madison stepped forward, her long golden locks of hair flowing gracefully down and over her shoulders. Queen RhiAnne motioned to each of her children and Benjamin to sit.

"Benjamin, you were called because there is something you need to see. Yes, you were also correct. Here we address you as Benjamin, as we should. What you need to see is something very significant for The Guardian, as well as for you. For tonight, under the full moons of Kalamar, he shall cry The Tear of Tears, creating The Tear of Healing.

He had prepared a long time for this. He started when the moons began to rise. His ritual is sapping his strength, taking far longer than we imagined. But he knew. I can see his power gradually ebbing from within and dimness in the light that beamed from his face."

"Tear of Tears? Weakness?" Benjamin repeated after the queen.

"Explaining would be too difficult and take too long, Benjamin. It is better that you watch and experience for yourself. Together, we shall watch The Guardian do his work. When it is time, you will know what you need to do." Queen RhiAnne stood and began to move; the others immediately stood and followed her. They walked through the meadow until Queen RhiAnne motioned for them to stop. Gathering close to the queen, the four of them watched the Guardian. In a hushed tone, Queen RhiAnne spoke, "Allow me to briefly explain, Benjamin. For as the night progresses, we will become one with The Guardian to help him complete this task." Reaching out, Queen RhiAnne motioned for them to hold hands. Reverently, she began by touching the minds of the others with her thoughts. While only a thought, the words were crystal clear in Benjamin's mind.

Queen RhiAnne took a moment to provide Benjamin part of his history and the history of The Chosen. "A long time ago, written in the book of The Seven of Sevens, was the first mention of The Chosen Ones. From the moment when all things began, the male child was given the voice of thunder and the female child the breath of magic. The first time they meet, they will stand together by the water, and she shall part the sea with her gift. These are The Chosen Ones, chosen by me. I, The One of Ones, knew My Chosen before they were born. They are My Chosen Ones. Freely I bestowed on them gifts and powers that I alone had set aside for them from the very beginning. Part of what has been given to them is the Reward of Rewards, to be used in the Battle of Battles."

When her last words faded, Queen RhiAnne pointed to a spot in the meadow. There, a single rock protruded from the lush green pasture. The Guardian stood high atop the rock, his hands outstretched toward the heavens. He was illuminated by the light cast from above by the moons of Kalamar. Even at this distance, it was unmistakable how much effort The Guardian was expending. His purple robe was covered in a mixture of his own sweat and the mist in the air. As they watched, his hands moved from side to side. While they observed The Guardian's movements, he called forth the mist that began to form and thicken in the meadow. At his guidance, the mist started to encircle both the rock and The Guardian, responding to his call. From The Third Plane, he had called the mist from The Great Lake. Massaged by the Guardian and a ripple in time, it had become part of his magic. His hands moved faster. The mist, following his direction, began to swirl. The Guardian opened his hand and directed the mist upward. It climbed toward the stars, joined by large droplets formed from The Tears of Healing.

Silently, Queen RhiAnne squeezed Benjamin's hand tightly in hers as they watched the Guardian. The Elven Queen explained what created The Tears of Healing. The mist, used to form each tear, was wrapped in the assurance that The One of Ones found no fault in those who are touched by this tear. All faults were placed in The Great Lake and existed no more. Some call this lake The Lake of Forgetfulness or The Lake of Healing. The Guardian was one of the few that could call the mist from The Great Lake. The tear, once shed, gives back to those what was stolen or taken away by Zorleg. They may be gone, but none have ever been forgotten.

The Tear of Healing:

Pure Love from the One of Ones,

A sliver of the Everlasting Hope,

A spark from the Eternal Flame from the heart of the Guardian.

The Tear of Healing:

For those who were loved,

For those who were lost,

For those who will always be remembered.

Benjamin listened intently as he absorbed every word while the Queen told the story of The Tear of Tears. She motioned Princess Madison and Wren to join The Guardian. There was no reason in Benjamin's mind to explain why he knew The Guardian's arms needed to remain uplifted. For as long as his arms stretched to the heavens, the tears would continue to flow. When the elves joined The Guardian, it was evident how quickly his strength returned. From his stooped appearance, his body now stood fully erect with the two elven princesses supporting his arms, keeping them pointed towards the stars above.

"The Guardian had placed and encapsulated his story, making it a personal story and plea, to each person. It makes no difference who, what or where. Each person has faced the end of the road they choose to travel. They felt trapped with no way out. Death, darkness, loneliness is all they must look forward to. Others look at them and see someone who is broken beyond all conceivable beliefs, wondering how they could have gotten into such a position, but offering no help, no hope. There is no pity or sorrow to be shared."

The Queen paused for a moment, looking at Wren and Madison supporting The Guardian. "Every person is different, yet all the same. They feel they have reached as low as they can go, when the essence of life feels as though it has started flowing from them with no way to stop it. What has caused the demise and fall? Throughout time, the reason changes. Alcohol. Drugs. Adultery. Self-righteousness. Lying. Cheating. Stealing. Infidelity. Self-centeredness. Greed. All of them, none of them, or was it something completely different? It was not a list of their own choosing, but it was Zorleg who created the list and was behind it all. The Lord of Darkness and Deceit had taken each weakness and created a crutch, working continually until they were solely dependent on him. How long have they been tormented? How long have they faced the demons and destruction Zorleg has placed in their life? They feel a deep loneliness, a darkness that stings their very souls, creating indescribable and unrelenting pain that has tormented their souls, night and day. From their torment, pain, and loneliness, Zorleg gathered and drew strength, sapping their very souls."

Queen RhiAnne paused again, asking Benjamin to join her as they walked towards where The Guardian stood. "A point in time comes when all can look and see their own torment and feel their own pain. In the deep, dark depths of loneliness, it will begin. Then, and only then, do the eyes begin to tear freely. Nothing Zorleg and his army of dark witches do can stop the flow of the tears. It is the moment when they become broken. From every eye of Child of Darkness will flow the Tears of Healing. They have been brought to that point in time in their life to find the strength to turn from the ways of darkness and seek the light. The path they chose was not the path The One of Ones desired for them, but He also would not deny them their freedom of choice. As with all things, some decisions are not correct. It is now that, from broken, painful agony and despair, they reach out for The Tears of Healing. The One of Ones brought them to this point for the simple reason that, of however low they are, He is there to greet them and welcome them home. Home is The Great Meeting Place and when called, they shall come. They shall come with a broken heart pleading to be mended, desperate to be rescued.

They have been wounded and come seeking a healing they do not understand. They shall return and answer the call. They shall come empty, looking to be filled."

They were all gathered at the large rock, listening in reverence to The Guardian as he spoke into the darkness, "This is my Moment of Moments. Many nights have I sent forth into the universe the tear that holds exactly what the lost soul has been missing and now craves. The calling of the tears was their choice. They have reached this moment in time that was prepared for them. They do not understand, but they know it is what they must do. The unbearable pain, the anguish, the crying of the question: 'Why did this happen?' The realization they were to seek the One who has always been present. When The Tear of Healing shall run freely down their cheeks, then they shall become aware their hope has been restored, the warmth of His never-ending love, and the glow of the flame will once again begin to grow within their own heart, snuffing out the darkness of Zorleg. The One of Ones has heard the cry of his lost children. For it is only The One of Ones who can wipe away their tears. With His touch, they shall feel His love flowing from his heart to theirs. A very small part of His Love was placed in the tear and waited to be called. The tiny spark now has become a bright flame burning within each person that has been fanned by the flame of eternity. Its warmth will spread throughout their body, its flame growing brighter with each beat of their heart. The flame of eternity shall begin to shine brightly from within their heart, casting aside the darkness and shadows. The eternal flame will put an end to what has held them prisoner for so long. Surrounded by His hope and renewal, their faith now restored, they run to the Feast of Feasts at the home of The One of Ones. While they run, The One of Ones is overcome with emotion and joy. He turns, allowing only his flowing white gown to be seen. His face and cheeks are now soaked by a stream of His own tears of overwhelming compassion and joy as He welcomes His Children home from the darkness, standing to greet them at The Great Meeting Place."

Benjamin began to move even before Queen RhiAnne spoke, sensing exactly what was needed next. He moved to a spot in front of The Guardian where he could see how His Face was covered in anguish and etched in pain. At the same time, a huge smile conveying love, life and happiness was glowing from His face. Benjamin stepped upon a stone to The Guardian's right as Queen RhiAnne stepped on one to His left. In the silence of the moment, they placed their hands on His. Queen RhiAnne looked at Benjamin and nodded.

Benjamin lifted his head upward and began to speak. With each word, the countryside began to shake from his voice of thunder. Trees swayed from side to side and the ground reverberated for miles around them. Benjamin spoke in no more than a whisper as he uttered the words he knew must be said at that moment. His words of thunder awoke the sky, with each word bringing forth bolts of lightning. His words rolled across the countryside in all directions. How many times were the words spoken? How many times did the mighty thunder shake the countryside? Where did the bolts of lightning come from and go on this cloudless night? These questions were meant to be answered and talked about outside of the forest as another tale of tales. With their hands joined together, creating multiple sets of three, a soft light began to glow. With each passing moment, the light intensified, growing brighter and brighter until they all were surrounded by a pure white light. While they stood motionless, the light began to shimmer. At precisely the correct moment, the light shot skyward, creating a dazzlingly brilliant beacon, cutting through the darkness, caressing the stars above.

Benjamin opened his lips again while he lifted his eyes skyward and repeated, *"**Sela Nu Amore. Keisa ruilea nesta. Telnadana**."* As his lips closed, the moonbeams joined the beacon of pure white light, changing it from white to a light blue. The beacon generated a low soft tone, calming to the ear, providing a feeling of comfort and reassurance. Around them, the mist continued to swirl as it joined with the light. Benjamin repeated, *"**Sela Nu Amore. Keisa ruilea nesta. Telnadana.**"* After he repeated the words a third time, Benjamin noticed Madison's face. Her face was covered with tears flowing freely and running down her cheeks. Her tears joined with the Guardian's before they were lifted upward with the mist and flowed into the fountain of light.

Benjamin closed his eyes, lowered his head, and whispered, *"**Fini**."* As quickly as it had appeared, the beacon was gone. He lowered his hands and silently stepped down from the stone as Queen RhiAnne, Madison and Wren followed his lead. The Guardian remained on the rock, motionless. His weakened state was clearly evident to each one of them.

Queen RhiAnne turned to face Benjamin. Her eyes met his as Madison and Wren returned to her side. Her lips never moved, but again Benjamin heard every word she said. "Thank you, Children. In one of his weakest moments, you again came to his aid." Smiling at Madison, Queen RhiAnne stroked the long golden locks of her hair. "Would you have ever dreamed, when he gave you your gift, that this would be one of the moments he needed you for? Your tears of healing mixed with his?"

Madison bowed her head before her mother, the Elven Queen. "I knew it was special, but not until I became part of this ritual did, I realize just how special of a gift it was. I couldn't tell if anything had happened to me or through me. Is The Guardian going to be okay? Should we do something?"

"No, Child. He has those who will tend to him. Our work here is done."

Queen RhiAnne turned to Wren and asked, "Would you like to take Benjamin to Reevus now? Reevus can explain how the rings, the bracelets, and the amulet all came into being. His skill forged the magic of the forest, the touch of the unicorn horn, and the captured moonbeams into each. Through his craftsmanship, all those parts were forged to make the items needed for the future. They shall be used for your future, Benjamin, her future and our future…the Future of Futures!"

Jerking up in bed, sweat pouring profusely down his face, Ben felt his chest heaving as he gulped for air. Turning, he saw Marcie staring at him and then felt her hand on his back.

"You are soaked again. Is there anything I can do?" Marcie softly asked.

"No, no, it was only another dream. I'm sorry, really. I am so, so sorry. I didn't mean to wake you!" Ben slowly sucked in another breath as he felt the coolness of the night against his soaked body.

"You were shouting and screaming again, Ben. Sometimes mumbling, but I couldn't understand what you were saying. It was like you were speaking in a foreign language."

Ben patted Marcie on the back. "It's okay, Sweetie, only a bad dream. Now let's go back to sleep."

As he rolled over on his side, he wondered about his dreams, and felt he was there, again. How many times had he awakened in the middle of the night, soaked in sweat, only to hear Marcie tell him how he was speaking in a language she didn't understand? As his breathing slowed,

Ben slowly drifted back off to sleep, completely unaware of Zorleg's attempt to invade his dreams and disrupt his life.

In his place, in another time, the Seer ran his fingers down his beard as he looked into the mirror. Thinking out loud, his voice filled the room. "Benjamin may not know of your presence again this evening, Zorleg. Like all things, I see all. The Guardian's work is not finished, with much still to do. For now, there is only a minor setback. We all know his strength is failing him, but there are many things yet to happen. Your men may have him, but he is not alone." The picture in the mirror slowly dimmed until it looked like a pane of smoked glass. A soft sigh escaped from his lips as the Seer maintained his constant vigil, always watching, listening, and waiting.

Part 5

Zorleg – Who Is in the Courtyard

Zorleg paused again and chuckled to himself. Rubbing his hands together, he relished his memories. *Oh, how happy those days were, but they pale compared to what lies ahead.* For years he watched his Zorean army grow in size and strength. When they stood shoulder to shoulder, they stretched farther than the eye could see in all directions. While he may destroy the Sisters of the Mist...stopping, he caught himself. *No*, he corrected himself; *I have destroyed the Sisters of the Mist. All shall hear and then see the vastness of my army as it approaches what once was the Great Gathering Place. They shall come from every direction, the south, west, and north. With the Great Lake to the east, there will be no escaping.* Chanting softly, he repeated to anyone within earshot, "***Time after time, death to the soul; the soul is mine.***"

Far below Zorleg's chamber window, the courtyard was empty except for a single figure who sat motionless on one of several stone benches. The gloominess of night was enhanced by the low-hanging clouds and the heavy mist dripping off everything, puddles of water standing everywhere in the courtyard. When the guards performed their normally scheduled rounds through the courtyard, they noticed someone sitting on one of the benches. Immediately, they approached him and took up positions on either side of the lone figure. Both looked at him, then at each other, then again at the uninvited guest. They watched him for a few moments without speaking. There really wasn't much to see. He appeared to be elderly, slender, with long strands of silver hair that disappeared inside of his hood. His beard extended downward from his chin before resting on his robe. Dressed in deep purple, he remained quiet and motionless as the guards began to bellow loudly.

"What be your business here? How be it that you be in his inner courtyard?" one of the guards asked gruffly, pressing his face close to the stranger's. Both guards began to shuffle slowly, methodically, around the stranger and the bench. The water splashed, sloshing with every step they took. Leaning forward, first one, then the other looked closely at the stranger's face before they turned to look at each other.

With arms crossed, in unison, they spoke. "Humph, something be different here," they said before turning to the stranger and asking jointly, "Where ye come from? Why ye be here? No one walks the land of Zorleg freely!" The guards moved and stood on each side of the stranger, their dark black attire with the Gold Z on their pant leg clearly visible in the dim light. "Tell us, stranger, so that we may please Lord Zorleg…how is it that ye be here in the middle of his courtyard? How is it you able to get in? Why it be all ye garments be dry?" They looked around the bench at all the mud and water leading up to the bench. At the same instance, both noticed as they peered down at the ground, the only footprints in the mud belonged to them.

The stranger spoke softly. "Oh, I pretty much come and go as I wish. However, it is not you that I wish to speak with. For your own good, it would be in your best interest to let Zorleg know I have a few things he should be told. In all his greatness, there are things that even he does not know."

The two guards laughed uncontrollably at the stranger. "What? Zorleg not know? Impossible! He know everything!" They looked at each other in disbelief at what the stranger had dared to speak.

Above the laughter, they now heard the stranger's voice again. It was clear as if a bell ringing in the night. When they turned and looked at their uninvited guest, his lips never moved, but each word rang clearly and distinctly in their ears.

"Heroism and chivalry are not dead. Go tell the one who prefers to be called the Dark Lord these words." The stranger stood before he continued. "You are planning to go where you should not go. You are planning to take that which does not belong to you nor has it ever belonged to you. It would bode you well to remain away from the Great Queen and the Enchanted Forest." As silently as he stood, the stranger returned to his seat on the bench before he placed his hands comfortably in his lap. "I shall wait here for you to pass my message along. As you found me, I shall remain steadfast and await your return."

Astounded, they looked at each other and thought *How could someone be so brazen?* Neither said a word but knew the thoughts of the other. The stranger's lips did not move, yet they heard his every word! *How can that be?* Together they pushed their faces close to the stranger's ears, one on each side, as they agreed and said out loud, "Not gonna trust him." Both had the same opinion that one must stay with this foreigner while the other reported his strange words to Lord Zorleg.

Swiftly, one turned and sprinted off to Zorleg's chamber. As he ran the sloshing of his footsteps as they landed in the pools of water filled the air, echoing off the inner walls of the courtyard. Stopping outside the chamber door, he lifted his hand to grasp the knocker. There was nothing he could do to stop the uncontrollable shaking. Before extending his arm to reach for the knocker, he heard Zorleg's booming voice. "Who dare knock upon my door? Open and enter slowly, knowing full well that you are here only because I allow it."

Lifting the latch, the guard timidly entered Zorleg's chamber with extreme caution. After he entered, he bowed in reverence and obedience in honor to his lord while he lowered himself to one knee.

"Your Majesty, I come begging forgiveness." The guard paused before he continued as he waited for Zorleg to respond.

"Rise and share your news!" Zorleg bellowed as he rose from his throne.

The guard lifted his head, then moved slowly to the base of the steps until he stood upright before Lord Zorleg. Stammering, stuttering, the guard began, "Your Highness, within ye sacred walls a stranger be. Where he be from, we know not. Strange attire, strange, Your Lordship, very strange, but even stranger be the words he speaks." Pausing, cowering, he awaited Zorleg's approval before he continued.

Silently, Zorleg wondered who it was that had arrived unannounced and sat in his courtyard. Like the guard, he too questioned not only who he was but how he had gotten into his inner courtyard. Leaning forward, Zorleg waved his hand as he motioned the guard to continue.

The guard stammered and stuttered again, picking up where he left off, "My lord, the stranger be sayin' to us you should not seek the queen of the Enchanted Forest. We not know or understand what he means, Your Lordship." As he finished his words, the guard fell to his knees and placed his arms up over his head as if to protect himself from being struck.

The last word no more than left his lips before the room filled with the bellowing and shouting of Zorleg. "How dare he! How could anyone know my innermost thoughts?" With a rage burning within him, Zorleg continued to yell at the guard, "Go! Bring him to me at once! The door will remain open until you return." Seething, Zorleg's fingers firmly clenched and dug into the stone arm of his chair.

Picking himself up, the guard ran as quickly as his short, stubby legs would carry him back to the courtyard. Splashing through the puddles, he returned to the courtyard, his partner, and the bench where the stranger sat. He stopped, panting and out of breath. "Your presence before our Great Lord now be required, not be an option. Get up! Move." Both guards stood on either side as the old man rose.

"Gladly…that is my purpose here." The words were spoken calmly, softly as he rose.

He walked with the guards as they navigated through the courtyard and into Zorleg's castle. After the three had entered the dark lord's chambers, the door closed and locked itself behind them at Zorleg's silent command. Zorleg made sure no one would leave until he allowed them to leave, and by his command. Bowing before Zorleg, the guards tried to force the stranger to his knees in the presence of Zorleg but were unsuccessful.

Leaning forward, raising an eyebrow, Zorleg softly asked, almost in a whisper, "So tell me, stranger, how do you know of the Great Queen of the Enchanted Forest?"

The stranger looked at Zorleg. Once again, his lips did not move, but his words filled the room. "While you are no lord of mine, and I do not bow before you, I know 'Your Lordship' is how you expect to be addressed. I said nothing of knowing the Great Queen. My exact words were, 'You are planning to go where you should not go and take that which does not belong to you. It would bode you well to remain away from the Great Queen and the Enchanted Forest.' You may ask your guards to confirm I speak the truth."

Zorleg looked at both guards questioningly. "Well?"

In unison they replied, "'Tis true, Sire, as he said." Puzzled, they looked at each other. "Well, 'tis what we think he said, but as we hearin', his lips moved not!"

Turning back to the stranger, Zorleg continued. "I find it extremely interesting. Those very thoughts were in my mind mere moments ago. Are you some sort of mind reader, magician, or sorcerer?"

"None of those terms would be how I would be described, nor do they apply to me. I know things. Such as your unanswered question about things, you will do and have done to others. Or perhaps the simple spoken word of a child and how much of a change a child can make. From The Great Lake, even after the destruction of Kalamar, The Child of the Lake has moved the sands of time exactly where they should be, not one grain out of place. Even now as my words are spoken, The Child shifts the sands of time again. The theft of the keys will do you no good. It was only an unfortunate turn of events for your own joy and glee. Was there more you wish to know?"

Rage built from within, Zorleg's glaring eyes as his cheeks turned a deep color of red. He moved his hands, motioning his guards to join him. After they turned their backs to the stranger, Zorleg leaned forward, toward the guards. His words were more of a whisper, as he spoke softly so only they could hear what he said.

The stranger stood silent and remained motionless. He watched the three of them gesture wildly, before injecting his own words and warnings. As he spoke, the three turned and looked in his direction. "You will use your rolling thunder, along with the clouds and mist, as a mask to disguise what has happened to The Great City. It was a monumental effort on your part to destroy it, but the walls, while damaged, did not fall. From your own hand, others shall come and go. Maybe it will be your soldiers, perhaps those left behind, but all will be able to hear the subtle change over and over again. Your rolling thunder shall stop momentarily, replaced by the crisp, methodical sound from the heavens. It will be faint at first, then start to grow louder as they approach, then fade again to silence as they leave. When they have departed, a question will be raised. What was it that passed in the heavens? What was it that came, was it coming or going, or did it exist at all? If it was something, where is it coming from and where is it going to? Why are they coming and going? Or is it only the minds playing tricks on so many? What is the secret behind the storytellers? Who are The Chosen? These are only questions I leave for you to find the answer to, Dark One."

Turning his back on the stranger again, Zorleg shifted his focus and asked the Guards, "And he got into my inner courtyard how?" drawing out the "how" into a very long word.

"Sire, our rounds take us by the square where we find him every quarter mark. He not be there during our last crossing of the courtyard. Nay, not a soul has been allowed entrance through your outer gates, just as you have ordered. Sealed and locked by your command, Your Lordship. Where he be from be a mystery to us as well. How he be in your courtyard, we know not. We find it odd his attire, his hair, nary a sign of being wet. Dry, as dry as if he had never stepped outside, but yet there he be in the middle of the courtyard without a drop of water on him. Look at him now and look at us. We still be soaking wet! And we tell you something else that is odd, very odd, Your Lordship. Not a footprint around him or the bench, nothing to show how he got there. Not one footprint, no Sire, not one. But we could see our own leading up to the bench he be sittin' upon clearly outlined in the mud. Makes no sense, no sense at all how such a thing could be Your Highness. How could he simply appear without leavin' no footprints behind?"

Silently, all three heads turned in unison. To their amazement, the room was empty. The stranger had been only a few feet away, standing at the bottom of the steps, but now he was no more, gone, and vanished. Looking at the door, they saw the latch was still securely fastened and locked in place. All eyes scanned the room. His chamber now empty, Zorleg felt the inferno rage as it once again began to burn within.

He looked at his two guards as he willed his chamber door to fly open. "Leave me, leave me now!"

They did not need him to say it twice. Quickly they exited his chambers, the door slamming shut and locking behind them.

How is it possible for anyone to know my thoughts? It was only on this evening, Zorleg pondered, that he was planning the attack. *How did he know what I had planned for The Great Forest?*

His final thought turned to the cave of keys. *Again, it was only this night that I laid out my plan. How? How could he have known about my planning the theft of the keys?*

Zorleg was so infuriated; he had no answers to his own question. Now, more than ever he was determined he must find this enchanted forest and the queen who lives within. He will prove this old fool wrong!

No man or woman can harm me. I have nothing to fear! And I must find out what this secret is that I have heard about the storytellers. Zorleg wondered, *what was the secret I have been told on several occasions by my soldiers about the storytellers. Do the storytellers have additional power for me?*

After thinking of the additional power, he would gather from the storytellers and the Queen and the Great Forest, Zorleg bellowed, "I must have all power!"

The Seer, now safely back in his place in time, chuckled softly. He knew before he left that Zorleg would not be able to figure out how he arrived or how he departed. A gift that would also be bestowed on the Chosen when it was needed.

Nafari - The Witch of Darkness

The two minions of Zorleg, Grink and Pounce, ran as quickly as their legs would carry them, arriving at the door to his chambers completely out of breath. Loud sucking noises could be heard as they recovered from their long run.

Grink bent over, placing his hands on his knees. "We run fast, real fast. We come like we be told."

Pounce, standing next to Grink, was also gasping for breath. "We run that far before? Why we run so fast? We not be doin' that again soon I hope!"

Both remained bent at the waist with their hands grasping ahold of their knees. "We hope we be pleasing Your Lordship we be here so quickly," Grink stammered in between panting for air.

Zorleg was pleased they had arrived before him so quickly as he peered down at the closed door. He raised the index finger on his right hand and the door swung open.

Grink and Pounce looked at each other in fear as the door slowly creaked open. Without much fanfare, Zorleg motioned them into the room from the seat of his throne.

Zorleg looked down at the two of them menacingly. He scowled before his voice broke the silence. His deep voice boomed, reverberating off the stone walls when he spoke.

"Tell me what you have found this time." He paused, staring at both of them with a look of disgust, before he continued. "Be sure you choose your words wisely or you, too, will suffer the fate of others who failed me and did not have the correct answer! But I feel I need not warn either of you again. I know you oh too well."

The two minions looked at each other, both too terrified to speak. Finally, one of them stepped forward and bowed. Grink moved before Lord Zorleg and started but stuttered and stammered before he finally was able to speak.

"Your Majesty, we be findin' the boy." Grink, after saying only one sentence, retreated a step back and rejoined his companion. His body shook uncontrollably as he awaited the upcoming response.

Zorleg looked at them both, a wicked smile spread across his face. A slight chuckle escaped from his lips as he leaned forward. He raised his fist and pumped it victoriously in the air as he exclaimed, "Well now, that is good news! Tell me more. How old is he now? Has he started his training? What all does he know?"

The two looked up at him as they continued to shake uncontrollably in fear. Grink, again the bold one, took a small step forward and timidly spoke again. "Your Majesty, he be a boy of around five, six maybes. We feels he don't know nothin' and 'pears to be normal, nothin' special we be seein' in him, Your Lordship. We be sayin' it 'peers he be startin' something of some sort but not appearin' to be anything special that we could see. How far he be, what he be doin', more things we not be able to figure. We be certain though, without question, he be doin' something of some kind. We be keepin' ourselves well-hidden and out of sight in the cistern, just as you instructed. We did hear the one, what you be callin' him? Oh yes, you be callin' him The Guardian sayin', You have stopped the messenger, but not the message.' We not be knowin' the meanin' but thought it be somethin' we needs to lets you know."

Zorleg jumped up from his throne, moving so quickly he almost knocked both off their feet. Returning as quickly as he left, he slipped back onto his throne again. His hand reached up unconsciously, and he started stroking his chin. They remained silent as they both listened intently to Zorleg.

"So, The Guardian has started his training, has he? He is aware of how many times I've been successful in removing his messengers before. What makes him believe that I won't find and do the same with this one? So many before, but none of them were the correct one. Let me see if there isn't something that can be done to disrupt things just a bit." Zorleg paused before he continued to think out loud. "Now that I have found where he has been hidden in time, what is it that I can I do to instill so much fear in this child to completely discourage him and bring as much disruption as I can into his life?"

Zorleg sprang from his throne again, catching Grink and Pounce off guard, startling them. Before his feet had touched the cold cobblestone floor, he began to shout and yell, "Prepare the Dreamcast!" He looked at Grink and Pounce, then screamed at them, "Dolts, I don't need you anymore! Get out of my sight, now! You have done all that was asked of you! Leave me, NOW!"

The wicked grin covered his face as Zorleg walked out of his chambers and hurried down the hall. He stopped and opened one of the many doors in the corridor. Inside the room, he slowly looked around until he saw exactly what and who he was searching for. Zorleg moved with a slow gait until he stood behind her. Cocking his head to one side, he whispered, "Now it is time."

She turned and looked back at him through her white eyes. Her skin was pale white, her pointed nose and chin protruded outward. Her facial features were accented by coal black hair that flowed freely over her shoulders and down her back. She wore a long black dress that covered her from head to toe, only her neck and hands left exposed. "How well you know me, My Lord. The name you have given me, Nafari, your Witch of Darkness, like always, is ready to serve you. It gives me great pleasure knowing my successes are the results of what I have been trained to do. Every scar upon my face, each hideous feature that are so appalling to others, I owe to you." Nafari fell silent and bowed her head in respect to the Lord of Darkness.

Zorleg let out a small laugh. "Ah, darkness. I like that, witch. For it is in darkness that I shall use you. I have chosen a special task for you to complete. This task, unlike all the others I have sent you on, is a very, very important task. The most important!" Zorleg took Nafari by the hand and led her to the middle of the room. With a wave of his hand, a projection of the boy appeared in front of them. "This is your subject. I want you to invade his dreams, fill them full of fear to terrorize him. Do all you can to disrupt his life. Make him useless!"

Zorleg paused for a moment to allow his order to sink in before he asked, "How many times have I sent you to instill fear in others? To make them bow and cower before you. This, however, will be your greatest task ever and is much, so much more important to me!" Zorleg bellowed out as his laughter filled her room.

Nafari turned silently and slowly before she looked at Zorleg, then spoke firmly but not loudly, "The child's name?"

"His name is of no significance for you to do your task," Zorleg replied ungraciously. "Unlike other trips you have taken for me, this time there is no need to kill or maim, only instill fear in the boy's heart. He must feel fear like he has never felt before!"

"As you have commanded, I shall make it so. I will report to you on my return." Nafari closed her eyes, whispered a few words, conjuring up a spell that immediately transported her from the presence of the Dark Lord to exactly where she needed to be.

Zorleg's face was covered with a grin of wickedness. He anticipated his huge victory in this ongoing battle with the Guardian. "How can this child be a threat if he is filled with fear?"

The Gifts

Reevus sat alone with his thoughts. Skippy curled up in a ball on her bed in the corner, sound asleep. The oil lamp sat in the middle of the table, giving Reevus just the right amount of light that he needed. Reverently, he bowed his head before he began to recite from memory.

"It was written in the Seven of Sevens eons before the first mention of The Chosen Ones. The words that were written and recorded were, 'From the moment when all things began, he was given the voice of thunder and she the breath of breaths.

"His voice, when called upon, shall boom through the air, shaking the very foundation of all that is around him. To those near him, his voice would sound greater and more powerful than thunder. For her, the spell of casting her breath would cause water to churn and divide. For both, their gifts come forth when they are called. Both shall be taught the nature of the special gift and how to best use it."

Reevus paused to take a drink of water before he continued.

'"Between these pieces of parchment, it was written about the first time the two shall meet. Each will be a formidable foe standing alone. When they are paired together, coming together as one, it will become even more so. From each other, the combining of the different gifts will cause their strength to grow. At the edge of The Great Lake, he shall call out to her with his gift, and she shall use her gift to part the raging waters. When he speaks, the power of his voice shall echo throughout the land. There will be no mistaking who they are and that they have arrived as foretold within these pages.'"

Reevus was visibly overcome by emotions as he recited the words of The Seven of Sevens, words that were given to him to speak at this moment in time to usher in what is yet to come. Reevus took another gulp of cold water before continuing.

"'They are The Chosen Ones. They were chosen by me, The One of Ones. Before they were born, I knew them and laid upon them special gifts for a very special purpose. I bestowed on them gifts and powers when I stood at The Great Meeting Place, and they were brought forth from their birthing tents in The Great Forest. I have given them the greatest gift I could give, the Reward of Rewards. The day is coming when they will use their gifts against the one who has turned the beauty and serenity of The Third Plane into his darkness. They all shall gather in The Battle of Battles.'"

Reevus bowed his head and whispered a few more words before taking another sip from his glass of water. He sat upright in his chair and stared at the light from the oil lamp, then over at Skippy.

"It is all I can do. Recite the words, tell the stories, prepare those whose ears hear for what is yet to come. You know, girl, it would be nice if everyone was relaxed as you are. But I am afraid, very afraid, so many hear but do not believe. They listen but do not hear."

Reevus took another sip of water. "Oh yes, I know, Skippy. I hear the words people say about me, too. It's nothing but the babbling of an old fool. He's telling wild stories."

Reevus ran his hand over his face and then down his neck. "I can only do what I was meant to do. Thankfully, there are some that listen, hear, and do prepare for what is yet to come. I will continue to do what I do, using the gift I was given.

"Well, Skippy, you beat me again. I hope that I'll be able to fall asleep as easily as you do. Now I think I'll join you." Reevus took one more drink of water, leaned forward and blew out the lamp. “I’ll be with you in dreamland shortly, Skippy.”

Reevus slipped into bed and, just as he told Skippy, sleep came quickly. The sound of both snoring filled the room.

The Krazac

Rose smiled contently, slowly walking down the path she had traveled many times before. She could feel the warmth of the Three Suns as they lightly caressed her skin. She gazed off into the distance while she walked, each footstep falling silent when it touched the grass. Her long green dress swung freely, barely an inch above the grass of the lush green meadow. As far as her eyes could see, there was nothing short of perfection. Gently rolling hills were covered with many types of flowers that she found brought warmth to her heart. When she reached the top of one of the many small grassy knolls, she paused and gently lowered herself until she sat upon the ground. Her hands felt the coolness of each blade as she slid her hand through the rich green grass. Even though she sat alone, she never stopped smiling, nor did the feeling of someone being with her ever leave her.

Rose loved sitting here in the warmth of the day, listening to the sweet, melodious songs of birds serenading her. With each breath she inhaled, the fragrance of the roses greeted her. How long ago she wasn't certain, but she was pretty sure it was Reevus who was responsible for planting every rose bush so many years ago. Rose paused while she enjoyed the moment. She remembered the comforting feeling of the sand as it ran between her toes on the shore of The Great Lake, one of the many fond memories of days gone by, but memories firmly etched in her mind.

Rose often wondered how long she had been tending the herd. Looking out over the meadows allowed her mind to be filled with the pleasant memories before the attack. Slowly they formed another picture of a perfect day on Kalamar. There were many things that had seemed rather odd and out of place too many before it happened. She vividly recalled how some of the farmers spoke repeatedly of the numerous strange travelers that had appeared. No one knew who they were or where they came from, but they showed up unannounced across the land. What struck the farmers as so odd was that they appeared precisely at harvest time. Rose remembered hearing more than once how the strangers bought up all the crops, paying an outlandish fee for the grain and anything else they could buy. After they had completed their transactions and bought whatever they could, they quickly moved on to another location. Everywhere they appeared, things began to change as soon as they had departed. First, all the fishermen's boats started returning with empty nets. Time and time again, the fishermen journeyed out onto the lake, but when they came back from their journey, the results didn't change…empty nets and saddened faces. Next, the birds that filled the air were gone. It wasn't that they had quit singing…rather they were gone. They had completely vanished. It was as if they had never existed. First the fish, then the birds, both inexplicably gone. It begged everyone to ask what would happen next. A great silence had fallen across the land without the cheerful songs of the birds filling the air. It was a very eerie silence without their songs. Not a soul was aware or knew that what they had already experienced was only the beginning of a dreadful change for The Third Plane of Kalamar.

Rose considered herself to be one of the lucky few. She still didn't understand why she was chosen out of so many. Tears welled up in her eyes as she thought of all of lives that were lost.

Again, she wondered, asking out loud, "Me, why me? Why was I chosen, out of all those available to be moved here and allowed to live?"

The tears cascaded freely down her cheeks. Rose struggled with her thoughts, unable to figure out why, why her. The memory served as a constant reminder of someone special.

As Rose looked off in the distance, her mind tugged at her memories of so long ago. She allowed her mind to be filled with memories of her days of Kalamar before she had been chosen to be here. While she found comfort in where she was, she had no idea where "here" was. Her thoughts were broken when she heard her name being called, someone shouting for her to come quickly, to run. She didn't understand why, but Rose ran as fast as her feet could carry her. How far she ran she didn't know before she stopped and slowly turned to look over her shoulder.

Wow, how did I do that? Rose wondered. She was shocked to look at the long path behind her and the distance she had traveled. It was a very long path that led from whence she had come to where she is now, from there to here. After gazing far in the distance, she paused briefly and closed her eyes. *How was it possible I covered such a vast distance in so little time*? she thought. Rose took a few deep breaths to calm herself, then opened her eyes and she saw her Companion for the first time.

Shocked, Rose softly whispered "Where did you come from? You weren't there a moment ago. It was like you appeared out of thin air." After speaking, Rose slowly lowered her head in respect for an elder. Before she could say another word, she heard a soft soothing voice of comfort.

"I know it is difficult for you to understand, Rose. I could not save everyone," her Companion said. "On that day, at that time, you were the one that I chose. Take heart, my dear child: things are not always as they appear."

Her Companion wrapped her right arm firmly around Rose. As soon as her hand touched Rose's shoulder, the Companion shared the vision of that fateful day. Together they both experienced the vision of giant fireballs plummeting from the sky all over Kalamar's Third Plane. Everything the fireballs touched instantly burned, turning the land a charred black. The Companion slid her arm down from around Rose's shoulders, clasping her hand in hers.

"I am so sorry, Rose. So much was lost then, but yet even in loss we have so much to gain. You must always remember things are not as they seem," the Companion said.

Together they watched in silence as a dark cloud began to hover over all the Third Plane, shrouding it in darkness. Far off in the distance, they both watched in horror as the jasper walls of the Great City of Kalamar were repeatedly battered by large stones and fireballs. Rose looked on intently as she watched the jasper walls crumbling from the assault, exposing The Great City. To her horror, she watched as The Great City became engulfed in flames. Even as the flames roared and consumed many of the buildings, the remaining walls of the city stood strong, repelling the assault. Even with vast portions of the wall and the city severely damage, they refused to fall or burn. Rose and the Companion stared in amazement as the city slowly faded from view, obscured by the smoke. While the city faded from view, they detected a strange mist that had started climbing up from The Great Lake. They watched in amazement as the mist rose from the lake, completely engulfing and obscuring The Great City, keeping it hidden from view.

Rose had been mesmerized by what she saw and continued to stare without blinking. She didn't notice the slight movement of her Companion's hand. Rose followed the new direction and looked at the vision of the Great Meeting Place where the Sisters of the Mist once stood. Unending and unrelenting, giant balls of fire had rained down from above. It appeared that a magic word or incantation had to have been spoken when a huge ball of fire landed directly on each of the four Sisters. It appeared the Sisters were gone, but were they? Had all four been consumed by the fireballs? As Rose watched, she noticed a mist rising from where the Sisters had stood and from The Great Lake. The mist had appeared right after the fireballs started landing and now had started creeping across and covering the land. Rose watched the mist as it moved. Never once did it rise higher than her waist above the ground. As the mist moved, it covered all the land, moving at its own pace. Rose noticed that around the base of The Great City, the mist started to climb until it had completely shrouded the city, obscuring it from view, joining the mist of The Great Lake.

Pulling her hand free, Rose turned and took some time to look at the one who had rescued her before she started peppering her with question after question.

"What happens to me?

"What do I do now?

"What about my family, my friends?

"Where are they?"

"All could not be saved, Rose," the Companion said. "Come, let us turn our back on what was, and what we cannot control, and prepare for what is yet to come."

Rose turned with her Companion as they began to move. Rose could sense she was moving, but there was something very different about how. She knew they were not walking, yet they were moving. She did not struggle to understand or know what it was, nor could she explain it. In the blink of an eye, they were here. Exactly where "here" was, and/or is, Rose did not know, but knew it was exactly where they were supposed to be. It reminded her of the peaceful, serene, warm sandy beaches and crystal-clear water that was destroyed on Kalamar.

"What is it that I am to do here? It reminds me so much of The Great City of Kalamar, but I know it can't be because I just watched it being destroyed." Another tear slowly fell down Rose's cheek as the reality of the situation sank in.

Stuttering, barely able to speak, Rose timidly asked, "Who…who...who are you?"

The Companion smiled warmly as she stretched her arms out from her side as a welcoming gesture. Rose could see the long golden locks of her hair as it flowed down the small of her back. "I am known by many names, but tell me…who do you think that I am? For it is not important who I am, but rather *what*…and that you believe. You do believe, don't you, Rose?" Pausing, she stopped and laughed lightly. "Yes, I know you do, my child. So, tell me, what would your answer be if I said Cna, Dorlie?"

"Oh my, all know the story, the flying horse Pegasus, Dorlie, and the unicorn, Cna."

Rose immediately paused with her response as she remembered, only a few moments ago, the vicious attack on Kalamar.

Screaming, "No no…it can't be! Please tell me they did not perish in the great fire, too."

Unable to control herself, Rose dropped to her knees, tears flowing freely down her cheeks. Without anything to stop them, they dropped silently to the ground. Her green eyes puffed up as the reality of the events struck her. The tears still flowed down her cheeks unending and unrelenting as Rose composed herself long enough to ask. "Please, tell me, please…are they gone?" Rose sobbed uncontrollably now, knowing the pain of the loss of family and friends that stabbed deep within her very soul.

The Companion could sense how intense the situation had become. She took a step backward before she turned her head, took a long deep breath, and turned back to face Rose.

"Rose, do you remember what I told you earlier?" the Companion asked.

Still sobbing, Rose stammered, "I…I…I'm not sure."

"Things are not as they appear. Today, our great planet has been attacked by the Lord of Darkness, Zorleg. First, he emptied our great ocean and seas, and then he took the birds. Finally, it was the children. Like you, those who had not reached the age of servitude, I was able to rescue. They have been placed where they are safe. Sadly, on this day, to all of those who could not see and believe, both Dorlie and Cna are no more. They, too, were victims of the attack. But to those who see and believe, both have been placed here, hidden in time."

Upon hearing this dreadful news, Rose immediately began wailing in pain as she cried uncontrollably. After a moment, she felt the firm hand of her protector on her shoulder followed by warmth as it filled her entire body. The tears quickly dried, the racing of her heart subsided as she experienced an inner peace that began to grow and encompass her entire body. Standing, Rose looked towards her new friend, the Companion.

"Thank you. I don't understand what has happened but thank you. I've never felt such peace."

"My dear Rose, that which was given to me, I now have passed on to you. Today was a day of great loss but also a day of the new beginning. All believe both the unicorn and Pegasus, the flying horse, are gone. But here, you will watch over a new creation. The wings of one, the horn on the other…now together as one majestic animal…the Krazac. As it has been written, 'For I tell you to remember these words…*it is not who, but what*. The Krazac will return. When they come, He will be with them…The Chosen One, stepping out of time to return, to return to break the darkness that holds The Third Plane in its grip.'

"It is here that you will watch over the herd. They will produce many offspring and grow great in number. When it is time, he will call them to rebuild the city, and you will be their guide. At your direction, my child, you and the mighty Krazac will haul the resources needed from here to The Great City so it can be rebuilt."

Rose looked on, uncertain of what to ask. "How?"

A smile crept over her face as Rose realized the answer to her own question. "When it is time, then it will be revealed to me. That which is needed shall be given to me when it is needed. When it is not needed, it shall be locked away in time."

Rose closed her eyes before she took one deep breath, then another, as she calmed herself. When she opened her eyes, she was back in her place in time, overlooking the lush meadow. As far as her eyes could see, the Krazac grazed, wings tucked in against the massive bodies, magical horns shimmering in the bright sunlight. She remembered before how both were a brilliant white, but now, combined, they were black, black as the darkest night. She also knew they were larger, much larger than before they were joined to be one, a new creation.

Rose wondered aloud, "How long has the herd grown?"

Rose answered her own question…" A number too large to count."

Rose wondered how many of the Krazac would protect The Great City, hidden by the mist.

Smiling inwardly, her green eyes and auburn locks glowed brightly as the suns kissed her. Her hand gently caressed her flowing locks as she inhaled and exhaled repeatedly, enjoying the fresh fragrance of the roses. For now, she waits with the magnificent herd. Waiting to be called by the One Who Is. Then the mighty steeds will fill the heavens with the army of The Chosen for the Battle of Battles.

Nafari – Invading Benny's Mind

Nafari stood in the corner of Benny's bedroom, right next to the dresser. Dressed in her flowing black gown, her black hair flowing down her back, you wouldn't see her unless you looked directly at her. She had found Benny in a deep and peaceful dream on her first visit.

"Exactly as you should, child, sleep. From this time forward, it belongs to me." Nafari watched Benny, hearing his deep breathing.

He slept peacefully as she moved around his bed, but Cosmo was another story.

"You!" she exclaimed, pointing her bony finger at Cosmo. "He may not know, but I know what you are!"

She cursed when Cosmo started to bark. For now, the only way she had to silence him was to leave. His presence would make it much more difficult for her to do what she needed to do. Not impossible, but more difficult.

"It is not by accident you are here, my four-legged friend. I have my ways of dealing with you." Nafari knew his presence, his being with the boy, was intentional. Nafari was aware he was the perfect alarm for Benny anytime he was approached by someone from The Third Plane of Kalamar that had anything to do with Zorleg.

"Yes, you are a problem, my problem, but I will deal with you as I need to. Your presence will not stop me from filling his mind with torment and fear." Nafari had moved closer to the bedside, looking down at both Cosmo and Benny.

How long she stood there was no concern to her. She wouldn't let a small dog stop her from invading Benny's mind. She had been tasked with filling his mind with unbelievable horrors.

For a child that has almost reached the age of servitude, it shouldn't be too difficult flooding your mind, Nafari thought that while she relished her power.

"You will see how proficient I have become at torturing others to get what I need. You will not be an exception." Was it a smile that spread across her lips as she looked down at Benny? Her mind flashed back to many of the villagers, even some of Zorleg's own army, upon whom she inflicted ghastly spells, disfigurement, and pure terror.

"Soon, very soon, the same torments as others have suffered will reside in your mind." Nafari chuckled internally. There were so many who said she created horror, unspeakable dread wherever called upon.

"It will be an easy task when I return. I will enjoy filling your mind with things you could never imagine."

"I am not just a witch, Child!" Nafari paused for emphasis, her voice as cold as ice. "I am his witch!" Again, she paused to allow her words to sink in. "I am the Witch of Darkness!" Her final words cast deep into his mind; Nafari gave her words of self-proclamation time to embed themselves deep within Benny's mind.

"My powers have been honed over the years on subjects great and small. Because of what I have done and my expertise, I have risen to become the most powerful and feared witch under Zorleg." After her final words, she contemplated what her actions would be, while lost deep in thought.

She didn't remember when it happened; all she cared about remembering was that it happened. Zorleg had shared one of his darkest, most closely guarded secrets with her, his creation of dark matter. "It truly has significant power, doesn't it?" Nafari had asked after he had revealed it to her.

Even though it was only a brief moment, Nafari felt she understood the power of dark matter far better than Zorleg ever would.

"Your Lordship, with your permission, I would be honored if you would allow me to add the power of dark matter to my tools." She knew he wouldn't refuse or ask questions. It had served her greatly, far beyond her wildest dreams.

But for now, she needed to prepare herself for the tormenting and harassing of Benny. She would proceed slowly over time, terrifying him more with each visit. She was also determined to take care of that wretched dog and its ability to warn Benny of her presence, too.

On her next visit, Nafari stood silently and observed, watching Benny as he slept. She knew Cosmo would be a major problem, and she hadn't figured out what she needed to do to quiet him yet, but she would.

"Go ahead and bark, my four-legged friend. I will deal with you in time." Nafari pointed her left index finger at Cosmo. "For now, I shall allow your barking to continue." Nafari reached out and touched Benny's mind for the first time.

"Yes, you sense my presence, don't you, Child? I am in no hurry." Nafari stood motionless in Benny's room, next to the dresser. "Yes, I will go slowly, Child, gradually increasing my disturbances in your mind. Fear you shall see and feel every time I visit."

Many things ran through Nafari's mind as she stared at Benny lying in bed. "Yes, unspeakable fear to make you cower when you are awake. Maybe I'll use a spider, perhaps a rat, or darkness itself."

Her list could go on and on, describing all tools of her trade to instill and stoke the fear in young Benny. She would repeat her visits to him while he slept. With the darkness and stillness in his bedroom, Nafari slipped deeper into his mind.

"Here, my child, something to grow while I'm not visiting. Nothing serves me better than planting my seeds of doubt, fear, and uncertainty. You will find, young child, it will become like nothing you've experienced before." Nafari wondered how many times he would wake from his deep sleep screaming and crying in fear.

"Nightmare, hah!" Nafari chuckled as she spoke to Benjamin. "Yes, to you it was a nightmare, but it was my nightmare! One that was created specifically for you, and I shall play it over and over and over again."

Nafari determined this night would be different.

After she entered the room, she cast a simple spell she had created to take care of Cosmo and his barking.

Her hands moved in a circle as she rolled them in front of her. When she opened her hands, a short flash appeared. "Silence," was all she said as the flash struck Cosmo. She knew it wouldn't harm him and would be gone when she left. For now, in the stillness of Benny's room, she was ready to begin her work.

Holding out first her left arm, curling her fingers in a beckoning motion, she called out to Benny.

"Come. Come to me."

She dropped her left arm and repeated the same calling with her right, her fingers curling back towards her.

"Come. Come to me."

Nafari had invaded Benny's sleep, deeply embedding herself into his mind, walking around freely. For the first time she allowed him to see her…her face, her flowing black dress and long black hair, the wickedness in her laugh piercing the stillness in his room. From within the deepest recesses of his mind, she started calling again. With her right arm outstretched, her long bony finger pointed directly at Benny, he heard her calling.

"Come, my child. Come to me." As she spoke, a red mist spread from her lips and began to fill the room with a reddish fog.

Benny woke with a start and remained frozen in bed. His heart pounded, but he held his eyes tightly closed, afraid to open them, clutching Cosmo in his arms. *How many times have I had this dream?* He wondered silently as he stroked Cosmo. He thought there were many nights where Cosmo woke him from a deep sleep, barking at something he hadn't heard, but for some reason he hadn't heard Cosmo barking at night for a long time.

Slowly, carefully, Benny opened one eye slightly and peered around his room before opening the other. It appeared everything was exactly as it should be, but it didn't feel right. Taking a deep breath, he slowly gathered all his courage before he released Cosmo and slipped out of bed.

"Cosmo, was that a dream? Did it frighten you too? My throat is parched! I need to get something to drink. You wanna come with me?"

Benny's heart pounded as he walked down the stairs, hoping it was all a dream. Cosmo followed close behind as they headed down the stairs. Benny walked into the kitchen, grabbed a glass from the cupboard, then opened the refrigerator. Cosmo sat, staring at Benny, watching him pour himself a cold glass of water.

"Would you like some too, Buddy? Did you have the same bad dream? I don't know about you, but I sure am getting tired of the same dream." Benny reached down and scratched Cosmo behind the ears. There was no rush to return to his bedroom, so Benny took a seat at the kitchen table. After a few minutes, he decided to head back to bed, filling his glass up before he did. With slow, steady steps, he started his return to his bedroom, his heart still pounding. He was curious to see how much attention Cosmo was paying while they walked back to his bedroom. Benny would stop, look down to see if Cosmo also stopped. Every time he tried, it was the same result. Cosmo mimicked his every move.

After they had returned to his bedroom, he held his cold glass of water in his hand until he carefully set the glass on his nightstand.

Benny turned his head and gazed out the window. His mind churned as he tried to remember what he was told.

"Cosmo, can you help me remember? How many times or years has that same witch appeared in my dreams? You know it, too, don't you, Boy? Every time she stood in the exact same spot, too." He shuddered with the thought as he remembered. Her words never changed. She always recited the same words over and over, coaxing him to come to her. But why, why did she want him? Even Cosmo shivered as the thoughts of her presence filled his mind.

Benny picked up the glass and took another sip of water, then placed it back on the nightstand. His mind was filled with many thoughts as it raced, as he again tried to remember.

Benny looked again at Cosmo. "What was it the Old One said? Rub the stone and repeat, "Dreams are not forgotten?' What came after that? What was the rest of it?" Rubbing his head with his hands, Benny tried to recall the whole phrase. Time seemed to stand still; thoughts of what The Guardian told him slowly began to return, slowly filling his mind of that moment years ago. One word at a time they drifted back to him, one, then another, until finally he softly whispered:

"***Dreams don't last forever, but dreams are not forgotten.***"

Benny reached down and picked up the jasper stone from his nightstand. He held it firmly in his right hand, paused and wondered what he was supposed to do next. For the first time, he looked down at the stone and began to examine it. In the darkness he wondered who she was as he looked at the stone.

Benny asked himself, "Do I rub the stone? Do I just hold it and say the words?" He thought back to when the Guardian had given the stone to him. Benny wished now he had asked for more specific instructions on what or how he was supposed to call him. But that was so many years ago. What was he, five? He doubted he would remember what he was told at that age anyway. He really wasn't sure why he was remembering it so vividly now.

Cosmo let out a small yap, coaching Benny on what he should do. Benny held the stone in his hand and spoke softly into the darkness.

"Dreams don't last forever, but dreams are not forgotten."

After he spoke the words, he waited. Nothing. He waited longer. Still nothing. He let out one sigh, then another. Cosmo seemed to know beforehand nothing was going to happen and now lay fast asleep on his pillow. Time appeared to have stopped for Benny. He continued to wait, not knowing what he should do or how long he should wait. Finally, feeling very foolish, he placed the stone on the windowsill, not the nightstand, and slid back into bed. As soon as he laid his head on his pillow, the room filled with a light blue. Startled, Benny didn't know what to think or do. Thinking it was another nightmare, he was immediately overcome by fear. He grabbed Cosmo and timidly slipped down further in his bed, pulling the covers over his head to hide. He clutched Cosmo tightly, hugging him close for comfort.

From his hiding spot under the covers, he heard the soft comforting voice of The Guardian.

"Thank you, my child. I see you have finally seen a need to call me?" The Guardian stood at the foot of the bed, his words comforting

Benny's ears. Benny's head popped sheepishly from under the covers, followed by Cosmo.

"Tell me, how can I help you, my child?" The Guardian quietly and calmly asked. He reached out his hand and called Cosmo, "Come On, Boy, it's been a long time, hasn't it? Yes, I know you've helped a lot."

Benny retold his story of the recurring nightmare, as far back as he could remember, to The Guardian.

"She is hideous. She appears dressed in black, with long, pitch-black hair flowing down her back, with black eyes and pale skin." Describing her to The Guardian, Benny felt the fear and torment well up in his body as he described her and the recurring dream.

"In every dream she pointed her bony finger directly at me. Every time!" Benny described how her finger felt so close to his face before she filled the room with a red mist. He shook in fear from simply retelling the story.

Benny took a deep breath to calm himself, looked up at The Guardian and asked sheepishly, "Am I being a big scaredy cat? I'm almost twelve, I really shouldn't be afraid of a dream, should I? But it bothers me a lot because I've had the same dream for so long. The things I saw and felt still scared me and made me shake and tremble. Sometimes I thought Cosmo was barking, like he was sounding a warning, but then he stopped. I thought it was all part of the dream, I guess."

The Guardian moved and took a seat at the foot of the bed. He smiled and motioned for Benny to come and sit. The Guardian did not say a word until after Benny was seated next to him. Silently, he reached out and touched Benny on his forehead with his right index finger, right between his eyes. The touch was very brief, only for a moment. After he removed his finger, The Guardian placed his arm by his side.

There was something very special about the touch from The Guardian. Barely above a whisper, he said, "When it is needed, then it will be given."

Turning, he looked at Benny, then continued. "Benny, you now have the power within you to tell your uninvited visitor she will no longer invade your dreams nor ever bother you again. What you weren't aware of was how simple it would be. Tell me, has she always stood in the same place in your room when she invaded your dreams?"

Benny nodded as Cosmo curled up between them. "Yeah," he said, his arm outstretched as he pointed across the room before lowering his arm and petting Cosmo. "She always stood in the corner between those two windows and next to the dresser."

The Guardian stood up and walked over, standing next to the dresser Benny had pointed at. "Have you noticed anything different or new on the dresser since this dream started?"

Benny paused to think, "Well, nothing has changed since it was moved into my room years ago. There was that old glass inkwell filled with ink. I don't know where it came from, but they came together. Maybe the dreams started after the dresser was moved into that corner and the inkwell placed on top of it!"

The Guardian looked at Benny. He intentionally paused before he spoke firmly, giving him words of wisdom. "Here is what I want you to do the next time the witch visits you and you have the same dream again. I want you to bravely slip out of bed, walk over to the dresser, pick up the inkwell and give it to her. Look directly at her, and call her by her name, Nafari. She has been sent to torment you in your dreams. For now, it is not important that you understand who sent her or why. After you hand her the inkwell, here are the words I need you to speak to her: 'I am no longer afraid of you, witch. You have no power over me.

Get behind me, now!' Then reach up and place your right index finger on her forehead, just like I did to you. After you do these things, I don't think you'll be troubled by her in your dreams, or ever again."

"I don't understand. That's it? I only need to say a few words and a simple touch?" Benny asked questioningly.

The Guardian patted Benny gently on his head. "Now, back to bed, Young Lad! All you have to do is believe."

Benny didn't know how long it had been before the dream returned. It could have been days, weeks, months. It really didn't matter. What he was certain of was, when the witch finally reappeared in his dreams, there was no mistake in his mind that she had returned. Exactly as each time before, her bony finger pointed directly at him, her black hair cascading down her shoulders, flowing down over her black dress.

Nafari called out his name, continuing her haunting while he slept. Benny wondered to himself as he listened to her call, *Should I continue to let this witch, Nafari, haunt my dreams? Or should I do as The Guardian instructed me and stop her?* Cosmo nudged him as if to give him the courage to do what The Guardian had instructed him to do. "Well, enough is enough!"

Benny threw the covers back, jumped out of bed, and walked over to stand directly in front of the witch. Reaching down, he picked up the inkwell off the dresser top, exactly as The Guardian had told him. With the inkwell in his hand, he turned and looked directly at the witch. With courage, he said, "I know who you are, Nafari. You are the Witch of Darkness. Tonight, it stops." Raising his voice, Benny continued, "GET BEHIND ME, NAFARI…NOW! You shall haunt my dreams no longer. For as it is written in The Seven of Sevens, so it shall be!"

As he spoke, his voice reverberated through the room like the sound of thunder. Benny wondered if he was still dreaming - or did his voice actually shake the entire house? Benny questioned where his words came from. Why did it seem like his voice was so loud? It did, however, get the witch Nafari's attention.

Benny continued to speak to Nafari, emboldened by The Guardian's words. "For as I say, your look of wickedness shall be no more. Gone shall be the evil that has lived within you, your deformity, gone, too, the wickedness, and your hideous features that have bound you to him. I cannot change what you have done, but I can change you. For as you once were Nafari, so shall you be once again. From this moment on, and forevermore, changed. Look into your secret place, deep within the recesses of your heart, and there you will find me. This day, your secret room has been unlocked by the only one who has your key."

Benny reached up and placed his finger on Nafari's forehead, just above her nose and right between her eyes. Confidently he spoke the words given to him.

"Be no more, you are free! As you were, so you are now. The One of Ones has made it so." Benny didn't understand where his words came from, but knew they were exactly the correct words for that specific moment in time.

A loud shriek from Nafari broke the silence and filled every corner of the room. *Am I the only one to hear it?* he wondered. The crying, the pain, and the agony Nafari exhibited washed over him, and then suddenly she was gone. Benny stood motionless for a few moments before he slipped back into bed, Cosmo curling up next to him. He enjoyed the most restful night of sleep he'd had in a long time. When he awoke in the morning, he wondered if it was all part of his dream or if it actually happened. Benny looked over at the dresser and noticed the inkwell was gone, leaving no doubt in his mind it was both a dream and real.

Part 6

The Creation of The Seven Stones

There was never a date written, or at least a parchment has never been found, to place the exact date and place in time. The story, acutely familiar to everyone, makes the date of *when* rather meaningless. It happened on the grounds of The Great Meeting Place. All eagerly recited the story over and over again.

"On the day chosen by The One of Ones, He spoke worlds into existence from His place between The Seven Stones of Kalamar. This is the exact spot The One of Ones chose, the place where it all began. He made this the very center of The Seven Planes of Time of Kalamar. The One of Ones named this very special place, The Great Meeting Place. The existence of all planes has remained a mystery to all but a very select few. To Him, the Third Plane was special. It was here He decided the Great Storytellers would call home. What the majority failed to realize was that they were more, much more, than just plain old storytellers. It is true they painted vivid images with their words in the minds of those who heard. But there was more to what they told. The storytellers told of what was, what is and of things that are yet to come. The majority had chosen to ignore the stories, happy their children were occupied with them, which left them alone to enjoy conversations with family and friends after a delicious meal at the inn. Some who sat within the audience of the storytellers listened intently and believed. Likewise, there were others who scoffed and ignored the stories and the warnings some contained. Regardless of the stories they chose to believe, the stories were told time and again. The greatest storyteller of them all,

Reevus, had captured the ears of many and pulled them in by the crafty weaving of his words.

"The One of Ones chose the number seven as His number of perfection, for He has always been perfection. When you looked at The Great Meeting Place, The Seven Stones appeared to be quite distinctive. Every stone had a different shape but was blemish free, the stones perfectly made by His hands and completely smooth. The One of Ones placed each stone exactly where He deemed necessary. Each stone represented a different plane of Kalamar, perhaps, as some have speculated, even a different place and time. They have been perfectly aligned for a reason known only to a few. There have been stories of some who have tried to travel between the planes, but the travel was a closely guarded secret known only to the ones He chose.

"Other than The Great Fleet of Kalamar, few have been given the gift of moving freely between the planes. No one had actually watched, or saw, when The Great Fleet of Kalamar sent its packed fleets, heavily loaded with harvested crops, to other planes. Once The Great Fleet had sailed over the horizon and out of sight, they magically disappeared and moved to another plane before returning empty, ready to be loaded again.

"The Seven Stones at the Great Meeting Place have been forever guarded by the Sisters of the Mist, called by name from the beginning of time by the One who created time. Each of the Sisters are known by secret names: Love, Faith, Belief and Hope. Together, they are known as the Sisters of the Mist, or the Guardians of the Great Meeting Place of The Third Plane of Kalamar. Regardless of the name they have been called, they are one and the same. Why they are referred to as 'The Sisters of the Mist' remains another mystery. Some believe the name came not from What Was or What is, but from What Is to Come. For on Kalamar, there was no such thing as a mist. Their place of origin was another of the mysteries surrounding the Four Guardians. It is believed by some that when He created The Great Meeting Place, they, too, were created. A question flowing from that thought was: Were they always with Him? It is known to all what each represents.

"Hope…for she brings forth Courage. Courage for all of those who are and those who are yet to be.

"Faith…forever untouched to all who have come to the Great Meeting Place. Honor is placed into the hearts of those who stand to protect the secrets.

"Belief…all of those gathered are here to protect this sacred ground. Great is the patriotism of all who support and believe in the magic of Kalamar.

"Love…the gift of Sacrifice they will give to one and all."

There were two questions that continued to resurface. *Are the guardians supposed to be from the past, the present or the future? Why is it that on any cool evening, with the naked eye, you can see a mist rise from the Great Lake of Kalamar?* It was told the mist moved from the Great Lake and surrounded the Seven Stones and the Guardians. This mythical mist rose nighty and covered the Great Meeting Place. Reflecting the moonlight, the Four Sisters were highlighted and illuminated as they appeared to be standing guard.

Each of the Sisters was adorned with a special wreath. Those who have seen them describe each to be dressed like a warrior ready for battle. Aye, ready they stand! Hope with a helmet, Faith with a wreath, Belief with a civic crown and Love with a winged star. Oh, but the size of the Four Sisters is beyond measure, rising to over seven feet tall! The swords they yield appeared quite menacing, with blades longer, wider, and greater than any spear or sword. However, as the story is told, they come not to fight but stand to protect. The Sisters were the keepers of the

Secrets of Time and the Seven Planes of Kalamar. Erect they stood, awaiting the call from the One Who Has Walked Through Time. *For when they are called, they stand at the ready to come to His aid. And yet we find a question that leads us to ask another question. Who walks through time?*

There have been many who have observed the Sisters standing guard. They stood like the points on a compass; each pointed in a different direction…to the north, south, east, and west. Over time, many questions surrounded the mystery and magic of the Four Sisters, questions never answered or resolved.

Why are there only Four Sisters when there are Seven Stones?

Were they, in fact, Sisters at all?

To answer these questions, the scholars had pondered and researched far and wide, using all resources that had been made available to them. One answer repeated most frequently came from many, if not all, of the scholars. The remaining stones that sat upon the Great Meeting Place, it was said, are for the One Who Was, the One Who Is, and the One Who Is Yet To Come. One appeared to be the constant, but it is also where the great story began to diverge with more questions asked.

Who are the three?

Are the three one and the same?

Are they the Chosen Ones mentioned by the Seven of Sevens?

Question begat question – with nothing positive presented as an answer, the door of speculation had been kicked wide open. *The One Who Was, Who Is and Yet To Come…what will the meaning of the trilogy of questions be?*

The Cave of Keys

Looking out through the stone archway, the Seer smiled as the stars twinkled, illuminating the darkness slightly. He inhaled casually before taking a deep breath. He enjoyed the cool air as it filled his lungs before he exhaled. Quietly sitting beside his feet were two small puppies, heads cocked to the side as they gazed at the stars with him. Nonchalantly, the Seer bent down until he rested on one knee, his pure-white robe flowing effortlessly across the stone floor. He reached out with his right hand and caressed each of his four-legged friends gently before grabbing them both under their bellies and lifting them as he stood. Turning his head from one to another, he spoke to each puppy as though they understood every word. Both puppies cocked their heads from side to side, licking his hand, letting out a soft yelp.

"Look, my four-legged friends, see how the stars have aligned?" The Seer chuckled as he continued, both hands full of puppies as he lifted his hands slightly upward. "And you, Young Lady, can you see it, too?" The Seer scratched Sophie's head lightly, kissed each puppy's head, then lowered them back to the floor.

"Yes, my little friends, it is time now for our work to begin. Our visitor will arrive shortly. Among the four of us, we shall discuss events that have occurred, those that will occur and what we can do to help those that have yet to occur. I do not know if our discussion will be vague or very in depth. I never know what depth our conversation could go. Be that as it may, little ones, the time is now at hand."

The Seer turned his back to the archway and walked into the darkness of the cave. With each step first one puppy, then the other, continued to lovingly lick his hand until he reached his stone chair. The Seer stopped, turned, and slowly lowered himself into his chair. After he had securely seated himself, he reached over the armrest, carefully placing both puppies on the floor. Both of them moved instinctively to an overstuffed pillow, climbed on, and curled up next to each other.

In front of the Seer appeared to be a giant window suspended in midair. The Seer raised his right hand, reaching into the air that separated him and the display. Methodically, he moved his fingers back and forth. The Seer waved his hands, his fingers slicing through the air but never touching the display. The images moved slowly at first and then began to move faster as they kept pace with the movements of his fingers. He continued until he heard one of the puppies give a small bark. The Seer turned his head and looked down, then smiled. The puppy's head moved from side to side as she excitedly wagged her tail. Their eyes met as they looked at one another before he continued.

"You are very observant, little one. This is exactly what we needed to see. Now we wait for The Guardian. It won't be much longer."

Sitting upright in the saddle, his cloak firmly secured around his neck, the Guardian sat comfortably on Cna's back as they traveled. Beside them, galloping in stride with them, each hoof landing silently in the air, was Dorlie, the unicorn. Traversing the heavens, they were protected by Dorlie's magic bubble that surrounded them as they traveled.

With each beat of Cna's mighty wings, they moved faster through time. Only a slight touch to either the right or left side of Cna's neck changed the direction of their flight. In the distance, The Guardian could see the Seven Stars twinkling brightly before them. He chuckled to himself. He was amazed at how easy it was to find his way back to the Seer's home again. For longer than he could remember, the Seer had been hidden here, in a time and place of His choosing.

The Guardian paused for a moment to remember one of the teachings from the Old Ways. He repeated the ancient words that were shared with him long ago. He spoke the words softly and clearly.

"Things are not always as they seem."

After his words left his lips, the star's intensity around them grew. In the distance, his path had now been specifically illuminated for his arrival. What started as a very tiny speck and appeared to be nothing more than pebble floating in the great expanse of space was their destination, the home of the Seer. Effortlessly, silently, they closed the distance toward the rock.

The Guardian's eyes caught the very faint blinking of a small blue light. Patting Cna on her neck, he leaned forward to reassure her.

"Almost missed that one, didn't we, friend?"

His eyes now fixed on the blinking blue light, he guided Cna in her turns with a slight pressure from his knees on either her right or left side. A few short moments later the three found themselves in front of the Three Moons. They sat like orbs, one above, one to the left, and one to the right of the blue light. When all three moons came into full view, they outlined the Seer's pathway in the stars. The transition from their travel to their destination was now almost complete. Again, The Guardian repeated the ancient words out loud, "***Things are not always as they seem.***"

The Guardian's hand caressed Cna's neck again, her movements following his instructions, turning when needed until they arrived at the pathway. Without a sound, the travelers softly set down and began to follow the illuminated path. After several steps, The Guardian slipped off Cna, with Dorlie alongside him, walking with the majestic steeds beside him.

How many steps they walked was uncertain. A few? Many? It mattered not. Now they stood before a large opening and a flight of stairs carved out of stone. The Guardian caressed his friends on their necks, softly whispered a few words in their ears, then turned and approached the steps. Both horses knelt, one on each side of the steps, as they awaited his return. Giving them one final gesture, The Guardian waved, turned, and continued his walk up the steps into the darkness. With each stride, the steps illuminated a soft light on each side of the stairway to guide his movement along the darkened path. After he passed underneath the archway at the top of the stairs, he entered a vast open room. In the middle of the room sat the Seer, raised several steps above the rest of the floor, and his two little helpers still resting comfortably on their pillow. The Guardian approached the center of the room, before stopping at the bottom step. The Seer stood to greet him.

"Welcome, my friend, come, sit. We have much to discuss," the Seer said as he motioned for The Guardian to join him. The Seer turned to his left, waved his hand and another chair instantly appeared directly across from his. He gestured with his hand in the air, as if to guide The Guardian to his seat.

The Guardian moved up the stairs and sat down across from the Seer. Their eyes were at the same level as when they started the long-awaited conversation.

"Was your trip an easy one, my friend?" the Seer asked.

"Effortless." The Guardian beamed. "How true the saying, 'Things are not always as they seem.' On the outside, this really does look like it is nothing more than a giant rock floating in space. As soon as I saw the beacon, things began to change. Truth be told…I just about missed the beacon. But after that, it was simple to follow and allow it to guide us along the path. The moons appeared from behind the cloak of hiding when, and not before, they should have, revealing our pathway in the stars. Everything was exactly as written in the Seven of Sevens and taught to us in the Old Ways." The Guardian paused and looked at the Seer as they both chuckled for a moment or two.

When the laughter had subsided, they both gazed at the other and smiled. The Seer spoke first. "Yes, I don't have many visitors, but at the same time I have many guests." His hand lifted into the air and moved around the room, the room becoming illuminated in the same blue hue that guided the Guardian. As the Seer's hand moved around, he pointed to hallway after hallway. "Within each hallway reside many rooms. Within each room are many keys." The Seer fell silent and bowed his head reverently, a tear slowly trickling down his cheek.

The Guardian slipped from his chair, took a couple of steps, and placed his hand on the shoulder of the Seer.

"It is difficult to think of those who lost their souls to Zorleg. It is, perhaps, the most difficult part of our job for all of us."

The Guardian began to list those responsible.

"The Three of Threes, The Seven of Sevens, The Chosen…all of us to bring back all that we can. From the darkness Zorleg has imprisoned them and uses them for his dark and evil purpose."

The Guardian took a much-needed pause before he continued.

"The dark matter and Zorleg have created such evil, removing all the light that caresses and blesses the Third Plane. Our job is to restore the light Zorleg snuffed when he stole their souls. It is important that we remember our great storytellers were more than storytellers; they were our friends."

The Seer turned his head to the side and wiped his tears away. He stood and moved across the room to position himself in front of the giant display. "It was only by pure luck that Zorleg found this place. Or perhaps it was not luck at all; someone may have guided him here. However, even once is once too often. Here, hidden in time, my location is only known by the measurable quantities to an extreme level of precision. That is why he was only able to raid the one room. Out of pure luck, he was able to find my exact location in time." The Seer's voice trembled as he continued to speak. "But they have never been able to repeat his feat because he doesn't understand the descriptive laws of physics. You and I, we have no problem with being able to repeat over and over again the measure we need, unquantifiable, to move through time, based upon laws of physics. Zorleg has never, nor will ever, understand any laws. He always has felt he's above any law. It's part of his makeup that has made him so arrogant, hostile, and self-serving. It is all about him and the capturing of souls to serve him for his purpose. Unlike the One of Ones, who is the exact opposite, always giving, caring, and loving." A soft sigh escaped the lips of the Seer.

The puppies had walked over and were nuzzling against The Guardian's legs while the Seer talked. Looking down, The Guardian smiled. "And what of these two?" he asked softly as his outstretched hand, caressed each of the puppies gently.

The Seer picked both of the puppies up, kissed them on the forehead, and smiled. "One for each of The Chosen. They are both very unique. They will not age, they will always be aware of any of Zorleg's minions, and they will be able to send out a warning should either of The Chosen need assistance. Through my looking glass, I shall always be able to see The Chosen and any dangers around them. Your task now is to deliver one to him and the other to her. As for me, I shall always be aware and watching both, as well as you."

The Guardian reached out, took both puppies in his hands, and spoke softly to them.

"Well, my little friends, it looks like when I leave, I won't be leaving alone."

The Seer rose and walked over to the giant display with The Guardian beside him. Pointing to a spot on the display, the Seer turned and looked at The Guardian. "This is where you need to go, where it all needs to begin. It will serve as a good spot to use for our purpose. Always remember, I will be watching over them and you."

Dropping his hand and turning, the Seer began to walk toward the wall lined with multiple hallways; The Guardian fell in step and walked beside him. "Come, let me show you the room of keys. While it may sound like a room, it is, in fact, rooms that began with time and never end. Contained in each room are the keys to every soul and heart created by the One of Ones. Each room has been filled: keys for those who were, those who are, and those who are yet to be. There are also rooms that were designed to contain the keys for the lost. Part of what I do now is to move them. They all began in His hand. Regardless of the why, things change and some fall under the influence of Zorleg because each has the freedom of choice. There is only one who can use the key to unlock the hidden rooms and free them from what Zorleg has done. With these keys, there is always hope that the last room within the heart of the lost will be opened. When that room is opened, all fear will be gone and the light will once again shine as they are led away from the darkness of Zorleg, back into the light of The One of Ones. On your return to the calling of Benny, you shall see the beginning of the work, the Laws of the Old ways that have come into play, and the impact it has on what is believed to be Zorleg's most powerful of witches, Nafari."

The stillness of the moment was broken by the soft whimper of one of the puppies. The Guardian reached down and picked her up. Petting her softly, The Guardian's hand ran over the head, comforting his new friend.

Looking toward the Seer, The Guardian wondered out loud, "You have special rooms here, don't you? Zorleg wanted to come here again and raid your special rooms, didn't he?" Without stopping to allow an answer, he continued, "Special rooms that allow those you have rescued to live in peace, to enjoy life again, to help and assist you. Is this not so?"

The Seer's lips parted with a small smirk before he filled the room with laughter. "Yes, my friend, within these walls and this place, *Things Really Are Not as They Appear*. But now it is time for you to leave and begin your journey. Remember, my eyes will always be watching over all of you. As you instruct Benny, let him learn on his own. Many of the teachings from the Old Ways have a life of their own and appear when needed by the Chosen."

"Guide him well, my friend. Zorleg is so overconfident in all that he does. For him, it is only one. But from The One of One flow all, first to The Three of Threes, who in turn pass it to The Seven of Sevens. Many parts are integrated and always part of The One of Ones. It is for this reason that it is so painful to Him when He loses even one soul to Zorleg. Many times, has He left the many to retrieve the one! I have been part of many of the feasts for those whom He has rejoiced over when they returned, sparing nothing to show His happiness and joy when another one of His children returned home. For The One of Ones, His work in threes leaves His mark wherever He has been. The same as He used threes, He also uses sevens. The Three Moons, the Seven Stars, you, Cna,

Dorlie. I'm sure you can see a pattern beginning to form. Sadly, Zorleg sees none of it, nor cares."

The Guardian stroked his beard. "Yes, it is true the depths that to which Zorleg will stoop. He will stop at nothing to deceive, blowing the winds of confusion and deception to cloud the mind of the unknowing. Lies, cheating, stealing, nothing is off limits to what he does. He takes great pride in being able to turn the heart and the inspiration from those that desire the warmth and love offered by The One of Ones. Zorleg's desire and his world of darkness are only for him and about him. A stark difference between the two. Perhaps this is also one of the reasons behind his hatred for the Great Storytellers. While I am not the one I used to be, I shall continue to use all my powers to help prepare those who have been entrusted to me. I may have been young once, but now I'm older and much, much smarter."

The Seer moved and stood next to The Guardian before they walked together to the opening of the chamber. Standing under the archway, the Seer pointed to the Seven Stars.

"These seven stars," his arm moved as he gestured, his fist balled with the first finger extended, "the ones that are shining the brightest, were placed exactly where they are by The One of Ones. His hands moved them to where you see them now. The position, shape, and color are all parts of the design to keep this place hidden. Created in time by Him, for His use, and to hide His children, for He created time."

The Guardian turned and looked at the Seer. Softly he asked, "But you are not hiding, are you? This is where you dwell, doing his bidding with the ability to touch all points in time. The mirror allows you to see and watch all, doesn't it?"

The Seer hugged The Guardian. "You see far beyond your years, and the last I checked, they stopped counting your years a long, long time ago. But you will see that The Chosen has been given part of my gift. It will appear when it is needed most."

Together, they both enjoyed a deep laugh as the puppies stuck their heads out of the deep pockets in The Guardian's robe. They looked down, then up at each other and chuckled.

"It looks like your travelers are ready to leave. The word shall pass quickly throughout the lands. For now, the preparation for the battle has officially started." The Seer turned and patted each puppy as he bid them farewell. We will be in touch, my little friends! And for you, my big friend, I wish you well! Remember, use the colors that fill this room and the power of the moon as you instruct your child. It shall serve you all well."

The Guardian walked through the archway, finding Cna and Dorlie waiting for him exactly where he left them. Both of the puppies secured in his pockets, he mounted on Cna's back with Dorlie falling in beside them. After a few steps, they were airborne again, Cna's powerful wings moving through the air effortlessly. The Guardian's journey officially began as he moved to another point in time. His mission: to mentor the boy while leaving her mentoring and guidance to another. *For it shall be as it is written in the book of The Seven of Sevens.*

Prepare the Way

The moonbeams danced across the stone floor, highlighting a solitary figure sitting by the fireside. Flames danced with delight, the fire crackling at each movement of his hand as though he were calling flame to dance for him. A smile of contentment spread across his face while he became lost in that moment.

A soft, timid, yet firm knock on the door broke the trance. Leisurely, he moved his large frame out of his favorite chair and walked to the door. The sound of each step echoed off the walls as he made his way from his chair by the fireplace to the front door. He reached out with his left hand and grasped the handle firmly. With his thumb, he pushed the latch down then pulled the door inward toward him. As the door opened, his face beamed with delight.

"Oh, thank you, thank you, for coming so quickly! Please, please, come in, come in," The Guardian said as he stepped aside allowing his guest to enter and then closed the door behind them. Reaching out, he grasped his visitor strongly in his arms and gave her a deep embrace. "It has been far too long, my friend. Come. Sit. I have much to tell you, and there is much to do."

Together, they walked across the floor to the fireplace and took a seat. Turning to his guest, The Guardian asked innocently, "Still enjoy three lumps of sugar in your tea? Or did I convince you that honey is so much better and dissolves so easily?" A smile spread across both of their faces as they enjoyed a brief chuckle.

“A hot cup of tea with honey would be fantastic,” she softly replied.

The Guardian looked at her as he poured her tea, the steam rising slowly above the cup. “Thank you for coming so quickly. We have much to do. If it wasn’t for you, I’m not sure I could do anything at all. While I have said ‘we,’ it is really you and your special talents. I want you to know you are free to be as creative as you wish. If we can’t have fun playing with the timeline and add our events to it unnoticed, then we must be slipping!” They both laugh at The Guardian’s joke.

“So, tell me, my dear friend, what have you in store for this journey? Anything special?” asked Wren, the oldest daughter of the Queen of the Elves, RhiAnne.

Leaning forward, drawing close, The Guardian motioned Wren to bend her ear to his lips. In a voice no more than a whisper, he said, “My friend, it has begun. Now is when I need your talents and skills the most.”

Wren looked up at The Guardian as she leisurely sipped her hot tea. “This, I believe, is what you have been telling me for some time, is it not?” Pausing, Wren smiled before she continued. “So, tell me more of what you have. I know time is short and there will be much to do.”

The Guardian took a deep breath before he leaned back in his chair. The steam from his hot cup of tea rose steadily as it drifted upward. The Guardian took a sip, then began to share his plan with Wren. “I have chosen a place very similar to Kalamar. Unlike Kalamar, it has many different climates, huge oceans, and abundant wildlife. My plan is one I think you will like. Your job will be to go back in time and begin to tell stories, planting seeds of imagination, both here on Kalamar and where I have chosen. All of your actions will be used to guide the Child.”

Setting his cup down, The Guardian paused for a moment before he continued, "I want you to create some diversions he will be able to use to his advantage. With your skills, I know you will use it so it plays on the fear, giving them something to talk about. I will send Cna and Dorlie ahead of you to add to the stories of enchantment. They will refer to Cna as Pegasus, the horse that flies. Dorlie will become known as a unicorn, one with magical powers in her horn. Now you see them, now you don't. Leaving them to wonder if they really exist. Are they really magical?"

Wren leaned forward, her eyes fixed on The Guardian's lips as he spoke, soaking in every word. As she listened, the excitement began to build in her. "And what is my part in all of this?" she calmly asked.

"Ah, this I feel is the best! With your small stature, and coming from such a strong bloodline, you shall remain as you are, the eldest daughter of Queen RhiAnne. Like Cna and Dorlie, the same will be said of you. Do Elves exist, or do they not? What is this Elvin magic everyone speaks of? What is the power of The Great Forest and who holds the power? I respectfully ask your permission for what is to come. Gifts created especially for you." Reaching to his left, The Guardian picked up a long emerald-green bow and a matching quiver full of arrows with red feathers. "I asked your mother if you could take this along. This is a very special gift she has prepared for you, and I give it to you now, little one." He stretched out his arms and handed Wren the bow. "As you know, an arrow fired from an Elven bow never misses its mark," he explained. Reaching down again, he picked up the matching quiver full of arrows. "From the spells placed upon both the quiver and arrows by your mother, the Great Queen RhiAnne herself, this quiver shall never be empty." A smile crept across the face of The Guardian as he handed Wren the bow and quiver full of arrows. “These, too, are part of the history you will create.”

The Guardian rose, turned, and spoke excitedly. “Oh, Wren, my dear child, there is one other thing you should know. My hope is I have not offended you, I have your permission, and you enjoy the subtle change. Your mother did give me her permission, and while it is common in The Great Forest, outside it is not. It will help immensely when tales from times past are told. It’s a vision I have created to add to the stories of enchantment, magic, and belief. Please, come, look in the mirror.” The Guardian motioned toward the mirror as he guided Wren across the room until she stood directly in front of the mirror.

As The Guardian beckoned, Wren moved across the room until she stood in front of the mirror. Blinking, she turned her head from side to side, her short brown hair moving with each turn. She chuckled slowly, “Oh my, my, my… What have you done this time? This has never been seen outside of The Great Forest. No one has ever seen the pointed Elf ears. I am so honored. They look beautiful. Thank you, my friend!”

“Tell me,” The Guardian paused, fearing he had offended his friend. “Do you like the look? It was only a subtle pointing of the ears. It seemed appropriate for an Elf, and your mother did approve it.” He tilted his head from left to right as he observed Wren’s ears.

“Why did I do this?” he said. “I don’t know, but it adds so much more to the mythical story you shall weave. The how I leave up to you, but the Elf is only one part. I am so happy your Queen Mother allowed me to let others see the pointed ears.” The Guardian paused to allow the thought to sink in before he continued.

“Another of your gifts you have been allowed to take with you is your ability to run fast and far without tiring. A step, a mile, several miles, it doesn't matter. Just as you ran in the forest, you will never tire. But now, perhaps, I say too much…I want you to use your ideas, add to what I've given you to create your own story. For me, I've only given you a sprinkling of ideas. The rest remains up to you and your imagination. I can't thank your mother enough for allowing me to use what is natural in The Great Forest for you on our journey."

Wren smiled as she listened and asked, almost begging, "My, you have put a lot of thought into this, haven't you? So, you want me to accidentally be seen as I move from visible to invisible. Hmmmmm, perhaps translucent would be best so they could see right through me. I can see this as a perfect way to add to the mystery both here and there." Wren paused and caught her breath, containing her excitement. "Tell me more, please, if you can. Or would it be best that I not know what the future timelines hold and how you want me to blend in?" Wren bubbled with excitement in anticipation of her journey.

The Guardian continued, "We also must have a means to instill fear in people through stories, legends, myth. You need to make them believe something is there when it is not…a haunting or a ghost, so to speak. Allow them to see you only when you want them to." The Guardian paused. "I do like the thought of 'now you see me, now you don't.' A very good choice, Wren. Now to continue – think of something you could do before you completely disappear from view."

The Guardian picked up his cup to take another sip of tea before he proceeded to weave his story. "I will give you some ideas as to what I believe will work. The rest will be left up to you. You have always had such a great imagination. Already you have shown me a touch of your creativity. I challenge you to use it to the fullest. Become one with the story you weave, the tale you tell. Let it be etched in the minds of men for centuries to unfold. As I feel now, I stress to you the importance of having the same feeling within you." The Guardian grew silent to allow all he shared to sink in and be absorbed by Wren.

"For you, your biggest challenge will be placing the rings, the bracelets and the amulet exactly where they need to be when they need to be there. Like The Chosen, all are to be hidden in different places in different times. When needed, then and only then, will they be discovered. It will not be easy for them either. This is why there will be different corridors in time for you to do your work without being detected. They will know they are hidden somewhere in time, but not where. Many times, they will be so close they can sense and feel you but never see you."

Mesmerized, Wren's eyes remained riveted on The Guardian as he continued to lay out his plan. Unconsciously, she continued to sip from her cup while she listened, her eyes twinkling with delight. She felt the warmth from the tea fill her body with contentment and the excitement of the challenge being laid out before her. It was difficult, almost impossible, for her to contain her enthusiasm as she realized how big her part would be.

How long had The Guardian spoken? Entranced by his words, she listened attentively. It felt like time was standing still. With bow in hand and the quiver draped over her back, she stood with The Guardian as they rose to leave the room.

As they walked, Wren turned to look in The Guardian's eyes. "Tell me, what different things do you have in mind for me to do my work? What seeds have you already planted that I should know before I begin my journey?"

Their gait was not fast as they moved down the hall. Pausing before they entered the room, The Guardian looked at Wren and spoke, "This is where your journey shall begin." Unnoticed, his hand slipped into one of his many pockets. "Last, but not least, use this rune should you ever need to contact me."

Looking down at the coin, Wren noticed the inscription. On one side… "*Dreams don't last forever.*" And on the other… "*Dreams are not forgotten.*" She noticed there was a very notable coolness when she touched the coin. The Guardian urged her to rub the rune firmly. When Wren rubbed the coin, it began to give off a blue glow. Smiling, Wren looked up at The Guardian. "Ooooooo, you old dog, you. They have been enchanted with the ancient language and sealed by the moonbeams, haven't they?" Wren asked excitedly.

Smiling, The Guardian placed the coin in Wren's hands. "As with the other gifts given to you, these, too, will help to do my bidding. Once they have been planted in the past, they shall aid us in the future. This is what was foretold."

Reaching into his waistband, The Guardian pulled out a small cloth bag and emptied the contents in his hand. Wren looked on attentively, wondering what each represented. In his large hand she could clearly see three rings, three bracelets, and an amulet.

In a hushed tone, The Guardian spoke as he took her hand into his, first placing the rings in her hand and reading the inscription inside the rings. "For the One Who Was." Next the bracelets joined the ring in Wren's hand as The Guardian continued, "For the One Who Is." Last, the amulet joined the rings and the bracelets as The Guardian concluded, "Yet To Come." Firmly, he closed his hands over Wren's as he completed his short incantation.

"When it is time, you will know what to do with each of these."

The Guardian raised his eyes, and with a soft gentle laugh, a smile spread across his face. "Have I not piqued your interest, little one? Perhaps, I believe, far greater than it has ever been before." As he continued to chuckle, they stepped onto the balcony and into the moonlit night. “Always remember, if you need anything from me, all you need to do is ask the coin and read its inscription.

“I do, however, need to stress the importance and significance of what we need to do. We have laughed and enjoyed good conversation. I don’t want to downplay what is at stake. The balance of all Kalamar rests in the hands of a few. The Dark Lord has grown strong and powerful. I push the thought from my mind and erase any doubts. It doesn’t mean they are not there, though.” Wren felt the grave concern shared by The Guardian and nodded without speaking, acknowledging what was at stake. The very balance of Kalamar, as they knew it, was held in the hands of the few.

After some moments of silence, The Guardian waved his hand. “I need to show you something, Wren.”

As she looked on, she saw an evening sky filled with the same blue hue given off by the coins. The blue hue cast its light down upon a bed. Lying in the bed, dressed in a pure while silk gown, her long, flowing golden hair spread out over the pillow, was a young lady.

Wren looked down and immediately knew who she was. Looking up, she commented, “She is so beautiful and so young, but she is older now. My Mother has always been so beautiful.”

Smiling, The Guardian chuckled. “You are correct; she looks young, but do not let that fool you. I now introduce you to RhiAnne, your Queen, when she was but a child. As you know, her age is immeasurable. Before you is your mother, RhiAnne, Queen of the Elves, with unknown powers. All that you possess and have been given, she has given you. She will be your constant ally and confidant. Both of you shall pass through time together. For when she awakens from her sleep, you both will be in your new home in The Great Forest.

"As you can see, you both have much to do. There is one other that will join the two of you. Your sister, Madison, will make you a threesome of both knowledge and power."

They walked out of the room and down the hall. Reaching out, The Guardian opened the door, and they arrived at their destination. Smiling, he asked, "Are you ready to begin your journey? There is one last thing I leave you with. You shall be as nimble as a cat and move with a quickness that will befuddle any opponent you should encounter."

Elders of The Seven Planes

The Elders were called from each of the planes and had gathered in the middle of the town square next to the well. Taking a seat on the stone benches surrounding the well, they waited in silence. Each of the Elders was dressed in a long white robe with leather sandals. Hushed tones and whispering from those passing by gave rise to the significance of the visitors. It was uncommon to see one of the Elders in public, but to see all of them all together was extremely rare.

The esteemed scholars had gathered to discuss what had happened on The Third Plane of Kalamar. A water bucket rested on the ground, the wetness on the cobblestones evidence of its recent use. The position of the benches around the well presented a loosely formed circle. One by one, the Elders took a seat on different benches. Leaning forward, they placed their hands together and intertwined their fingers. With voices no more than a whisper, the Elders started to discuss the reason they had been called and why they had come together. After several minutes of hushed conversation, the tallest of the Elders, the one from the First Plane, rose, looked around, and began to speak.

"The Guardian has already moved The Chosen. The reason they have been moved was for their own protection and to begin the process of mentoring them in The Ancient ways. He also did one other thing which we all had agreed to. We referred to it as an added layer of protection, placing them at separate points in time. Since they both have been positioned at different points in time, this should make detecting and locating either, or both, extremely difficult. The Guardian has chosen, and again we agreed, their ages and where along the timeline would not be revealed even to us. When needed, they will be called forth as was set forth in our writings of The Seven of Sevens." His voice fell silent while all nodded, grim looks covering their faces as they listened intently, waiting for the appropriate moment for their turn to speak. As silently as he rose, the Elder from The First Plane returned to his seat, an unspoken signal for the Elder from the Second Plane to speak.

The Elder from The Second Plane, a bit younger than the first, lifted his head, nodding in agreement and continued the conversation where the first Elder had left off. "With his gift, the Seer has been following how all the events are unfolding. Even now, as we speak, the Dark One's authority has continued to grow since his rise to power. With each passing cycle, Zorleg has continued to grow stronger, converting more to become his followers of darkness. He has abandoned all that has been, making things to his liking and his desires. Zorleg wants only for himself, for it is all about him, his desire to be all formidable and ruler overall." Following the cue of the first, he too returned to his seat and awaited the Elder of the Third Plane to speak.

All the Elders remained silent while they digested the profound details of things penned by their hands that were now coming to pass, foretold in their writings. The eldest of the Elders came from The Third Plane. After he rose, he broke the silence before he slowly raised his hand. Unlike the others, his ears had a distinct point hidden under his flowing brown locks. With his right arm outstretched, he pointed to each of the Elders one at a time. After turning in a circle, he raised his right hand and clasped the back of his neck, massaging it. Deliberately, cautiously, he continued the conversation started by the other two.

"As it was told to me, as we have written, the slow process has been ongoing over time. When he was young, Zorleg showed so much promise. For reasons we may never fully understand, he developed a desire to be all-powerful, and this desire continued to grow with the passage of time. From the beginning, his heart developed a deep hatred for the teachers and the storytellers, and he developed a love of darkness. We do not understand why he detested the way the storytellers could take words, magically mold them into a picture and share those words, painting pictures in the minds of others, planting seeds of inspiration. What he found even more troubling is how they were able to tell their stories that, to him, were not stories at all but described events of the future. Jealousy, hate, discontent, all described the feelings of Zorleg, who, even at his young age, started to develop his power of darkness even before he had discovered the additional power from dark matter. The how of his discovering the dark matter has always bothered me."

The Elder from The Third Plane paused, reached down with his right hand, and grasped the handle of the ladle in the water bucket. Silently, he lifted the ladle to his lips and took a sip of the refreshing cool water before he continued. "My memory dates back eons before the youngest of you joined the inner circle of elite Elders." Slowly, his steel-grey eyes moved from the youngest to the oldest of the Elders sitting around the well. He paused again, signaling the next Elder to speak. He moved to his bench and calmly took his seat.

The Elder from The Fourth Plane stood on cue, looking to be somewhere in age between the oldest and youngest. His look was a bit different than the others with dark red hair, green eyes, and a flowing beard. Like the others before him, he picked up the story where the third Elder had left off and added his part. As he spoke, he turned his head, so his eyes met each of the Elders. "Even before the age of servitude, Zorleg had snuck off the path, away from The Great Meeting Place. Instead of partaking in the learning, he chose to develop his powers that I feel were not his own. He chose to learn what he wanted, but I ask you, who was his teacher? Others were learning to create life. He, on the other hand, took an immense pleasure in taking life. He started with a beautiful flower; somehow, he learned how to turn it to ashes after he removed all of its life. Again, we have the question of dark matter. I echo my colleague's concern. How had Zorleg discovered it, and who was behind his teachings on how to use dark matter?" He shook his head in both disbelief and shame as he fell silent and returned to his seat. To his left, the fifth Elder stood and picked up where the Elder from The Fourth Plane had ended.

"With each small death, Zorleg's power gradually increased. First, a small flower, then he moved on to something larger. A bug, a worm, whatever he could find to torture or kill in the niche of rocks not far from the Great Meeting Place. His hiding place was so close to those who were doing well. Instead, his goal was to choose to do for himself and his own gratification. At first, he boasted proudly of his newfound power, and then started a process of recruiting others to follow him. Many were aware, but they followed the writings and the option of allowing one to exercise free will and choice. They did not interfere but were acutely aware and gravely saddened by his actions and growth. It was painful then, it is painful now and will be more painful in the future." The fifth Elder stopped, the signal for the next Elder to continue.

Being the shortest of them all, the sixth Elder sat on his stone bench. Like the others before him, his long grey hair and beard flowed freely in the gentle breeze. Before he spoke, he hopped down off the stone bench and began to pace back and forth on the cobblestones that surrounded the well. "I share neither your age nor wisdom, but I feel the intensity of what we have shared and what shall be. As a reminder to us all, there is nothing we can do. We cannot give a warning; we have been bound not to interfere. As grim as things will become, we must allow things to come to pass. We ourselves wrote in the Seven of Sevens of what shall come and what we cannot do. Those who are The Chosen have a monumental task before them." At the mention of the monumental task, his eyes moved from Elder to Elder. Each nodded in agreement. Like the others, the sixth Elder grew silent and returned to his seat.

All had spoken except the seventh Elder. He stood and moved toward the well. Before he spoke, he took the ladle from the bucket and enjoyed a sip of water. After placing the ladle back in the bucket, he leaned against the stone wall of the well. He took a deep breath and then provided his thoughts for the conversation.

"All things have been placed in motion. It is now time for us to leave this plane and allow things to evolve. There are things we know, but our words cannot be spoken. We have been forbidden to interfere with the freedom of choice. All we can say, collectively, is great will be the destruction and disruption to all our planes caused by Zorleg. Should he succeed, things will become far graver, I fear. Everything will start here, on the third plane. The Chosen have been hidden in time, but the question passing through all our minds is, will they be able to restore The Third Plane to what it once was? The one who wants to control all Planes has selected The Third Plane as the starting point for his quest to conquer all planes of Kalamar. Great is the power that was given to The Chosen! Unlike Zorleg, the mentoring provided to The Chosen by the great ones has reached deep into time itself. For The Chosen, how true will ring the words to make them famous… '*Things are not always as they appear*.'"

He ended his words shaking his head as he trembled and mumbled, "But will it be enough? Will The Chosen be able to overcome the Dark Lord and the power of dark matter? If they fail, what becomes of Kalamar as we know it?"

Slowly, all the Elders rose and joined together, forming a small circle. It was important that all spoke freely about what was on their minds. They said what needed to be said. Now the time for their departure had come. Each reached out and clasped hands together, fingers interlocking tightly. Softly they chanted, again barely above a whisper. With each word, their bodies shimmered, before growing dimmer and dimmer until they were no more. For as they arrived, so, too, had they departed. Uncertainty hung in the air over events yet to unfold. Off to observe from afar... *Things are not always as they appear.*

Zorleg - Attack of The Great Forest

Queen RhiAnne, Madison, and Wren had quickly returned to the Great Forest and had taken their respective places in the Tree of Life. With her children now secured beside her, Queen RhiAnne lightly tapped the trunk of the tree three times. With each tap, she whispered a different word. She tapped, spoke her words softly, then fell silent for a few moments before she repeated the process. After she whispered the last word, the trees within the Forest began to sway and take on a life of their own. Vines appeared and started themselves from branch to branch, tree to tree. The openness of The Great Forest had begun a significant change, and it was happening rapidly. Where there was nothing, now a thick wall had formed. The new wall got thicker as the vines interlocked and reached skyward.

Within a few moments of their return, the mighty Elven Queen had created a solid, thick wall designed to protect her Elven homeland. The three moved in unison and took up a spot behind the Tree of Life and the Wall of Protection. Floating high above the barrier, The Great Fleet of Kalamar magically appeared, answering her call. All the great ships moved as if they rode on the waves of The Great Lake. Another spell cast by Queen RhiAnne quickly filled the ships with her Elven warriors in full battledress, not the battle of this day, but for a day that was yet to come.

Madison looked at Queen RhiAnne and asked a question she already knew the answer to.

"Mother, what is happening?"

Queen RhiAnne smiled.

"My child, we are never alone. Lord Zorleg has declared the Great Forest to be his. As we speak, he has sent more legions than I care to count to destroy and burn The Great Forest and our home. He has filled his mind with a lust for more power, and he has come to take what he believes is his for the taking, the magic that lives within our forest. What he has failed to realize is he is trying to take something that is not his and something that cannot be removed from our home."

The Great Queen paused for a moment before she continued.

"For Lord Zorleg, it is but one of a million mysteries that he cannot solve, even though he was warned not to come. For it was decreed that we were given this land, and it shall be ours and no others. It is disturbing to see our great fleet leave, but they leave and wait in safety, to come forth on another day when our warriors will return. The day of their return has already been set forth, the great calling...calling home the lost, the forgotten, the great warriors and so many more. It is then all shall return and return in numbers far larger than Lord Zorleg ever imagined. I have taken the steps needed to ensure our forest has been sealed and protected. It is now, and shall forever remain, our Great Forest. Watch, my children, and see how our home shall appear exactly as they believe it should, but things are never as they seem."

Queen RhiAnne's voice tapered off while the sky continued to be filled with brilliant flashes of light. With each flash, another ship from The Great Fleet of Kalamar appeared. Its cargo, the Elven warriors, were safely sealed above and below deck before the ship vanished as mysteriously as it had arrived. All the movements of the ships and warriors went unnoticed by Lord Zorleg as they moved through the darkness. The Great Queen allowed another smile to cross her face as her eyes twinkled in delight.

Queen RhiAnne looked at the heavens. The last of the ships from The Great Fleet was now hidden in time with the One Who Walks Through Time. Her legions of soldiers, the great Elvin warriors, are with him. They are away from what appeared to many as her forest being destroyed. Like Wren, each warrior's sheath was slung over his shoulder, all covered with the spell of a full quiver that never empties and arrows that never failed to hit what was targeted. Today was not the day, but they had gone to wait. When it was time when they would be called, they would return just as they left. *From out of the darkness, they shall reappear in numbers so great they will numb the mind.*

Queen RhiAnne paused once more, allowing herself a small, quiet chuckle before she continued. "How great will be the surprise when Zorleg's forces are unable to enter the Forest or destroy what is here. As I speak, and as we stand by the Tree of Life, strains of time have woven themselves to each tree, branch, vine and leaf. What can be seen from within is not visible to those who look from the outside. The magic of my incantation causes a deception, allowing them to see and believe what they wish. For what they see is destruction and fire, believing they have destroyed our forest and all that has surrounded it. However, not one blade of grass, no, nothing, has been harmed, and nothing shall change except for the warriors who have joined Benjamin as part of his army."

Queen RhiAnne reached out and took Madison's and Wren's hands in hers. As they turned, a doorway appeared in The Tree of Life. Without hesitation, the three quickly walked through the opening before it closed and secured itself behind them. As fast as it had opened, it was now covered with branches and vines. The vines quickly camouflaged the door and then the entire tree. Through her spell, the Tree of Life was pulled into the same thicket until it disappeared from sight. The Great

Forest was now protected by the spells of the Great Elven Queen herself. "Protected it shall remain until the day comes when those called shall join in the rejoicing and herald the return of the Great Storytellers."

From every direction, the enormous armies of the Dark One marched toward the Forest. The grinding of wheels on the trebuchets, catapults, ballistae, and wagons filled the air. The ground shook as his armies and machines of war moved forward, inching closer and closer to the Great Forest. Legion upon legion stretched as far as the eye could see in every direction. A signal torch for each legion dotted the landscape, a different color for each. The torches were visible, leading each army as they moved toward their goal, the Great Forest. The torches would be used to coordinate the attack when all had gathered, and the Great Forest was surrounded. Lord Zorleg formulated his plan and this quest long ago. He was here to obtain all the magic from this forest. Yes, he had been warned not to go to the Forest, but the warning only made him thirst to take all its power, adding it to what he had already developed with the use of dark matter.

He was a far distance from the Great Forest. It was there where Zorleg waited and contemplated his next move. He had already determined he would stop at nothing...anything and everything was for his taking to increase his power. For him, this was but another domino to fall since starting his campaign. How vitally important to the Lord of Darkness was the magical power of the Forest he had heard so much about. He stared off into the distance, wringing his hands together while he anticipated the new power flowing through his veins. Short, quick breaths replaced his slow breathing as he anxiously awaited the attack to begin. He broke out in maniacal laughter. He smiled as he felt the closeness of his new-found power tickling his body. Overfilled with joy, his mind could feel how it would be to conquer The Great Forest and obtain the reward that it would provide him. Scoffing, he raised his eyebrows while his mind replayed the events that had been reported to him.

Two of his Elite Guards, Grink and Pounce, had been overcome by Elves and pinned to the floor. There must have been many to shoot with such precision to pin both of them down. Zorleg felt it could have only been accomplished with the assistance of the magic from this very forest. He fumed with anger as he paused and remembered hearing the report. Now alone with his thoughts, he began to shout, taking his outrage on anything within striking distance as he began to lash out.

"It is important, no, vital…the power from The Great Forest must be mine! Those from the Forest will pay!!! No one will be able to withstand my great army! On more than one occasion it has been reported to me these Great Storytellers are also the Gatekeepers to Kalamar."

Zorleg wondered if this was another secret that had been held from him. He must have the power of the Forest to help with opening the gateways to all seven planes.

"Once I control the gateways, all seven planes shall be mine."

It was not long after Zorleg had received the report of the sighting of the Chosen at the inn that he sent more soldiers to follow the trail. Conjuring up his own black magic from the dark matter, Zorleg sent several legions from his Elite Guard. When they arrived, they reported seeing some sort of great beam shooting into the night sky from The Great Forest. That really piqued his attention. It wasn't long after the special ceremony concluded that his troops finally captured The Guardian. He had a problem understanding how they captured The Guardian but not his staff. The Guardian's staff surely held the type of power he could add to his own, but why wasn't it captured as well? He turned his attention back to the Forest. He had planned and plotted how he would remove the magic of the Forest for himself. What happened to The Great Forest was no concern of his, only taking what he had wanted and desired for quite some time. Lord Zorleg continued to move about, lost deep in thought, before he returned to his throne. He had planned and plotted how to use the magic of the Great Forest for himself. Patiently he sat and waited for the reports and updates about the progress of the ongoing attack. Soon, the runners would tell him what had happened and the results. He anxiously awaited hearing how successfully his plan had been carried out.

Red signal torches illuminated the sky. All across the horizon, red was the only color visible, the color Lord Zorleg had designated for use to halt all movements of his army. The Great Forest was now completely encircled by Zorleg's army. With the pause, each of the large weapons was prepared with balls soaked in oil. Archers were readied and stood with arrows wrapped in creosote-soaked rags. Both were intended to set fire to the Forest and burn every tree and bush in it to the ground. In the darkness, all torches were systematically extinguished one by one.

With the last signal flare snuffed out, everyone knew it was only a matter of time before a green signal would rise high in the darkness. A single torch of green would be the signal for all the archers to commence shooting the flaming arrows into the Forest. If there were two torches illuminating the night, it was the sign to unleash a barrage of fireballs. When signaled, all would commence the bombardment of the Forest, designed to engulf the Forest with flame and intense heat. Just like Kalamar, the Forest would be turned into a pile of burnt rubble with an acrid aroma of sulfur filling the air. Some of the trebuchets would be loaded with pigskin filled full of oil. Once launched, they would burst on impact, to be ignited by the archers' flaming arrows or fireballs shot from the ballistae or catapults. Well prepared, the army of the Dark Lord has come. Legion upon legion of soldiers and archers, thousands upon thousands of trebuchets, ballistae, and catapults to pound the Forest relentlessly. Should anything happen to venture out of the Forest alive, soldiers had been positioned to ensure nothing lived, neither man nor beast. Those hidden within the trees shall feel the torment and affliction of Lord Zorleg, his plan executed to the letter by his vast army.

Without a word being spoken, a single green torch was illuminated and broke the darkness. Surrounding the Forest, arrows could be seen being lit before they illuminated the night sky with a trail that arched through the blackness of night towards the Forest. With only the swishing sound of the arrow strings, wave after wave of burning arrows arched upwards into the darkness then rapidly rained down on the Forest. Volley after volley of flaming arrows from all directions illuminated the night sky, turning the darkness almost into the brightness of daylight.

Without a moment to delay, two green torches replaced the single green torch. A deafening swoosh filled the air as the balls of oil-filled pigskin hurtled through the darkness. The splashing of each ball splitting open could be heard over and over again. Seconds later, the oil was ignited by the flaming arrows. An enormous whoosh from the explosions was unmistakable. When each ball of oil burst into flame, the flames shot skyward, drenching the trees of the Forest. Unceasing, unrelenting, they did not stop. Wave after wave was launched, adding more fuel to the fire before it exploded when it ignited. The Forest appeared as a great fireball from every direction as far as the eye could see. Runners were summoned and sent to report back to Zorleg the status of the attack on The Great Forest. From the intensity of the flame, each commander had the same thought. There was nothing that could possibly survive the heat and destruction from the burning oil raining down on the Forest. How glorious would the reports to Lord Zorleg be on how successfully his plan was carried out and how the Great Forest was now ablaze.

Part 7

The Great Deception Revealed

The spies had traveled through numerous villages with the same result. Many far from the Great City of Kalamar knew nothing of The Chosen's death. It was worrisome to the spies that they were not hearing reports that would verify that he was dead or alive. Zorleg's spies found it very interesting, many of the villagers scoffed at the existence of The Chosen at all. They all thought it was nothing but a story from the storytellers. Who, they offered, could believe such stories from the likes of a storyteller? Perhaps with that mindset, they could be recruited to join Zorleg's forces.

Zorleg's spies proceeded carefully and cautiously as they moved across the land. Many of the Zorian spies thought it was extremely odd that many of the villagers had heard these stories yet did not believe. It would be important for them to include those thoughts when they reported back to Zorleg. His orders were explicit. "Bring me proof. That is all I ask. Bring me proof the male child of The Chosen is dead. Alive, dead, I don't care, bring me proof!"

Grink and Pounce were two of the Zorians who had been sent to spy across the land. Pounce was the first to speak. "You knows, we knows we killed him once, didn't we? We not check, but he be dead, no?"

Grink responded, "Course he be dead. We know he be dead; now we find proof. We be so proud tellin' what we know."

"Grink, we don't be knowin' it be true or not. You be tellin' Zorleg he be dead. Me, me never sure he was. Still scared of what Zorleg do with us when he finds out he be alive. Be our fault, Grink, our fault."

"Pounce, why you worry so? Me take care of it all. Look, let's be goin' to that inn. I be hungry. You be hungry?"

While Grink and Pounce readied themselves for their return, Benny tossed and turned, suffering through a night of sleep evading him. His head rested gently on his pillow, but sleep continued to escape him. Finally, his mind drifted slowly off and allowed him to fall into a deep sleep. With each breath, his chest rose as he inhaled, followed by an unhurried exhale. Deeper and deeper Benny drifted off to sleep...

From the comfort of his sleep, Benny heard the unmistakable calling. It was not a calling of his name, Benny, but he knew the name belonged to him. Crisp, clear, and concise, his name was called again, *Benjamin.* Approaching his thirteenth birthday, Benny had become accustomed to being called Benjamin. Without questioning, he sat up and responded, opening his eyes. "Your Majesty." His eyes felt like they were stuck in a thick fog from his sleep, but he was amazed how quickly his vision cleared with each blink of his eyes. His senses returned, his eyes bringing his surroundings into focus. It didn't take long for Benny to realize he was no longer in his bed or in his room. He wondered why Cosmo didn't bark, alerting him to something that was going to happen.

Benny wondered aloud before he spoke in a voice barely above a whisper, "This place. The trees. The forest. Reevus brought me here before when I was little. How can it be that I have returned?" His deep steel grey eyes scanned the countryside before he continued, "So much has changed, yet so much remains the same."

Finding himself standing alone in the middle of the road, Benny looked to his left, then to his right, instinctively knowing exactly which way and where he needed to go. Off in the distance he could see a familiar hamlet visible in the twilight of the day. The faint glow of candlelight twinkled from the houses in the distance. Quickening his steps, Benny covered the ground from his arrival point to the town's inn in the twinkling of an eye. Standing outside, he paused to look at the structure. *So familiar* he thought before he firmly grasped the latch, pushed down, opened the door, and stepped inside the inn. Instinctively, he scanned the room before his eyes settled on a small table on the back wall near the window. Politely, Benny smiled at the barmaid, Miss Katie, and then moved swiftly to the table and took a seat with his back towards the wall. Miss Katie followed a few steps behind, and as soon as Benny had settled into his chair, she placed a large glass of cool spring water on the table.

"Will someone be joining you, or will you be eating alone?" Katie softly asked.

Benny looked up at Katie, ignored her question, and asked one of his own, "Do you know a cobbler named Reevus?"

Katie paused, thinking for a moment before she answered. "Reevus, oh goodness sakes, yes, we do. And what a cobbler he is! He has a brother that is a blacksmith, too. Tales have it, the metal he used in his work was mined from the elf mines deep within The Great Forest. Many have told the story that anything made with those metals has been enchanted by the Elvin Queen RhiAnne herself. Men have been known to travel great distances for his skill and those metals." Katie paused, leaned closer to Benny, and whispered in his ear, "Tell me, traveler, have you come from afar? While your clothes are familiar, I sense there is something very different about you, but I can't quite put my finger on it just yet." Smiling, she stood upright as she awaited Benny's answer.

A sheepish smile washed over Benny's face before he responded. "Yes, you could say I have traveled far. But as I speak, I am not sure why I have traveled here or exactly what I'm looking for. All is so familiar to me. This inn… When I was a boy, there was a storyteller named Reevus who told stories of The Great Forest, along with many more. My exact age for that particular memory isn't clear, but I believe I was around five. While I fail at remembering my age, I do remember that night well. I am positive it was from here that I made my first trip into the forest and met Reevus. It was a night of many things that I've failed to find an explanation for." Benny paused again, as he took a sip of the cool water before he continued. "From this inn, this is where Reevus told his tale of a night in The Great Forest. It was a night and a story that I have never forgotten."

The quiet and silence of the night air was broken as the doors to the inn were thrust back and slammed against the wall. Startled by the noise, Miss Katie jumped and quickly returned behind the bar. Two squat, ugly deformed men walked into the room. A golden stripe traveled down each of the men's pant legs, broken in the middle by a golden Z before the stripe disappeared inside their boots. In unison, the two began to yell at the barmaid. "Food! Drink! And we want it now!" Frantically, Miss Katie scurried around behind the bar to fetch both food and drink. The two squat men slowly walked through the room, glaring at first one person, then another. Suddenly, they stopped in front of a table. Shouting loudly Grink and Pounce demanded, "You! That' be our table. Get up! Now!"

Sitting at that particular table was a petite young lady. Benny wondered why he hadn't noticed her sitting there when he had entered. She lifted a spoon full of soup to her lips, then nibbled on a broken piece of bread before she sipped from her cup of tea. Without looking up, her soft voice spoke, "I am afraid you are mistaken. This is my table. As you can see, I am already eating and enjoying my meal." Her hand and arm moved slowly as she removed the cup from her lips and placed it gently on the table. No one noticed her lips as they parted slightly, or the sounds which were less than a whisper being spoken in the old language, but Benny heard. He heard every word she whispered. Once the words were spoken, she bowed her head and closed her eyes. With a brilliant flash of light, the two minions of Zorleg, Grink and Pounce, were instantly blinded. The petite lady shoved her chair back, jumped up and sprang high into the air, somersaulting in a graceful arch. With one fluid motion, her hand expertly pulled her bow from her shoulder and an arrow from the quiver draped on her back. When she completed her arch, with blazing speed, arrow after arrow was pulled from the quiver, nocked, and launched toward the two intruders. Not an arrow pierced the skin, but both Grink and Pounce now found themselves pinned to the floor, flat on their backs, unable to move, not one arrow having missed its mark.

She lowered her head to the spy closest to her, Pounce. A voice one would not expect from one so small in stature filled the room. "Return with your lives this time, minions! Tell Zorleg those he seeks are not here. Come again, and neither of you will escape with your life. You will not be spared! We are not a warring race but tell Zorleg we shall stop at nothing to protect The Chosen Ones and Kalamar from his hands of evil, of destruction. This plane is the plane of the storytellers and shall remain, forever, theirs!"

Benny watched carefully, unaware that during her short battle, he had risen from his table and now stood with his back pressed firmly against his new friend's back. He heard a voice not with his ears, but it was in his head. His eyes scanned the room, confirming what he thought. The words spoken were for his ears and heard by no others.

"The Guardian awaits you. Allow me to apologize for the slight interruption. They will cause no further problems to us or anyone else for some time. Zorleg will not be pleased to find his underlings have failed him again."

Benny silently replied. "I know you, don't I? Reevus introduced us. But how can that be…that was so long ago…or was it?" Benny's thought trailed off, but again he heard her voice as she spoke.

"Remember, things are not always as they appear." Her head tilted to the side and with the slight movement of head, her hair brushed back and revealed her pointed ears. The memories began to flood Benny's mind as she spoke. "We must go now. The room has too many eyes, too many to ask questions. We need to go and allow those who will, tell tales of this night."

Benny placed several coins on the table for Katie, to pay his bill for something he did not order. After the coins landed on his table, the two quickly departed the inn. Outside, Benny placed his hand on her shoulder and asked, "Wren, isn't it? The daughter and right hand of Queen RhiAnne, Queen of the Elves?" Shaking his head, Benny tried to understand how quickly his mind had been filled with memories.

Smiling, Wren's brown eyes twinkled. "Reevus was right; he said your memory would return in a flash. While this may look familiar to you, this is a different place in a different time. Here, Reevus' brother is a master smith. From his skill as a smith, he has crafted a set of rings. Because they are special, perhaps magical, they have been hidden in time to protect both you and the rings. Zorleg will stop at nothing to find them. He knows they are a key to the Gateway of All Planes." Pausing for a moment, Wren continued, "Don't forget the two at the inn. They were sent to look for you and the rings. To give you insight into why the rings are special, they were made with the metal from the mines deep in our forest, but not this forest. Both the mines and the forest are filled with magic and enchantments from The Great City of Kalamar. Both rings were crafted with magic and enchantments thanks to the special skill of Reevus' brother. To ensure these rings are not mistaken for another, each was engraved with the true phrases from The One of Ones. The rings were originally given to me by The Guardian before our journey from Kalamar, but the craftsmanship of Reevus' brother cannot be hidden by time. To ensure they remain hidden, we have added the magic of our Elven Queen RhiAnne to conceal them. When the time comes, as soon as you see them, you will know."

Benny stopped to wonder, and asked aloud, "How did you know I would be here? How did I get here? It is all so strange and different to me. One moment, I'm in my bed, and as soon as I fall asleep, I hear my name called. But it isn't my name, it's Benjamin's name. Here I'm Benjamin, not Benny. It's so confusing to me. How is a thirteen-year-old supposed to understand such things?"

Wren calmly interjected with her soft voice, "But you are Benjamin. You have always been and will always be Benjamin. The name you go by, Benny, has been part of the plan to hide you in plain sight where you cannot be found. It allows us to call you when we need to introduce you to something new, give you more insight and knowledge of the Old Ways, or let you see something to help you understand. Tonight is a night for understanding. We shall join The Guardian as he works. It is a very special time for him, for us all really. But I shall allow Queen RhiAnne to explain as it happens."

"But how did you know? It's almost like someone was watching, knowing my every move, perhaps watching me through a mirror," Benny commented haphazardly.

A smirk crossed Wren's face as she turned and looked at Benny. "That may not be too far from the actual truth, Benjamin. In a few brief words, there is one who does have the means to watch. We all are able to peer through time in a very special way. That piece of magic is constantly guarded by the one we call the Seer. You haven't met him yet, but one day you will. His job is to watch over both of you and alert us when we are needed. He is one of the few who knows how to move through time as it was meant to be used. From him, you will learn his magic of how he is able to move through time." Wren stopped, reached out and placed her hands on Benny's shoulders. "I know it is difficult for you to understand. You are who you are because He said so. She is who she is because He said so. The two of you are The Chosen Ones because He, The One of Ones, said so. Our job is to help and prepare you as we teach you the Old Ways. We must hurry a bit now; the moon is rising, and Queen RhiAnne is expecting us - or more precisely, you."

Stopping in the middle of the lane, Wren reached out her hand to Benny. "Take my hand and run with me." With the words barely out of her mouth, they were off and running. Benny couldn't believe the ease and speed as they moved. His mind suddenly returned to his childhood as Benny, another time where he was uplifted and ran faster than he had ever run before when he was returned to his bed.

"You will be with me again, when I'm in high school at the league track meet, won't you? You will help me again, won't you? Reevus will be there, too. He sent a little girl to tell me to be ready."

As they ran, Benjamin noticed how rapidly they traveled. The countryside had become a stream of colors as they passed, yet neither breathed hard. Wren continued to fill Benny in, her words touching his mind as if they were spoken aloud. "When that day comes, like today, Zorleg will have sent some of his stooges to disrupt things. I will tell you no more of what is to come. I will tell you The Guardian will be extremely pleased with you that day."

"Thank you for explaining why things feel so familiar to me, Wren. But still, I have so many questions."

"Yes, I know you do. We shall be with Queen RhiAnne shortly, and she can answer and explain many things that I cannot."

Grink and Pounce arrived on The Third Plane and were busy walking around one of the many villages. They, along with many of Zorleg's spies, were busily about carrying out their orders from the Dark Lord. "Seek and find out the truth…are the stories of the Chosen's death true? Was he actually dead?" They had been instructed to not wear their normal Zorian attire, but to wear clothing that would allow them to blend in with the villagers. They needed to remain unnoticed, without attracting attention to themselves or the questions they asked. Sent out in groups of two or three, they were meant to remain undetected and undiscovered.

Kay-Lee Meeting on The Lakeshore

The wind blew across the Great Lake effortlessly and quietly, and fog slowly pushed toward the shoreline. High above, the stars twinkled brightly as they leisurely became hidden, one by one, as the fog thickened. A cold chill returned with the night air.

In the still of the darkest of night before it turned into day, The Ancient One's questions were silently spoken as the moon rose on the horizon. When viewed from above, the moons illuminated the landscape, lining the lake with silver.

Pondering in the silence of the night, he spoke, perhaps only to himself, as he paused between each question, asking methodically, almost in a religious tone. "How long has this been? How long will it be? Was it? Is it? Is it yet to be?" He asked the same haunting questions over and over with the stillness of the night providing no answer to his questions.

The fog parted briefly to reveal an unimpressive large stone overlooking the lakeshore. The Ancient One moved unhurriedly and stepped upon the single large stone. Draped in a deep purple robe, he carefully climbed the few steps to take his place at the highest point on the stone. Behind him, his robe flowed freely down his back, his head covered by a thin hood of purple matching the robe, hiding his long grey locks. Behind him, the moonlight bounced off the fog-covered lake, illuminating his shrouded figure. His words were distinctly heard by the moonlit night without moving his lips.

Slowly The Guardian turned and looked out over the lake. His fingers slipped one at a time from the sleeves of his robe, first his right hand, then his left appeared. With both hands now free, he raised them over his head and pointed towards the lake. Like a conductor directing a symphony, his hands began to move across the moonlit sky - to and fro...left, right, up, down to a very specific sound that only he could hear. The fog reacted instantly, as if being called, joined the movement of his hands, and danced, following his gestures. The fog rose and fell with his every movement. It spiraled upward, changing from a thick ghastly gray to an illuminated light blue. It shimmered in the crispness of the moonlight. With the shimmering intensifying, his robe began a subtle change from its deep dark purple, to a glowing brilliant white. His movements continued to flail the night air, the fog obediently dancing under his direction.

With the passage of the night into day, on the horizon, the sun's rising began to break the moon's hold over a new day. As the sun rose higher, its warm rays began to dissolve the fog, leaving The Guardian alone on the rock. His robe, however, still glowed brightly, a silver lining to begin a new day. He looked to his left, then to his right, gazing up and down the shoreline. While he could not yet see them, he knew they would be coming shortly, but he didn't know in which direction.

Strolling along the shoreline, a young girl of nine, Kay-Lee, walked hand in hand with her mother, Mori. Unlike other morning walks, this morning Kay-Lee could hear music filling the early morning air, something she had never heard before on their morning walk. She slowly turned and asked her mother in the innocent voice of a child, "Momma, why is there so much music in the air? Can you hear it? It is so beautiful."

Mori stopped and looked down at Kay-Lee. Smiling, she asked her daughter in a soft loving voice that only a mother has, "Kay-Lee, what are you talking about? I don't hear a thing. Quit talking such foolishness, Sweetie." As she spoke, her voice began to change from the soft loving voice of a mother to her child to a harshness only the child could detect.

"Momma, you don't hear the music? It's so beautiful. Can't you hear it?" Kay-Lee stopped, turned, and pointed. "Can't you see the man on the rock? Can't you see his arms moving? It's like he's a conductor and I hear the music, but I don't see any musicians. Are you sure you can't hear it, Momma?" Kay-Lee asked.

"Kay-Lee, I think your imagination has gone wild again! I don't hear a thing!" Mori tugged on her hand gently, then looked down at Kay-Lee sternly and said, "Now be still and come along. We need to finish our morning walk."

From his perch atop the rock, The Guardian turned and looked at the little girl without stopping the movement of his hands and arms. From the distance, his voice was as clear as if he were standing next to her. While Kay-Lee was being pulled along, she watched and listened as she heard his voice call out, "Kay-Lee."

Wondering, Kay-Lee looked up at her mom and asked, "Mom, don't you hear it? He's calling out for Kay-Lee. Why is he calling out for me? How does he know my name?"

Feeling the pressure of her mom leading her along, Kay-Lee turned and listened intently. She heard more words being whispered, but they must have been meant for only her ears. "Kay-Lee, you hear what others cannot. You are seeing what others cannot. On this day, I have for you a gift."

She continued to listen intently as he quietly said, "This I give to you now. What you see, what you feel…all of this is your beginning, your awakening. Remember this day, little one. Remember your walk by the lake…for there shall be another time, another place, and another great lake for us. Then we shall have this talk again. It shall be at that time, my child, all that I do, all that I am, will be revealed to you. Then you will know your purpose in life."

Kay-Lee looked up at her mom again, pondering what she had been told. Before she could say a word, more words touched her ears. "Kay-Lee, your mother knows. She does see as you see, but for now, she has chosen to ignore for a different set of reasons. In time, it will be explained to you, and you will understand."

The Guardian turned and looked out over the water, the fog now completely dissipated. He lowered his hands to his side and allowed all that he had conjured up to come to an end.

Feeling a hard tug on her arm now, she heard The Guardian tell her, "Before you go, remember these words: '***Dreams don't last forever, but dreams are not forgotten***.'"

Kay-Lee felt confused as she listened to the words before she felt another strong tug on her arm. Mori continued to walk at a fast pace, putting more distance between them, the rock, and The Guardian with Kay-Lee's hand firmly clutched in hers. As they hurried along the path, Kay-Lee turned one last time to look at the stone…only to find it wasn't there. The large stone and the one who stood on it were gone. The sweet chorus of beautiful music had been replaced by the sounds of the waves splashing against the shoreline.

Mori moved faster, quickening her pace as she hurried along with a firm grip on Kay-Lee's hand. They had moved down the sidewalk closer to her car before she slowed their pace. Her mind shot back through time as she took a deep breath. Oh, how well she remembered the old man. Muttering to herself, Mori thought it was funny how he always seemed to appear as an old man. Even now she wondered if this was the form he enjoyed taking to give an illusion for more flair and mystery. Silently, she wondered how many times this ritual had taken place since they first met. Mori's task had always been different. Like the Ancient Ones, she, too, had transcended the bounds of time for the same reason. How she had hoped this day would never come. Even hiding in time had not helped Mori to protect the young female of The Chosen. Seeing The Guardian, Mori was completely aware of what it meant. Her calling, Kay-Lee's, has begun. Soon, her awakening will begin, and it would be up to Mori to protect her until she is ready.

When they reached the parking lot, Mori opened the car door and secured Kay-Lee in the back seat before she slipped into the driver's seat. She buckled her seat belt and looked in the rear-view mirror. Softly she spoke, "It's ok, Sweetie. Our fun little walk today will just be our secret, ok?" She turned the key, started the car, slipped it in gear, and pulled out of the parking lot and into the light flow of early morning traffic. It was a silent ride with neither Mori nor Kay-Lee speaking. To fill the void, Mori turned on the radio as she drove. She hoped the music would sooth her mind and calm her down, but it didn't help. Her mind continued to race, churning nonstop after their encounter with The Guardian. This was the day she knew would come but one she also dreaded and hoped never would. Mori wondered how much time remained before things would begin to move at a pace far greater than she, alone, could handle. She also wondered about the safety of Kay-Lee, from the Dark Lord. Was this the reason why The Guardian picked today to reveal himself to her? Should she take it as a warning of impending danger? Mori pushed the thoughts from her head and made the remainder of the drive home in silence.

Nafari's Failure

Zorleg was so angry, so furious. He had looked everywhere for Nafari. Everyone had become accustomed to his screaming, so his rampage this time was no different. He screamed at the top of his lungs. "Where is she? Where is my witch, Nafari? WHERE IS MY WITCH OF DARKNESS? She should have returned by now!"

Out of the corner of his eye, a soft glow caught the Lord of Darkness's attention.

"Who allowed this light!" he bellowed.

It appeared out of nowhere in the corner of the room, followed by a soft warm voice.

"Zorleg, there is no need to shout. I am here."

Zorleg continued fuming before he started to lash out, yelling in the direction of the voice he heard. The voice was completely unfamiliar to him.

"Who are you? How did you get in this room?"

Zorleg called out for his guards to come posthaste. Someone uninvited was in his room!

The sound of footsteps filled the hallways in response to his command. Calmly, coolly, the stranger spoke.

"You do not need your guards, Zorleg. I have returned."

Looking at her from head to toe, Zorleg continued to allow his rage to flow, shouting, screaming.

"You! Who are you? I've never seen you before! I don't know you!"

Calmly, Nafari gave him his answer. “I was your Witch of Darkness, Nafari. For what I was, I am no more. I have been changed.”

“What? What has happened to you? What do you mean you have been changed? Who changed you? How? You have failed me! Do you hear me? You failed me, Witch! You said it could be done! Tell me why your Dreamcast did not work!” Zorleg’s face grew redder and redder the angrier he got and the more he shouted.

Nafari lowered her head before she continued to speak softly.

“He is one with powers far greater than I. He was told how to rid his dreams of me.” Nafari slipped her right hand into her pocket and removed the inkwell.

“The Child found the inkwell, picked it up off the dresser, and handed it to me. He told me to get behind him. It was never our design; never could a witch work from behind someone. It has never been the nature of any witch. No one can see what is behind them, only what is ahead. This one, I fear, has far greater power than even you can imagine, especially for being so young. For within him, I felt and saw great things. Even you, Lord Zorleg, will find difficulty with this one. When he spoke, his voice caused the room to shake and was a voice of thunder. The words he spoke were from the ancient language of The Seven of Sevens. Look at me! Look at me now! With the brief touch of his finger and one spoken word, he instantly took away my hideous features that took you so long to create. He has taken from me the untold years of your work, the hideousness you created. He took it all away, all that you had done, and replaced it with the exact opposite. Fear this child, Lord Zorleg, for he truly is a Chosen One!”

Zorleg exploded in a full rage and filled the room with his fury. He shouted at Nafari, “You, witch, or whatever you are! Get out of my sight! Witch, hah! I don’t need a failure like you to tell me what I’m up against! You are a miserable excuse for a witch! Leave me! I need time to think!"

Nafari looked up at Zorleg. "Before I go, there are a couple of things that I feel compelled to share with you. From this child, it is important you should heed these words: 'You can stop the messenger, but the message will go on.' From The Guardian, though I did not see or speak to him, are these words. 'From the One Who Was, giving to the One Who Is, awaiting the One Yet To Come.' You may not yet know the meaning of these words but now is the time for you to ponder them."

Promptly after sharing, Nafari silently left his presence. Never before had she felt a power so great as what she had experienced from the young boy, telling her to get behind him. Nafari smiled as she walked out of the room and left Zorleg's presence. Why, she wasn't certain, but she thought deep in her heart, *This one shall be the One Who Is and is being taught by the One Who Was.* She shuddered as she remembered his voice of thunder, its power and the words spoken in the ancient language of The Seven of Sevens. Passing by a polished stone as she walked down the hallway after she had left the chamber, she looked at her reflection. Just as the Child had spoken, gone was her long nose and pointy chin, her white skin and hair and eyes. *How long has it been since I looked like this?* she wondered.

She talked silently to herself as she walked down the hall to her chambers, "Hail the One Who Was, Who Is and Is Yet To Come. For the Child only touched my forehead with his finger for an instant, and all my years of torture, mental anguish, and disfigurement were removed. Zorleg's lies, his deception, the Child removed with the simple touch of his finger. From the ancient language of the Seven of Sevens, he spoke the words and made the heavens thunder. As I was, now I am again…he has made me whole. He truly is one who is most deserving, yet he is far more than the messenger."

Nafari's Escape

Zorleg's wrath could be felt throughout the palace. A cold chill passed through the thick dark walls and pierced every corner.

"How many years have I spent? Was it centuries, a millennium, or more?" Zorleg questioned how long he had spent molding, corrupting the mind and the body of his creation, his Witch of Darkness, Nafari.

"She was my greatest work. I took from her the youthful innocence and beauty. People cowered in fear, trembling at the mention of her name. She became my great deceiver and temptation." Zorleg's mind whirled as he tried to understand. "How hideous her features had grown over the years. I was proud, so proud of what I created. This shall be only a minor setback!" Zorleg mentally patted himself on the back on how he had disfigured her. Many of the other witches he had created were overcome with fear at her appearance and power. Her disfigurement was a testament to the power he gave her and how he ruled over the world of darkness.

Zorleg paced around in his chambers, his anger rising with each step. He stopped to wonder how she could have been changed so quickly and by whom. When he looked at her after her return, all evidence of what he had manipulated over the years was gone.

Standing in front of one of the many open windows, Zorleg's eyes were fixed beyond the horizon as he felt his wrath continuing to build.

"Why did I allow her to walk out of the room?" Zorleg continued to stare into the distance.

“Why didn’t I command her to stop then?” Zorleg blinked.

“Why can’t I sense her presence now?”

The more Zorleg pondered his decision to let her go, the more intense his anger grew. Finally, he could take no more. He remembered how fear-built walls instead of bridges, and now he needed to build a wall, a huge wall. He quickly left his chambers, shouting as he ran down the hallway past his throne room.

“Send all my Elite Guard to me now!” Zorleg shouted as he moved down the hallways. His rage increased with each passing moment and was evident in his contorted face.

When Zorleg reached his throne of darkness, he quickly took his seat and waited for the arrival of his Elite Guard. One by one, they entered the room and formed into rank and file, row by row until the room was filled. Sensing when the last of his guards had entered and taken his appropriate position, Zorleg stood and began to speak.

“The Witch of Darkness, Nafari, is no longer with us. Somehow, someone has changed her, no longer is she what I created. She was one of my finest, no, she was the greatest of my works. I don’t understand, but now she has somehow been changed. You need not know either the how or the why.”

The Elite Guard cowered in fear as they listened to Zorleg’s words. The longer he spoke, the louder his voice became. They could see the rage etched in his face, the veins protruding from his neck, pulsing with each beat of his heart. The anger and rage of his words reverberated within his chamber.

“All you need to know is you are ordered to go to her chambers! Do not knock! Kick down her door and bring the witch back to me! Bring her back to me now!”

Zorleg swiftly swiveled on his heels, hiding the rage from his elite guard, gazing off into the distance. With only his back now facing them, his army rapidly filed out of the chamber and moved quickly down the hallway to Nafari's room. The sound of their boots hitting the stone floor echoed in the hallway, deafening as the sound bounced off the wall.

Zorleg took his seat, gazing slowly around the empty room. He listened to the sound of the footsteps of his Elite Guards growing fainter as they moved down the hallways. He knew his guards would move to surround Nafari's chambers both inside and out. It won't be long before they return. Silently, anxiously, Zorleg waited, wringing his hands together in anticipation.

"Defy me, witch! I will show you how much power I have. You were nothing before me and, like the flower, I shall turn you into nothing now!" A snarl had formed on Zorleg's lips.

Zorleg's Elite Guard arrived at Nafari's door. Two ranking guards placed themselves at either side of the doorway. They looked at each other and then held up their hands to begin a countdown from five. At "one," they both turned and kicked the door so hard it caused it to shatter and splinter before they rushed into the room. They charged through the splintered door as they moved into the space of Nafari's room. Quickly, they slipped to the side as more guards poured into the room through the shattered doorway. Methodically, they began to search the room, the closet, the balcony, and the inner and outer chambers, leaving no corner unturned.

"Nothing? Nobody is in this room. Can anyone be positive the witch returned to her chambers? Nothing that belonged to her has been touched, and everything appears to be in its proper place, except for this large stain on the floor." One of the guards bent down and touched the stain. "This stain is dry, no telling how long it's been there."

A shuffled noise came from outside the door. Two guards looked at the door to see a man of very small stature being pulled into the room. The small, timid man was pushed from behind as the guard prodded him, "Speak now, and tell them what you saw."

"Nothing, I have nothing to tell you." He looked at the two guards who towered over him. First his eyes looked at one and then the other before he continued.

"The Witch of Darkness, Nafari, did return to her chambers. Well, I assumed it was her anyway. I didn't see her face, only the back of her white robe. But I did see her walk in and close the door behind her. I thought to myself it seemed odd that she was dressed in white and not black. Her arrival could not have been more than a few moments ago. I swear, no one else has gone in or out of that door, nor has anyone else been down this hallway from either direction, except for you." Cowering before them, the little man asked softly "May I go now? I have nothing else to tell you."

With a nod of the head, the guards motioned for the little man to be released. They walked to the balcony and yelled to the men below.

"Did you see anything? Anyone see anything? Have you found anything?" They watched the heads turning from left to right.

Standing alone on the balcony, the two senior-ranking guards began to discuss the problem they now faced.

"How do we tell Zorleg she wasn't in her chambers? We aren't sure that she's even in the palace. What type of wrath will we face?"

They looked at each other, both knowing they mustn't hide the truth from Zorleg. Regardless of what may happen to them, they cannot fail to pass along their findings. Nodding in agreement, they dismissed all the guards and began the long, slow walk back to Zorleg's chambers. As they walked, neither spoke a word and remained silent as they approached Zorleg's chambers. Alone in their thoughts, they pondered their fate.

Zorleg stood and turned when they entered. He raised an eyebrow, and then asked, "Only the two of you return? Where are the others? Nafari has many powers, but I have never known her capable of taking on so many at once. Did she kill all your troops?"

The two guards turned and looked at each other, and then one stepped forward, bowed on one knee, and spoke. "Your Majesty, she is gone."

Zorleg looked down at the guard as he ran his hand over his chin. "Gone? What do you mean gone? Did she escape you?"

"No, Your Highness. We searched her chambers, and everything was in its place and undisturbed. It was as though she never returned to her room. We did find one of your servants in the hallway who said he witnessed her enter the room. No one had been seen in the hallway or been through her door after she entered. Even her robe was found on her bed."

The guards felt Zorleg's rage building once he heard the news. Fearing for their lives, both began to tremble.

The sounds that came from Zorleg's lips were deafening. Both guards fell to their knees, reeling in pain and agony, too close to the rage unleashed by Zorleg to protect themselves. Turning quickly, Zorleg left the room and walked down the hallway to Nafari's room to see for himself. After he entered her room, Zorleg used his powers to scan the room before he realized what he had been told was true.

"She is gone? How was she able to leave?" Zorleg vowed then and there that he would not let the loss of one witch foil his plans. "I have more important things to worry about than one worthless witch. I made her; I can make many more just like her, perhaps even better."

Zorleg turned abruptly, walked through the shattered door and left Nafari's chambers. He returned to his throne, realizing there was much for him to do.

Seasons of Life

Nafari moved quickly, her feet barely making a sound as she scampered across the stone floor and down the hallway. She slipped into her chambers and quickly closed the door behind her. In the stillness of her room, she could hear her heart as it pounded, amplified by the quietness of the moment. With her back pressed against the wooden door, she sensed something, or someone, that she had never felt before. She was uncertain exactly what it was, but her senses had never failed her. One thing she was certain of, it was not Zorleg's presence she felt. The presence was different, but powerful, and she knew it was very close.

Nafari heard her name being whispered softly, quietly, a soothing caress to her ears in her moment of terror.

"Nafari."

Then she heard it again.

"Nafari."

Timidly, she answered the calling. "Who calls my name?" Nafari replied hesitantly. When she heard it the second time, the voice she heard became clearer and louder. She listened intently, engaging in a conversation with someone she could not see, but unquestionably could hear. Again, she asked "Whose voice is it that calls my name? His Elite Guard will be here shortly. I have no escape."

The voice spoke again, "Yes, you are correct and fully aware that Zorleg will come after you shortly, aren't you? He means to have you, to turn you back to what you were, redoing all of what and how he molded you over time, or perhaps even worse. You were his greatest work of deception and disfigurement. Oh, how numerous were the times he boasted about you!" The voice grew silent. Nafari was unable to think of anything to say or a question to ask.

"Were you not amazed how you were changed by the single touch of a young child? His finger placed briefly on your forehead has changed all that you were, changed you, hasn't it?"

The voice fell silent again, as if waiting for her answer. Nafari felt a sense of comfort and calm when she heard the voice reminding her mind of the touch of the Child. The cold chill of the stones within the castle had kept her cold for years, far longer than she could remember, but now warmth had begun to spread over her body, a feeling she hadn't experienced for a very long time.

Nafari began to speak aloud to her unknown ally. "Yes, it is no longer safe for me here." Almost as if pleading, she continued, her voice trembling, "But I have nowhere to go, no place where I can hide where he can't find me." Tears began to flow down her cheeks, her body trembling. She paused to wonder as her body continued to shiver; her hands and legs shook as she began to gasp for breath…*How long has it been since I've cried*? Nafari walked to the middle of her chamber and took a seat at the end of a faded sofa, flinging her robe to her bed.

"It is possible for you to come to me. Come here, here, where you will be safe. He has never found this place except once, and that was by accident. All you need to do is tell me you want to leave his darkness and help those like you who are held captive." Again, the mysterious voice trailed off.

"What? What is it?" Nafari heard herself pleading to her unknown accomplice as an excitement filled her soul. "What? What is it I need to do?" Her mind raced as tears continued flowing down her cheeks. Nafari sensed the rage of Zorleg, knowing it would not be long before his guards would come for her. As she finished speaking to her unseen guest, she turned and looked at the door. This is the one time in all her years in this palace that she wished it had a lock. Once again, she heard the words of instruction break the silence.

"Do you still have the inkwell?"

"What? You mean the one that was in the boy's room? Yes, it's here in my pocket. Why?" Nafari replied hesitantly.

"Take it out of your pocket and pour the ink on the floor. After you have poured it on the floor, it will create a puddle. Once the puddle has formed, I want you to step into the center of it. It shall appear to be a circle of dark black ink, but once on the floor, it will generate a portal I've created to be used, only once and only by you, to bring you to me. When you step into the circle, you will no longer be within your current plane of time. It will take simply only a second or two for the process to complete. As time passes, you do not need to be alarmed. You will be safe in my hands."

Quickly, Nafari pulled the inkwell from her pocket, removed the cork stopper and dumped the contents on the floor. The ink began a life of its own as it ran across the stone floor before it formed a perfect circle. Without waiting for another word, Nafari moved towards the circle and stepped into the center. As soon as she stepped into the ink circle, she watched in awe as a soft blue light completely engulfed her. The process was painless as the light swiftly began to move from her feet to her head, then back to her feet again, showering her in its warmth. The cold chill and dampness from the palace of the Dark One had been completely washed away.

Nafari stood in the center of the circle motionless and watched in horror when the door to her chambers was knocked off its hinges and shattered. Without question, it had to be the result of hard, swift kicks of the Elite Guards. Of that she was quite certain.

Shouts and screaming from the Elite Guard quickly filled her chamber, echoing off the walls, as they poured into the room. Petrified with fear of being taken captive again, she watched as the guards ran directly towards her. Nafari closed her eyes; she felt her end had arrived at the hands of the Elite Guard. She gasped as the guards walked right past her. No, not past her, not up to her, not around her, but right straight though her. She watched as Zorleg's guards tore her room apart looking for her. She didn't understand why they couldn't see her. Then she quickly remembered the words spoken to her by her unseen ally.

Softly, but firmly, she felt the unknown friend touching her mind. "Come to me now, child. With your eyes closed you are still able to see all that is happening around you. As you have surmised, they cannot see you. Your safety has just started. Now you are in safe hands. Keep your eyes closed and come to me. The blue light shall be the path the portal will use to bring you to me, but you must keep your eyes closed and place your trust in me."

Without questioning him for a second, Nafari kept her eyes closed. Suddenly she felt a warm breeze moving over her entire body. She could sense a slight movement, and then as quickly as it started, it was finished.

"Now, my child, open your eyes. For here you are safe. May I welcome you to the Seasons of Life? Here you will find no sunshine, instead only the shadows of night. The illumination of the stars and moons fills my world. From your work in darkness, I felt you would be most comfortable here as we begin the process to rid you of so many years of pain and suffering. Go ahead, my child, open your eyes."

Nafari opened her eyes to see a vast room with stone walls illuminated by the same soft blue light she saw before. So many questions instantly filled her mind. At this moment she felt only a peace, serenity, and calm. She knew her questions could wait.

Gathering her composure, she heard the voice tell her, "Now is not the time. I know you have many questions that you want answered. In time, my child, in time. For this moment, you only need to rest and get comfortable with the new you. Go ahead, child, relax, you are safe now."

Nafari panned the room, her eyes looking at the vast opening in the wall leading to an unending expanse. She moved slowly and walked over to stand in front of the opening and peered out. In the darkness, her eyes had quickly adjusted to the soft but brilliant glow of seven stars. Turning around, she was startled to see a presence dressed in a long flowing robe standing behind her.

Softly, barely above a whisper, her voice trembled as she spoke and asked, "You? You did this? Are you the one responsible for bringing me here? There is no reason or need for me to ask how. I know in time you'll tell me. But I must ask, who, who are you?" Nafari stepped back into the room, her eyes moving from wall to wall, ceiling to floor, then returning to the one who stood in front of her.

"I am known as the Seer. This is my place in the great expanse of time. We are not located anywhere in time, but in many planes between time."

In a voice of pure peace and calm, the Seer continued to speak. "Zorleg cannot find you here, nor can he find this place. To the untrained eye, where we appear, we look like nothing more than a giant rock floating in space. But for those that know or seek the pathway to the stars, they see the signs and are able to follow the path to the way home."

The Seer reached out and took Nafari's hand, continuing to comfort her. "Here, you will never be alone. This place is above the clouds of deception. We are beyond the reach of doubt and the confusion that Zorleg used to deceive so he can lure others into his world of darkness to join his army." The Seer paused, turned, and began to walk towards the center of the room, holding Nafari's hand as they walked side by side.

"But how do you know me? How did you find me? Why did you come for me?" Nafari asked her questions in rapid-fire order as they walked towards the center of the room.

When they reached the center of the room, the Seer waved his hand, and two seats magically appeared out of thin air. He took a seat and motioned for Nafari to join him. She obeyed. The Seer again took her hand in his as he looked into her eyes and began to speak.

"I have always known you, Nafari, long before Zorleg deceived you and filled your mind full of false promises. During your journey into his world of darkness, there was something that never left you, wasn't there?" The Seer paused as he waited for her response.

Nafari's mind spun as she tried to remember. Regardless of where she was, what she felt, there was something that massaged her from within, creating minute amounts of warmth and a glow from within her heart, the warmth and glow that she kept buried deep within her heart so not even Zorleg could see it. Nafari's head snapped as she jumped up and turned, looking at the Seer. She could see the smile spreading across his face.

"Regardless of what happened, in my heart I knew that one day I would be free of Zorleg, free of his power and free from his darkness. My heart knew…that's the answer you were looking for, wasn't it? Very few know Zorleg cannot see deep within a heart. He thinks once he has deceived you, that you are his. This, I believe, is a great weakness of his and one he fails to acknowledge."

The Seer was still smiling when he stood, and he reached out to Nafari before taking her hand. "How true, my child, how very true. It is this weakness that you shall use against him. Instead of using the Dreamscape to haunt one's dreams, I'm going to task you with using the Dreamscape to place a tune into the dreams of The Chosen Ones. The tune shall be a bond between them and guide them to each other at the time that has been predetermined. For as it has been written in The Seven of Sevens, so it, too, shall come to pass."

Nafari tilted her head slowly. "The Seven of Sevens also mentioned a child who shall speak with the voice of thunder. I have heard his voice and even told Zorleg, but it didn't seem to concern him. Zorleg didn't think it was anything for him to worry about."

The Seer released Nafari's hand as they moved toward one of the walls. Nafari noticed a number of hallways spreading out from the center of the room in all directions. The Seer raised his hand and gestured toward them. "A bit confusing isn't it, child? Think of it this way: each corridor is filled with rooms. Each room is a room full of keys. What did the Child tell you when he touched you? He mentioned the key to your secret room, didn't he? Your room, like all others, is the one you have always been afraid to enter. Regardless of how strong you thought you were, it was still the one place you would never go, wasn't it?"

Pausing, the two continued to walk before the Seer continued. "Benjamin took you to that room, didn't he? When he opened the door and you looked inside, he was both inside the room waiting for you as well as standing by your side." The Seer paused again. "In these rooms are many keys just like the one he used for you. Another part of your job is to place into the minds of all you touch *There is one who holds the Key of Keys.* Now, you are a great reflection of His wonderful light. Each of them must know and remember that whatever happened, the doubt, despair, the blowing of the winds of death and destruction, through it all they will be able to feel and experience the same thing you have. They will know their hearts, know the truth too, and it is the truth that shall set them free. Not only will they see with their eyes, but they will realize they must also see with their hearts. As you have been set free, you will be the instrument using the keys we hold to set forth and free our army. From the deepness of Zorleg's darkness, The Chosen shall set them free to join the Army of The One of Ones."

They turned and moved back to the center of the room again. The Seer continued to explain what he had planned for Nafari. As they walked around the vast space, Nafari suddenly stopped dead in her tracks. Turning in circles, she looked and took in everything in the room…its immensity, the never-ending corridors between rooms, not to mention the endless keys they each contained. Then she paused as she noticed the huge transparent screens in the middle of it all. Surprised, she found they weren't hanging from anything, but instead were suspended in space, floating.

Nafari turned and looked at the Seer, her voice no more than a faint whisper. She asked a question that she knew she had to ask, "I'm the first, aren't I? I'm the first one that has been touched by the Chosen. I am the first of the Army of the One of Ones." Feeling a weakness in her knees, Nafari slowly slipped to the floor, overcome by the realization of the events. Her experience with the Chosen, Zorleg, her departure from the palace, the rescue by the Seer was more than her mind could fathom. Putting the pieces together, she realized she was the first of the army of The One of Ones. The Seer asked, no, told her to use her skills to teach The Chosen and the many whose keys of the soul are contained within each room. Barely able to breathe, Nafari was overcome by how large her task had become. She felt the Seer's hands helping her to her feet.

Brushing her hair back out of her face, Nafari looked at the Seer as she spoke. "For what you ask, I know I am ill-equipped and completely incapable of doing. But I also know that while I may not have all that is required, I have what is needed. I have the will and the desire to do what has been asked and when it is needed, then it will be given. For so much has been done for me, setting me free, it is the least I can do. I will proudly be the first of the willing to build the army to battle Zorleg and his Force of Darkness. While now we may be few, with each dream, a new key will be used to unlock the soul of another and set them free."

Nafari stopped speaking, clearing her mind before she walked back and stood in front of the giant translucent screen. She turned to the Seer and asked, "This is where you watch, isn't it? Tell me how you watch, please."

The Seer stood next to her and began to move his hands through the air, as though he was touching something only he could see. With his movements, images flashed across the giant screens. Nafari looked up at the Seer. "How is it I am able to comprehend all that is passing before my eyes? It is not one place or moment in time, is it?"

Smiling again, the Seer released a small chuckle. "You are quite perceptive, my dear. These are my windows, or mirrors, in time. You are right, in a way. It is not a moment or place in time, but it is time. Many planes of existence, all separate, but all on the same time. One of the abilities possessed by me and The Guardian and The Chosen is the ability to move between the layers and hours of time, in and out of the planes. Few know the magic teachings of the Old Ways to travel. There is another way to travel as well. But those are stories unto themselves. Can we save them for another day?"

"Please, I want to know all you can teach me. I want to share that, as far away as I was from The One of Ones, he still came for me. My story can only give encouragement and hope for those who are discouraged and without hope."

Taking Nafari's hand again, the Seer began to lead her down one of the halls. As they walked, he continued talking. "It has been difficult for you today. So much has happened in your life. The winds of change have blown and touched you in a great way. Through it all, under the nose of Zorleg, you never lost the feeling, and your heart always knew."

Walking towards her chambers hand in hand with the Seer, Nafari heard the sound of rushing water. Pondering how she was hearing running water, it was as if the Seer read her mind. They stopped in the hallway, as the Seer turned and looked at her.

"You hear the roar of the river, don't you, my child? You wonder how a river could be here, in the midst of time. Perhaps you also wonder why it is that only now you are hearing the rushing water. Would those all be valid questions?" The Seer looked at Nafari as he awaited her response.

"I know it has been a long and trying day, but will you show me? Will you answer the questions whose words have not escaped my lips?"

The Seer led her to an overhanging cliff. Below, basking in the blue hue like the rest of the room, was a vast river. On one side, elves were picking up stone tablets, black as coal, stacking them next to the river as they were prepared to be washed in the flowing water. As one tile was lifted from the pile and placed in the water, its blackness was instantly washed away, leaving a pure white tablet.

"What are they doing?" Nafari asked.

The Seer continued his explanation. "Since your arrival, they actually have just started. When you look at the black tablet, think of it as those being held captive by Zorleg. The black represents his darkness and wickedness, the lost. What you are seeing is the washing, or cleansing, of the tablet. All that is evil is being washed away in the river of life, the Crystal River. For those that were, are no more. The old tablet is gone, replaced with a clean, pristine slate, a new beginning. You were Nafari but are no more, for your tablet was the first to be washed. The One of Ones inscribes each new name on every tablet." The Seer's voice rose as did his hands. Every elf stopped working and turned to look at the Seer. The Seer then proclaimed, "The Witch of Darkness, Nafari, is no more. Behold, the first of the Army of the One of Ones, I present to you the Queen of the Seasons of Life!"

An elf stood, picked a black tile, and washed it slowly in the river. All the other elves stood motionless and silent as they looked on. After a few moments, the elf stood and held the tablet high above his head. From out of the darkness, a finger appeared and began to inscribe on the tablet. "The Queen of the Seasons of Life, first of the Army of the One of Ones."

The Seer looked into Nafari's eyes, pulled her close, and firmly hugged her before he stepped back. "Tonight, is a night for you to rest, my child. Tomorrow, we have much to do. Come, let me show you to your quarters." They walked in silence until they reached her door. "Enter my child. Your room has been waiting for your arrival for a long time. Sleep well, for when you wake, you wake with a new purpose, *the Queen of the Seasons of Life.*

Shaken - Kay-Lee

It had been another long, grinding day at the office for Kay-Lee. How sweet it was to finally walk into her apartment, shut the door, and fall on the sofa. Even before Kay-Lee could get her shoes off, her puppy came running at full speed to greet her. Sophie's tail wagged rapidly from side to side as Kay-Lee reached down to pick her up. Together, they lay on the sofa and shared a tender moment, both happy the workday had come to an end, and they could enjoy some special time together.

Kay-Lee scratched her puppy playfully behind her ears. "Heh. Sophie, need a treat for being such a good puppy?" Why Kay-Lee still called her a puppy was something only they understood. Yes, Sophie was small, but she'd had her for as long as she could remember. She was as full of energy now as when she really was a young puppy. Her silver hair hadn't changed since she grew her adult coat.

Sophie's tail continued to wag back and forth in anticipation of her treat. Her excitement grew as she began to jump from side to side, barking softly, begging. Kay-Lee slipped off the sofa and walked into the kitchen. She opened the one container that held the treats Sophie enjoyed the most, her DreemeBones. Kay-Lee walked back to the sofa. Sophie raced ahead of her, jumped up on the sofa, and waited as patiently as she could. Kay-Lee held her treat in her hand, taking a moment to tease Sophie. "What, you think I have something for you?" she softly murmured.

Sophie's tail wagged rapidly while she waited for Kay-Lee to drop her DreemeBone. After Kay-Lee dropped it, Sophie playfully snatched her treat off the sofa, tossed it on the floor and began to play with it. This was her ritual, tossing it, and then quickly running to grasp it in her mouth before she threw it again. This was her special time of playing her own little game. After what she considered a proper amount of playtime, she wasted no time shredding the DreemeBone, devouring it until it was gone. When her treat was gone, she jumped onto the sofa, lying down next to Kay-Lee, and falling fast asleep.

"Hmm. Now that you've had your treat, what am I going to eat?" Kay-Lee got up, leaving Sophie on the sofa. Walking into the kitchen, she opened the refrigerator door and scanned the shelves for something appealing when her eyes fell on the leftover pizza. She pulled a slice from the box, slipped it on a plate, and put it in the microwave. As the pizza heated, Kay-Lee opened the refrigerator door again and pulled out a bottle of water, then opened the cupboard and pulled out a glass. Her hand pushed the glass against the ice dispenser, filling her glass with ice before she poured the water from the bottle into the glass. The timer on the microwave beeped almost at the exact same time she had finished filling her glass. She pulled the pizza from the microwave and returned to the sofa. After she had settled in, she grabbed the remote control and switched on the television. Slowly, she nibbled on her pizza with Sophie, content, curled up next to her. Sophie's head rested softly on her leg as she ate, her eyes staring at her as if to say, "Give me a bite." After sharing the last bite with Sophie, Kay-Lee set the plate down on the coffee table and took a drink of water before resting her head on the pillow, gently petting Sophie. Her eyes slowly began to droop, until she had fallen sound asleep.

Her mind drifted to her walk along the lakeshore with her mom, seeing the old man standing on the rock. How vividly the images of that day were.

Why the memories filled her mind she wasn't sure. But now, she tried to focus her eyes. Was the day at the lake and this dream related? How many times has she experienced seeing the moonlight as it cascaded down from a cloudless star-filled sky? Her eyes panned the landscape illuminated by the moonlight. Kay-Lee felt the crispness of the night air as she walked but was not chilled. Her path was illuminated by the moonlight as she moved slowly but with self-assurance.

In the distance she saw the soft glow of a campfire illuminating the darkness with its warming orange glow. Her eyes were able to make out someone sitting close to the fire. She was still too far away to make out who or what it could be, but as she looked it had a feeling of familiarity.

Kay-Lee wondered with each step, *Why do I keep having this dream? Why did I remember the lakeshore walk this time? It's all so recognizable, yet still so different… I'm just not sure, but still, I'm so positive.* Moving forward, she sensed something she had not experienced before spreading over her body. Stopping, she turned and looked around, wondering, feeling, knowing this time, there was something different.

The night was silent. Not even the sound of her feet touching the grass broke the stillness. She knew the words weren't spoken out loud, but in the quietness of the moment, Kay-Lee distinctly heard, "Welcome Kay-Lee, my child. Come and sit. Join me by the fire. I have been waiting for you and for this moment." Then again, the same words filled her mind: "Welcome, my child. Come, for now the time is at hand."

Kay-Lee approached the fire cautiously, only to see an old man stand and motion her closer, beckoning her nearer to him. His outstretched hand and bony finger pointed distinctly towards the old log next to the fire. A memory flashed through Kay-Lee's mind. "The robe, the hands…I have seen them before! I know I have. We met at the lakeshore. I remember you!"

The Guardian remained silent, turned, and joined her as they both took a seat on the log. "I'm sure you have many questions, my child. In time, perhaps we will find the answer to them all. But before you ask your questions, allow me to tell you a story and ask you a few questions."

The Guardian began to ask question after question, never allowing Kay-Lee to speak. "Do you remember when you were a child and you walked with your mother, Mori, by the lake? Do you remember the music? Do you remember how it made you feel, how it inspired you? You told your mother how beautiful it was. You were hearing and seeing it all, but she told you it was your imagination. That is when I knew it was time for me to reveal myself to you. So many days, so many years, the same place, as I went through the same gestures. But it was only you Kay-Lee, only you have heard." The old man paused, took a breath, and continued. "Did you ever wonder where the inspiration comes from for each word and note of a song? Or who gave the inspiration for the words in a book? How did the magic work that would turn words into a song? From one person's circumstances they were created and turned into a tune that filled the hearts and lives of so many. The burning desire to create something to share with others that would tell a story in words, songs, paintings…all were given to an artist."

Unable to speak, Kay-Lee listened intently while The Guardian spun his tale, drawing her in with each word. Captivated by the tone of his voice, Kay-Lee enjoyed how every word spoke clearly to her, almost as if he were performing a ritual as they stood next to the fire.

Slowly The Guardian turned, looked at Kay-Lee and spoke reverently. "For as I was, for as I am, you now shall be. Many listen, but few have heard. The gift that was given to me, I now give to you."

Watching as he knelt by the fire, she saw The Guardian call the flame, coaxing it to jump from the fire and into his hand. Did she gasp? Kay-Lee wondered if it was her own moment of shock that broke the silence?

Reaching out, he called the flame and guided it into his hand. The Guardian stood, turned, and faced Kay-Lee. He extended his hand, the flame flickering, reaching out to her. With his hand outstretched, the flame changed from an orange hue to a brilliant white that burned brightly. Silently, he motioned for her to stand as he moved in front of her. She watched the flame in hand, burning white hot, but it did not emit heat or burn his hand or their clothing.

Kay-Lee's eyes were fixed on the flame in his hand. Frozen, unable to move, she watched as his hand reached out. She saw, watched, and felt the flame jump from his hand and into her chest. Her eyes locked on his, she heard him softly whispering an incantation.

"Our flame is bright, our flame is light. That which was given to me, I now give to you. What you have heard, you will now pass on to others. As it has been, as it is now, as it yet shall be... Kay-Lee will be what I have been."

Her gaze slowly traced the outline of his arm to his hand, while she replayed the flame jumping from his hand and into her heart. She could feel the flame massaging her heart and her most inner being with a warmness she had never felt before. Kay-Lee's body began to tingle as she listened intently to every word spoken by The Guardian.

"For within the flame are the Words of Words, the Song of Songs. The flame has been passed…and now you are another keeper of the magic of inspiration. The power that was mine is now yours. As it was, as it is, as it shall be... for now you are!"

Sweating profusely, breathless, Kay-Lee bolted up from the sofa, visibly shaken from her dream. She paused to think for a moment. Was it a dream? This was not the first time this vision had filled Kay-Lee's sleeping hours, but each time the dream became clearer and more precise. This was the first time she had the dream of the lakeshore and the forest together.

Looking down, Kay-Lee wasn't aware of her hand softly rubbing Sophie's back as she wondered, *How long have I been having this dream? Since I was a child? Is it a dream? Is it my imagination? Can this be? Wasn't I only having a dream? Didn't I wake up? Am I still dreaming?*

In the darkness, Kay-Lee sat up and slowly took a drink of water from her glass. Sophie nuzzled her head under her arm as the glass touched Kay-Lee's lips.

Kay-Lee - Imprisoned

The Seer could not believe what he was seeing. His hands moved feverishly, panning from window to window. How could he not have seen this coming? Not how, but why didn't the thought even cross his mind? There, on the giant displays, he witnessed, helpless, while Kay-Lee was grabbed by two of Zorleg's guards. It mattered little how they got where they were or how they found her. It is a major problem. They have her now. What will this situation do to the timeline? She is supposed to be in so many different places, but now all those events have been plunged into chaos.

Kay-Lee was on her way home from the office, finishing another productive week. She sang along to the music while it played softly on the radio as she drove home. Her fingers thumped the dash keeping beat with the music. She was looking forward to a week of rest and relaxation. She had nothing special planned other than catching up on things around the house. She had stopped at the store on the way home yesterday, so groceries were not a problem. There were plenty of snacks to enjoy as she cuddled up on the sofa and enjoyed a movie or two with Sophie.

Kay-Lee was jolted from her peaceful ride home by a loud pop. Immediately her car started to veer from one side of the road to another. She firmly grasped the steering wheel and took her foot off the gas. Her car had a mind of its own, determining which way it was going to go regardless of how she tugged on the steering wheel. Kay-Lee didn't feel a pressing need to figure out which tire had gone flat. That was the least of her worries. She would have plenty of time to try and figure that out later. Now she needed to gain control of the car, so she didn't hurt herself, or worse, hurt someone else. The car continued careening this way and that, with Kay-Lee struggling to control its path and direct it to where it would be safe.

Out of nowhere she heard the loud crash. The steering wheel was ripped from her hands, the seatbelt doing its best to hold her in place, the airbags deploying as the car began tumbling, rolling side over side. Kay-Lee felt like a rag doll as she was flung about in her seat, but thankful her seatbelt and the airbags were offering her some protection. How many times she rolled before she passed out, she wasn't sure. It wasn't long before darkness invaded her consciousness, surrounded by the noise from her crash, and the radio was gone. Her body was limp as she slumped over in the seat. The stench of burnt rubber from the screeching tires filled the air. Steam from the damaged radiator drifted upwards, the driver's side of her car bent in from the impact.

She had no idea how long she had been asleep. Would that be the correct word? She wondered, thinking the more likely story was she had been knocked out. With her eyes closed, she began to feel her arms and legs, searching to see if any bones had been broken. *Well, that's odd,* Kay-Lee thought. *I don't feel my seat belt. Maybe they had to cut me out of the car then. Why is it so cold in here? Am I in an operating room? Have I woken up from surgery?* Question after question filled Kay-Lee's mind. After several moments of self-assessment, she gathered the strength and courage to open her eyes.

Kay-Lee looked around her. This was not right. She kept her thoughts to herself as she turned her head. She found herself in a very small room with only enough room for a bed, a table, and a lit candle that burned dimly. Her mind pondered her predicament.

Where can I be? No, I know where I am, but why? Why am I here and how did I get here? This is not supposed to be happening. None of it makes any sense to me. The last thing I remember was one of the tires going flat and then being hit by another car. And now I wake up here? It really makes no sense, no sense at all. Kay-Lee put her face in her hands. *What, how am I supposed to get out of this place, wherever this place is? How am I supposed to help the others?* Her mind was filled with so much confusion, worrying how she ended up in the state she now found herself in.

The room was about as barren as barren could be. It wouldn't take her more than a few steps to walk from one end of the room to the other. A compact room with no windows, and a door that was latched from the outside only. Kay-Lee continued to ask herself why she was here. Regardless of how many times she asked, the same answer appeared. There was no other option.

Somehow, it was Zorleg. He had finally managed to find where she had been hidden, captured her, and had brought her here. There were too many pieces in the puzzle for Kay-Lee to figure out the how or the why. It was far beyond her means to even consider how to break out of a room with a door that only opened from the outside and had no windows. Kay-Lee took a big sigh. Oh, how she wished only, if only, she had the skills and talents of Benjamin. Then she chided herself. Well, if she had his talents, she wouldn't be in this mess in the first place.

There was no contact with anyone outside of the room. Twice during the day, a panel would open at the bottom of the door, only accessible from the outside of the room. The panel would only stay open long enough for her to retrieve the tray with food and water. She had no way of telling time, no way to gauge how long she had been held or how long she would be held. Imprisoned, she had no idea where, with no idea how to reach out to anyone. *Do they even know? Well, how could they know? If they did know, how would they even know where I am being held? Where to look, how to find me?*

Kay-Lee allowed her mind to rest. All she had accomplished was getting herself worked up into a panic, thinking of how hopeless her predicament was. She took deep breaths to calm herself and think of a logical explanation. All her efforts seemed to fail as she attempted time after time to figure it all out.

She Who Has No Name enjoyed her entertainment. How easy it was to take her from the comfort of her hiding place and bring her forth. Now, held within the domain of She Who Has No Name, it would be interesting to see if anyone would come. She doubted it. Her mind had the same thoughts as Kay-Lee. That fact that she had reached out from her place of imprisonment, snatched the female Chosen, and now held her captive in a location known only to her brought her great pleasure.

Time had no meaning for her. After all, she had been there how long? *Interesting*, she thought. *There doesn't seem to be anything so special about her. She hasn't shown any way to figure out how to escape her entrapment, which is for the best, since there isn't.* She put her in there, and Kay-Lee won't leave until She Who Has No Name deemed it so. All these names, all these people of significance, meant nothing to her. They were merely pawns in a greater battle. This was her battle, and she had taken the first step to remove a piece from the playing board. Now she wondered if she would be able to eliminate others whenever she desired.

The Seer was beside himself. To say he was upset would be an understatement. In all his years, he had never made a mistake. This, though, was so much more significant. "Significant" wasn't even the right word. This was a very tragic event. He thought, *If it could be done once, would it be attempted again? If tried again, who would be the target?* The only option now was to call a meeting of the others and tell them what had happened to Kay-Lee to put everyone on their guard. He wondered, *Would it be possible for Queen RhiAnne to cover them all with an enchantment to prevent losing more to this unknown black power?*

The Seven Planes of Kalamar – Battle for The Third Plane

List of Characters

Benny/Ben/Benjamin – from his birth on The Third Plane it was his destiny as one of The Chosen to learn from his mentor and to cultivate the gifts that were set aside for him before his birth. He hears, he feels, his is the cry of your heart. His birth name from Kalamar, the male child of The Chosen. While he is hidden on Earth, he is Benny. Whenever he is called, he knows he is Benjamin and never questions The Guardian's use of his birthname. While on earth, an American English voice, while on Kalamar, speaks with an Irish tone.

Cosmo and Sophie – from times past to times present, they have always been more than just a Morkie. Gifted from The Seer to The Guardian for The Chosen, they have the power to detect Zorleg and his minions. Both are faithful companions presented to Benny and Kay-Lee, specifically to watch over and protect them.

BrarinEar – The Ancient Language for a magical three…the amulet, the bracelet, and the ring.

Cna – a shimmering white and majestic steed, the mighty flying horse Pegasus. One of the targets of Lord Zorleg to remove from existence.

Dark Matter – Exactly how it was discovered by Zorleg has always remains a mystery. After he discovered its power, his own powers of darkness expanded immensely.

Dreamcast – the means Zorleg uses to invade one's mind for his evil and dark purposes.

Dorlie – Another magical beast of Kalamar, the Unicorn. Like Cna, a shimmering white coat and a magical horn. Targeted by Lord Zorleg, like Cna, to be removed from existence.

Grink and Pounce - two of Lord Zorleg's minions. Neither were known for having much intelligence, always talking in a cockney accent. They have been able to do what others before him have not…they found where the male child of The Chosen, Benny, had been hidden in time.

Empress Katherine and Emperor Daniel – The rulers of The Great City of Kalamar, loved by all and a close friend of The Guardian. Speak in educated and proper voices but never condescending to those around them.

Joe –Keeper of the mirror and bound with Mori by the bracelets of time. While Mori protects Kay-Lee, Joe watches over Mori. Fully Irish voice.

Kay-Lee – Born at the same time and place as Benjamin in The Great Forest, she is the female child of The Chosen. Like Benjamin, she, too, was gifted with gifts that were set aside specifically for her, gifts that had never been seen or heard of before. She is special in her own way, different from Benjamin but still a very skilled adversary. To ensure the safety of The Chosen, they were both hidden on Earth but at different points on the timeline. While on earth, an American English voice, while on Kalamar, speaks with an Irish tone.

Lord Zorleg, the self-appointed Lord of Darkness – He mysterious rose to power on The Third Plane of Kalamar. Over time, he crafted his dark skills and converted his followers. He constantly interfered and despised anything that inspired happiness or brought light and goodness to The Third Plane. His power mysteriously took a quantum jump in power after he discovered Dark Matter. Raspy voice, hard accent.

Grink and Pounce – underlings of Zorleg. Uneducated, speak in a cockney accent. You have them down perfectly.

Madison – One of the daughters of Queen Rhianne, queen of the elves. What would an elven princess be without magical powers? As an elf, soft spoken, a voice of enchantment with Irish overtones.

Miss Katie – The barmaid/server at the inn of Carillon. She has the unique ability to know what a patron will order before they place their order. All, that is, except for Reevus. She's able to peel away his gruffness and coax out exactly what he'd like for the evening meal.

Mori – She was appointed guardian of the female child of The Chosen, Kay-Lee. On Earth, it appears as a mother daughter relationship. In the other world, she is the one who the wind is named after – Moriah, who was banned from Kalamar by Zorleg during his attack. On earth, speaks as an American.

Nafari – What her real name was had never been mentioned. She was created by Lord Zorleg as his most powerful Witch of Darkness. Before he had disfigured her, he continually convinced her that no one would ever want her. After her beauty had been stripped away, Nafari, The Witch of Darkness, was feared by Lord Zorleg's Elite Guard and all the citizens of The Third Plane. Her deeds of wickedness and ruthless torture proceeded with her. Her voice changed rapidly over time sliding from a pleasant, blue eyed blonde teenage into the repulsive cackling voice like the witch from The Wizard of Oz.

Queen RhiAnne, **Queen of the Elves -** Her likeness appears on one side of the Rune Coin that was forged within The Great Forest of Kalamar. From deep within the hidden forest, she reaches out to aid Benny and Kay-Lee in their times of need. Though they have never seen her, both of The Chosen are acutely aware of her presence and power. Benny is the only one who hears her voice when she calls him to return to The Third Plane. Another of The Preceptors. Voice tender, mild, soft Irish. However, when angered or in battle, a voice similar to Galadriel in The Hobbit.

Queen of The Seasons of Life – The first to be transformed by Benny by a simple touch to her forehead. Escaping from The Dark Lord, she is transformed from the Queen of Darkness, Nafari, to The Queen of the Seasons of Life. Soft spoken Irish.

Reevus – The town cobbler of Carillon who would be found every evening at the village inn. Not only a cobbler, but a storyteller. He wasn't simply a storyteller; he was the greatest storyteller of them all. After he had finished his evening meal, he would work his magic, leaving the audience to wonder whether he had told them another far-fetched tale, or had he shared a story of what was, what is and what is yet to come. Another of the Preceptors. Jovial, joking, Welsh accent

Relocmor – The Captain of The Royal Fleet of Kalamar and the younger brother of Reeves. He was the first to notice the strangers that had started to appear across the land, buying up crops at outlandish prices. Welsch accent.

Rose – There was nothing special or magical about Rose. She was one of the few that were rescued from The Day of Destruction, the day Lord Zorleg attacked The Great City and all Kalamar. Rose never tried to understand where she was but rather accepted her place in time and the task she had been given. Like her, Cna and Dorlie were saved. Hidden in time, they would create The Krazac. A horse over twenty hands tall with the horn of the unicorn and the wings of the flying horse. The magical Krazac would be the instrument to ferry the needed supplies to rebuild The Great City. Irish accent

Rune coin – inscribed with the secret binding "Dreams don't last forever, but dreams are not forgotten". A coin given to Benny by The Guardian, a coin that begins to change his life.

The Child of The Lake – An anomaly existing in what cannot be. The Child of The Lake walks through the great lake on the dry lakebed, moving the sands of time to precisely where they should be at the exact moment. He is surrounded by billowing waves around him. He shares a closeness with The Great Mothership and always refers to her as Mother. Childlike voice of innocence throughout, American voice.

The Great Forrest – home of Queen RhiAnne and the elves. A target of Zorleg to acquire that which is not his for the taking.

The Great Storytellers – those with the ability to weave and craft a story, taking over the imagination of the listener and transporting them to a place in time of great joy and entertainment. Reevus was the expert and was the greatest storyteller of Kalamar. All storytellers were despised by Zorleg!

The Guardian – Gifted by the One of Ones with the knowledge and language of The Ancients, he was tasked with mentoring The Chosen by The One of Ones. His ability to cast enchantments may only be overshadowed by Queen RhiAnne. One of the Preceptors. What you are using for The Guardian is perfect!

The Isle of Innisfree – an island full of mystery and home to Mother and The Great Kalmarian Fleet and The Child of The Lake. Created by incantations in The Ancient Language by Queen RhiAnne. The isle has been hidden and offers privacy, secrecy and miraculous healing powers to those who are invited to visit. It was created to serve The Chosen and The Guardian in their darkest hour of need.

The Mirrors of Time – Far from anything but a mirror. They allow The Seer to watch over The Chosen and all Seven Planes of Kalamar. Through The Mirrors of Time, The Seer sees far more than reflection. He peers into times past, times present and times future. The Seer is always watching.

The Mothership of The Great Kalmarian Fleet - To those who have seen her, she appears to be nothing more than the last of The Great Kalmarian Fleet, floating alone in The Great Lake. She is more than a ship though; she is the Mother of The Isle of Innisfree. Gifted by The One of Ones, she changes appears from a woman wise with age and magic, to The Mothership of The Great Kalmarian Fleet. Strong, compassionate, kind, all knowing.

The One of Ones – it was by his words that all things were spoken in to being. The story strongly suggests he stood at The Great Meeting Place to put things in motion. Thundering voice of authority.

The Preceptors – They were selected by The One of Ones, charged with mentoring, teaching and protecting The Chosen. Each of The Preceptors was given gifts of magic and knowledge to help them with their task.

The Three of Threes – designated by The One of Ones to transcribe into The Great Book the beginning, creating a history of The Seven Planes creation.

The Seer – watcher of all things in a world and place all of his own, hidden in the starts. Long time friend and companion of The Guardian. Another Preceptors. Slow and deliberate speech, medium soft, no accent, highly intelligent.

The Seven of Sevens – also referred to as The Great Book. Within this book are the recordings of time past, the history of how The Seven Planes came into existence. There also lies within the warning and The Prophecies of what is to come.

The Seven Stones of Kalamar – uniquely arranged and placed on the grounds of The Great Meeting Place. Precisely when The Seven Stones were placed and why is described in The Great Book.

The Seven Planes of Kalamar – created by The One of Ones and placed exactly where He wanted it. A galaxy many light years from our world but easily within the blinking of an eye with the correct incantation speaking in The Ancient Language. Carefully selected his Preceptors, those who would be charged with mentoring and protecting The Chosen. Even before the creation of The Seven Planes, The One of Ones had planned for The Chosen's birth and special gifts to prepare them for The Battle of Battles. His one rule to The Preceptor's…there can be no interference!

The Sisters of The Mist – like the points on a compass, each of The Sisters were positioned around The Great Meeting Place. They were The Guardians of Kalamar before the great attack and were thought to have been destroyed. But were they really? The storytellers have said shared they, in fact, were not destroyed but changed and now surround The Great City of Kalamar, protecting it.

Wren (pronounced Ray) – The eyes, ears and loyal servant and daughter of Queen RhiAnne. Dressed in Elven battledress, she is a skilled archer and fighter. More than once, she has come to the aid of young Benny, watching over and protecting Benny as part of her duty. Voice like Tauriel from The Hobbit.

Zoreans – the name Lord Zorleg gave to his black army. The Zoreans are great warriors, taking what they want and ruling out of fear. Instilling fear in the citizens across the land and the fear of punishment at the hands of Nafari for failure. Cockney accident.

The Seven Planes of Kalamar – Battle for The Third Plane

Ancient/Magical Language Translation

"Drema cest non fevore da drema no fegistn." Dreams will not last forever. but dreams are not forgotten.

"Brestee' un mea" –

" mhuscailt" (her awakening)

"Neathe eine de Soula, De Soula ist Minnen" (death to the soul, the soul is mine)

"Sela Nu Amore. Keisa ruilea nesta. Telnadana"

"Fini" - finished

Things are not always as they appear

"an whispser ghaoth d`ainm" (the wind whispers your name)

"Saoghal dorchadas," (world of darkness)

"Bidh e mar a thuirt mi" (it shall be as I have spoken).

"Nuair a tha feum air" (when it is needed)

"an uairsin bheirear seachad e" (then it will be given).

Bhí am ann" (There was a time)

"Tá am ann" (There is a time)

"Beidh am ann" (There will be a time),*"*

"Glaoitear orm anois dul tríd an am" (Now I am called to step through time).

"an breathe de draiochta breathes," (The breath of magic breathes)

"an whispser ghaoth d`ainm" (the wind whispers your name)

"Drema cest non fevore da drema no fegistn." (Dreams will not last forever, but dreams are not forgotten)

"an breathe de draiochta breathes," (The breath of magic breathes)

"Cle ni tri more sa". (From Morning's First Light)

"LaNa de, cous fa ti". (Til Evening's Last Star)

"Sela Nu Amore. Keisa ruilea nesta. Telnadana."

"Do slabhrai' ata imithe', Ta tu saor in aisce curtha ar bun." (Your chains are gone, you are set free.)

"Ni ainm Grace. I gcas anch bhfuil se bhfuil Grace. Ach Cad e Grace." (The name is Grace. In case it is, it is Grace. But what is Grace?)

"whisper ta se in am" (It is time).

"Cle ni tri more sa.". (From Morning's First Light)

"LaNa de, cous fa ti." (Til Evening's Last Star)

"Cla Nigh,"

The Saga Continues

by HANSFORD ROBERT HULL

The Seven Planes of Kalamar –

Battle for the Third Plane

Book 2 - Rescue Times Three

www.ingramcontent.com/pod-product-compliance
Lightning Source LLC
Chambersburg PA
CBHW081131300726
48982CB00005B/928

* 9 7 9 8 9 8 6 0 2 4 0 0 4 *